Book 2 of the award-winning *Troubadours* series

'Evocative and thoroughly riveting. A vividly-written, historical saga.' The Wishing Shelf

'A walk through time! That is what it was like to read this fine novel. It drew me into the pages and would not let go of me until done! Bravo for a wonderful read!' Arwin Blue, By Quill Ink and Parchment Historical Fiction blogger

'A remarkable achievement.' Deborah Swift, *Pleasing Mr Pepys*

'You will not find any better historical fiction, nor a more powerful evocation of a vivid past than in Gill's brilliantly written series.' Paul Trembling, *Local Poet*

'The whole quartet is well written, well plotted and beautifully composed... highly recommended.' Cristoph Fischer, *Ludwig*

'A thrilling page-turner and very hard to put down.' Deb McEwan, *Unlikely Soldiers*

'Gill's skill at moving from culture to culture, savoring the distinctive colors of each, is breath-taking.' Elizabeth Horton-Newton, *Carved Wooden Heart*

'Fascinating history – the plot was ter Novels blogger

GW00584981

JEAN GILL

BLADE SONG

1151: THE HOLY LAND

THE TROUBADOURS
BOOK 2

Cover design by Jessica Bell

Jean Gill's Publications

Novels
The Midwinter Dragon - HISTORICAL FICTION
Book 1 The Ring Breaker *(The 13th Sign)* 2022

The Troubadours Quartet - HISTORICAL FICTION
Book 5 Nici's Christmas Tale: A Troubadours Short Story *(The 13th Sign)* 2018
Book 4 Song Hereafter *(The 13th Sign)* 2017
Book 3 Plaint for Provence *(The 13th Sign)* 2015
Book 2 Bladesong *(The 13th Sign)* 2015
Book 1 Song at Dawn *(The 13th Sign)* 2015

Natural Forces - FANTASY
Book 3 The World Beyond the Walls *(The 13th Sign)* 2021
Book 2 Arrows Tipped with Honey *(The 13th Sign)* 2020
Book 1 Queen of the Warrior Bees *(The 13th Sign)* 2019

Love Heals - SECOND CHANCE LOVE
Book 2 More Than One Kind *(The 13th Sign)* 2016
Book 1 No Bed of Roses *(The 13th Sign)* 2016

Looking for Normal - TEEN FICTION
Book 1 Left Out *(The 13th Sign)* 2017
Book 2 Fortune Kookie *(The 13th Sign)* 2017

Non-fiction
MEMOIR / TRAVEL
How White is My Valley *(The 13th Sign 2021)* ***EXCLUSIVE to Jean Gill's Special Readers Group***
How Blue is my Valley *(The 13th Sign)* 2016
A Small Cheese in Provence *(The 13th Sign)* 2016

WW2 MILITARY MEMOIR
Faithful through Hard Times *(The 13th Sign)* 2018
4.5 Years – war memoir by David Taylor *(The 13th Sign)* 2017

Short Stories and Poetry
One Sixth of a Gill *(The 13th Sign)* 2014
From Bedtime On *(The 13th Sign)* 2018 (2nd edition)
With Double Blade *(The 13th Sign)* 2018 (2nd edition)

Translation (from French)
The Last Love of Edith Piaf – Christie Laume *(Archipel)* 2014
A Pup in Your Life – Michel Hasbrouck 2008
Gentle Dog Training – Michel Hasbrouck *(Souvenir Press)* 2008

For Heather
in hopes we'll make Hay again

CHAPTER ONE

His world was a small white chamber, dazzling him with light after days in the darkness of a blindfold. Large cushions of rich, silk brocade offered ruby-and-ochre relief from the whiteness, and rest for his body. An empty pail for his needs in one corner, clean rose-scented water and a towel in another, were the only other furnishings.

Stripes of sun and shade slanted through the arched window, filtered by the vertical iron bars rooted in the stone sill. The room was well protected from invaders. Wrought in the iron were flourishes of spear and ball but the man was in no mood to appreciate the exquisite craftsmanship of his prison and cared not whether someone could attack him from outside.

His enemies would come through the door, not through the window. Wearing black robes and swathes of black around their heads and faces, speaking soft Arabic, they would bring some kind of spicy pottage. They would untie his hands so that he could use them to stuff the mash into his mouth and they would give him a cup of water. He'd be allowed to wash his hands and face. Then they would bind him again and bow before taking leave of their 'honoured guest'. Strange hospitality.

Escape attempts had failed so far, although it was a compliment to his perseverance and ingenuity that three anonymous attendants always stood outside the door with their curved swords. Rubbing bonds against the rough wall merely fretted his skin to bleeding, as did the shattered fragments of his water-cup after he'd kicked it against the wall. After that, they'd not left the cup with him.

Biting into the cushions and scattering their contents – feathers – advanced him no further than when he'd kicked over his chamber pot. Unless disgust in his jailers' eyes counted as an advance. Fasting for a day while they were absent and lower mortals cleaned his mess, struck him as no advance at all but he added their obsession with cleanliness to his observations on the fine scimitar blades. The filigree patterns on the steel were no ordinary pattern welding and they teased his memory. Who knew what would be useful, or when.

His hands were tied and his balance was badly affected, but he was starting to adjust. Lying on his back and repeatedly scoring the wall under the window-sill with a big toe, he could mark the passing of nights, a dirty smudge for each, without it being noticed by the guards. The toe-marks tallied twelve already but he couldn't guess at time lost before he started counting. Time when he also lost his clothes, his precious horse and the book entrusted to him by a wise Jew; the book he was supposed to guard with his life and deliver to Abdon Yerushalmi in the dye-works in Jerusalem; the book on which his own future depended. His ideas about that future were changing rapidly in the white chamber but it was still possible he might have one. If they meant to kill him, they would have done so. Wouldn't they?

He crouched and straightened, exercising his calves and thighs, rotating his ankles, strengthening his riding muscles. His hands bound behind his back, he could do little for his arms but stretch them sideways or lie prone and arch hands towards feet but whatever use he could make of a cushion and a wall in keeping active, so he did.

For his restless mind, his usual release was unhampered and he shut his eyes, breathed deeply and sang. He roved through spring-time and kisses, goat-girls and fatal sword-thrusts. When memory threw him lines last sung as a duet with the sweetest partner he'd ever known, he accepted the pain and let it flow into the song of morning-after, the aubade and a lovers' farewell. Discipline for the heart as well as the mind.

Another lyric, not his own, floated into his mind; a song born in Occitania and carried into the crusade by its maker.

'Lanqand li jorn son lonc en may,
M'es bels douz chans d'auzelhs de lonh,
E qand me sui partitz de lay
Remembra.m d'un amor de lonh.'

'When days are long in May
I hear
the sweet-tongued birds so far away
And near
Things leave me dreaming
Only of my love so far away.'

The far-away lady-love of the poet, Rudel, had been here, in the Holy Land, although he had never seen her. His fancy had been fuelled by stories of a matchless beauty, the Comtesse de Tripoli. The captive knight mouthed the plaintive Occitan.

'Iratz e gauzens me.n partray
S'ieu ja la vey l'amor de lonh,'

'I would leave in joy but also pain
Should I but see my love so far away
Just once, again,'

He deliberately altered the words, thinking of his own Estela, no unseen, unknown lady.

'I know not how nor when,
The lands between so far away,
The roads uncertain to her door –
No more!
I cannot speak! Inshallah!'

He sang the Arabic, ironically, instead of *'Diau platz.'* It seemed to him that the God of the Muslims held more power over him at this moment than the God of the Christians.

He let the sounds of the street below accompany his first attempts at shaping a new lyric, clashing tin pans for a tambour and a muezzin's call instead of the plaintive flute, to the rhythm of a rolling cart. Everything was a song if you knew how to listen.

Whatever the anonymous guards thought of such music, nothing showed in their demeanor as they entered the room, seemingly in the appointed way, at the appointed time. When they'd taken off blindfold and gag, after a head-splitting journey, the first thing he said was, 'If you harm my horse, may God, Allah and Yahweh spit on your children's future, and on their children's future, to the thousandth generation.'

'He is fed, water and stabled, honoured guest,' was the reply, with a bow.

Then the knight tried questions. 'Where am I?' he asked them in Arabic, accented with Occitan. Like most Franks of his standing, he could read the language and speak it fluently, along with his Occitan mother tongue and Latin.

'In the care of Allah,' was the response, 'may His Name be praised.' The guards' own Arabic was odd, the words difficult to understand but the overall meaning was clear enough. Always accompanied by a deferential bow and no expression in eyes that dipped quickly to avoid his, and were all he could see in the swathes of black.

'Who are you?' he asked them.

'The servants of Allah, may His will be done.'

All his questions were answered in this way, politely, a fog of nothings from which he tried to give shape to his enemy. For he was surely in the hands of the enemy, however soft-voiced. Three years had passed since the humiliating end to the second crusade and nothing was more easily explained than Moors capturing and holding a Christian knight foolish enough to venture alone across their territory. It would certainly explain the respect with which he was treated and which usually preceded lengthy negotiations over a suitable ransom, after which he would be free to continue on his way. As heir to extensive lands in Aquitaine, and until recently Commander of the Guard and troubadour to Aquitaine's infamous Duchesse Aliénor, Lord Dragonetz los Pros was worth several coffers to those who could afford to pay. Such a sum might even attract someone rich enough to replace the chewed and tattered cushion immediately with another, larger, and even more sumptuously woven.

However, Dragonetz had not been on Moorish territory. Three days after disembarking in St Jean d'Acre, he'd been ambushed in an alleyway and knocked unconscious, and now here he was, wearing a striped linen robe instead of his armour. Perhaps he should have been more vigilant but, in a city swarming with Templars and Hospitalers, his main concern after a month at sea was to avoid questions and to stock up for the journey to Jerusalem. There was no reason to fear Moorish attack in the heart of Oltra mar Christendom and although bad blood remained from the second crusade, the war had ended two years ago. As a defeated veteran, Dragonetz was an unlikely military target for such a premeditated attack, however profitable he might be as an opportunist catch on the road.

He had to face the possibility that someone not only knew who he was but what he carried with him. From the moment when he accepted the book from the Jew in Narbonne, he also accepted the danger that came with carrying such a priceless treasure Oltra mar, overseas, to the Holy City itself. Jerusalem was under Christian rule but across disputed lands, and the journey there was perilous.

On the long sea voyage, he had time to wonder why the book was so important, to unwrap the oilskin and study the parchment pages, which were covered in the even script of the Hebraic letters. Accustomed to reading Arabic, with its curves and loops, Dragonetz could make nothing of this square alphabet, words hanging like washing from a line running across the column. Between the three columns were squiggles, obviously the annotations that Raavad told him were the most precious feature of the Codex. What else had Raavad told him?

At the time, Dragonetz had been too shocked by the death of Arnaut, his aide and friend, and the fire that ended his paper mill, to take in all he was told by the leader of Narbonne's Jewish community. Dragonetz owed money he could not repay and was bound against his will to this strange mission of the book, bound to put thousands of miles between himself and the woman he loved, as well as between himself and his enemies. Or so he'd thought. Maybe the book had brought him new enemies, or maybe old ones were harder to shake off than he'd expected.

The book was a Jewish bible, two hundred years old and precious in itself but the annotations made it a sacred and irreplaceable treasure. Raavad called it the Keter Aram Sola, perhaps the oldest Torah in existence.

'These,' he'd pointed with reverence to the squiggles in the margins, 'are the work of Aaron Ben Asher and they represent years of work and study by a brilliant mind. They tell us not only how to read the Torah but how to sing it. This Codex is the sacred guide to the Torah and must be preserved. It has been stolen, ransomed and given into my care. It has fed the learning of my people in Provence and I have great hope that something special has been born here, thanks to this book. But it is no longer safe in Narbonne, or even in Occitania. It is perhaps the only copy after the desecrations of the last decade in the Holy Land and it must go back there, all four hundred and ninety-one pages still in one piece, to somewhere that is safe. *'Blessed be he who preserves it and cursed be he who steals it, and cursed be he who sells it, and cursed be he who pawns it. It may not be sold and it may not be defiled.'*

Then Raavad had given the book and the mission to Dragonetz, along with the name of Abdon Yerushalmi and a way to contact him in Jerusalem. From the moment the book was out of his hands, and in Abdon Yerushalmi's, Dragonetz would be free. His debt of honour paid, he could go home to Estela and to – what? His dreams of making paper were in ashes and the Church would never allow him to start again.

If not in making paper, then in what lay his destiny? He could reclaim Estela from her position in Dia with the Comtessa, and return to his father's lands, where he would await his inheritance and play at estate management. His face screwed up wryly. He could reclaim Estela and they would tour Occitania, singing and juggling

at the great courts, Aurenja, Barcelona, or head north to Champagne and its strange whining language. They could even cross the seas to learn the songs of the barbarians living in the Pais de Gallas. He sighed. If only such a future were possible! But a warrior of his experience could not lay down his sword and stay in the world. He would be challenged wherever he went and if he declared no allegiance, blood would spill to make him choose sides.

He could reclaim Estela and take her to war with him, while he fought once again for Aquitaine and Christianity, fighting with his kind against the Moors and the Jews, fighting against the very civilisation that supported his dream, fighting against all knowledge, against science, mathematics, medicine, astronomy. If another crusade erupted, he might be forced to do just that, but there must be a better choice for him. For when he was free.

Free! He laughed aloud. He couldn't even move his hands! He just hoped that a few of the book's curses would land surely and quickly on whoever was holding him. As he tallied another mark under the window-ledge, he tried not to think of knights held to ransom for years, their beards grown to their knees. At least he would remain beardless if he continued to accept the efficient ministrations of his guards, whose only turn of the knife against him had been to smooth his cheeks and chin, without so much as a nick. If ever he lost hope, he only had to jerk his head violently enough and a Moorish blade would end all. A blade patterned with silver swirls that ran impossibly deep into the metal.

Swirling steel and stiffened silk, he mused. And then it came to him, the one word to describe both silk and steel – damascene – and suddenly he knew where he was. When the door opened, his guess was confirmed. Accompanied by the usual guards was someone he recognised and had hoped never to see again. He was in the oldest city in the world, Damascus, a city Dragonetz had last seen from outside the walls, where he led besieging Crusader troops.

'My Lord Dragonetz los Pros.' If there was a hint of irony in the nickname 'los Pros', 'the Brave', it was too subtle to be sure of the mockery. A low bow in greeting and then the newcomer turned to the guards. 'Leave us.' The men hesitated, hands on their sword hilts. 'I am in no danger from your guest! Go!' And, as an afterthought, 'Bring us tea.'

Although he too wore black robes and a scarf hood, the man who spoke was bare-faced, sun-trenched wrinkles deep in his ageing face. Dark skin and hooked nose suggested his race but not his religion. Damascus was not only the oldest city in the world but the oldest seat of the Christian Church, founded by St Paul himself. In this land where allegiances shifted like the sands it was no surprise to find a Syriac Christian giving orders to Muslim guards.

'Yohana Bar Philipos.' Dragonetz returned the greeting with a grimace as the instinctive movement of his hands met only rope. 'You have me at a disadvantage.'

His eyes steady on Dragonetz, Bar Philipos unsheathed his scimitar and said, 'Turn your back'. A shaft of sunlight caught patterns on the blade. There was no hesitation in Dragonetz as he turned his back, not because he trusted Bar Philipos but because this was the one man who had the right to kill him. If Dragonetz condemned the Archbishop of Narbonne and Toulouse for his crimes, how much more did he blame himself for the torture and death of this man's daughter, in the crusade that shamed all those involved.

Three years ago, Bar Philipos stumbled into the Crusaders' camp, demanding to see Aliénor's Commander in person so he could tell Dragonetz to his face how a beautiful girl had died, never betraying her lover's name, nor how to find him. It was not the details of torture that unmanned Dragonetz but the knowledge he hid deep in nightmares for the years that followed; he couldn't even put a face to the girl let alone a name. She was merely a pleasing body come to him in the dark, along with her giggling friends, who'd sneaked a ladder down over the city walls to pleasure the young soldiers outside, bored with their siege. How could he know that their wild trysts could be used as a way to trap him, a way that failed because of the courage of one young girl who refused to speak. Who, according to her father, loved Dragonetz and had died for him.

So his jaw hardened and he turned his back. A breath of air and one whistling swish upwards was all it took, so sharp was the blade. There was a rush of pain as circulation returned to his wrists and Dragonetz rubbed them hard. 'Thank you.'

'If you give your word not to attack your long-suffering guards, and not to try to escape, I can ask that you be left unbound.' Bar Philipos dragged two cushions from the pile and placed them as seats, gesturing to the other man to take one. The sliced rope on the floor was unravelling from its thick plaits into strands. Dragonetz picked up a section, puzzled at its fabrication.

'Silk,' Bar Philipos confirmed, his hand never straying too far from the steel that had cut the knot. Dragonetz' own sword was solid, well-tempered and proven in battle often enough, but it was no match for Damascus steel. Occitan smiths had forged their versions, relying on descriptions from returned Crusaders.

Dragonetz had seen swords that were pattern welded, clumsy mixes of iron and steel, twisted in the making. He had seen pretty etchings on blades, filigree swirls of copper or silver on the surface of the steel. But no-one outside Damascus had come close to making steel like this, patterned through to the very core, like watermarked silk turned to weapon. It was hard without being brittle, durable without softness and could be sharpened to an edge that cut through flesh as if it were goat cheese. And oh, but it was beautiful. Not since he held a sheet of paper for the first time had Dragonetz felt such a longing, such a need to know how something was made but he knew better than to ask directly.

'The craft in your sword sings of Damascus,' he told Bar Philipos, the Arabic shaping his compliments in the manner a language has of forming thoughts in that culture.

'It is our heritage. Damascus has passed on its skills for centuries and will continue to do so, God willing.' Bar Philipos had switched into a language that was not quite Arabic but its sister, the same spoken by the guards.

'Your sons are blessed.' Dragonetz winced even as he spoke the tactless formula.

'My sons are blessed,' Bar Philipos agreed, then he answered the wince, 'and I have other daughters. Although you will forgive me if I do not introduce them to you. The world has moved on in three years, Lord Dragonetz, as have I. A child who shames her family no longer has a family. A child raised in virtue, who behaves as a whore, deserves to die as a whore.' His voice rose and broke, resuming in flat tones. 'This is an example to others in the family and in the community. It is not something worth speaking of. She did not exist.'

Dragonetz blinked. If he had a sister who'd slipped over Ruffec's walls at night to play the oldest game with some man, and had died for it, would his own father have spoken like this? A foolish thought. No sister of his would have been so careless of her honour. 'You are speaking Syriac?' Dragonetz hazarded. Bar Philipos nodded. 'Please, continue. I need to learn.' Until he spoke the words he had no idea that he needed to learn and he was still not sure what he needed to learn. Know your friend, perhaps, and, of course, know your enemy. He was unsure which of the two sat on the cushion opposite him but he already knew that this man would not speak of love with anything other than contempt.

'I was asked to confirm your identity,' Bar Philipos continued. Dragonetz frowned in concentration and the Syrian spoke more slowly. 'Please, ask me if there are words unknown to you in my speech. It is said by the Muslims that their prophet Muhammad asked to learn Syriac and it took seventeen days. I think you will be quicker. As to my purpose here, I have permission to answer some of your questions but not others.' He broke off to admit a guard, who carried a silver tray, on which were a bowl and two brown-glazed cups, themselves decorated in silver trace. Was everything in this city crafted in metal magic?

Bar Philipos placed the tray on the floor between them, politely indicating the cup of hot black liquid nearer to Dragonetz. A blade in the back was one thing, poison quite another. Dragonetz leaned forward and turned the tray, copying the Syrian's gesture and offering the same cup. Bar Philipos smiled and shook his head, reaching out to the cup. 'No, my friend, there is no difference between the cups.'

'Good,' said Dragonetz, beating Bar Philipos to the cup he'd chosen. 'Then I'll change my mind again and take the first one.' The Syrian showed neither disappointment nor triumph as he reached across for his own cup and raised it in a toast, saying something that sounded like 'fisehatak', 'to your health'.

'Santat,' replied Dragonetz in Occitan and took a sip, scenting an overlay of flowers and feeling a bitter aftertaste on his tongue. 'What is it?'

'Herbs and honey.' Bar Philipos shrugged. 'Some say it calms the spirits and eases repose. I have no interest in herbal lore.' Dragonetz thought wistfully of al-Hisba, his Moorish friend, who had been as talented in medicine as in engineering. He would have sniffed out the composition of the drink, known every property of each herb in it. Al-Hisba and Estela would then have argued the merits of each situation in which the drink could be used, from childbirth to amputation. Dragonetz disciplined his rambling thoughts. Such friends were a time and an ocean away. He had other questions to pose this strange intermediary.

'You said you 'have permission'. Who gives permission? By whose name am I held here?'

'That I can't say but he is of noble birth.'

'Why me?'

'Your worth as a warrior is known, my Lord Dragonetz, and the situation here is precarious. Should you accept one of the offers which will surely come to you, like the last grain of salt on the scale you will tip the balance towards whomsoever you choose. It is considered safer that you enjoy your stay here while events unfold.'

'What and who are in the balance of which you speak?'

'Now that is something we can speak of at length when I come again but, in short, since the Crusaders failed Damascus –' Dragonetz winced but could not contradict the statement – 'we have held our city against our enemies through the strength of our walls, of our skills and of our trade. No-one wants to see Damascus razed and everyone wants to possess it. To the north, the Saracen force grows ever stronger under the Aleppo ruler, Nur ad-Din. To the south, the King and Queen of Jerusalem are increasingly at odds, dividing the Christian kingdom of Jerusalem between them.' Bar Philipos flushed, stumbled over his words. 'But we will speak more of this next time.' He rose abruptly to leave. 'Before I leave you unbound, do I have your word?'

'I will not attack the guards. I swear.'

'That is but half an oath, Dragonetz, but you cannot escape, so don't try. It will go ill for you and worse for anyone you try to subvert to your purpose. There are no serving-wenches here to charm with a song. Nor any other wenches.'

The light retort had to be stifled, each word allowed to cut, and accepted as his due. As if reading his mind, the Syrian said, 'Be assured, my Lord Dragonetz, you will be treated exactly as you merit.' Bar Philipos bowed and left Dragonetz wondering whether it was only his permanently guilty conscience that made the words sound like a threat. He felt a sudden nausea and put it down to the emotions of the encounter. He would feel better if he lay down.

Closing the door behind him, Bar Philipos leaned against the wall, feeling giddy. One of the guards moved quickly to support him and warned, 'Not here – come.' When they were far enough away from the others, in a chamber protected by walls thick enough to hold all secrets, the guard dropped the Syrian onto some cushions and slipped off his black headgear.

'This stifles me. It's bad enough now but I don't know how your people wear it in the summer.' He shook free a mop of curly brown hair and revealed skin that was tanned and weathered brown but with paler origins. 'How long do we have?'

'The agitation has started but I have used the poppy before and will be lucid until sleep takes me.'

'Did he drink it all?'

'Yes. It was as we planned. It might not have worked if only one cup had been doctored.'

'You can control your own intake in the future?'

'Of course. Next time he will be more trusting and I will not need to partake of the poppy.'

'How long before he needs it?'

'That depends on his body and his mind, how strongly they bind to the poppy. With a small dose each day, I think we will quickly make him ours without him noticing. His quick mind will betray him because he is too interested in what I can tell him to realise what his body could tell him. The longer he stays with us, the tighter we bind him, and the more sluggish that quick mind will grow. When we let him escape, he is ours wherever he goes. We neuter him.'

'We are being paid well to keep him out of action but safe.'

'And we are being paid even better to kill him. This way, we satisfy both our clients. We let one know he is well and the other know that he will die whenever we choose, without a trace of our involvement. He will need to know where to find what he craves and he will do the rest himself. We will do nothing and he will die.'

'And if it becomes more expedient that he lives?'

'It is possible to arrange. But far more difficult.'

'What happens now?'

'Now, I sleep. And dream. Leave me.'

CHAPTER TWO

E stela knew how much she'd changed and she felt ugly, as if she was a huge impostor, but the guests at table were looking at her as they always had, confident that their songster would complete a pleasant evening in the Great Hall of Dia. She gave an involuntary gasp, then hid it in an emotional rendering of the next verse. If her audience was surprised at the intensity of their troubadour's feeling for a shy maiden being wooed and won, so much the better. After only six months entertaining the Diois lords at the court of Comte Isoard, surprise was already Estela's hallmark.

As her voice soared for *'No m platz plus'*, she mentally admonished the source of the gasp, 'Little trouble-maker!' When the next fierce kick came inside her, followed by a punch and ripple as the baby changed position, she was ready for him – or her – and didn't miss a note.

As she sang of Rudel's *'amor de lonh,'* his far-away love, she thought of her own and there were tears in her own eyes as well as her listeners' as she finished the tale of doomed love. How wonderful that Rudel had managed to see the lady he'd dreamed of, for whom his song was written, even if it had been to die in her arms. How romantic.

The baby kicked her again, hard. If this was the result of being in a lover's arms, she would never ever again let a man near her unless he was wearing full body armour. She would wear a literal girdle of chastity and let the dog keep the key attached to a spiked collar.

She glanced at the huge white fur-mat half-lying under the trestle table where she'd recently finished eating. Nici's eyes were shut in the comfortable dreams of a dog who'd scavenged his fill of under-table scraps and was now blissfully unaware that he'd cleared five people away from his end of the table, using a combination of ripe dog smells and sheer physical occupation of space. No-one ever liked to move Nici.

From the moment he'd run away from home and found Estela doing likewise, he'd assumed they were a good team and, somehow, she'd never convinced him otherwise. Nor was she going to convince him that he should be guarding sheep like a good patou, and wearing the spiked collar. A complete failure, he'd liked people too much to stay out in the fields. So the chastity belt plan was doomed too. And yet there was no shortage of wolves in the Vercors mountains, requiring both Nici and Estela to stay on guard.

Estela glanced round the hall as she curtseyed the end of her performance, accepting the tribute she had come to expect. Tonight she had sung others' compositions, but as her confidence and reputation grew, she included her own work in her repertoire more often. She could rely on any of Dragonetz' songs to warm up the audience – and usually the baby! – or to rescue a choice that fell flat. People wanted novelty yet responded to what was familiar so Estela had learned to include only one or two new songs, and repeat those in her regular programme a few times, before adding more.

After the first performance of her 'Song of Arnaut and al-Hisba', she had cried herself breathless in her room; her greatest work, her most personal work, received with disapproving mutters. And she had lain awake, remembering all Dragonetz taught her, all al-Hisba had taught her, remembering Arnaut's love for his friend – and for her.

Then she'd sung it again, the token Arnaut had worn as her knight, a talisman around her neck. This time the murmur had a different note in it. Then, another night, she'd sung it again, and seen people mouthing the words with her, singing along. The evening someone called out, 'Sing us the one about Arnaut and the Moor', she knew she'd won, and not just for herself.

That evening, Estela had looked to where her men were sitting, her self-appointed guardians; Gilles, who'd saved her life and paid for it with his right hand, finding and following her with the same loyalty as Nici; and Raoulf, Arnaut's father, his shaggy black head lowered to hide his face as Estela sang a song of love and courage, brotherhood across the divide of race and creed. It was Gilles who told her, 'That was well done, Roxie,' using the real name of her childhood that she'd abandoned for her troubadour persona. Raoulf couldn't speak beyond a gruff grunt and nod, but that was more than enough.

If she never composed another song, this one had brought her all the reward she could ever want, easing her own heart in carrying the debt she could never repay. They were all changed, she, Gilles, Raoulf and Dragonetz – wherever he might be. Even al-Hisba, or Malik as she ought to call him now she knew his name, had tangled his life with theirs before he returned to some fabulous inheritance in al-Andalus – or wherever he might be now.

A summer in Narbonne had come and gone with the swallows, leaving Estela in the mountain fortress of Dia, troubadour to its young heiress, Bèatriz, alone but for her serving-men and a large white dog, and about to give birth to Dragonetz' child. She'd followed his advice at their forced parting, attached herself to Bèatriz' party and returned with them from Narbonne to Dia, in anticipation of Bèatriz' marriage.

The serious fourteen-year-old whose musical talents Estela had encouraged, had grown into a young woman who spoke only of duty but still sang of love. She had been betrothed at seven, so was perfectly prepared for her highly suitable marriage to a local Comte, Guilhelm de Poitiers. She could explain at length to Estela the importance of joining her future lands to those of the Comte, which fell under the sovereignty of the Holy Roman Emperor, not of France like her own. But for all her political astuteness, Bèatriz was also a fifteen-year-old who'd tasted the sophistication of Narbonne.

She'd witnessed the court of Ermengarda, not just the intricacies of trade and alliances, but the quality of everyday life, and of the music there. The Court of Love. So they'd called it when they'd staged an elaborate entertainment, part-show and part-debate, dazzling with wit and beauty, attended by the young troubadours whose names were already passed from one stronghold to the next. Whose names had touched lightly on Bèatriz, herself a young troubadour to be reckoned with, apart from one. A spark between like minds, a flame catching between a girl's serious brown eyes and a man's, full of laughter. Raimon d'Aurenja. If Bèatriz spoke the name, it was quickly, before it could burn her. Estela had seen the looks, interpreted what wasn't said, and understood all that went into her young mistress' songs.

And here they both were in Dia, incarcerated in grey stone, ringed with snow-capped mountains. A city solid in ancient inland values, not dancing with the newest fashions that were rushed by the traders from port to palace, as in Narbonne. There had been thick snow for months in Dia and even though the bluebells could be seen round the woods, this far north was still cold, at a time when Narbonne would be shaking the lavender bags out of silk gowns. Here, the women were still wearing their furs, making it easy for Estela to conceal her growing belly under voluminous winter clothing, even as close to the birth as she was now. A month, she thought, if all went well. And then? As always, her mind hit a wall. Other than there being a baby, she could not imagine her life afterwards.

Some day in the future, she and Dragonetz would be together, arm-in-arm, while a small child played on the grass beside his proud parents, but how she would get from where she was today to this appealing scenario, she had no idea. As things stood, she was married to a vassal of Ermengarda's, a man she'd seen once, on her wedding day, and who would be the nominal father of the baby she carried, despite never having touched her. Dragonetz had no idea she was pregnant.

When she'd first found out, she'd contemplated sending Gilles or Raoulf to find him, with the signet ring he'd given to her 'for protection in need.' He'd said, 'Send it to me and I will come to you no matter where I am or what I do,' and how she had longed to summon him. Then she had thought what it would mean for Dragonetz. His return Oltra mar, on some mission from the Jews, was his only chance of paying off the enormous sum he'd borrowed to build the paper mill. His absence from Narbonne was all that was keeping him safe from his enemies, Toulouse, the Archbishop, the Church itself, all conspirators in destroying his dream. Al-Hisba – Malik as she must think of him – had been right, and she would not be the one to drag her lover back from his quest for honour, into danger.

She fingered the chain round her neck, the one Arnaut had been wearing when he died. Once, it had carried the bangle she had given him as token. Now it held Dragonetz' ring. Tokens and reminders, friendship and love.

'My lady?' Raoulf interrupted her endless mill-race of thoughts.

She managed a smile for him. She would always manage a smile for him. The scowl lines of his bear-like face softened and he spoke for her alone to hear, amidst the hubbub of the Great Hall. 'Forgive me, my Lady, but I've taken the liberty of seeking a woman for you, a wet-nurse, and I've found someone I think you'll like.' Her smile wavered. Of course those closest to her knew her condition, and perhaps many not so close to her, but in common courtesy no-one drew attention to it. Feminine modesty alone demanded such respect, and her somewhat unusual situation merely added another level of discretion. But Raoulf and Gilles were all the family she had, and took the associated liberties. Of course Raoulf would know all the practicalities associated with childbirth, being many times a father himself.

The familiar ache at losing Arnaut changed to dawning awareness. She was about to become a mother. How would it feel? She met Raoulf's eyes. How did it feel to have lost your child? How she wished her mother was here! However, her mother was not here and she had no option but to carry on without her, as she had since she was a little girl. Gratefully, she told him, 'You are right and I need help with this. Perhaps you can tell me what else I need to do.'

Relieved at her reaction, he smiled back, and was about to launch into a detailed account of her practical requirements when she stopped him. 'Tomorrow,' she said firmly, as the Comtessa and Bèatriz approached with their entourage. Raoulf took the hint, bowed and left her.

'The songbird of Dia excelled herself tonight,' was the extravagant judgment of the Comte de Lans. One of the more colourful examples of Dia's court, he bent over her hand, his mouth lingering in its imprint.

'The blackbird sounds sweet when the skylark is silent,' was Estela's reply, as, with the ease of practice, she deflected the compliment towards Bèatriz, who had not sung that evening. No, Dia was not short of wolves, even when she was eight months pregnant. The baby kicked her again. Not long to go now, surely.

It took both Raoulf and Gilles to drag Nici away from Estela and lock him in another room so the midwife could get anywhere near her, and it was just as well they were wearing gauntlets, boots and leather jerkins. Estela could still hear Nici's furious scratching at the door and outraged yelps at being shut away from his mistress when she clearly needed him.

She had known when she woke in a pool of liquid that it was time to send for the midwife and, after a scurry of servants, Bèatriz' women had ushered her to a chamber well away from the daily bustle of castle life. The purpose of the room was clear enough. Apart from the blazing fire, which barely took the chill off the air, there was a bed, a birthing stool, chamber-pot, wash-stand and ewer.

In her own home, the mattress would have been stuffed with our lady's bedstraw and the fire strewn with juniper branches but Estela didn't know what herbs were used here, if any. The only light came from the fire and the pitch torches on the wall, as if the business of birthing should be in darkness, like the act that produced it.

Estela's gloom deepened into panic as her body spasmed. She had a rough idea of what would happen, thanks to visits with her mother, a healer, and thanks to a Moorish physician, who'd held science above prudery and discussed medicine with her. If only her mother or Malik could have been with her now, instead of women whose names she could barely remember. She hadn't felt so alone since she'd woken in a ditch after running away from home.

And then Nici appeared as if by magic, bounding to her side, anxious brown eyes and insistent tongue, her only friend now as then, licking the salt of her tears as she indulged in self-pity. In between the waves that racked her, Estela trailed her hands in the coarse white fur but when the midwife arrived, Nici made it clear that no-one was going to touch his mistress when she was so clearly vulnerable and incapable of making any decision. It was unquestionably his job to take charge.

Usually an easy-going lump of a dog, who was as happy milling around with any of the hunting packs as he was dozing hopefully under a trestle table at meal-time, Nici was unrecognizable. Hackles raised, eyes bright as pebbles in water, he fixed the midwife with an inimical glare.

The midwife made it equally clear that she was leaving unless someone removed the growling monster from the room. Helpless with contractions, Estela's half-hearted attempts to reassure Nici seemed merely to convince him that she was not herself.

At which point, Raoulf and Gilles braved women's territory and took matters into their own gauntlets, ignoring the scandalised squeaks of the attendant women as much as the furious complaints of the huge dog, whose muffled barking from his solitary confinement accompanied Estela's involuntary shouts of pain.

'Jasmine oil,' she begged the midwife, whose face looked like a child's dough sculpture, lumpy and white, with raisin eyes. Eyes that narrowed, weighing her up. In the birthing chamber, the only queen was the midwife, whatever the rank of the mother-to-be.

'Jasmine oil,' the midwife repeated flatly.

Estela couldn't keep the desperation out of her voice as she felt the beginning of another wave. No longer a baby kicking; more like a herd of horses pounding her into the dust. 'Inhaling oil of jasmine helps with the pain...' she tailed off, biting her lip bloody and doubling over, half-falling onto the bed.

'Well we don't hold with such fancy things here and babies get born just the same. You'll manage,' stated the midwife, moving Estela to the birthing chair to see how wide open she'd become.

Estela felt the screams rising as if they belonged to someone else, except that Nici joined in, so they must be hers. She knew Raoulf and Gilles were just outside the door, hers in a way that none of these women were, and she was overwhelmed by longing to call them in, to grab onto a hand of each, to anchor her body in this world to the rock of their loyalty. To have them with her when she brought Dragonetz' baby into the world.

She almost called them but enough thought remained to know she mustn't. This dour woman was her baby's herald, able to doom – or bless – him or her with a word. Let it be said that men had been at the birth and the baby would be cursed, hag-ridden, switched, any of a thousand insinuations that would make themselves into truth. Men would cross themselves and avoid touching such an ill-fated child, and if he sickened from so much as gum-fever, it would be the devil's work and no-one would lift a hand to make him better.

Estela knew the way people's minds worked. When visiting cottages with her mother, with salves and potions, she'd listened to the rhymes and prayers that her mother advocated applying with the medicaments, knowing that the patients' minds played a part in the healing. So Estela gripped the chair arms instead of her friends'. She would bring this baby into the world, whatever it cost her.

Hours, days or years later, adrift and dazed in the distinction between more pain and less pain, exhausted beyond obeying the midwife's impossible instructions, Estela nevertheless realised that the purse-mouthed enemy was about to stick some kind of irons into her most tender parts, irons more suited to turn a pig on a spit than a baby in its mother.

Bursting her lungs, Estela screamed and pushed one last time, Nici no longer barking but howling with her, a wolf-call of solidarity. The irons were dropped on the stone flags as the midwife caught the baby and, astonishingly, smiled up at Estela.

'A fine boy, my Lady.' Transformed from enemy to ally, the dumpy woman dug into her bag with her free hand, rubbed parchment across the baby's head, folded it carefully and showed the parcel to Estela. 'Born lucky, my Lady, with a helmet on his head for a warrior. The caul will dry in the parchment and do you keep it safe, for his luck is in it.' She cooed to the baby and shook him, then, thin at first, but building in strength, the cry of a newborn announced the arrival of a human being in the world, as the midwife finished severing the baby from all that still connected him to his mother's womb and swaddled him loosely.

'Can I hold him?' asked Estela, hesitant.

'For a moment,' assented the midwife, who was now an angel, the firelight a halo round the kindness of her expression. 'Chew on this,' she instructed, responding to the query in Estela's eyes with, 'Angelica root, to clear your body of what's left.'

Relieved that some expertise had reached this far north, Estela obediently chewed, and held her son in the crook of her arm, marvelling at the pulse showing through the thin skin of his head, at the tiny hands, balling into fists and flailing against her. His eyes, screwed up against too much light too suddenly. His skin, traced with blue like the veined goblets brought to Narbonne from Oltra mar, Damascus or some such place. Perfection. Somewhere in the distance the midwife announced that all was well, that the nurse could be fetched. Estela just felt pleasantly warm and stupid, like a cow, she thought as she finished chewing.

'Does he need to be baptised now, good wife?' The grave tones of the priest jarred on the moment and both Estela and the midwife said, 'No!' sharply.

'No,' the midwife repeated, more smoothly, 'I have the right to baptise the baby, as you know, good sire, and neither he nor his mother have need of your services this day.'

'Praise be to God.' The priest fingered his crucifix then left the chamber and death, ever present at a birthing, went with him.

'You need rest, my Lady,' the midwife told her kindly. 'You have done as hard a day's work as a body knows and you have done it well. My Lord will be proud of you when he knows. They tell me he is far away.'

'Yes.' Tears glittered but Estela would not let them fall, not today. 'But I have family here. Raoulf! Gilles!' she called and they were beside her in a second, their faces white and strained, as hers was not. She could feel the glow in her own, the warmth of bringing this precious morsel into the world. The midwife let her do as she willed and she let each man in turn hold the baby. Raoulf, many times a father, who could not but remember holding Arnaut once this way. Gilles, a better father to her than her own, but a stranger to babies, holding the infant as if he were a marchpane sculpture.

'Let Nici in!' Estela ordered and despite protesting, Raoulf opened the door barring the dog from his mistress. Three bounds and he was by the bed, sniffing warily at the new being in her arms. Estela stroked the dog's head with one hand as she held the baby relaxed in her arm. 'My darling,' she murmured to him in Occitan, 'this is our baby, to live and to die for.' The dog nudged the infant with his nose, testing its response, smelling who it was, then, satisfied, he started a thorough cleaning of its ears and tail, which made Estela giggle and drew horrified gasps from the midwife. She moved to rescue the baby but Nici had not forgiven her and rumbled a low warning.

'Enough, Nici,' Estela told him and the dog sighed. His mistress was herself again. He could relax. He pottered off to a corner and slumped in a heap, as exhausted as the two men.

'Now mistress, the baby must to the nurse and you to sleep. Don't worry – he will be brought to you tomorrow again, and the day after that. Your boy is healthy and strong. Do you have a name for him?'

The room waited, cosy as a womb now, logs sparking and crackling in the stone fireplace. Light-headed with effort and blood loss,

Estela watched the flames dance themselves into her lover, bright sword in hand as he leapt and parried, turning to smile the special lop-sided smile that was only for her. What should she call Dragonetz' son? The flames conferred and whispered to her in little puffs of smoke. What else could Dragonetz' son be called?

'Txamusca,' she murmured to the baby, then louder for everyone to hear. 'Txamusca', the Occitan word for 'fire'. What else would his father produce but fire. The silence around her held disapproval.

'It's a very ... unusual name, my Lady,' said the midwife, but now that the birth was over, she was returning to her rank. Anything that did not directly concern the child's health, or the mother's, was hardly her business.

Gilles had no such reticence. 'Are you sure, Roxie? You want him to carry such a name?' Raoulf put a warning hand on the other man's arm before he finished *'a name that shouts who fathered him, to anyone with half a brain?'* Secrets spoken in the birthing room found their way quickly to the banquet hall.

'Yes.' Estela's chin jutted stubbornly, with just a hint of wobble, and the men exchanged glances, saying no more. The midwife held her arms out for the baby, and Estela reluctantly gave him up to the rite of baptism in the one situation where a woman had sacerdotal powers. Then, a new soul formally admitted to the world, Estela sank deeply and quickly asleep, even as the entourage tiptoed out of the chamber.

Six weeks later, Txamusca de Villeneuve was christened with due ceremony in church; the young heiress of Dia was his beaming highborn godmother; Raoulf and Gilles beaming even brighter as his lowborn godfathers. Neither the mother's husband, the Lord Johans de Villeneuve, nor the baby's father, were able to attend. As neither of them knew of the boy's existence, this was hardly surprising.

CHAPTER THREE

O ver the following weeks, Dragonetz caught up with
Damascan politics as told him by Bar Philipos. They danced
around the subject of the siege during the crusade, when Dragonetz
had been among the forces outside the city walls. The Syrian had
been one of the Christian inhabitants inside the walls, defying the
city's Moorish administration to help their brothers in faith. Dragonetz and Bar Philipos did not discuss why the siege had failed, nor
why a young girl had died.

They did talk about Unur, the leader of Damascus' Moorish army
and, through absence of the city's ruler, the man responsible for
keeping Damascus independent throughout the crusade. He'd fought
off the marauding Christians without the aid offered by the northern
Muslim leader, Nur ad-Din, aid that would always be a mailed boot
in the doorway. Dragonetz had first-hand experience of Unur's military tactics and knew he'd been out-manoeuvred by a man who
combined strategic thinking with charisma. If Unur had been Occitan,
he was the one who would have gained the title 'los Pros', the brave.

It was during the siege of Damascus that Dragonetz gained his
nickname, and also discovered how much he had to learn. He knew it
was un-Christian to admire his heathen adversary but what
commander would not admire the tactics that cost four Crusader lives

for every Damascan killed, in the sorties led by Unur against the city's attackers? Bar Philipos' Damascan pride in Unur showed no Christian restraint and Dragonetz was saddened to hear that Unur's death had ill-matched his life. His last meal had cost him dear, infecting him with dysentery that was beyond his body's or his physicians' resources.

The current ruler was the very man Unur had represented in his absence for all those years. Mujir ad-Din was no fighter, and Damascus was weakening while he dithered. The Syrian could not hide his bitterness. Damascus had lost its ports to the Frankish kingdoms. The caravan routes between Syria and Egypt were barred by Frankish forts, and the ways around were vulnerable to attack by nomadic bandits, many of them Frankish. Trade was suffering and only thieves benefiting, where before there had been mutual understanding. In the past, Syrian caravans had been accompanied to Egypt by Muslim pilgrims, to mutual advantage, but now the Franks made life difficult. There were those who wished to find again the balance that allowed prosperity for men of all religions. There were others who sought to eliminate the cause of the imbalance and find peace through war and winning lands.

The more Dragonetz learned of Levantine politics, the more convinced he became that the fate of Damascus would decide the future. This city, which had defied him and the joint crusading armies, stubbornly resisting all subsequent pressure from Jerusalem, and from Nur ad-Din, and suffering attacks on its trading routes from outlaws of all colours and creeds, was finally showing the cracks. However coldly the Syrian presented the facts, Dragonetz could not ignore the implication that failure to capture this city, his failure, had cost the Franks a strategic fortress that was becoming further and further out of reach. What part he would play, Dragonetz knew not, but that he would *have* a part seemed to underlie the very existence of these privileged conversations.

He guessed at who might be behind Bar Philipos in holding him here but was offered no clues by the Syrian. If Dragonetz was being kept out of play, for fear of him choosing the 'wrong' side, maybe it was Mujir ad-Din himself, the weak leader of the city, who held the knight captive. The Christian Syrian might well take orders from his Muslim ruler, and the guards were of that faith.

Bar Philipos was bitter at the changes brought about by the Crusaders. Maybe he wanted to strengthen Mujir ad-Din and his city, even against the Franks, his brothers in religion. Nothing united men like a common enemy and maybe the threat of Nur ad-Din was pushing Bar Philipos to bolster the Seljuq rulers of Damascus, either Mujir ad-Din or whoever might replace him, perhaps the leader of the earlier mutiny.

Although he got no further in finding out who was behind his capture, debates with the Syrian ranged wide, reminding Dragonetz of his time with al-Hisba. Bar Philipos was a Christian who had grown up in Damascus, with Moorish leaders and fellow-citizens, and his way of thinking was as different from Dragonetz' as cat from dog. The knight came to look forward to the times when the guards accompanied the Syrian into his chamber, and the days when the guards came alone, were longer. Dragonetz even grew to like the black, honeyed tea and found himself missing that too.

When Bar Philipos brought Dragonetz the instrument he'd last seen packed into his saddle-bags, his own oud, he willingly gave his word that he would not try to escape. Now he was able to accompany his new songs, strumming the Arabian lute as he matched melody to words and his prison was transformed completely to sanctuary, even though an enforced one. No monastic retreat could have offered such a haven. The more Dragonetz let go of the outer world, and reflected on his inner one, the more he felt at peace with himself.

Only the book troubled him, pricking his conscience over the mission he had accepted. He still had no idea whether his captor knew of the book's worth and he couldn't ask Bar Philipos without revealing it. The more open they seemed to be with each other, the bigger the shadows from the two topics not mentioned; the book and women.

It was clear from the way the oud had been re-wrapped in its protective cloth, that someone had rummaged through Dragonetz' belongings, and it was impossible that the Torah had remained hidden. That it was valuable would be apparent, but only a connoisseur would know just how valuable. If some underling had filched the book, Dragonetz might yet recover it quietly, in time. If, however, it was a sophisticated man like Bar Philipos, or, presumably, his master, things would be more complicated. No, the book could not be mentioned first by Dragonetz.

Nor would either of them wish to talk about women. If a discussion arose on Persian poetry, Dragonetz instinctively censored his quotations, away from sensuality and love. He could not tell whether the other man was also deliberately avoiding these topics. Bar Philipos was difficult to read.

If thoughts of the book, and a certain delicacy in directing conversation, were all that troubled Dragonetz' waking hours, his dreams were less gentle with him.

'You pass too much time with Dragonetz, Bar Philipos. The information you give him will sharpen an already dangerous weapon. One might worry that you are growing fond of him. He has a reputation for charm as you have for certain ... weaknesses.'

Bar Philipos laughed. 'Were he ten years younger, maybe! But I confess I find pleasure in the twists of his mind and his recent knowledge of affairs across the sea sharpens my own weapon. Dragonetz holds one half of the world in his head and I the other. When we look at the whole together, I see possibilities for the future that I would not have considered otherwise.'

'And will these possibilities please my mistress – or your master?'

'Possibly.' Bar Philipos smiled but didn't elaborate. 'By then, our sharpened weapon of a knight will be dulled by the poppy, which makes him safe for my amusement. A condemned man in isolation can be trusted with my speculations about those in high places.'

'As can I, Bar Philipos.'

'Indeed.' The Syrian bowed in acknowledgement, hiding his eyes.

'The poppy is working?'

'Only the initiated would notice the signs but they begin, the rhythms of dullness and agitation. Now that he has his music, his enthusiasm for debate is more marked, his contentment in his prison seems normal to him. He has suffered recently I think, more recently than his campaigns here, and he has wounds in his mind that have not healed. This makes him doubly receptive to the relief given by the poppy. And doubly receptive to the dreams. He will indeed find the healing he seeks, though he knows not that he seeks it. Physical pains will not be felt. And the songs he composes will make the very walls weep or dance, as he chooses, for want of other listeners.'

'You make me want to try the poppy myself!'

'It is all true, at first, and it is why our doctors prize this medication. But no-one can control it except by stopping it, and no-one can stay free of the craving.'

'Does he crave it yet?'

'This is why I spend the time with him, so he will take tea and so I can observe him. He is going deeper all the time. It is possible now to watch him while he dreams, without him knowing anyone is there Such is the violence of his visions, he has begun to cry out and even my men can pick out the name he calls again and again. Estela. She is someone important to him. We can use this weakness.'

'We should note all that he lets slip, any such names, what they mean to him. You are right. It could be useful.' The other man brooded a moment. 'Does the poppy impair his manhood?'

'At first it will increase desire, and the capacity to remain inside a woman's body before climax. His dreams will add to his waking fantasies and he will be able to perform more than he ever imagined possible. Then all this will be so but without any climax, and finally, as the poppy takes hold, his lance will be limp and he will forget that desire ever existed.'

'Then we should act sooner, to find out all we can, make the most of his weakness.'

Dragonetz made obeisance to his Seigneur, only half-aware of the words fluttering in air that crackled with the excitement of the coming hunt. Like his brethren, Caradoc and Perceval, he had vowed to make the Grail his unswerving aim but if he should chance upon lively game in pursuit of his mission, he had the Seigneur's permission to hunt in the royal forest and by the rood he would make the most of it. After all, sighting deer was more likely than sighting the elusive artefact, which seemed to prefer Perceval for reasons Dragonetz chose not to dwell on. Since his visions, Perceval had seemed more and more a man apart, not one to feel the call of sunlight through trees, the rush as silence turned to a frenzy of movement and the baying of hounds.

When the old mage stopped Dragonetz en route to the stables, there was an urge to shake off the hand on his arm but he was not so far gone as to ignore the Seigneur's mysterious advisor. True to form, Dragonetz received counsels that made no sense whatsoever. 'Chance will bring the Grail near you, young Dragonetz but only if you rise above your body's needs. What do you seek?'

'The Grail,' Dragonetz replied, irritated at a riddle which was none.

'Remember that,' the sage nodded, 'for you will be given what you seek. And guard well your hounds. As long as you hear them tell, the forest's hold will not be strong enough to affect your choice, but you will always have a choice, merely one that grows harder, the deeper the tendrils twine in your mind. Remember that too.'

Along the broad tracks between forest and field, then the narrowing trails of boar and deer, fox and badger, spurring and galloping, spurred on himself by a glimpse of antlers and white flanks; never had Dragonetz seen such a magnificent head. The rack of antlers at full size, the carriage and movement of the beast showed a male in his prime, and never before had Dragonetz seen a white hart. Luck was with him.

Vague warnings fretted him but old men's caution was for palaces, and the thrill of the chase cleared his head of all else. Never had he felt so alive, so at one with the hounds, the hart and the forest itself, whispering secrets in the wind. Whooping, yelping, chasing he rode deeper until the trees raised their limbs into a canopy high overhead, blocking the sunlight, whispering, Lost, lost, lost…'

His throat was dry as dust and his leather water bottle long since empty. He whistled the dogs but only the rustling of leaves answered him. After whistling and calling till his voice cracked, he knew that the hounds were gone with the hart. 'Woof,' mocked the trees amid the silence of dogs. He beat his leather-clad fist against the saddle, causing the grey to skitter. How could he have been so stupid? The dogs were too young. He should have matched one of them with an older, more experienced dog for such an outing. All that training by the best fewterer in the kingdom wasted! Dragonetz would not be welcomed in falconry and stable with such news.

'Lost,' rustled the trees. If he ever found a way back at all. It wasn't just the dogs who risked starvation and drought. Dismounting, Dragonetz led his horse through the woods. If he could only find water! The shadows in front of him flickered as the wind and leaves sculpted unearthly shapes that changed into stumps and stones as he neared them.

Weaving through the darkening trees, his lips chapped beyond any normal day's thirst and his throat closing, unable to swallow, the knight heard the pounding of a cascade long before he saw the water gushing down from rocky heights at the far side of a clearing. He had taken one step out of the forest when the earth trembled and a night-black destrier pounded along the banks of the river, snorting great breaths of steam and pawing the ground between Dragonetz and the life-giving water. On his back was a knight in full armour, impossibly black, from the black plumes streaming on his helm to the black leather of his boots. Three white wavy lines were the only blazon on his black shield.

'What do you seek at my waterfall, stranger?'

Dragonetz didn't have to think. 'I would drink at your waterfall, good knight,' he replied, his voice rasping and sore. The trees shook with laughter.

'A second time I ask you; what do you seek?'

'To drink but a drop,' was the answer, as quick as it was painful. The trees reached a crescendo at the joke.

'For the last time; what do you seek?' The point of a black lance was levelled at Dragonetz as the knight shouted his challenge.

'Water.' Though his voice was a croak hidden under a wild wind through the trees, Dragonetz' words must have reached the black knight for the great steed reared and stamped, and, 'You must best me in the joust first!' was the reply and the knight of the waterfall drew back into position to charge. The setting sun filled Dragonetz' vision blood-red and his veins coursed with rage, thundering through his body like the water down the fall. He leaped onto his mount and found himself fully armoured in white, even to his blank shield and jousting lance.

'Who challenges me?' roared the black knight. 'Your shield tells of your shame yet you dare challenge me?'

'I am errant and seeking my name. Let my deeds speak for me.' Each word rasped Dragonetz' throat but seemed to carry on the breeze, float on the wind and the water, echo in the rustling leaves. He quickly summed up his best line of attack. His grey warmblood charger was smaller and faster than the black destrier, was accustomed to the joust and had a tenacity of spirit that held steady before charging boar or marauding outlaw.

This was no practice with the quintain, or game with a scarf dropped to start the charge, and with one roar, the black knight rode full tilt at Dragonetz, who stopped thinking and dug his long spurs into the charger. The clash on both shields rang around the clearing like a funeral toll.

As he eased his sweating horse to a stand, Dragonetz couldn't decide whether his right arm was the more numb from his hit against the black knight's shield or whether his shield arm had suffered more from the hit he had taken. Both spears were still whole but the dent to his shield and body left him breathless. He hoped the black knight had fared worse.

Although crazed with battle and drought, he wasn't going to be caught off-balance a second time and he was the first to turn, shout a warning and charge back along the river bank they had made their tilting ground. This time, he watched the angle of the other man's lance and shield, leaving his own shield dropped just enough to let the black knight think he had an opening, until the last moment, when he raised his shield and lowered his lance, unseating the other just as his lance shattered on Dragonetz' shield, sending shards in all directions.

Dragonetz leapt off his horse, waiting for his opponent to yield as he must. 'I claim victory.' The words trickled out of his mouth like a raven's caw. Still the black knight lay on the sward, oddly still.

The strike had been clean, unhorsing him with a body blow and should have winded rather than wounded him. There had been no intent to kill and Dragonetz had hoped to avoid switching weapons and continuing. All the man had to do was yield and allow him a sip of water, in Christian charity!

Dragonetz ignored his own throbbing shield arm and approached the supine form. He nudged it gently with his boot and heard a moan in response. Kneeling, the white knight found the answer to the mystery, splinters of the man's own spear piercing bloodied eyes that had been clear grey.

Dragonetz' pulse raced. He eased the helmet off the black knight's head, groaned in disbelief. 'Arnaut,' he cried, his dry throat grated raw as bleeding flesh.

As the grey eyes clouded over, his friend's voice whispered, 'Why do you always have to win?' Dragonetz held him, unable to speak. 'Drink or you will die,' the black knight told him, and once more the companion of all his campaigns died in his arms and once again, it was his fault.

Shaking, not sure he cared whether he lived or died, Dragonetz walked to the cascade, took off his own helm and obeyed Arnaut's last wishes. He drank. Then he drank more. Only when he had drunk the waterfall to dry rocks, the river to a bed of stone, only then did Dragonetz stop drinking and start to weep.

As if in response to the sound of their master weeping, his two hounds bounded into the clearing, ran to the man on his knees and licked his face, yelping with excitement. At the sound, all the sage's words returned and he realised the depths of his failure. Three times, Dragonetz had been asked what he sought and he had replied, 'Water'. Despite the sage's warnings, he had forgotten his true quest.

If he'd asked for the Grail what wonders might he have seen, what treasure brought his Seigneur, what honour gained. They said the Grail gave life. Would Arnaut's have been spared, if only…? His tears fell into the dried riverbed, sparkling like precious jewels. They gushed and flowed upwards, up the barren rocks until they formed a cascade.

And then they stopped. The cascade and the river and Dragonetz' tears froze as in a painting, so that he could not tell which way the water flowed before, nor which way it would flow afterwards. And while his world was motionless, a girl walked towards him, a girl who wailed when she saw the dead body of the black knight but continued walking towards Dragonetz, her golden eyes meeting his without fear. Her robe was deepest pink, strangely multi-layered, and as she reached him, so did the scent of roses, headier than any perfume he'd ever smelled before.

The world moved again, the water flowed in its natural course and Dragonetz breathed 'Estela'. The diamonds of his tears were in her eyes, a sad gift between lovers. 'Oh, sweetheart,' she said, 'what have you done?'

'I don't know,' he replied. 'Tell me.'

'You must guard the waterfall now,' she told him. 'You caused the harm and you must earn again the honour you lost when you listened to the forest and forgot your quest. You must wear black and no-one will know who you are. Even if men seek you, they will know you not in your black. You will be able only to say the words of challenge.'

'How can I escape?'

'When another comes to replace you. The same way Arnaut escaped. Let the Seigneur's will be done.' A tear silvered a track down her cheek. 'But we have until dawn tomorrow. Then she kissed him and each pink layer swirled onto another in a spiral around her golden eyes, until all she wore was her long black hair. Longing took him, stronger than his earlier thirst, stronger than his earlier remorse and he doubted the feeling for its very strength.

'This cannot be wrong?' he asked his love.

She stroked his cheek, made armour melt and flesh burn, murmured, 'It is not wrong.' She pulled him down onto the bed of pink silk and he let himself flow into her, as right as the river. If he doubted, if he opened his eyes once and saw a stranger's face, he forgot his doubts in his need. Never had his pleasure matched his urgency for so long, an endless ripple; an eternal rhythm, the stars conjoined.

'Estela!' he cried out, finally.

'I'm here, my love. I'm here,' came the soft reply.

And if a girl swore in Arabic as she eased herself away from the cushions where she had lain with a young knight, Dragonetz heard nothing, as he had fallen asleep once more. The girl dressed quietly and went to report to her father, having done his bidding.

'… along with what the guards have told us of what he calls out in his dreams, that's all the names and fragments of sense Yalda has been able to pick out. She goes to him in the mornings, when his manhood is strong and his mind weak, especially just after the poppy. His ramblings as he half-wakes gave her all that I have told you. She is a clever girl and will do as I bid,' Bar Philipos stated coldly.

'She has done well.' The other man looked at the Syrian, curious, but made no comment on the relationship that allowed a father to make such use of a daughter. He had known much about Bar Philipos before approaching him.

'Like all women, she is useful, if she is obedient,' Yalda's father acknowledged. 'And the knight is drained by such dallying.'

'If his Estela is so important to him, she would be useful to us…'

Bar Philipos' lip curled in contempt. 'Surely no man could be so weak! I have more faith in the poppy than in the girl but the more we bind him, the easier it will be to let him loose and reel him in should we choose – or let him spin into the black of his own despair and ending, should we choose.'

'I hope you haven't forgotten our common interest.'

'Damascus.' Bar Philipos bowed his head. 'We bait our hooks with the book and the knight, bind our allies to us though they hate each other, and where trade profits, we profit.'

'As long as you remember that. We must work together or lose all. I need to go to Jerusalem. I don't dare send any messenger and she will be anxious for news.'

Bar Philipos didn't need to ask who 'she' was. 'Tell her she shall have a book that makes her priceless psalter look like a common charter.'

'And you will tell your master that he shall have a book that makes the Koran of Damascus' Umayad Mosque look like a camel-drover's purse.'

'We understand each other. The book must not go to those dung-beetles, the Jews, who are never satisfied with the quarters they are given, or the trade they are allowed. Whatever they get, they want more. If only their curse was not on the book!'

'Superstitious nonsense.' Bar Philipos flinched at this bald dismissal of the words binding the book, and the other man continued, 'Your master can rest easy as, with the knight's assent, we shall not be stealing. In fact, now I think of it, we shall earn the blessing on those who preserve the book!'

Bar Philipos did not join in the laughter and his farewell was subdued. 'I wish you safe journey, de Rançon. My support goes with you to your lady for as long as her support meets the needs of my city.'

'Quite. And your master need know nothing of me.' The two men parted.

Treading barefoot back to his private chambers, Bar Philipos chided himself for feeling dirty. The young Frank always had that effect on him and yet the dark knight locked in his stifling chamber aroused no such reaction. Rather he felt stimulated by the way Dragonetz thought. What had he said? Expedience makes strange bed-fellows.

Expedience had brought him and the Frank together and neither suffered any illusions about their strange partnership. The Frank had so much to learn about the Levant, newcomer as he was, and perhaps he would make the right choices of his own accord, the more he understood what was at stake. As the legitimate bearer of the book, Dragonetz could make choices but ignorance of the Kaballah would not protect either of them from its power.

Should Bar Philipos obey that power and approach the Jews to whom the book truly belonged? He whispered to himself, *'Blessed be he who preserves it and cursed be he who steals it, and cursed be he who sells it, and cursed be he who pawns it. It may not be sold and it may not be defiled.'* He shivered as he knelt in front of the cross, and prayed to Jesus.

CHAPTER FOUR

E very time the wet-nurse Prima brought Musca to his mother, his perfect, miniscule fingers curled deeper into her heart and every time he was carried away from her, he took part of her clenched in his tiny fists.

Estela had seen motherhood. She had visited the cottages with her mother, seen love and hope creating magic and miracle, seen despair over death, and the worse despair, over unwanted life. She'd administered the herbs to soothe after-fevers and melancholy, or the holy thistle if the mother's milk wouldn't come. Estela's own herbal lore had grown from the knowledge Malik had passed on, but she had no need to add his recommendation of fenugreek to holy thistle, for Prima. No problems there for the wet-nurse, whose generous body doubled its output with ease to feed Musca along with her own son, Simo, a week older than his foster-brother. *What would it be like to suckle a baby?* Estela wondered, her own breasts newly unbound and no longer aching.

When Musca's face screwed up with hunger screams, the nurse held her arms out for him and would have left the chamber to feed him but Estela stopped her. 'There is nothing that you need hide from me,' she told Prima, who protested at this breach of custom but gave in, settling on a stool, closing her eyes peacefully as the grasping hands and mouth latched onto their one goal. From agonised screams to total contentment in three seconds, such was babyhood. There was a kind of peace in the simplicity of it. Food, sleep, wiping up mess. Again. And again.

Yes, Estela had seen motherhood. But nothing could have prepared her for how she, Roxane de Montbrun, felt as a mother. Even the word seemed full of strange flavours as she turned it on her tongue, to savour it. The word 'husband' had slipped down her throat, tasteless as stale water, but 'my son' jerked a string in her deepest core.

Estela pushed the reluctant Prima to talk to her and what began as an interrogation became shyly two-way. The nurse's name had come from an unimaginative peasant father, who still farmed Dia lands, with the five sons who had luckily followed his disappointing first-born. Her own man had died in the summer sickness, leaving her with a baby on the way and a place at her father's hearth. Even though she had a baby, sometimes it was useful to have the extra protection of her father and brothers. Prima flushed and looked away as she spoke.

For the first time, Estela noticed the young woman as a man might. Her honey-brown hair escaped in curls from under a demure cap and the curves of her body, enhanced by childbearing and the glow of happy motherhood, were equally rebellious under the constraints of dun homespun. Her manner, too, attracted. Comfortable with who she was and how she was, Prima knew how to behave in keeping with her rank. Unlike Estela, who continued to ask unsuitable questions.

'How did you meet Raoulf?'

Prima blushed once more, fetchingly. Raoulf had chosen her wetnurse well, Estela thought cynically, her suspicions heightened.

There was a hint of a stammer in the response. 'He was collecting dues for my Lord of Dia and I was helping my father with the tally.'

'I see.' Whatever pleasure Raoulf might have in mind with the farmer's daughter, he would see she was better off from his attentions, Estela was sure of that. And a soldier far from home was never likely to worry too much about his wife. Or children. Her heart squeezed in that new way it had acquired. She shrugged it off. Raoulf was not the sort of man to worry too much about his wife even if she were at his side. And Dragonetz? What would he be like as a husband? Another train of thought to cut short. Had her fancy been so unruly before the baby? Pff. All that mattered was that Raoulf had chosen a good wet-nurse.

Frowning, Estela demanded abruptly. 'How old are you?' hiding her surprise at the answer, 'Seventeen.' So they were of an age but Prima had been weathered by farm-work outdoors and chores indoors, her skin brown and her hands calloused.

In her turn, Prima asked Estela hesitant questions about her family, most of which were smoothly evaded. No outright lies were required as the key question never arose. And if anyone ever did ask Estela 'Who is the baby's father?' she had all her answers prepared, depending of course on who did the asking. As the women grew to know each other, Estela made a decision.

'I want you to bring Simo with you,' she told Prima, whose mouth made a frozen 'O' in shock. 'We're sharing one baby,' Estela pointed out, 'so I don't see why we can't share two. That way, you can spend more time here, I can spend more time with Musca, and with Simo too. Why not?'

Unable to pit, 'It's not done', against the force of Estela's will, Prima accepted the new arrangement and whatever the Chateau of Dia thought of the new craziness of its latest troubadour, 'artistic temperament' was held responsible.

No-one was foolish enough to speak to Estela of convention and respectable behaviour, although the young Comtessa-to-be did speak of new songs. 'New songs?' Estela repeated in a dazed voice, hearing tambours and cymbals, lute and rebec, over the imagined sound of a baby wailing. Impatient brown eyes fixed hers across the gulf of maternity.

'You've talked about nothing but the baby for two months now,' snapped Bèatriz, 'and it's boring! I can't believe you're turning out just like the other women. I really don't care whether your offspring slept for an hour or a month, or whether his dribble alchemised into pure gold! He's just a baby. And I'm stuck on the repeated end-rhyme of a canso! I need you to help me finish it.'

'Two months,' Estela repeated. Had she been living in baby-world for two months? She smiled, feeling cow-like dreamy happy. 'End-rhymes ... canso...' Her brain stood to attention. 'Sing it to me.'

'At last!' Bèatriz breathed a sigh of relief and launched straight into the passage that was tormenting her. Eyes shut, Estela teased apart the words and the melody, feeling for the wrong sound, finding the right syllable, the right note, the way Dragonetz had taught her. 'Play on 'ion',' she told Bèatriz. 'You could use 'jazion', 'volon', 'des-iron', and try dropping, not rising. More passion, less jollity. Languish a bit.'

'Thank you!' Bèatriz rushed off to experiment alone, leaving Estela humming a melody that had come to her, which she was still singing hours later when she cradled Musca in her arms. He smiled his gummy smile and she sang his future to him, a life of daring and damsels. Like his father's. Estela was back to work.

It was on just such an afternoon of babies and melodies that the visitor came. Nici was dozing in a corner, one eye flicking open occasionally to check on his people. Since Musca's birth, he too had changed. From the moment he risked approaching the new-born that mewled on Estela's lap, sniffed its sicky-milky smell, he had grown fully into the role for which he had been born. The role for which generations of selective breeding had prepared him, however scatter-brained he had been when sent to do his job with the flocks on the hillside.

Or so Estela saw the change in him, as she watched the great white dog and he watched her baby. Nici roamed less, spent little time with the packs of curs scavenging round the chateau environs, alert in a second when Musca whimpered. The appearance of a second baby seemed to have merely confirmed his belief that here was work worthy of a good dog. On this particular day, he was peacefully stretched out on the stone flags.

Prima was feeding Musca while Estela tested out a trill on Simo, skipping a dance step round the chamber and shooting him in the air for the high notes. 'He's too young!' protested Prima but Simo remained defiantly contented while the world whirled round him. 'You're turning him against his mother,' muttered Prima half-heartedly.

'Turn, turn,' sang Estela, suiting action to words. Simo gurgled, wriggled and waved his arms, blinking in the bright light that came in when the great oak door swung open, seconds after Nici had transformed into the Beast of Gévaudan. He'd leaped impossibly from semi-sleep to full alertness, glancing once at Musca on Prima's lap, then placing himself between Estela, Simo and the door. Hackles raised, teeth bared, legs braced to jump, Nici's low growl prickled the small hairs on the back of Estela's neck.

'My lady,' squeaked a page, and was interrupted by the figure behind him, whom Estela had not recognised with the sun back-lighting him to silhouette. Evidently, Nici did recognise him, and that was enough to warn Estela.

'I'll introduce myself,' interrupted a voice with the warm accent of Estela's southern home. But there was no warmth in this voice. Instinctively, Estela pulled the baby close to her and Prima covered up the suckling Musca in a layer of shawl. The growling dog waited, tense.

'No, Nici,' Estela told him, but she didn't add, 'It's a friend'. The dog stayed where he was, waiting, fixing the visitor with unwavering brown eyes.

'So you even stole one of father's dogs when you ran!' sneered the man. 'Ever the thief, and too stupid to know how useless this one is – though it seems you found out. You should both be called 'Nici'.'

Thinking rapidly, Estela told Prima, 'Take the baby and leave us,' holding out Simo towards Prima, but it was not to be.

'Take your own brat and leave us. The bastard stays with his mother,' came the cold counter-instruction.

Prima looked to her mistress, made no move, said nothing, for all of which Estela could have kissed her. Instead, all she could do for now was to nod and dismiss the nurse, along with Musca. And to promise, 'The baby will be safe. Trust me,' as Prima left the chamber, her precious son in Estela's arms.

The man had moved aside to let them pass, watched closely by Nici, then he closed the door after the nurse, restoring the balance of the light and shutting Estela in, alone with her brother, her nurse's baby and an angry dog. Should she choose to set him on the intruder, Nici was as dangerous a weapon as any sword.

'Miquel,' she said flatly, shifting the baby to her left hip as if naturally, leaving her right hand free to delve into her undershift if need be. She smoothed her gown lightly, feeling the hilt of the dagger hidden under the layers of stuff, and she tugged her fingers into the fold that was really an opening.

That gave her access to her second weapon, one that was not vulnerable to Miquel's sword. His hand had been on the hilt ever since he'd entered the chamber and although she didn't doubt Nici's courage, neither did she doubt her brother's ability to kill the dog without thinking twice. She didn't want to test who was faster unless there was no other way. If she had a third hand, she'd hold the dog to make certain he didn't make a move unless she wanted him to. 'No,' she reminded him firmly, clutching the dagger.

'Big sister,' he sneered, his face losing its initial resemblance to Estela – Roxane, as he knew her from childhood. They had the same straight black hair, although his was shoulder length and hers swept below her waist when unloosed; the same topaz eyes, wild as a mountain lion's, their mother's eyes.

Female softness and male angles made less of a difference between them than the tracks left by their habitual expressions. Bitterness and suspicion drooped Miquel's wide mouth – also from his mother, but curving upwards in her and in his sister. His eyes were hardened to chips of glass and made him seem far older than his fifteen years. The face Estela saw in her precious mirror could be serious, her generous mouth straight and pensive, could be wistful and hint at tears, but retained a belief in people, which glowed in her eyes, in her smile, in her curiosity about the world and everyone in it. She took the measure of the young man in front of her, the stranger she knew intimately, and it came to her that the doors to his soul were locked. She shrugged off the foolish fantasy.

'My dear, *dead* big sister. The mourning for you was as fake as your death.'

'I don't doubt it.' She looked him straight in those cold eyes and held his gaze. She had to try. He was her brother after all. 'Miquel, there's so much you don't know, so much that you've been told that's just not true. If you would just listen and think...' Simo gurgled sleepily, his fuzzy brown head nodding, and Estela shuggled him gently, crooning nonsense words, pacing a little to lull him with the movement. This seemed to ignite whatever burning issues Miquel had brought into the room with him.

'Whore,' he hissed, provoking a warning bark from Nici, 'flaunting your bastard, seeking my inheritance for *that*.' His sword was unsheathed in a clang of anger but he came no nearer.

Estela still had time to throw a dagger before he made a move, and she could throw a dagger to lethal effect – Gilles had made sure of that. Thanks to Gilles, the dagger through the placket was of best steel, however pretty it looked – and it had to look pretty because it was Miquel's dagger.

Pretty mattered to Miquel. Too closely watched by her stepmother to keep or hide her own blade, Estela had stolen Miquel's the night she'd run away, relying on his usual carelessness. The servants who daily searched her bed and her clothing, who watched her every move, had not thought of her hiding Miquel's dagger under his own window, to be reclaimed from there in stealth while he slept in his usual liquor-ridden stupor. If he were in his own bed at all.

'The misbegotten brat of a stable-hand,' he spat at her. 'What would you know about truth? Rutting in the straw, tainting the name and the blood of de Montbrun with that animal!'

Estela blinked and flushed, wounded despite herself, for there was some truth in the words flung. How could she have forgotten? He thought she'd conceived from her stupid, youthful notion of becoming a woman in the hands of a boy working in the stables. Once and once only. No, there had been no consequences for her. Or at least, no physical ones apart from the loss of her virginity. But the consequences for him!

With an effort she remembered his name. Peire. Yes, that was it. A shock of brown hair, bright eyes. A mistake. A stupid, youthful mistake, that's all it had been. She'd been married after all. To a man who'd made his vows and then quietly, kindly abandoned her as he'd arranged with the ruler of Narbonne. A marriage of convenience. So she'd had the right to become a woman, her own way, with a man of her own choosing. But it had not been what she wanted at all. It had been exactly what her brother called it.

If Dragonetz had not healed the damage caused, she might never have become a woman, in the richer senses of the word. And then Peire had been found murdered and mutilated, in such a way that made it clear why he'd been killed. Executed by someone unknown, for his folly with a lady of higher rank.

Her nerves on edge, Estela remembered her suspicions. No unknown would have murdered Peire as a message to her, a message underlined by sending Gilles to find her, falsely accused, his right hand amputated, with words from her stepmother Costansa, hoping she had received both messages. She studied this brother of hers. Who else would jump to Costansa's bidding, like the lapdog he'd become?! Better that he believed Peire to be her baby's father. But she must try, for their mother's sake. She made the mistake of saying the words aloud.

'For our mother's sake,' she began and his face burned white with hatred.

'Don't dirty our mother's name from your whore's mouth! Spare your poisonous breath. Costansa told me every lie you'd tell. That you'd pretend you never stole her jewels, you'd say that she hid them, that she accused you so our father would whip you, that she wanted you out of our lives. She knew that you'd blame her for every evil thing you've done.'

Estela snapped. 'Including swiving her husband's son?!' she hurled at him and saw she'd hit home. Simo woke at the shouting, crying with baby-fears. 'There, there,' she shushed him, wanting to change hip for carrying him but not daring to put the dagger out of reach.

Miquel rallied, suddenly sounding young as his years, and Estela remembered them climbing the big apple tree together, playing 'who could go the furthest' along an ever thinner branch, to reach the furthest fruit. 'I don't have to justify the love between Costansa and me. Someone like you could never understand. What she puts up with from *that man*.' He shook his head, shaking spittle with the movement.

So much anger! *Look out father*, Estela thought, and then the question she didn't want answered spoke itself, a cold statement of fact. 'You killed the stable hand,' she heard herself saying.

'Hurt, did it? Seeing your lover like that, your little love toys covered in blood. No more playing.'

'You are mad. Possessed.' Another cold statement of fact.

His smile was worse than his sneers. 'Costansa told me you'd do that too. That you'd try to shake my confidence in my own mind. Won't work, big sister.

I've enjoyed our talk but I'm not stupid. Your servant has had the time to fetch your man and no doubt the cripple can find someone with two hands to help him out, so I'll not finish the job here, where my way out might be blocked. That wouldn't be very clever, would it.

I want you to sweat. I want you to wake in the night knowing that I'm out there, that I'm coming for you, that people will always let me in to see you because I'm your brother.

And don't rely on your watch-dog. Dogs die so easily. Who knows when a bit of poisoned meat will be Nici's final treat?' He gave a spectral grin, opening the door behind him, about to leave.

Thank God, thank God.

But not without a parting shot. 'And when I choose, I shall kill you both.' He pointed his sword at her chest. 'You.' He twirled his sword in a flourish, while Estela's grip tightened on the dagger, but he never moved closer. 'And the bastard.' He assumed an attacking pose with the point towards Simo.

Outraged, Nici barked and sprang but the distance between them allowed Miquel enough time to escape, vanishing with the light as he heaved the great door to. Nici stormed round the perimeter of the chamber, rearing on hind legs and barking his rage while Estela expressed her feelings in one anguished war cry as she threw the dagger to stick good and true in the oak where Miquel's heart had been seconds earlier.

When the door started to open again, she thought she'd been tricked and rushed to retrieve her weapon, joggling an irritated baby into full screaming complaint.

Daylight streamed in again and Estela fell into the solid arms, one-handed or not, of Gilles, who had always been there, always, from when she was a baby. Nici rushed past her, barking and sniffing, searching.

The tears came, anger and relief, as she told him, 'In the apple tree. He used to cheat. He always went first so he could cut the branch when he thought I wasn't looking and then I would fall before I got as far as he had. I fell twice, then I knew what he was doing. I'm not falling again! He cheats!'

'Where's the whoreson?' Raoulf demanded, drawing an ironic laugh from Estela.

'You mustn't speak ill of our mother,' she told him, light-headed with shock. 'Legitimate, I assure you, and I'm equally certain he's long gone.' Nevertheless, Raoulf took all but two of the armed men with him to search the environs, leaving Gilles and the wet-nurse with Estela.

Prima had extricated her squalling son from Estela's arm the moment she'd arrived with the men, and she was soothing him in a corner, unlacing her bodice for his preferred comfort. 'With the Comtessa's women' she answered Estela's unspoken question.

The need to know Musca was safe was swiftly replaced with an overwhelming desire to see him, to hold him in her arms, to know he was safe and to keep him safe. The two armed men followed her as she stormed through the passage to the women's quarters. Would anywhere ever be safe again?

CHAPTER FIVE

Dragonetz knew who the girl was and she had a name, Yalda. She also had a father. When she'd told him she was the daughter of Bar Philipos, he should have told her to go. He should have disciplined his mind against the easy response of his body to warm skin, but what was the point when he'd already explored her body with a thorough wildness new even to him.

Perhaps it was the months of chastity, perhaps captivity itself, but he'd responded like a parched man to water, even when he knew she was not Estela, even when he opened his eyes to see all the differences; the long black hair coarser to the touch, like a horse's mane, the skin darker, less even olive-brown; limbs rounder and shorter, muscular thighs gripping his hips; breasts smaller with dark swollen aureoles and tips.

Even cataloguing the differences aroused him and, although he knew this was no kind of love at all, he took what was offered. Before he even touched her, she showed him that her place of Venus was opening to him already, a rose in dew, and the dark kohl-rimmed eyes mocked him even as they invited – dark eyes not golden ones – but he took her anyway.

When he found out who she was, it was already too late.

'Does your father know?' he asked.

'He would kill me.' Her eyes widened and her sweat smelled of fear, unmistakeable as the sexual musk it replaced. That she was afraid of her father seemed indisputable yet there was something hidden.

'How can he not know?' Dragonetz persisted.

'I know the guards and their families. I know how to reward them.' She lowered her eyes demurely and Dragonetz chose to believe she meant monetary rewards.

'Why? Why are you coming to me?'

Then she looked straight at him, eyes flashing with that hint of mockery, and something darker, that he couldn't identify, something that challenged and aroused him again. 'I wanted to know what my sister, Aini, thought worth dying for.' Dragonetz knew he was being dared to cross boundaries but it was too late for him to care, too late for him to back away and pretend they had never met, never tasted each other's sweat.

'And?' the devil in him replied, pulling her on top of him as he adjusted the cushions for a new experiment.

'I don't remember,' she murmured. 'Remind me.'

Dragonetz studied the board. He would never beat Bar Philipos until his familiarity with the pieces and rules was automatic. He had quickly grown used to the plain board, without the chequered squares customary in his homeland. He had played with different sets in the past, from the carved wooden figures of his childhood to the crystal courtiers in Aliénor's Palace, so he was adapting to the strange ivory shapes in front of him.

He knew the principles of shatranj from al-Hisba, who'd told him that the old Persian game was still played in al-Andalus rather than its modern derivations such as the Occitan jòc d'escacs. From the same source, he knew that depiction of recognizable human or animal beings was unacceptable to Allah, hence these stylised Damascene chunks for shah and rukh, instead of the crowned king and castle.

What Dragonetz could not get used to was the complete absence of queens. Brought up to play escacs, his strategies were all full of holes, missing the most powerful figure on the Occitan board. He could challenge Bar Philipos but he was far from offering an equal game, still very much a learner.

The Syrian moved his white faras, the knight, in its devious side-stepping attack, threatening Dragonetz' green-stained shah without offering a direct check. Increasingly, Dragonetz found it difficult to distinguish between moves made purely to teach him all the elements of the game and those made in genuine combat. The better he became, the more skill Bar Philipos unleashed against him.

The knight's move made Dragonetz frown. It left black with no legal response. Then it dawned on him that this was exactly the situation Bar Philipos had told him about, the previous day. 'Strangled stalemate,' he observed.

The Syrian nodded, waiting.

'So I can exchange places between the shah and any other piece. If that's not possible, I lose.'

Another nod.

Dragonetz looked at his options, then flung back his head and laughed, appreciating the play. As a learner, he played it through, just to imprint the moves in his visual memory but it was a foregone conclusion. Whatever exchange he made only prolonged the game a few moves more. Bar Philipos had every outcome covered. The game was his.

They played it through anyway. With another jagged move of his knight, the Syrian pinned Dragonetz' shah in check-mate, saying, 'You had a book in your saddle-bags.'

'Had?' Dragonetz looked at his dead shah, playing once more for time.

'I thought it safer to put it where it could not be stolen. It is of great value, as I'm sure you know. Too great to stay with you, or with me. It is a book that destroys people, and chooses others. I would like to see it move onwards.'

'Then give it back to me and let me complete my journey.'

Bar Philipos shrugged, apologetic. 'That is not possible. It would be a disaster. When you know more, you will agree and thank me.'

'Then tell me more and let me be the judge!' Dragonetz struggled to control the rush of anger, aware that he was being measured, his weaknesses noted, while Bar Philipos' hands unerringly re-set the board.

'I think it unlikely that you will become Dragonetz Oath-breaker until you know the full consequences of carrying out your oath. How can you make your moves without knowing the game? I will show you the game first and when you truly know our rules, then you will see your moves differently. This will take time.

Already you have changed. In acknowledgement of this, the door is now open to you. The guards outside are no longer there to keep you in. They are your bodyguard and will follow you wherever you go. Don't try to shake them off or I will be forced to lock the door again. If you are still alive.

You should cover your head and move like the wind on the water, of no interest to those who watch. You will not be armed but my men will be quicker than you could ever be if there is trouble. They know the streets here.

You may take your horse, you may gallop wherever you will, but know that the book is with me and you must return to it. You must return here, for food, for sleep, for your oath.

First, a re-match.' He picked up two pieces, one in each hand, and held the lowly baidaks behind his back to swop and re-swop them, then he held out his closed fists towards Dragonetz. 'Choose,' he ordered.

'I will learn and I will win.' Dragonetz spoke between gritted teeth as he took the white pawn from the open palm.

'Then learn this,' replied the Syrian, opening his other palm to reveal an identical white pawn. Dragonetz glanced at the board again to see all black's pieces on the board already. His jaw set, he made his opening move, ignoring the gesture with which Bar Philipos threw the extra piece onto the floor, where it rolled back and forth until finally coming to rest.

Dragonetz' head felt clearer than it had for weeks, or was it months? He had no doubt felt so clogged from being confined to one chamber, with its permanent scent of roses. Wrapping the scarf around his head, an end trailing loose, in the manner of the man he followed, he stepped over the threshold to the outside world with only one thought in his mind and one destination, nothing to do with the book whatsoever.

The guard moved too slowly for Dragonetz' impatient feet and the minutes they took to reach the stables seemed hours. The whicker of welcome reached him before Dragonetz saw the glossy black nose hanging over the stable door, eyes liquid soft, ears pricked forward in welcome. He rushed to the stallion, murmuring to him in Occitan, caressing with words before hands continued the sweet process of reunion.

'Have they treated you well, my beauty, Sadeek, my true friend?' he asked softly, earning a coquettish toss of the head and the shake of a silken mane. Dragonetz unbarred the closed half-door of the stable, and went in to his horse. With the habit of years, he checked hooves for stones, feet for tender spots and legs for cuts or swellings. He ran finger and thumb along the spine, pressing to find any sensitivity. One hand lightly on Sadeek's withers, talking to him throughout, he felt the underbelly, for worn skin, for the start of sores from girth or saddle. Ears, nostrils and eyes were clear and clean. Above the young teeth were healthy pink gums and a pinch of skin quickly regained shape. No signs of dehydration. Flanks showed a hint of ribs, no more, so Sadeek had been fed and exercised, to judge by his overall condition. Dragonetz stroked the big cheek, crooned, 'All's well, my boy. All's well,' and he felt his own heartbeat slip back to normal, only then realising how anxious he'd been.

'Where's my saddle?' he asked his two shadows and the growing number of stable-hands gathering round.

'Better that you use ours,' replied one of the guards, looking significantly at Dragonetz' robes. 'It's safer if you're just another local, exercising his master's mount.'

'As long as I can take my horse out, I don't care if you saddle him with silk cushions, just get something here for me now!' Sadeek and two other horses were saddled up efficiently, while Dragonetz breathed linseed oil, hay and leather, the universal scent of stables. The guards' horses were Arabian mares, faster, lighter and shorter in the back than Sadeek, more like the forebears of Dragonetz' crossbred Andalusian stallion, which was itself lighter than the traditional heavy-hooved war-horses of the seasoned Crusaders. It had taken only one pitched battle in the first year of the crusade for Dragonetz to realise the superiority of the Moorish light cavalry over the slow solidity of the Christians, so he knew what these little horses were capable of.

Belting his linen robe higher above his breeches, Dragonetz watched the stable-hand saddling his horse, then mounted and allowed one of the guards to shorten his stirrups. And shorten them further again. Although used to riding *à la estradiota*, Dragonetz had seen the Moorish style *à la jineta* often enough to know how to adapt. He was used to armour, straight legs and high protection of pommel and cantel so it was strange to be so open before and behind him, and to have bent knees in short stirrups. It added to his feeling of vulnerability, without arms or armour, but the freedom of movement was a revelation. Leathers around his breeches protected his calves but he could feel the horse's movement in a way he'd never done before.

All three horses were high-gaited, not comfortable for walking for long and it was a relief to get out of the crowded city streets, where people scattered to the sides on hearing the curt orders of Bar Philipos' guards, who cleared the route swiftly to the southern gate. Once outside the city walls, Dragonetz knew only too well where he was, and eased into a canter. Past the lush orchards, onto the grey plateau and open space, he allowed Sadeek his head. His two shadows whooped, dug in their light spurs and followed, losing ground but staying with him as the wind pounded them all into a mindless gallop.

How far he rode like this, Dragonetz had no idea but he cared too much for his horse to forget there would be a return journey or to allow his horse to sweat into fatigue. He stopped to rest and to allow the guards to catch up with him. He cupped a little water in his hands for Sadeek before swallowing his own draught from his leather flask. Not enough for either of them to risk cramps. Sadeek was more interested in the apple he was given, and which was also a measure against dehydration after such exercise. The day was mild so there was little risk of fever from cooling sweat. Dragonetz tethered the horse in the shade of some huge grey rocks, to avoid too much mid-day sun. Bar Philipos' men followed suit with their own mounts when they joined him, then respectfully chose a place apart to sit and rest.

'My water is your water,' Dragonetz told them, raising his leather waterskin, inviting them to join them. They hesitated, and he added, 'I have nothing left but my horse and my word, and I treasure both equally. I've given my word not to harm you nor try to escape you. May my horse's life be yours if I break my oath.'

Then the two men joined him, sitting cross-legged beside their prisoner, in awkward silence.

Used to soldiers and their ways, whatever their religion, Dragonetz eased the moment from a jolting walk to a smooth canter. 'You ride well and I would know more of your style. How do you train your mares to dodge and turn in battle as they do? How do you avoid a lance with such a saddle, that offers but a bump in front of a man's gut?'

Within the hour, Dragonetz knew his guards as Aakif and Shunnar, and they had offered to show him tricks on horseback the next day, when they would ride only a little way, to a training ground just outside the city. They all agreed that Sadeek could never be as fast as the mares but Dragonetz was adamant that the stallion's intelligence and fire would make him win any competition the Moors wished to name. Somehow, they'd not only named a day for a friendly horse-back tournay in lance, archery and swordsmanship, avoiding their respective holy days of Friday and Sunday, but they'd even laid bets on the outcome.

The silence that followed, while the men broke fast with crisp meat-filled pastries, was that of brothers-in-arms, watchful of each other's back but needing no words. Replete, sitting in the wilderness with his erstwhile enemies, Dragonetz was free to follow his own thoughts on the uncomfortable track he felt necessary. To untangle his present, he needed to review the past. He was sure that somewhere in the events of three years ago lay the answer to what was going on now. It was time to face up to his past.

CHAPTER SIX

1148.

The crusading fires lit by Bernard of Clairvaux were already dampened when the Frankish army reached the Holy Land, but then Dragonetz was no naive boy looking for glory on earth and in heaven. At twenty-one, he was a seasoned warrior, accustomed to leading forays to protect his father's lands in Aquitaine, or to suppress warring barons for his liege lady Aliénor, his Duchesse. He'd laid siege, organising the great rock-throwing manganels and wooden towers; he'd led cavalry charges and he'd killed without compunction. His father was a harsh teacher, a mailed glove concealing an iron fist, but his lessons kept Dragonetz alive and turned him into a leader who checked whether there was clean water and a safe haven for blood-gorged soldiers, before he waved his sword and ordered the attack.

It was therefore with great frustration, rather than loss of illusions, that he endured the trek across land that turned friend to foe, before the army even reached enemy territory. Following in the wake of their German allies meant marching through black lands, pillaged and wasted by the troops before them. Every village was emptied before them, the people running scared or banding to take a small vengeance on anyone leaving the main group. Skirmishes and starvation diminished the enthusiasm of those with the holiest fires.

Dragonetz gritted his teeth and soldiered on, under the orders of his superior. Geoffroi de Rançon, Aliénor's Commander of the Guard, was a neighbour of the Dragon domaine at Ruffec, a man in his fifties and a veteran of the battles following that of the Field of Blood. His experience of fighting Oltra mar would no doubt be essential to their victory once they reached enemy territory. Or so Dragonetz thought at the time, having great respect for his Commander from riding out with him in Aquitaine.

The road to Byzantium was long in months and hunger, alienating ever larger numbers of people, and ending any possibility of returning this way. Dragonetz was clear in his own mind, even if others were only speaking of the route to victories and the glory of God; the way back would have to be by sea, whatever the level of glory or ignominy. In the event, Byzantium provided neither the haven nor the allied force expected by the German Emperor Conrad and King Louis. The two rulers finally met up there and combined their troops, whose idea of forage took little account of what would be left when they were sated.

It was hardly surprising that Manuel Komnenos, the Emperor of Byzantium, encouraged Conrad to take his troops onwards as soon as possible. No doubt Komnenos would have preferred all of the crusading troops to leave Byzantium as soon as possible. What was surprising was that Komnenos should have told Conrad how easy the route would be. The all-powerful ruler of Byzantium was apparently totally unaware of the danger that Seljuq Turks would waylay Conrad's army, as they in fact did, destroying it. Someone less trusting than Conrad and Louis might have thought that the Byzantine Emperor preferred a truce with his Turkish neighbours to new negotiations with German ones.

Meanwhile, Aliénor and Louis enjoyed the sophistications of the Byzantine palaces, hot spring water running under chambers to warm them, hanging gardens to delight the eye and birdsong in closed courtyards for the pleasure of the ear. After four months' trek, to sleep in a bed, to eat at table and to drink good wine, were riches more valuable than the gold leaf dripping from cornices and tableware alike but Dragonetz was uneasy. Beneath the hospitality lay only questions and disagreements.

Louis was lulled by lavish hospitality and devious arguments into forgetting that he had expected a Byzantine army to fight alongside his own. He would now be grateful for a promise of future appearance by some Byzantine troops as soon as they could be released from their duties. If Louis stayed in Byzantium much longer he'd be grateful if Komnenos sent as much as a basket of fruit to the Holy Land with his 'allies'!

When the remnant of Conrad's troops limped back to Byzantium with their Emperor, the catalyst was only just enough to stir Louis out of his torpor, with or without Komnenos' men. Weather was no excuse as even in January the routes were clear, so onwards marched the joint armies, or rather what was left of them. From the hostile lands of their allies to the lethal territories of their foes they marched, informed by the German survivors of what they could expect from the Seljuq Turks ahead of them, blocking the route to their next haven, Antioch. It was more practical to split the huge force into three, with baggage and supplies in the middle contingent.

Aliénor argued her way into the vanguard, as liege lord of the Aquitaine cohort, which was probably the most disciplined and cohesive force in the combined armies. Her red hair flying, she wore breeches for riding astride and was glowing with excitement, the one Crusader whose fire could not be dampened.

When Aliénor had taken the cross, a strip of fabric from Bernard de Clairvaux's own robe, Dragonetz saw her face light up at the prospect of action. Louis' face changed too but what was religious duty for him was sanctified freedom for his wife. Dragonetz knew his lady well and he was not the only man to worship her. As seasoned in what was called love as in battle, Dragonetz never found any other word for his feelings about Aliénor when he was twenty-one. He'd worshipped her. Had worshipped her from the moment she dubbed him knight, when he was still dizzy from sleepless vigil and looked up to eyes that claimed him as hers, even as her mouth stated the fact.

Every song he'd written was for her, his Patron. Four years older than he was, already Queen of France and versed in her role, her hands shook while she took his oath. She was human and he was her knight. And troubadour.

Whenever Aliénor came to Poitiers or another of her Aquitaine estates, Dragonetz was part of her entourage; composing, singing, and playing in the Great Hall or serving with the Guard. He watched her sparkling in her Duchy with her people, and dull with her Paris courtiers around her, like a buried diamond. The dalliance between Aliénor and her troubadour flashed repartee in Occitan and died into stilted foreign platitudes in the king's Frankish language, dullest of all in the presence of the king himself.

Dragonetz had sworn no oath to Louis and would have resented the kingdom of France anyway, whoever represented this greedy little region. Louis of France had only become Aquitaine's overlord by marrying Aliénor, and the nature of that marriage made it even harder for Dragonetz to stomach the king. Aliénor deserved the respect due to Aquitaine and the way she was treated by Louis, barred from councils and ignored in public debate, insulted both lady and land.

The king bleated his instructions from Archbishop Suger, his advisor, a shield against his Queen's pleas to be consulted and to take part in decisions. Louis made puppy-dog eyes at his headstrong wife, wanting to please her, but too scared to disobey his political nursemaid, Suger. Small wonder that Aliénor saw the call to arms as a heaven-sent opportunity to free herself of old advisors, who were fit only for tottering round palaces and abbeys. She would be a warrior queen, reclaiming Edessa from the heathen, inspiring a Christian host to work miracles.

If Dragonetz had misgivings about his lady's view of her role, it was not his place to say so. When she summoned him to private recital, and was moved to tears by his songs of courage and loss, love and loyalty, was he going to speak to her of wagon wheels and water barrels? Of horseshoes and harness? Would it have made her any more realistic about what she might face? Later events suggested not, but Dragonetz would always wonder. If someone, any of them, had been able to prick that bubble of naive idealism in which Aliénor existed, with herself the heroine of every story, would she have been less dangerous?

Instead, she was the heroine of his every story. Every languishing lover in Dragonetz' songs yearned for her and well he might. Tall, fiery-haired and fierce-tempered, with pale skin that flared red in passion, Aliénor was quick-tongued and daring, challenging all around her to keep up, hating it when they couldn't, hating it even more when she was confined by king and prelate to the women's quarters. She showed to advantage on horseback, threading through the soldiers, spreading golden words of encouragement, a goddess. It would have been churlish to reflect that she risked not so much as worn boots, protected as she was.

Dragonetz had made no such reflections at the time and had seen no clash between his unquestioning love for Aliénor, and his practical scepticism about his leaders' choices as the army progressed. The further they went from Paris, the stronger grew Aliénor's influence on her husband and it was typical of her to insist on being in the vanguard as they moved into Turkish Seljuq territory.

Riding with her Guard, Dragonetz knew she sizzled with excitement, like any raw recruit wanting battle to begin, convinced that her loosed arrow, her rallying call, or the mere sight of her brave example in the lead, would secure victory. That she had never killed, went without saying. That there were strict instructions to bundle her into a covered wagon at the first sign of danger, was also a given. Nevertheless, she was lord of Aquitaine, and was treated as such by de Rançon, if not by de Maurienne, uncle to the French king and placed in the vanguard to represent Frankish interest.

Dragonetz was at Aliénor's side when these two nobles cantered up to her. Although they were well into Seljuq territory, the day's journey had gone without incident so far, and, at barely mid-day, they were already approaching the crest of Mount Cadmus, chosen for the night's halt.

'We pitch camp here for the night, my Lady.' De Rançon steadied his grey beside her, snorts of steam showing the horses' efforts on the climb.

Two sullen frown lines wrinkled Aliénor's forehead. 'That would be a waste of the time we've gained. Our scouts have reported a plateau but a few hours ahead, flat and fair, perfect for our camp. We should profit from our speed and continue. The heathens will never expect us to be upon them so soon and the element of surprise is worth ten thousand men.'

Before de Rançon could respond, de Maurienne pulled a face that would sour milk and abort sheep. 'My King expressly instructed that we camp on Mount Cadmus for the night, where the goods-train and his own army will join us. Remember that the Germans were ambushed in this pass and we need to regroup as soon as we can.'

Twin points of hectic colour flared in Aliénor's cheeks. 'My husband,' she emphasised the title, 'has not seen the terrain here. Nor heard from scouts that all is clear. If he had, he would order this army to continue. The fact there was an ambush here three months ago means nothing! As the vanguard is under my orders, I command you, de Rançon, to continue with the day's march!'

Dragonetz held his breath, in no position to intervene. The silence stretched.

'Are you the Commander of my Guard or are you not, de Rançon?' The ice in her tone was cutting, the threat clear.

'At your service, my Lady,' came the unequivocal reply. He was going to order them to march onwards.

'No,' shouted Dragonetz, jumping off his horse, clutching Aliénor's bridle and stopping them all in their tracks. She glared at him.

'You overstep yourself, my Lord Dragonetz. Be careful what you say next lest I find I have a traitor in my Guard.'

'Dragonetz,' warned de Rançon.

There was no going back and Dragonetz hoped wholeheartedly

that there would be no going forward. 'No,' he repeated, more quietly, but the words still tumbled over themselves. Months of hearing bad advice leading to bad decisions welled up and poured out into this one attempt to stop lunacy. 'My lady, if we continue, we are opening up the baggage train to attack. We cannot abandon them like this! The Seljuqs could be anywhere in these mountains. Those behind us will be slower, losing more and more distance from us, splitting up our army and making each section more vulnerable. Our horses need rest and our men must rally their strength in case they are called upon to fight. Our gains will show if we need to act in our defence.'

De Rançon leant down from the saddle and struck Dragonetz across the cheek with his glove, drawing blood. 'You weren't asked to speak.'

Aliénor held up her hand, stopping de Rançon from striking again. 'He means well,' she observed dispassionately. 'We need men who care enough to speak out.' Dragonetz' hopes rose. 'Even when they're wrong. There has been no sign of these Seljuqs who are supposed to be everywhere. Our scouts have reported the terrain clear. Louis will catch up to the others for a night here. And we can ride a few hours more to be better rested and in full possession of a perfect campsite. You should be thinking of attack not defence!'

Dragonetz dropped to his knees in the dust, still holding the reins of Aliénor's mount. He unsheathed his sword and held the hilt out towards her. 'By my oath to you, by all that's sacred, I swear I would rather you kill me with the same sword by which you made me knight, than make this wrong choice.'

Her eyes flashed at him, impatient. 'Enough histrionics, Dragonetz. I am not so easily swayed.' She lashed out at him with a boot, kicking his hands off her reins and dropping his sword in the dust. 'Leave me. I want only loyal men beside me. Give the orders, de Rançon, then ride with me. Let those who see bog-sprites and nightmares go back to Paris where they belong!' As she spurred her horse into a canter, Dragonetz picked his sword out of the dust. His father's men were with him in seconds, bear-like Raoulf and his golden son Arnaut, ready to kill or die for him, as he was for Aliénor.

'You heard our orders,' he told them curtly. 'Tell the men.' They'd been with him long enough to say nothing, but do exactly what they'd been told. Dragonetz ignored de Maurienne's impotent clucking, mounted his horse and rode on along the Kazik Beli Pass, down the other side of the mountains until they reached an inviting plateau. There had been no attacks, not even one sighting of a Seljuq. The surroundings were clearly visible from the campsite and Aliénor was protected by de Rançon and her Guard, including Dragonetz' men. Raoulf would rage at being given the slip but then if Dragonetz was to suffer Raoulf's anger, they would both still be alive. He would take no-one with him and then he could take no-one down with him if he were wrong, for there would be a reckoning with Aliénor in either case.

Dragonetz apologised to his horse, left the army setting up camp and galloped like a raised ghost back along the route they'd just travelled, back to Mount Cadmus.

CHAPTER SEVEN

He heard the fighting before he saw the Turks controlling the crest, their backs towards him, concentrated on the battle below them and completely unaware of the lone horseman approaching from the east. Silent as a quick death, Dragonetz spurred through the Seljuqs, scything them aside with a wild sword. On foot and taken by surprise, the Turks barely had time to call the alarm before the knight was through and past them, galloping on to the source of screaming men and horses. Carving his way to a Frankish standard, Dragonetz dismounted and clasped the shaking hands of the bearer, a lad standing by an overturned and smoking wagon, while his friends protected their knights' mounts in the little shelter offered.

'Tell me,' he ordered.

'They jumped us when we reached the pass. Word went round that the vanguard must all be dead or they'd be here but no-one's seen bodies.' His eyes widened and he started shaking again. 'They're demons, Sire. They've murdered and eaten our brothers. That's why there's no bodies.' Dragonetz slapped his face, shocking the boy out of his hysteria.

'The vanguard is safe and well,' Dragonetz told him bitterly. 'I'm here to prove it.' He looked around the mass, distinguishing the spiked helmets of the Seljuqs from the flat plate of his own side, estimating numbers and progress as best he could in the chaos. Then his breath caught as he saw the king's standard in the thick of the fighting.

'King Louis is here?' he demanded urgently.

'Lord Odo went back to fetch them, sire, and they came but they're too late.'

'No they're not!' The boy needed something to do, not standing still with his fears creeping up like sabres in the mist. 'Boy, you and your friends will do something this day that will be talked of in every great kitchen in every Frankish hall. You will have any kitchen-maid yours at just the mention of your name.' He lifted the lad's head and met the spark of hope with a steady gaze. 'There is no fame without danger but, thanks to you, our army will live to see the morrow.'

He surveyed the white faces and chose the steadiest. 'You, stay here. Guard the standard and the remaining horses. The rest of you, mount, and ride like the wind, up the pass. Stop for nothing and no-one, not for the heathens, not for each other. If you're wounded, ride on; if you're killed, then your spirit carries on! Go to my Lord de Rançon and my Lady Aliénor where they camp down the mountain and bring them here. A thousand times you've dreamed of racing these horses, ducking past the enemy. Now! Sooner than now! Do it!'

The prospect of action galvanised the boys and they knew horses well enough to do exactly what was asked of them. Throwing themselves onto animals already restless with the scent and sound of blood and steel, the lads disappeared in a storm of dust.

'God speed,' Dragonetz murmured. This was no terrain for cavalry and he left his own horse with the others. The battle showed Louis and his elite knights winning a route for the baggage train to reach the crest, but at terrible cost. Dragonetz took his customary minute to prepare mentally, then hurled defiance at the world as his life narrowed to killing or being killed.

All close fighting in battles was brute and blind. Although aiming for King Louis, each path towards him was indirect and through bodies, so survival instinct led Dragonetz in circles back to the wagon where he'd left his horses.

A woman's scream broke through his concentration and he saw a knight, backed against the wagon, defending someone behind him against five scimitars. Dragonetz pushed harder and was near enough to hear the crude sexual jibes from the Seljuqs, unmistakable even in thick Turkish. He was near enough to see the anguish in the knight's eyes as he succumbed to the inevitable, but too slow to prevent a curved blade ripping the woman's gown from top to toe even as she sobbed for her husband. What happened next shocked Dragonetz as much as the Turks, who turned and fled, gibbering. The semi-naked woman displayed an unmistakably male set of genitals beneath her female clothing and after a moment to recover his sang-froid, Dragonetz threw 'her' a blanket grabbed from his horse.

'That is the most remarkable distraction I have ever been offered by a comrade but it has served its purpose now,' Dragonetz told the shivering victim. 'Wait with the boy. You can join Aliénor and the ladies,' he queried 'ladies' with a glance at her and received a nod, '...later,' he finished and left her.

This time he was more successful in making his way towards the king, his route made easier by diminishing numbers of men in his way. More Christian bodies than Turks, he noted, suspending all feelings until such time they would not hinder him.

His body thrummed with crazy energy, the sanguine humour unchecked. Heart hammering, he saw his king take a hit and rage flooded him. From that moment, he had no idea what happened in the battle but they told him afterwards that he drove back the last Seljuqs round the king and finished the work done by the coterie of knights dying beside their sovereign.

Noise from the east told of reinforcements, the vanguard returning, but the Seljuqs were already disappearing like dust, celebrating their victory. They didn't know how close they had come to ending the crusade before it had begun.

Louis had battled on even when wounded, a king worth fighting for, and already a name was whispered around Dragonetz, carried on battle-breath, attaching itself where it belonged, as nicknames will. 'Los Pros,' men nodded to each other. 'Dragonetz los Pros. Dragonetz the brave.'

Los Pros himself was stunned, sitting where he'd dropped to the ground, every joint catching up with the day's blows, every thought clanging in despair at what should never have happened. When he saw Aliénor and de Rançon riding up to the King beside him, he flinched, knowing he'd have to pay for insubordination, as he'd expected.

'Sire.' De Rançon threw himself to the ground on his knees before his sovereign. Aliénor was deathly white and silent.

It was to her that Louis spoke, ignoring the grizzled head of her Commander. 'You,' he said, for once with all the authority given to him by holy ointment, 'will choose a new Commander.' He struggled to his feet, supported by two of his men, and withdrew to have his wound taken care of, without a backward look at the Queen or the man whose reputation was in the dust beside him.

Set-faced, Aliénor made her public declaration. 'From this day on, Dragonetz los Pros is my Commander of the Guard. His orders are my orders.' Then she too left, in the opposite direction from the king, to join her women.

Dragonetz stumbled towards an overturned wagon, where he used the last of his strength to send a woman and a boy on his horse to join Aliénor and her ladies. Then he slept where he fell, while stragglers from miles around discovered they were alive and rejoined the camp on the crest; while Seljuqs sang their victory to the winds that blew confidence north across Rum and east to Damascus; and while de Rançon and his son began the long and rueful ride back to Aquitaine.

Although milder than his native land, nights were cool enough for a blanket to be welcome, especially on the heights of Cadmus, and when Dragonetz woke in blackness and stars, he found someone had covered him, put a rolled cloak under his head and arranged his armour in a neat pile. Raoulf of course, ever the nursemaid.

The background noises of night camp were underscored with the anguish of the wounded. Dragonetz didn't need to close his eyes to hear the song of aftermath, to re-live every beat of horse-hooves and heart. No man was ever more alive than the moment after he'd outfaced death, and the energy that stayed when its need had passed was more dangerous than swords. That energy raped, burned, stole, in the shape of men who crept back into their own souls, shamefaced, the next day.

A hundred times, Dragonetz had prevented his soldiers destroying the very citadel or village they'd just rescued from marauding bandits, and too often on this crusade he'd watched helpless while his Commanders unleashed the wolf in every man, with no chance of ordering it back to heel. Dragonetz knew what drove his men because he felt it too. A hundred times, he had unleashed his own inner wolf in battle and caged it after. He knew every discipline of mind and body, from punching sacks of grain to reciting all four hundred appalling verses of 'She who goes a-wooing', to tame the wolf.

The aftermath, lying under a blanket with every thrust of the day replaying in his mind, bloodying the wolf once more, was no time for a woman to glide like a hooded spirit to join him under the blanket. No man, certainly not Raoulf, would blame him for his animal response and rough selfishness. This was, however, no sack of grain, but the lady he worshipped who lay underneath him, and it was wrong.

The wild fury he emptied into her compliant body was replaced instantly with a flood of shame and disappointment. He disengaged as if afraid he'd killed her, and bit his lip to bleeding so as not to say the harsh words in his head. What was she thinking of?! What stupid, impulsive lack of thought had led to this?

'It doesn't matter,' she whispered. 'It doesn't matter. It doesn't change anything. I want everything to be the way it was. Everyone makes mistakes.' Nothing, was the kindest, most difficult response he could steel himself to give, desperate to be alone, desperate for the whole day and night to have never happened.

Aliénor wrapped herself once more in her mantle, hiding her face so even the darkness could not see her, and disappeared into her own world, wherever that might be. Dragonetz didn't imagine any further than her presence and her absence. Once she was gone, it seemed more and more a delusion that she had ever come to him at all, and clinging to this hope, he finally slept again. In the morning, Queen Aliénor summoned her new Commander of the Guard, passed on the King's orders for the day and everything was as it had been before. Only Dragonetz had changed.

Mount Cadmos hadn't been the last skirmish with Seljuq Turks but the crusading army was learning fast. Dragonetz consulted the Templar Grand Master, Everard des Barres, who was leader of the hundred and thirty Templar knights in their company, and yet whose experience in the terrain had been previously ignored. Taking their advice, Dragonetz was soon drilling his men to make a stand, then withdraw instantly, to order. The lightning raids by the Turks were unlike the ponderous cavalry clashes the Frankish knights were used to and they had to adapt to an enemy that left as quickly as it came.

Refining their technique from hard experience, the Crusaders reached the port of Adalia, only to be barred entry. Three months after they'd left Byzantium, the tensions between Komnenos and the Crusaders left the Franks caught between ongoing Turkish attacks and the outrageous prices demanded by the Byzantine citizens of Adalia, whether for basic provisions or for the ships desperately needed to get to Antioch and on to Edessa.

Helpless, Dragonetz listened to his king pontificate about their oaths to two-faced Komnenos that they would do no harm to Byzantines, while daily reports told of starvation and illness among men and horses. Torn between evils, humiliated by his failure to follow in the glorious footsteps of the first crusade, Louis bought the ships, buying passage for half his army and condemning the poor and the volunteers to take the land route.

At least most of them would die in the footsteps of their glorious ancestors, or so Dragonetz had thought at the time. He later found out that the Seljuqs offered food and shelter to the young foot soldiers left behind, not even demanding that they change their religion. Word reached Jerusalem that the three thousand men who made that choice were well treated, unlike those who thought to re-home in Adalia, where the Byzantines used them as slaves. A few did indeed make it along the coast roads, to meet up with the combined armies of Germany, Jerusalem and their own Frankish brothers-in-arms.

Before the armies were re-united, Dragonetz had to suffer Antioch, where they were welcomed by the man sung of as 'the most handsome and gallant knight of them all.' Unfortunately, Prince Raymond of Antioch lived up to his reputation. When he walked into a room, everyone else became invisible. When he laughed, the world was happy. When he broke bread, everyone felt replete. When he said that they should storm Aleppo and Caesarea, King Louis looked at his wife's flushed face and said that he would discuss strategy with his peers in Jerusalem. King Louis pretended he didn't care when he saw Aliénor running along a passage with her laughing uncle, her bodice undone, or leaning over a parapet while Raymond pointed out the mountains with her hands in his.

Dragonetz didn't have to pretend. Whatever romantic feelings he'd brought on the crusades with him had died on Mount Cadmus and he observed 'the whore of Antioch' as she was known in the streets, with dispassionate cynicism. That she could not take her pleasure in a less public way endangered them all. Otherwise, Dragonetz could not have cared less. When Louis finally gave up trying to persuade his wife to leave Antioch and had her carried on board ship to continue on the ill-fated route chosen by God's holy warriors, Dragonetz was merely grateful to have heard of it after the event. He'd not broken his oath of fealty to Aliénor, nor made the worse choice of letting her stay in Antioch.

The merry band continued on their way to Jerusalem, Aliénor in silence or fits of rage, Louis talking constantly of his duty, and Dragonetz caring only about his troops. He drank and diced with Raoulf and Arnaut, talked tactics with the Templars and turned aside their invitations to join them. Love might be dead but chastity did not appeal. Raoulf's practice of whoring when convenient seemed perfect. There was no shortage of willing baggage women.

When they reached Jerusalem, Louis found spiritual sustenance; Dragonetz found a woman for half an hour. Louis visited the Church of the Holy Sepulchre and glowed with his renewed faith; Dragonetz organised mass privies, grain and water, repairs to carts, armoury reviews. He gambled, trained and whored with his men. He laughed when he heard that Alphonse Jourdain had been poisoned in Caesarea, wondering coldly whether Aliénor was behind the death of her old enemy. If so, she had cost them the Occitan army that returned to Toulouse, and the sullen cousin in Tripoli who refused to join the crusading armies because someone had blamed him for the murder.

Dragonetz had a task to carry out, regardless of how difficult these rulers made it. He had no part in the Council at Acre on Midsummer Day, with its endless debates over what they should do next, so he simply waited orders. When they came, he laughed again, his mouth twisting, and told Raoulf, 'We're off on the road to Damascus,' and the combined armies of Louis, Conrad and young Baudouin of Jerusalem marched towards the glory they had dreamed of a year earlier when they left Paris.

No matter that they'd left Edessa to its fate and instead were off to wage war against a Syrian trader-city, which was in a truce with Jerusalem's Queen. No matter that Damascus was full of Christians living peaceably with Muslims and Jews; the Syrian Christians would surely be only too pleased to bring Damascus to the true faith. There was no argument against the true crimes of the city; it was too rich, too powerful and temptingly within the 'natural' boundaries of the state of Jerusalem. Its independence was an irritant to the Franks and their answer was to lay siege to the city in the name of Christianity.

Three years later, Dragonetz was finally inside the coveted city, walking its streets in his robes of invisibility, feasting his senses on the spice-sacks and dried fruits in the souqs, cinnamon-sweet and turmeric-yellow, frosted prunes and almond-candies. The sweet tooth of Oltra mar was evident everywhere, in sticky pastries and snacks dripping in golden honey or sugar-dusting. Multi-lingual haggling in the souqs vied with hammering by metal-workers and builders, softened by the work-songs of the women silk-spinners and weavers, interrupted by the clatter and crescendo of a camel train from the south, setting up market in the heart of the city.

The camel-traders sat cross-legged in the Souq el-Sarika, their goods around them, bartering Egyptian perfumes, pearls and paper for Damascene silk and steel. Dragonetz took a professional interest in the paper, but was no less keen to learn all he could about sword- and silk-making. While he listened to the city's music, and shaped its singing for lute and tambour, he also interrogated all those willing to detail their craft to him. Most were very willing, given such a listener. Bar Philipos' warning that Dragonetz should remain invisible could never have been heeded by a man whose deep curiosity was combined with a rare understanding of how things were made, and how they could be improved. More than one craftsman looked forward to conversations in oddly accented Syrian or Arabic with the tall newcomer to the city.

Even the roses drew his attention, those same Damask blooms that perfumed his prison, blowsy and full-bodied. Wherever a patch of earth allowed, these hardy shrubs grew to man's height, sheltering against a wall or doorway, seeking the sun with their new-formed buds. Discussion with a flower-seller, who pestered him to buy a rose 'for his lover', revealed that blooms could be forced, in sun and shelter, to be enjoyed out of season.

Dragonetz thought of the cold stone of Ruffec, and wondered whether it would be possible to duplicate the Damascus method in Aquitaine. He asked for coin from his dogged guards, bought two roses in gratitude for the information, and presented them with a bow to Aakif and Shunnar. Their outraged expressions amid the laughter of the morning crowd kept Dragonetz smiling all day, though the poor flowers were kicked in the dust by their ungrateful recipients.

When Dragonetz rode out of the city with his guards, they went through the small southern postern of Bab ibn Ism'ail, past the irrigated orchards and gardens, into the empty lands where they could test each other's strength and speed on horseback. They were quick to learn each other's habits and punish the predictable, forcing and sharing new tactics in lance, bow and the games Dragonetz invented.

Sadeek's strength could not be matched but the Syrian horses were more agile, both by breeding and training. Dragonetz was determined to work on this and one of his games was to stick the three lances in the soil, well apart, so he could ride Sadeek in and out the poles. Gradually, the men moved the lance-poles closer, until even the Syrians were concentrating in order to weave in and out. And then they increased the speed at which they approached the twist. And then they had to throw a scarf in the air on the first left turn and slice it in half before it landed, without missing the two turns more through the lances.

Somehow, the guards had found it within their duties to allow Dragonetz his arms, purely for training purposes of course. Aakif complained that it wasn't Dragonetz paying for all the ruined scarves. Dragonetz complained that Damascene steel gave an unfair advantage over his own duller blade. They all agreed he needed a better sword. As a concession to the cost of scarves, Dragonetz invented a new game; holding their lances vertically, points uppermost, they competed to bat a leather purse between two rocks, yelling at each successful aim, 'For the glory of Allah,' or, 'For God and St Prosper of Aquitaine,' depending on who scored. Allah was in the ascendant but Dragonetz cried foul for two playing together against one.

CHAPTER EIGHT

W ithin weeks, Dragonetz had hardened his muscles and tempered his mind to match his new blade. The swordsmith had excelled himself, following the knight's instructions for a straight, double-edged sword, just under a yard in length and with a cross-guard wider than usual, allowing for both hands, or either one. Shimmering silver were the unique patterns of Damascene steel and the more Dragonetz practised for the display, the more he appreciated the edge such a sword gave him.

He would be ready, whenever the opportunity came to reclaim the book and ride on to Jerusalem. If an opportunity didn't come soon, he would make one. He studied the city, every gate in its fortifications; all eight of its radial canals from Yazid in the north-east to Qulayt in the south; the Bustan al Quitt, or scented garden, watered by the Qulayt, where rose-growing was elevated to an art form that included other perfumed species, jasmine and oleander, and sun-loving herbs such as lavender and rosemary.

Dragonetz followed his ordained path, which led from inside knowledge of the city, through plum trees and roses, to the place where he had waited with an army, plotting to take Damascus by force of arms. The more he reconsidered the past, the more he could feel the wrong notes. It was more than the mess of his own mistakes but he had been too close, too damaged, to see beyond himself at the time. If he played the music of the crusade often enough, he knew he could re-write the song of memory and find out how to get the book back. He could choose where to go next, not be driven like a wayward goat.

Little by little, Dragonetz re-traced his steps during the ill-fated siege of July, in the second year of the crusade. He remembered the moment the three crusading armies first met opposition at Mizzah Jabal, on the south-west outskirts of Damascus. Morale was high at last, from finally combining forces, and from the prospect of a real battle instead of skirmishes with an enemy who attacked and vanished into dust before the Christians had even formed ranks. Warned by scouts of the welcome awaiting them at Mizzah Jabal, the three armies approached in battle formation.

Young Baudouin led the vanguard with Louis' more disciplined troops a solid centre, and Conrad brought up the rear. Despite the awkwardness of the terrain, split up by the fruit trees, canal and irrigation channels, the allied cavalry beat the Damascans back to the river Barada, but there the enemy made a stand.

Peasants with pitchforks fought alongside the Saracens and only those Franks whom Dragonetz had trained, switched to fighting on foot. Baudouin's Franks were as reluctant to leave horseback as most of Louis' army and had it not been for Conrad's Germans, the crusade would have ended that very day. Infantrymen by habit, the Germans broke through the ranks from the rear, and disrupted the defenders' lines, sending them back to the Citadel in chaos.

While some celebrated, Dragonetz secured the allied position in the river valley at Rabwa, controlling any approach from the west. He organised the cutting down of trees as field fortifications; prepared for the diversion or destruction of the irrigation canals should they gain control of the city's other water sources; and tried to control the wild raids by battle-energised soldiers.

Burying their dead diminished most men's destructive urges but there were always some who were merely more determined to make the most of what might be their last moments. The camp followers earned their keep and the sausage-skins used for protection from the pox were worn thin.

War had no day of rest and perhaps Unur of Damascus deliberately attacked the next day in full knowledge that it was the Christian Sabbath. He must also have known that Lebanese reinforcements were coming through the Barada Gorge, although Dragonetz still wondered at how much better informed the Damascans had been than his own armies.

Another question for Bar Philipos. Was it just a question of better scouts? Better knowledge of the terrain? Unquestionably, Unur had been well-informed and led a mass attack through the northern gates in an attempt to clear a route to the city. Dragonetz wasted no time remembering the bloody immediacy of combat, one death much resembling another, and best thought of as a number.

He did remember three days of reinforcements arriving from every direction to join the city's defenders, three days of harassment from Unur's crack ahdath soldiers and his mercenary 'askar troops. Whichever way the Crusaders turned, from another direction would come the Turkoman Seljuqs, flowing into Damascus like the life-giving water in its irrigation canals, unstoppable.

Dragonetz also remembered the first night after they'd set up camp by the river. He'd taken his men to patrol the northern wall of the city, where the Faradis gardens remained, although the suburb itself had been destroyed by pillaging Crusaders on the first day of siege. He was scanning the fortifications at dusk, searching each section for a weakness, when he noticed dark figures clumsily descending the wall.

Within minutes, his men, laughing, had brought him the would-be attackers and dropped them at his feet. Putting aside the guilt he had carried for three years, and its fictive embroidery to the scene, what did Dragonetz really remember of the six girls giggling at their adventure? Veils, robes and giggles, indistinguishable one from the other. Averring their Christianity and their support for the crusade, offering – more giggles – whatever encouragement they could give in an hour or two. Hoping they would see their new friends in the city soon and that their families would be protected when the city fell, as surely it must.

Naive but no virgins, Dragonetz had judged, licensing his officers to do as they wished. To his shame, and surely eternal damnation, one eager girl had stayed behind and he had used her as easily as eating a plum, probably with less pleasure, in earshot of Raoulf's porcine grunts. Just one more girl, best thought of as a number.

There had been a promise of repeated 'encouragement' the following night but Dragonetz was busy elsewhere and the men who waited, hopeful, told him no-one had appeared. Maybe the guards, who'd been happy to accept bribes the night before, had been moved to other posts, with tighter instructions in place. Why think more of it? Especially when Unur's messages from the Citadel showed no more hint of surrender than the destructive sorties of his men, which continued in the usual lightning style.

Even parading the holy relic of the cross, which had worked the miracles of the previous crusade, barely lifted the men's spirits. This wasn't the sort of fighting they were used to and they were confused. Dragonetz was no more able to work miracles than was a bit of old wood but he knew they had a strong position tactically. They had food, water, somewhere comfortable to sleep in good weather. All they had to do was to wait. The strongest minds would win.

On the fourth day of siege, Dragonetz was brought to his knees, begging forgiveness. There had been messages between the Crusaders and the Syrian Christians in Damascus, brothers in religion, who would obviously welcome the new lords of the city with open arms once the tyrant Moor was overthrown. The same kind of open arms their daughters offered, on their backs in the orchard at night?

The messages from the Syrians had been effusive in welcome, in mention of God's will, and completely void of any details that would help the allied forces take Damascus. Of course, it was too risky to commit such messages to people or papers that could be intercepted. The consequences for Syrian families trapped in the city were unthinkable – the Moors were infamous for their horrific tortures. Everyone knew they ate babies and bastinadoed old women.

Louis and Conrad were voluble about the goodwill of Christian Damascans, once freed, but Dragonetz had the impression that Baudouin kept some thoughts to himself on the matter. Baudouin's grandmother had been a Syrian Christian so maybe he had some inside knowledge? Whatever Baudouin's unspoken reservations, any messages from the Damascus Syrians were received by Louis, Conrad and Dragonetz himself, with the expectation that they would reveal some secret of the city's defences. Contact from a Syrian meant hope of entering the city.

This time, however, on the fourth day of siege, it was no message but an anguished Syrian father, who came to the camp in person, grief marking his face with reddened eyes, cracked lips and ashes. He was brought to Dragonetz by silent men, two of whom had been of the party by the northern gate. If Dragonetz had wanted to lie, he could not have, in front of those silent witnesses. Instead he bore publicly the Syrian's account of his daughter's torture, evident on the corpse that was rescued from the street dogs outside her father's house. It had been tossed there from a cart, which didn't even stop.

From her sobbing friends, her father uncovered the escapade over the wall, the rope ladder intended for more innocent times and used by those too innocent themselves to know the difference. It was said that she'd lain with the grand Frankish Commander, Lord Dragonetz and that she was in love with him, was going to meet him again. The father was told that armed men in the city had taken her for questioning. They'd been heard telling her she could save her city by meeting her lover one more time, with a little twist to the story. She'd been dragged away screaming that she would never betray Lord Dragonetz. Then she'd been dumped, without eyes and without fingers, for her mother and sisters to see.

Dragonetz crumpled to his knees, saying 'I beg forgiveness' over and over, knowing that his real crime was to learn her name only when her father spoke it, his voice breaking. Aini. Dragonetz didn't even know what she looked like. The veils had still covered her face while he hitched up her robes and took what he wanted.

Willing she might have been but there was no word low enough for what he'd done to another soul and now she was dead for his sake. He was still kneeling when his men led away Bar Philipos, speaking of 'war' and 'courage' and 'sacrifice for the greater good', using whatever words would change a rut in an orchard to a sweet love affair, that would make a cruel death heroic.

Events from there on made no sense to Dragonetz nor did he care. He'd reached his lowest point since Mount Cadmus so when he received the orders to break camp and move south, to the region outside Damascus where there was no food and no shelter, he made only token protest. He was told that the Syrians had made face-to-face contact with the message that the Crusaders could force entry at the south, that the wall could be breached easily there and that they would have inside help.

The Bishop of Langres returned to camp from the south, confirming what Dragonetz had already told his Commanders but still they ordered the move, despite the lack of food or shelter where they were going. The three armies pitched camp overnight mid-way to their destination, at Qayniya, where they still had good forage.

And then the new orders came – the crusade was over. The retreat was sounded and they were all to go home, tails between legs. Dragonetz didn't care enough to ask why. He was Aliénor's Commander of the Guard so that's what he did – he commanded the Guard. He built walls stronger than Damascus between himself and any man who risked talking to him of 'war' or 'courage' and, worst of all, 'girls'. Chastity was no longer a bar to his joining the Templars, should they invite him again.

He was no longer the young man who'd come on crusade. On the weary route home, Dragonetz saw Aliénor near-death in the storms of rough passage between Acre and Aquitaine, between the news of Prince Raymond's death and her return to her duty as Queen and Duchesse. He saw that whatever had been between her and her uncle ran deep, below the skin, and he forgave her, a little. Who was he to judge others?

Later, he forgave himself, a little, and found again the sweetness of bedding a woman, and then found something much deeper himself. He had never promised Estela to be faithful in his body. He knew himself too well for that. But he would never find his match in anyone else, his partner in song and sensuality, his equal in grief and guilt over Arnaut's death, with her own share of the burdens that come with leadership.

The man Dragonetz was now, with all he'd learned from living inside the city, reviewed the events of the crusade dispassionately. He heard the discord at the centre of the melody and then all the wrong notes jarred at once. It was all in the wrong key, all of it!

Starting with the certainty that Syrian Christians did not want now, and never had wanted, Frankish Christians taking over their city. They did not hate their Muslim fellow-citizens nor their administration. All Damascans had one priority, stronger than any religion; the city of Damascus itself. Change that key and what questions there were to ask of the past!

Would the daughters of Damascus have been any different from their parents? Would they really have been so keen on Frankish occupation of their city? What if Dragonetz had underestimated the girls. What if he'd fallen for their giggling act, dulled by his own appetite? What if they had come over the wall so easily, on a convenient ladder, because they had been sent. What more innocuous spies could there be, to report back on the besiegers' positions!

And if they had made use of the more intimate positions in which they found themselves, to pose innocent questions of their gallants, as to how soon they could expect entry to their city, what would have been easier! Dragonetz had no idea whether he himself had been asked and answered such questions but he owned it was possible. In that case, he had been too quick to feel guilt, too full of hubris and he had been punished. There had been no 'love', not even imagined. He had been played; he was not the player.

The logic led inexorably to yet more questions. Why then would the Moors have tortured and killed Aini? With gut-wrenching certainty, he knew, they wouldn't have. Not unless there were reasons that had nothing to do with him. Aini had not been tortured to give up his name, his details. She had not died trying to protect him. Bar Philipos had lied.

Dragonetz pictured the grief-ravaged face and knew no-one could act the feelings expressed there. Words could lie, and Bar Philipos must have done so, but his face had shown unmistakable grief. If the daughter was indeed dead, why? And why had Bar Philipos blamed Dragonetz?

All the wrong notes played together in his head into a crescendo of discord; girls, spies, murder, lies, girls, friends... girls! Girls close in age, in friendship, in background, trusting each other for such an escapade – whether spying or seeking lovers made no difference. Girls who told Bar Philipos where they'd been, what they'd been doing and what had happened to Aini.

Whether his story was true didn't matter; the girls knew the answers. Who would be in such a group of friends? Who would be the natural first choice of company for a girl in such an adventure? Her sister, of course, and Dragonetz would not be played a second time!

Dragonetz grasped Yalda's wrist, stopping her hand as it reached his skin. He ignored the instinctive response to her touch and tightened his grip, waiting for the answer to his question.

'Yes,' she said, 'I was with my sister and our friends in the orchard, with your soldiers.' Dragonetz let go and rose to his feet, thinking it all through, while she rubbed her wrist and said nothing.

'The guards dropped the ladder, let you down over the wall, let you back in, afterwards. You were sent to check our position and report back. If you were caught – which you were! – you were just giggling girls on an adventure, using your bodies like a jongleur to distract from what was really going on.'

'And it worked.' Her smile hit home.

'Yes, it worked.' The words tasted of his own gullibility. 'You were the very people we'd come to rescue, fellow-Christians threatened by the monstrous Moors, so of course you were overwhelmed by our heroic presence and so keen for us to enter your city – so keen for us to enter your bodies too!'

The smile vanished. 'Now you know better. I am Damascan. What would we want with your toy soldiers, squabbling with each other over who should have our fathers' land. You did well enough from 'rescuing' us, my Lord Dragonetz. Would you be the rich 'los Pros' without rewards from the Queen of France for commanding her Guard Oltra mar? Were you disappointed not to get Tripoli or Acre or even Damascus for your great leadership? Is that the real reason you're back? You missed out on your share of our land last time round!

Yes, we girls were sent, and we made the best of the idiots we found! You have no idea how proud your boys were of your wonderful training and troop placements – nor how helpful Unur found the information! It was a pity we didn't reach Baudouin's men instead and we might even have had a real conversation about ending the stupid siege. At least the Jerusalem troops had some idea of how we live together here, without being afraid of baby-eaters and dark arts. You Franks talk as if the Muslim religion is contagious!

You want to know who sent us? Damascus sent us! It doesn't matter whether it was my father or another of a thousand Christian, Muslim or Jewish fathers in our city. Damascus and its independence are all that matters.'

White-faced, Dragonetz accused her, 'Damascene, adulterated steel, watered silk, a slut.'

'And you, my Lord? Are you so pure?'

Dragonetz pursued his dogged thread. 'That doesn't explain your sister's death. Nor your father claiming it on my head.'

Yalda's laughter was ugly. 'You mean you don't believe Aini was killed for love of a man.'

'No.'

'Wrong again, my Lord, wrong again. You have learned a little more about us but not enough.'

'It makes no sense.'

Suddenly the defiance collapsed, leaving the unhealed traces of grief stark and unfeigned in the dark eyes. 'No, it makes no sense,' Yalda agreed. 'But we must live with it. Inshallah, as our enemies say.' The mocking bitterness returned so quickly Dragonetz doubted he'd seen anything else. 'I am tired of this conversation so unless you plan to torture me for more information, I will leave you.'

'She didn't love me,' Dragonetz repeated stupidly, knowing it was true, not understanding what it meant.

'Shall I come to you again?' Startled by the question, Dragonetz studied the face in the window light. The morning sun was gentle, erasing blemishes from the gilded skin, reflecting his own face in her eyes. 'Has it meant nothing to you?' she asked softly, open as a flower, turned towards the light and him.

'No,' he said, avoiding her eyes, avoiding the pain he told himself he must be imagining, as he fixed his gaze on the street below. He would not be caught twice. Long after the heavy door had creaked to, Dragonetz stared out of the window, seeing nothing.

CHAPTER NINE

'There is no other way,' declared Estela, her eyes red, her face pinched and lined. 'I've been over and over it in my mind. Musca must go to his father.'

'But –' started Raoulf and Estela cut him off, reminding him with a glance that Prima was in earshot, both babies asleep in her arms like bolsters on a well-padded bed. Estela had called her two men and her nurse to a private council, a very private council, behind thick oaken doors and stone walls.

'Johans de Villeneuve,' Estela enunciated her husband's name carefully, 'will provide a place of safety for *his son*,' also carefully enunciated, 'and an education worthy of the knight my son will become.' She glared at Gilles and Raoulf. The latter glared back at her, looking more and more like Nici and with the same instincts.

'I don't like it,' he growled. 'We should find this Miquel, and deal with him.'

Estela folded her hands in her lap, the air of calm contradicted by fingers lacing and interlacing as she spoke. 'You've looked. Nici's looked.' The dog opened one eye at the sound of his name, checked on the whereabouts of the two babies and his mistress, then relaxed again. They were here. There was no threat. All was well.

'My brother is a nobleman, adept with a sword, if not as skilled as ...

some of our friends.' Two pairs of eyes regarded her steadily, knowing full well the name she skipped. 'He is protected, respected and there are many in my home region who will tell you that I am neither. Even if you did find him and ... deal with him, there would be no honour for you in doing so and no safety for the little one. Lies breed. There would be law-suits for compensation, and who-knows-what attempts at revenge. Gilles knows what that woman is capable of!'

Gilles nodded, instinctively holding his right arm. 'She is behind Miquel and his death wouldn't stop her. Losing his only son would spur Tibau, Estela's father, to ever crazier action too. He believes everything Costansa tells him.'

'And Miquel is my brother,' said Estela quietly. 'He might be himself again, one day. I cannot sanction his execution, in cold blood or hot!' She suppressed the question as to what she would do, with dog or dagger, if Musca's life were at stake.

'I don't like it,' Raoulf repeated. 'You're sending the baby away from everyone who can best protect him. I am under oath to my Lord Dragonetz to protect you with my life'. He ignored the eyes pleading with him not to say too much. 'I will speak plain! If I'm to protect you, he would want me to protect,' he hesitated, '... your baby too. How can I do that if he's a thousand miles away, near Narbonne, closer to the very people who threaten him?'

Even whiter and quieter, Estela responded. 'Johans de Villeneuve lives simply, has other children, has a noble estate, but not enough to attract attention, has the favour of the Viscomtesse of Narbonne, is a kind man who will offer Musca what I cannot. No-one will ever think to look there for the baby and Johans has no place in public life, creates no ripples.

But you are right. My Lord Dragonetz would indeed want you to protect Musca, and so do I. You and Gilles and Prima are to go with Musca. This is what I want. These are my orders.'

This time Gilles was equally forthright as the two men slammed their fists on the table. 'By the rood, I will not!' 'Nor I!' Only Prima said nothing, listening, wide-eyed as her fate was discussed.

Stony-faced, Estela said, 'And Nici too. He is a good guard dog and I want Musca to be safe. Even Nici isn't safe here now.'

'And you?' Gilles demanded.

'I must stay here,' she said. 'Don't you see? Miquel will think that the baby is where I am. If he sees me here, he'll stay, looking, convinced Musca is somewhere around. He hasn't even looked at Musca so if he remembers anything about what the baby's face, he'll be seeking Simo, and Prima, which is why you must all go.'

'He wants to kill you.'

It was the simple truth. 'Yes. But he wants to kill the baby too. He needs to kill the baby. Musca is a threat to his very inheritance. This goes beyond personal, for him and for Costansa. They won't kill me while they think I can lead them to the baby.'

The silence deepened, full of the tiny noises made by sleeping babies, and the larger sighs of a contented dog.

'I know,' said Estela. 'But there isn't any other way. Don't you think I've tried to find one! It's not forever. Just for ... a while. Until things change. Until I can think of something.' *Until Dragonetz comes back to me,* her heart said but she felt the words heavy, a lump of false gold, not true coin.

Raoulf weighed his words, speaking with difficulty. 'I know what it's like to want to protect a son. I will do this. But only if you keep Gilles. You must have someone you trust.' The other man threw him a grateful look.

'Gilles?' Estela asked. 'What are your thoughts?'

'I stay. You can cut off my other hand for disobedience to my liege but even if you order me, I'm not going.'

'So be it.' Estela spoke curtly and rose, turning to hide the tears that threatened. 'Raoulf, go soon. As soon as possible. And with as little noise as possible. Go at dawn. You should take Nici on a rope to make sure he goes with you, far enough that he accepts it. I don't think he'll cause any problem after that, if the babies are with you. I leave you to your plans. Good night, all'. She forced herself not to run from the chamber, left them and threw herself onto the loneliest bed in Christendom. Or out of it, she thought, wondering where he was now, her baby's father, and whether he was still alive.

The mountain air of Dia was chill in the blue hour, the time between night and sunrise. The few people who hastened to their posts in the palace or in the gloomy streets paid no attention to the preparation of a wagon in a quiet square with two outriders' horses attached. No-one took any interest in those gathered there to leave with the wagon or to say adieu. If a flash of unexpectedly fashionable silk could be glimpsed below the homespun mantle of a young woman at the scene, if a whimper of baby and whuff of dog came muffled from the wagon interior, no-one stopped long enough to remark what was surely unremarkable. Just another small-time merchant off on a trading journey, to Lion no doubt, his relatives bidding farewell – and putting in their orders for damask and spices.

'Head north for a few miles,' Estela reminded Raoulf. Her face was pale and set but calm, tear-tracks powdered over.

Massive and anonymous in mail hauberk for his body and coif for his head, Raoulf's voice was distorted through the ventail he attached to cover his mouth – more useful against dust when riding, he'd told Estela, than against arrows. 'Leave tracks as if I'm heading for Lion, just in case. Then cover the horse's hooves with sacking, brush the turn traces away and head south. Don't worry; I worked long enough with young Dragonetz to know the tricks. No-one will follow our traces. And you?'

Estela took his meaning straight. 'Must account to the Lords of Dia for a missing baby and missing men. They will be offended of course. I will seek private interview this morning, with any luck before they discover you've gone. I'll tell them that my lord husband sent word to me that his enemies threatened our child and he wished the boy to grow up learning the skills of a squire, safe in a friend's keep. I was ordered by my husband to tell no-one of their travel so, unwilling as I was to hide such a matter from their lordships, I behaved as a dutiful wife. I will tell them freely, in confidence, that this friend resides in Paris and has access to the court, so I can be proud that my son will have the education that befits a man.'

Raoulf pondered this, then nodded. 'A double bluff. You tell their Lordships a new lie, let them think they are in your confidence, and should it slip out, it fits with our direction for the first lie, our merchanting in Lion. It should buy us months, a year, maybe more, but you know that word will get out if your stepmother and brother keep searching.'

'I know.' Estela unclasped the chain round her neck, Arnaut's chain with Dragonetz' signet ring pendant. Dragonetz' promise to her, *'If you should be in need, this will show that you are under the protection of Dragonetz los Pros. If you send it to me, I will come to you no matter where I am or what I am doing.'* Foolish girl that she had been, she'd not realised that she would be 'in need' from the moment he left the room, and that for his sake she would not call upon his token or on him. The greater the danger she was in, the more important that she deal with it herself while he was away. She was seventeen now, and a mother.

Estela balled up the chain and ring so that no-one else could see it as she gave it Raoulf. 'This belongs to Txamusca.' His full name sounded strange, as if he were already distant from her. 'It is his right, his lineage and his protection. Use it in need. Make sure it is with him in case you die, and in case I die.'

Raoulf showed no surprise at the Dragon crest in gold as he hid the ring and asked again 'And you?'

'I'm his mother. And will do what I must.'

Raoulf hesitated. 'Prima.' He paused again.

Estela nodded. 'Once you are safe. Away from her kin and the temptation to tattle. She is in danger too and has the right to know who her charge really is. I don't know whether the truth puts him in more danger or less from Costansa but it will be easier for you to judge if you share information with Prima.'

He nodded. 'She can be relied on.'

'She will need to be. It's time.' Estela had learned that the more you loved someone, the lighter you had to be at the moment of parting. Otherwise the fragile barricade of willpower would burst open and the torrent drop you to pleading on your knees that he stay, that you stay, that the world stayed put. Estela jumped onto the back of the wagon, leaned in and planted a cool kiss on Musca's cheek as he gurgled. She stroked Simo's baby soft hair and thanked Prima for being a mother to both. She faced the accusing brown eyes of a large dog, who was panting and indignant at being cooped up inside the wagon. 'Nici.' His eyes softened as she spoke his name. 'Look after Musca,' she ordered him, and she knew he understood.

She climbed out of the wagon and stalked back to the palace without a backward look. She didn't need to look. Her imagination showed her Raoulf mounting his horse, one of his men riding beside him, ahead of the wagon, itself driven by another two of Raoulf's men. Even though she was out of earshot, she could hear a whip cracked across the lead dray's neck, the clicking as the horses were urged to get going, the creak of wheels and joints as the heavy-laden vehicle started rolling. She saw the small party roll to a halt, answer questions at the gate, start up once again as the guards approved their exit, once more the clicking and creaking, then the smoother roll of continuous motion. And she could hear babies. Gurgling as Prima rocked them, pursing their mouths to suckle with small slurps, crying as the wagon bumped them. Even the silence of babies left its own trail of milky peace. No silence of babies for Estela now, only absence.

'My lady? Roxie?' her shadow, Gilles, queried.

Estela's pattens clicked along the cobbles. 'When Miquel went to live away, to train as a squire, I remember my mother became very quiet and my father was angry with her.'

'Your mother loved you both. She thought about your duties, you and Miquel, what you were born to, but the love came first. She worried about Miquel being out of her sight, growing up under someone else's influence. And of course she missed her little boy.'

'Do you think he would have been different?'

'If he'd never gone away? Who knows, Roxie? A good knife improves with tempering. You know that.'

'But we don't know how he was treated, do we. What was done to him, good or bad.'

Gilles followed her thoughts. 'You can trust Raoulf. And Prima.'

'But the man I am married to? What do I know of him but what I've been told.'

'Told by the Viscomtesse. By someone you can trust.'

'Second-hand. The truth is, I trust no-one with my son.'

'You're so like your mother.'

'Who left me.' Estela's voice broke.

'No, Roxie, she never left you. She would be so proud of you today. That was a hard thing and you did it well.'

'Needs must,' Estela quoted one of her mother's favourite dictons and set her mouth in a thin, tight line that made her jaw ache. It was the only way to stop her lips quivering.

Having survived the tense audience with the Lords of Dia, and the private reproaches of Bèatriz for not confiding in her, Estela was free to get on with her life. Free, that is, within the confines of her duties as troubadour and as Bèatriz' lady, with all that entailed in preparations for the wedding in six months' time.

Superficially distracted by the girl's chatter, which bubbled excitement at choosing linens and lace, and at seeing her initials intertwined with those of Guilhelm de Poitiers, Estela dutifully stabbed those same initials into endless pillow-slips. Embroidery had never been her forte and it was unlikely she would ever be promoted above pillow-slips, but even spots of blood from a clumsy needle didn't spare her the work.

Music was the only excuse for quitting ladies' work and her lute seemed strung with her own nerves, weeping its melodies into listeners' tears, hardly suitable for the lively bride-to-be. Instead of composing the songs of bloom and fruition that were expected of her, Estela's every note lamented the loss of her baby. Whatever gay words she phrased, the lute sang sad and true.

Functioning by rote, Estela relived her mother's death, knowing that the numb, grey days would lift into a pain beyond bearing before time accustomed her to whatever life she must live, the heart of it gone. The double heart of it gone. She couldn't remember what she used to do before the baby filled her world. People spoke to her through that same fog in which she lived, their words grey wisps that she walked through, feeling nothing. She wished her brother would come back, cause her pain, even – God forgive her – kill her. And she remembered her mother.

At first, the memories led her straight into the pain she'd known would ambush her when feelings returned. She was once more the young girl told by Gilles that the sickness had won. 'I don't believe you. My Mare makes people well. Why didn't she make herself well?' she had defied the man-at-arms.

'No man, or woman, is master of his fate, Roxie. When the time comes to die, so it is.'

She hadn't believed it, not even at the funeral, with the prayers and coffin, not till the new mother was sitting at high table with her father, who'd said nothing to his daughter about either her mother's death or his plans to wed again. Then young Estela had known that her mother wasn't coming back, that she'd done the unthinkable and abandoned her daughter. Then she'd cried her eyes and nose red, hid in the forest, practised knife-throwing with Gilles.

Even as she hurled all her bitterness into a knife-throw, against the mother who'd left her; as she killed door-jambs and trees, part of her was collecting the set of memories she needed to survive, her legacy. When she responded like an unwatered flower to pretty Costansa's friendship and femininity, part of her stayed aloof, detailing the herb lore and abiding by the principles which her mother had taught her.

Now, paying for motherhood, receiving as much pain as she felt love, Estela resorted to those same habits she'd been taught. She was no inn-keeper's daughter to dandle her baby into manhood for a mere repetition of breeding as his only mark on the world. She was a de Montbrun, her children would make their own futures, and fine ones – whatever Gilles said! – And they would be given the education that went with their status.

The Queen of France didn't blink at sending her babies wherever would best serve the realm. Estela smiled weakly at the thought of asking Aliénor whether she missed her daughters. 'What in heaven's name has that got to do with anything!' would have been the contemptuous reply. If the Queen of France could do it, so could Estela. Txamusca was going to be every inch the knight, worthy of his father, and Estela had sent him to just the right place. He had his beloved nursemaid, and men who would help him grow as he should, from squire to knight. Estela's grief was selfish, she decided, and should be conquered with action.

Ignoring every furry shadow that was never Nici, and ignoring the pangs that bit her, Estela sought out the midwife. Healing others was what she needed to do, and if she must be haunted by shades of the living, then taking comfort in her mother's invisible company seemed suddenly natural. As natural as anise and arnica, coltsfoot and cowbane. The litany of medicinal herbs was her childhood lullaby, a treasure handed down from mother to daughter, and her knowledge quickly won the midwife's trust.

Estela was more than just another land-owner surveying her estate, visiting the poor with one hand holding a basket of fruit and the other holding her lavender-scented scarf firmly over her nose. She was a healer, like her mother, someone who knew that what started with help at birthing continued with cures for coughs and colds, and – if you fell into temptation – with potions of love and death.

'Cowbane,' repeated Margaux, the midwife, wide-eyed. 'It grows in the monks' garden, where I may pick at set times, but it is deadly.'

Estela laughed. 'And why do you think it is grown by the monks?! In the right dose it suppresses a man's natural urges. It can also be used for cramps but I would not trust it for those of childbirth, or even monthly pains. It is too strong and as you say, can kill.'

'Aren't you afraid of speaking so openly of such things?'

Estela tossed her head, in the habit of girlhood, when her long black hair had swung unconfined. She frowned as the movement made a pin dig into the back of her head. 'No,' was the short reply.

The older woman whispered, 'You should be. The Lady of Dia eases my way but the priests watch.'

'The priests will always watch. And do worse, when they can.' *A paper mill in flames, a young girl stabbed in the back, a man dying for his friend, Dragonetz' exile, all the result of priests who watched.* 'We can spend our lives hiding or we can live and accept the consequences.' The midwife merely shook her head at rash youth. 'Rue,' continued Estela, pursuing her catalogue of herbs they needed to gather.

'Rue,' echoed Margaux. 'But it smells so awful!'

'Needs must,' said Estela, smiling to herself. 'A heal-all. Suddenly another living shade was at her side; al-Hisba, with his Arab knowledge. *Pliny says that if a man carries rue, he cannot be poisoned. This we know for a surety because the weasel eats rue before fighting a serpent. And ibn Botlan says that rue will turn off the light of Venus. Now that was more useful than protection against snake-bite.*

'Rue,' she repeated firmly, 'which has the same benefit for a birth-tired wife as does cowbane, if she gives her man a judicious dose.'

'Maybe it is worth the risk,' Frown lines deepened between Margaux' eyes. 'Babies are a joy but also a curse. More deadly than cowbane. I lose so many women.'

'Then let us help women make fewer babies and more joy,' prompted Estela. 'We only give them power to choose. We don't choose for them.'

A sigh. Then Margaux added rosemary to their catalogue, to prevent the fairies stealing the newborn, quickgrass against burning urine, sage as both heal-all and – as Estela pointed out, shaking her head with disapproval – aphrodisiac, and rose-water.

The practicalities of healing meant there was no point suggesting rose oil or expensive spices, so Estela suppressed the reminders al-Hisba whispered to her memory, of cloves for the toothache – often found with pregnancy and poverty – and ginger for energy. Golden Saffron for physical and mental recovery from childbirth was as much out of reach as if it were real gold.

Al-Hisba had not only had the treasures of knowledge; his doctor's box had been worth all the riches of Dia. Estela was only now appreciating what this man of many talents had taught her. Maybe one day, they would meet again. She hoped so. But for now, he and her mother walked beside her as she picked and dried herbs, re-stocked Margaux' jars, visited cottages that smelled of the sickness in them.

She was even excused embroidery for her charitable work and so the weeks went by, each filling her life to exhaustion until she could pick up her lute without wailing the loss of a child. Until she could hear a baby's first cry and smile at the new mother. Until she was curious about the newcomers to the court of Dia.

The chatter of Bèatriz' ladies had been background water-babble for months to Estela but in her determination to be useful once more, she reverted to the habits of Narbonne, when she had dug the nuggets of crucial information out of the flow of trivia. Lady Sancha had taught her to memorise each lady's birthplace and background, to know that Uncle Raymond was heir to Carcassonne, or husband Edward was fighting for Henri in England, so that news of uncle or husband was indeed the latest political news, to be discussed in full with Dragonetz.

Estela no longer had a companion to share news with but that didn't stop her gleaning all the information she could, and coming to her own conclusions about what might be the consequences. As Dia's troubadour, she had a duty to spice her songs with the latest gossip, to amuse her audience with satirical references and sly allusions to the leaders in current events. To work, she told herself.

CHAPTER TEN

'You sent your daughter,' Dragonetz stated.

Bar Philipos paused for a second, his hand holding the lowly baidak that had gained the furthest square on the board and that was about to be exchanged for a fers, the only option possible in shatranj.

'I wasn't responsible for her death.' Dragonetz pressed the point. The baidak was smoothly sidelined and the fers took its place, threatening Dragonetz' horseman with its diagonal attack.

'Ah, that daughter,' was Bar Philipos' instinctive response, quickly suppressed. 'You play a good game, my Lord, but you have yet to fully appreciate that an oblique move is preferable. That's why the fers is promotion for the baidak, even though each of them can move but one square.'

Dragonetz studied the board but saw no trap. His rukh swept along the baseline and took the new fers, returning the piece to the sideline. 'Sometimes a head-on charge gets results.' Then he held his breath. A flurry of moves later allowed him to smile. 'Your shah is bare', he observed, taking the other man's last piece.

'A win,' Bar Philipos acknowledged. 'If lacking in elegance.'

'You won't answer me.'

'No. I told you. She was a slut. She never existed.' His eyes were always on the board, inscrutable. 'You are starting to see my moves before I make them.'

'I'm starting to see the pattern of past moves,' Dragonetz corrected.

'It is the same thing, my inimical friend. It is the same thing. I think we are ready to go to market.'

'To sell a fat pig?'

Bar Philipos was not amused. 'Your humour is ill-placed Oltra mar. You offend citizens of two religions whenever you open your thoughtless mouth. But we will go to market and find out what you and the book are worth, and to whom.'

'I am intrigued,' drawled Dragonetz. 'I'm afraid you'll find the book better behaved than I promise to be.'

'And you really think that will reduce your price in the market-place? My buyers want a warrior, a leader, not a lap-dog.'

'Woof,woof.'

'You are not tired of inactivity? Of behaving like a woman, talking to shopkeepers and peasants while kings change the world? When you could be a world-changer? Are you really so content to plan your little games with two mediocre guards, when you could have a thousand trained men under your command? I am not selling you, my Lord. You will sell yourself while I watch.'

The Syrian reached for his cup and swirled the dark contents before swallowing. Reflexively, Dragonetz picked up his own exquisite lacquerware vessel and drained its contents.

The black knight of the waterfall knew no other name, knew of no time before the waterfall and no duty other than to fight all those who came thirsting for his lady's water. His own thirst grew daily. When he drank from the pool he guarded, the relief flooded him but, increasingly quickly, his thirst returned, black and bitter in his throat.

He no longer remembered his lady's face but he knew himself to be her true knight. Only sleep and fighting relieved his endless thirst, so it was with relief that he spied a wanderer coming towards him from the forest. He donned his helm, mounted a horse whose name he could no longer remember, and prepared to do combat.

The wanderer was not only on foot, he was barefoot. Dark-skinned and dark-eyed, hook-nosed, his head swathed in a scarf that left one end trailing, his body cased in loose cream linen, this was no Christian. Although a sabre hung at his side, he was not dressed for battle and would have no chance in combat, yet he walked without fear, his gaze steady. The black knight shivered. He felt as if he should know this man but no memory came. Perhaps they had been enemies in some past life. Still the intruder walked towards him, his pace measured, as if his feet felt no thorns.

When he was close enough for the black knight to see the travel stains in the cream linen, the man spoke. 'Sadeek,' he murmured, his voice like sand shifting and resettling. The word magicked into 'True friend' inside the black knight's head and he crossed himself. The black horse whinnied and pricked its ears forward, responding to the heathen's sorcery. Shaken by the strange wrongness, the black knight opened the ritual for battle.

'What do you seek?' he asked. Never, in his eternity defending the waterfall had he been give any response other than 'Water' but he followed the formula, dutifully. He had already dismounted, ready to fight a man on foot in all chivalry, to use sword and battle-axe to dispatch one more life. He would stop his ears against all words and carry out his duty to the lady and the waterfall. No-one should say that he broke oath. All he needed was the usual answer to his question.

The reply came in the harsh tone of one who was dying of thirst. The black knight had heard the rasping desperation too often to mark it but this time the words themselves defied possibility.

'I seek Dragonetz, my true friend. You have his horse. Sadeek.' At his name, the horse broke free of the black knight and galloped round the two men in a crazy circle, skipping sideways, shaking his carapace and his mane, finally stopping behind the Moor, nuzzling his neck.

Then the black knight fell to his knees, the poisoned water leaving his head, and the memories flooding back. Dragonetz was who he was. He remembered all that he had done wrong and he was ashamed. The man in front of him put out a hand, tilted his chin till eyes met eyes, and the shame was stopped before it let the poison work again. Dragonetz was who he was. And he recognized the man who sought him.

'Al-Hisba,' he said aloud, then tested the Moor's real name for its strangeness on his tongue. 'Malik.' The Moor who'd spent a summer teaching him engineering, constructing a paper mill with him, building a friendship on cogs and cogitation. The Moor who'd razed the mill to the ground to save Dragonetz from enemies who would stop at nothing to protect the Church's monopoly on parchment and literacy. The Moor who'd left a letter of explanation, with his real name and Sadeek as a present, a horse from al-Andalus breeding, worth a fortune. Sadeek, true friend. 'Why are you here?' Dragonetz asked.

'A feeling. I had a feeling that you needed a friend to walk beside you in dark places so I am here.'

'I killed Arnaut.' The words came without pain, just a fact to share with an old friend.

'No more than I did. But we all three would have given our lives for each other. It is not for the living to waste the sacrifice of the dead.'

'I have a quest.' Another fact. 'But I cannot leave this cursed spot. I gave my oath. It is my doom to defend the waterfall for the lady.'

'Your oath allows you to leave should another take your place.'

'There is no other. No-one can defeat me. If my match does come, he will kill me and my quest will be dead with me. There is no way out.' Malik's silence seemed assent. 'I love Estela.' The third irrefutable fact.

'I too,' Malik responded softly, 'like a daughter. To open the cage of such a songbird and teach her to fly, was as teaching the calculations of al-Khwarizmi to a man learning to make paper. The fruits of our summer together will ripen all our lives.'

'I too,' breathed a third voice, clear and cold. 'I love Estela. And you.' From the dappled shadows of the wood came a form that was more shadow itself than it was the armoured knight flickering in shape around it. Where the shadow knight walked, another world walked with him, one of strange colours, purple grass instead of green, crystal flowers that tinkled in the breeze instead of silken petals. Yet Dragonetz was not afraid, not as he had been before he recognized al-Hisba. From the shadow knight emanated serenity beyond this world. His voice was sparkling ice that turned the word 'love' into a mountain at dusk, looming above mere mortals, a beauty forever present.

Even before the helm was removed, Dragonetz knew the face beneath it, impossibly smooth and forever young, grey eyes once more alight, but with the same strange flickering blue light that made his whole person seem a human firefly. Tears had no place here where the dead walked.

'I will take your place,' Arnaut told Dragonetz. 'I am here so I must have defeated you. You may leave without breaking oath. I will serve the lady we both love. The water cannot hurt me. Nothing can hurt me and I am fittest for this service while you have work still to do. But you must lay this service on me, as my leader and as my friend, or I may not take your place.' He knelt at Dragonetz' feet, offering his sword to his Commander.

When he placed both hands on the mail-covered shoulders, Dragonetz could no longer feel them. He saw the blue fire playing around his own hands and the young knight's shimmering body. He willed his hands to grasp the elusive creature and make him rise but he felt only absence where his hands should be, like pins-and-needles. Arnaut stood, holding out his sword, which Dragonetz took, lightly dubbing the young knight in reminder of their past vows.

'So be it. Take my place, if you please.'

'Willingly,' Arnaut replied. The blue fires burned fiercely and lightning cracked the sky into sudden storm, a jagged flash striking the ground between the three men and the waterfall, raising a fine, dense mist. Then such song as Dragonetz had never heard filled the air, a multitude in strange harmonies, a melody that filled his heart with peace beyond understanding.

Through the mist he saw a gleaming goblet the size of a man, silver trace patterns on shiny brown and his forgotten thirst returned in tenfold force. He knew that this vision was the Grail, knew that if he could but sip from the cup his thirst would be quenched. 'What do I seek?' ran the question in his head. 'The Grail,' he shouted, 'the Grail, the Grail!' But even as he cried aloud, the mist blackened and an arm came down before the holy cup, accusing him, pointing, snaking words into his head that coiled and uncoiled through his veins. 'Not for such as you,' the venom told him, 'not for such as you,' and the vision changed again.

The music became one lone voice, a sweet one that he knew well, and the mist became a transparent silk veil, accentuating the beautiful body of a young woman, one Dragonetz knew intimately. 'Your heaven,' the venom told him, ' for which you are blind and deaf to all else.' And the desire to hold Estela in his arms filled Dragonetz to forgetting his thirst so that when the question came one last time, 'What do you seek?' he whispered, 'Estela,' and the vision vanished with no trace, leaving behind only emptiness and longing.

When the birdsong filled the silence again, pale imitation of the music still thrumming through Dragonetz' head, he asked Arnaut, 'What did you see and hear?' The blissful face answered before the unearthly voice. 'What I have sought all my life. You may call it the Grail. It is with me for always now.'

Dragonetz hardly knew what to ask Malik. What business had a Muslim in quest of Christianity's most sacred relic? But he needed to know. 'What did you see and hear?' he asked.

'A vision. And such music!' the Moor replied.

'What vision?' persisted Dragonetz.

Malik stared at him, puzzled that he should need to ask. 'What you saw too. The holy book, of course. We are all people of the book, are we not?' He whistled and into the clearing galloped Sadeek's twin, stamping and tossing his mane, raising dust as he stopped beside Malik, who jumped into the saddle and gentled the stallion in soft Arabic.

Dragonetz picked up Sadeek's trailing reins and followed suit. He looked back and raised his hand in a last salute to Arnaut, whose face still glowed in a fulfilment Dragonetz knew was not his lot. One glimpse only had been his, and he should be grateful. He knew his real quest. 'Let's find Estela,' he said to the Moor at his side, who merely nodded and, barefoot and spur-less, urged his horse forward.

It took time for Dragonetz to emerge from dream-sogged attempts to recapture a heavenly melody. Seven voices for the main themes would come close he thought, with a choir of angels to create the mood. He had a thirst from hell and downed three cups of water, then dunked his head in the basin for good measure. That cleared a little mental space to prepare his day.

Bar Philipos' words had hit home. Of course Dragonetz was tired of inactivity! But his daily sorties with the 'two mediocre guards' had toned his muscles and forged his partnership with Sadeek beyond any Frankish training. If his body missed Yalda's attentions, then there would be that much more energy for the 'little games' that day, in which a Frankish knight intended to give two Moors a spectacular return on their investment, even if the audience consisted only of a few of their friends watching.

As it turned out, the 'mediocre guards' apparently had rather more 'friends' than Dragonetz expected. When the three men reached the dusty terrain south of the city, demarcated for their display, they found silken pavilions erected all round and men crowding in the shelter offered. The vivid stripes shimmered in sun and wind; spooking the horses, which were already tense with anticipation. Trained for war, Sadeek knew better than to bolt, but unlike his predecessor Seda, he had faced only practice, and he trembled with the effort of self-control.

'Friends, you said!' Dragonetz called to Aakif and Shunnar, riding with him, even their sturdy mares rolling wide eyes and skittering sideways at the sudden movements and excited shouting which greeted the star performers.

'We'll take a slow turn in front of the tents,' suggested Aakif, his body easy in the position that Dragonetz no longer considered odd, knees high and bent, stirrups short, back straight and the low saddle allowing the movement they would need in the events to follow. 'Settle the horses and make obeisance.'

Dragonetz allowed Sadeek the concession of following the two mares and the stallion seemed reassured by their reaction, losing his fear of the flock of giant birds glimpsed in the corner of his eyes, which turned into mere men and strange extensions of their clothing as he neared the tents. Feeling his mount settle, Dragonetz also took the opportunity to observe his audience more closely.

There were no girls or women, only boys and men, some of the boys with painted faces, laying their thin arms on or round the older men as they fetched cups and sweetmeats. In his homeland, a tournay would have attracted as many ladies as lords, as many common women as men, and he would have worn his lady's favour on his helm, as would all the other knights taking part. Dragonetz suddenly felt a long way from home, a long way from his lady, any lady. Jerusalem might have a Queen but there was no sign anywhere here of a woman's power.

There were however signs of power aplenty and no question as to where to find its centre. One open-fronted tent was larger than the others, its silks richer, more colourful, demanding attention and getting it, as a trail of men clustered round the makeshift thrones within. Men knelt and moved on, replaced by others.

It was to this tent that the guards were leading him, and when they bowed before the men inside, their horses an excuse for not prostrating themselves, Dragonetz did likewise, musing briefly that such a bow from his old saddle would have blinded him, as he respectfully dipped towards his horse's mane. Risking a glance towards the interior he recognized Bar Philipos, in a lesser seat, attended by a pretty, painted youth.

The two fancy, carved seats were raised in carefully equal degree and Dragonetz guessed that one occupant was the ruler of Damascus, Mujir ad-Din, slight of body, haggard, his eyes darting everywhere but settling on nothing and no-one. It would take more than identical chairs to convince people that Mujir ad-Din was the equal of the man beside him, whose huge physical presence made everyone around him shrink to insignificance. Everything about him was bigger, his body, his laugh, his impact on those around him, while he himself had the same ease on his throne as Shunnar in his saddle. Although the man's torso was hidden under a robe, in the manner of his people, Dragonetz would have bet on a fighter's body under the swathes of linen. You could always tell by the way a man moved. The Damascene scimitar flashed at his side and no onlooker would think it was worn as an ornament.

With a glance of token query at Mujir ad-Din, the other man gestured the guards to begin the show, without looking once at Dragonetz.

'Who?' he asked Aakif, as they walked the horses back to the starting point they'd agreed.

'Nur ad-Din,' was the short, grim-faced reply. So the man known as the Guardian of Allah's country was here, and probably not because he wanted to watch Dragonetz play the fool on horseback.

It was no secret that Nur ad-Din wanted Damascus. Dragonetz remembered the threat to the Crusaders that if they didn't take Damascus quickly, they'd be caught between Unur's forces and those of Nur ad-Din, sweeping down from the north 'to help their Damascan brothers.' Unur had known well enough that such help came with a price and had kept Damascus independent. But Unur was dead. Dragonetz looked again at Mujir ad-Din, nodding and smiling, the ruler of Damascus – for now – and wondered how close Nur ad-Din was to his goal. And what else did he want? Why was he here?

'Dragonetz!' yelled Shunnar, formalities forgotten in the knowledge that weeks of practice were to be tested, and in front of such an audience! 'We begin.' Then there was no time for thinking of politics.

The wind had died down, the sun was behind them and the crowds watching had become mere landscape for the horses as the three riders started their planned routine. From weaving in and out the upright stakes, flourishing bright scarves that arced between them, they increased the levels of difficulty, each striving to out-do the performance of the man before him. They were now outside the parameters of their planning, improvising and competing, daring each other further. Aakif walked his horse backwards in and out the stakes and Shunnar repeated this while sitting backwards on his horse.

Dragonetz left a pause, long enough for the crowd to become restless. They guessed he was out-manoeuvred, and were convinced of it when he started merely repeating Shunnar's movements. Then, after the second stake was successfully negotiated, Dragonetz jumped to his feet, jump-turned and, balancing upright and backwards on the saddle, both man and horse completed the movement in and out of the stakes in reverse, to roars of approval from the pavilions.

Coming after the other two was both challenge and opportunity; if Dragonetz could both imagine and execute a higher level of difficulty than the man in front, and set a challenge too high to be bettered, then he would seem the best horseman. He'd already realised that Shunnar was sacrificing his own glory in setting a base which allowed Aakif to raise the level to whatever he thought within his capacity and too tough for Dragonetz. Two against one only spurred Dragonetz to crazier risks, drunk on the bond between himself and Sadeek, on muscle and agility, on audience appreciation. As if stretching after sleep, Dragonetz thrummed with life, pounded with horse-hooves, and craved danger.

The poles had been abandoned for games in the open. Scything ribbons with arabesques of steel, Shunnar and Aakif worked openly in partnership, linked by ells of ribbon as they galloped towards Dragonetz, threatening Sadeek with the billowing monster. At the last minute they whipped up the silk above the stallion's head, where it met his rider's blade, glittering overhead as the sword spun impossibly in the air and returned to Dragonetz' sure hand as he rode through the silken trap and out the other side. The two Moors galloped away, each trailing behind him a perfectly sliced half of silken ribbon, curving into dust as the men spoke briefly and returned to the game, their faces grimy and determined. They signed to Dragonetz to watch and follow suit.

Aakif dismounted, part of the ribbon stretched between his hands, his left hand high, right hand low, as far away from his body as he could hold it, sideways on to the galloping approach of Shunnar. Aakif stood as still as a desert rock pillar. The horseman dipped as he passed his comrade, the steel flashed and in a second the mare had galloped past.

As the dust settled, Aakif held aloft the ribbon, sliced once more, and showed to the crowd that he was untouched. He bowed to Shunnar, acknowledging the fine control and timing of the ride, then bowed to Dragonetz, pointing him out to the crowd as the next performer, while Shunnar dismounted, carrying the loops of his ribbon, taking up the same stance as Aakif had done.

Dragonetz weighed up the distance, the control and timing needed, the dip with his sword in a right-handed swipe that sliced the silk and not the man, but most of all he weighed up the crazy courage of his two comrades and rivals. His slightest misjudgement in one direction would kill Shunnar, an equal failure in the eyes of the crowd to missing completely, but not equal to Shunnar! Why should the man think that Dragonetz cared if the sword slipped into flesh? Or was it rather that life or death held no meaning for the man himself? 'If Allah brings you to it, he will bring you through it,' Dragonetz murmured to himself, one of the sayings he'd heard during training. Then, after preparing himself, emptying his busy mind of distraction, concentrating on nothing but the point where his sword must meet the scarf, he let instinct take over, increasing Sadeek's pace.

Shunnar was close enough for Dragonetz to see the eyes closed in concentration, or prayer, when he twisted in the saddle for one more act of showmanship. Attached to the horse only by his knees over the saddle, his upper body swinging further out this way, upside down, Dragonetz made the trick safer for Shunnar but at his own risk. He was already stretching out his sword-arm when Sadeek's fear alerted him. Then he saw and heard the cause.

Half-hidden by the silk, a rat lay dangling by its tail from Shunnar's left hand, squealing and scrabbling air with its front paws, a horse's nightmare. Dragonetz felt his horse's desperate urge to rear, tensing every muscle, sweat erupting rancid white on black hair, heart pounding to drown hoofbeats.

Murmuring lines of love poetry, willing Sadeek calm, demanding trust above and beyond, Dragonetz cut through squealing flesh and scarf, splattering blood on Shunnar and himself as he galloped past, twisting back up and into the saddle, completing a quatrain in soft Arabic, soothing his bright, brave Sadeek to a shivering halt.

If his victory gestures to the crowd took too long, as he wiped blood spots from his skin; if an abandoned blue ribbon was now lumpy and stained, who would notice after such a feat? If there was an odd quietness surrounding the three performers, who would be surprised after the physical and mental demands of the previous two hours?

As always after intense strain, Dragonetz felt the onset of shivering fatigue but he drew on his experience to postpone it. 'Later,' he disciplined his mind, as he had no need to discipline his beautiful horse, to whom he sent only waves of love.

Between himself, Aakif and Shunnar there was no need or desire to speak. Brothers in arms. They had expected to show him up. They hadn't. Theirs be the glory, for training him too well. Now they would return to the plan, an enjoyable display of cow work, the three of them forming a team, to round up the cow and the display. Nothing too difficult. Aakif stood in his stirrups, raised his sword high in the signal to servants unseen to release the cow and like a bolt from a crossbow it charged onto the training ground – black, horned and unmistakeably male.

One glance at the Moors told Dragonetz this was none of their doing. One glance at an enraged bull, wild-eyed and trickling blood where he'd been goaded, made it equally clear that cantering in circles as planned, reining-in to make neat patterns around the beast, would be suicide. The bull lowered its head, mad with fear and too confused to act, waiting. The sensible thing would be to admit defeat and quietly walk the horses as far away from this craziness as possible, leaving someone else to deal with it. An ignominious end to a spectacle. Like the bull, Dragonetz waited, and was not disappointed.

Walking his mare slowly up to Dragonetz, close enough to be heard, Shunnar told him what they were going to do. Dragonetz nodded. The plan was clear enough, even if impossible. Shunnar said it had never been done with three riders. But there was no time for what-ifs or pretty farewells.

Shunnar backed to join Aakif and the two Moors carefully reversed their mounts far enough away to be outside the bull's range, leaving Dragonetz the focus of red-eyed rage about to erupt. It crossed his mind that his death, gored by a bull, while Aakif and Shunnar looked on from a safe distance, might be their finale of choice, and would certainly please the crowd.

'Among the deeds most beloved by Allah is making a Muslim happy,' he quoted to himself, and prepared to make hundreds of Muslims very happy indeed. Then he shortened the reins and told Sadeek to rear up, balancing on his hind legs, pawing the air with his forelegs, challenging the monster in front of them.

Afterwards, men argued over what happened first and who played the best part. In a flurry of dust and movement, the bull charged, Sadeek side-stepped, a cross-footed dance whose elegance was not fully appreciated at the time. The bull's lowered horns met air and as it charged on, from sheer impetus, it was flanked by two sweating mares and men, equine beside bovine, body pulsing against body, trading fears. Aakif and Shunnar had circled wide while the bull was distracted by Dragonetz. They had galloped alongside the creature, were hemming him in, protected from the lethal horns as long as they were so close to him that he could not lower or toss the huge head in their direction.

Then Dragonetz and Sadeek joined them, adding the stallion's extra strength to the constraint on the bull's movements, delicately manoeuvring into place from behind, allowing Shunnar to join Aakif. Slowing the pace to a canter by physically blocking and containing the bull, moving always forward but wheeling a little to take the animal left of the tents, the knot of horsemen reached their destination in an eternity that lasted seconds. Sadeek on one side, the two mares on the other and the dynamics of forward movement took riders and bull to a crowd of youths, shouting and waving spears.

'We all peel away, but not till I give the word,' warned Shunnar. The others didn't need to be told that bad timing would leave one of them to the bull. Anticipating sport, the youths were vying with each other to see who'd get the first touch, but luckily they had enough sense to fall to either side of the bull's path, leaving it a view of freedom.

'Now,' yelled Shunnar and, as if forming one animal of three men and three horses, the riders wheeled away, with a whack on the beast's rump to propel it forward into an army of lethal spears and whoops.

Gathering the last of their strength, the three riders halted side by side in front of their ruler and his distinguished guest. They bowed obeisance, received a gracious nod in response. It had been a good show. Men were already squabbling over their wins, some claiming it was all fixed, when Nur ad-Din spoke in the ear of a boy beside him, sent him over to Dragonetz.

The boy's clear voice, not yet broken, carried across the dry earth between the pavilion and the black stallion. 'My master Nur ad-Din invites you to his pavilion this evening, my Lord Dragonetz, when you have bathed and recovered from your exertions. He would mark your courage with a feast in your honour.'

'It is I who am honoured.' Dragonetz replied, looking steadily towards the Guardian of Allah's Country before bowing polite thanks. He wondered if he was imagining the words mouthed by Bar Philipos, 'And so to market.' He wasn't imagining the slight to Aakif and Shunnar in ignoring them. Nor was he imagining the words quoted by one of the guards before they all parted, '*A friend cannot be considered a friend until he is tested on three occasions; in time of need, behind your back, and after your death.'* Whether Shunnar spoke to Aakif or to Dragonetz, or both, was not clear, but the quotation from Ali ibn Talib echoed in the knight's mind as he soaked in a hot tub, letting go of the death that had passed him by.

CHAPTER ELEVEN

F reshly robed, the swathes of fine linen around his head now second nature to him, Dragonetz was as ready to meet Nur ad-Din as he would ever be. Instead of guards, he now had servants, who could be distinguished from the former only by the fact that their faces were new to him and maintained the respectful blank expression common to servants of all races. What kept him in his chamber now, when the door was open, and he had a sword at his side? His oath to Bar Philipos? The missing book and another oath? Or just the desire to see how the game would play out?

As he waited, cross-legged on the cushions, spooning lemon sherbet and waiting for a summons, he mulled over what he knew of the man called 'light for the true faith' and 'fire for the infidels'. Clearly Nur ad-Din had a reputation for piety, amongst those who held 'the true faith'. In the name of Allah and all Muslims, this Turkish Atabeg preached a dangerous new idea, Jihad, a holy war. He also spoke of Jerusalem as the Holy City in the Holy Land. Such thoughts had never come from his father Zengi's mouth. Nur ad-Din had his warrior-father's spirit but religion was ever his first word. Perhaps the Crusaders had imprinted some aspects of their Christianity on their enemies after all.

A Sunni Muslim like the majority, Nur ad-Din was more at odds with the minority Shiites than with his theoretical enemies, the Christians. There were no circumstances in which Nur ad-Din would form an alliance with Shiites but even during the Crusades he had joined forces with Raymond of Tripoli against cousin Bertrand of Toulouse, now a guest of Aleppo's dungeons. Nur ad-Din's prisons were sometimes convenient for the Christians not actually incarcerated there. At least Bernard kept his eyes, unlike Joscelyn of Edessa, in that same impregnable prison.

Dragonetz had little respect for Comte Joscelyn, who had deserted his city, and – some said – betrayed his own father, but the story of his capture still had the power to shock. It was also likely to make a dinner guest think very carefully about what he might, or might not, say during the evening. When brigands captured Joscelyn, ruler of Edessa, on the road, and sold him to Nur ad-Din, the Muslim leader's response was unequivocal. With due ceremony, in Aleppo, Joscelyn was publicly blinded before being confined to a dungeon, in perpetuity. Nur ad-Din had made it clear that he had no respect for Joscelyn either.

A reputation for piety and justice, in hands that wielded more power than any Muslim had previously known. The sort of power that won battles, sent a man's head as a present to an ally, and bathed in the Mediterranean to show sovereignty of all the lands the water touched. In the name of piety and justice, such power could only be hungry for more, and the most glittering prize was Damascus. Just as the city had enticed the Crusaders three years earlier, so it shimmered its silks now, before the very man who'd helped keep it from them.

Would Damascan troops fight against Nur ad-Din if he made a move to take the city or would they see him as the answer to their problems? How independent would Damascus remain, under Mujir ad-Din as leader, with the Christian Franks and Nur ad-Din always vying for the city? Mujir ad-Din had already faced one rebellion from a rival inside the city and uncertainty was bad for trade. If Nur ad-Din was strong enough to unite the different factions in the city and protect it against the Franks, then his rule would end the uncertainty.

And what would happen to Bar Philipos and his ilk if Nur ad-Din took Damascus? How welcome would the Syrian Christians be within its walls?

A boy interrupted Dragonetz' thoughts, bowed and spoke softly. 'My master bids you join him.'

What any of this had to do with Dragonetz, he was about to find out. He followed the boy to where Bar Philipos awaited him. Accompanied by a small corps of guards, no-one Dragonetz recognized, the torchlight procession made its way to the city wall. The Watch accepted the password, and the men continued, on foot through the orchards, to the very river bank where Dragonetz had planned the taking of Damascus, three years earlier. The hoof-clop of their laden pack-horses rang warning of their coming over the criss-crossed irrigation channels to where fires flickered in the dusk and Nur ad-Din's camp came into view. As in Dragonetz' memories, there were grand pavilions pegged in the grey soil but this time their striped silks and alien pennants proclaimed a quite different provenance.

The austerity inside the tent was unexpected. Where Louis of France had transported on campaign all the luxuries his Commanders could strap to camels and pack-horses, his enemy travelled like any soldier, with blanket and wine-skin. Seated cross-legged on his blanket, the wine-skin beside him, was Dragonetz' host for the evening, the most powerful leader in the Muslim world, in embroidered slippers and a simple robe, tied loosely at the waist. His face was dark tan, firm-mouthed and strong-boned above the shaped black vee of his oiled beard, Turkish Seljuq origins showing clearly in his face. In his early thirties, with five years of command under his woven belt since his father Zengi's murder, Nur ad-Din wore leadership as his birthright.

After a pause that marked his choice to show respect by standing up, he uncoiled gracefully, rising to his feet in the courtesies of greeting. The fluidity of his movement suggested the tone of the muscle beneath the concealing robe. Even as he bowed and murmured the expected formulae, Dragonetz couldn't help wondering what the outcome would be of wrestling this man. It was a thought to be quickly dismissed before his imagination distracted him. A half-smile at an inappropriate moment in this Court would not earn him approval from a lady but rather the slice of a scimitar, severing head and neck.

'Not what you expected,' Nur ad-Din observed, gesturing at the plain interior, and confirming the need for Dragonetz to be on his guard.

'I knew not what to expect, my Lord,' he hedged.

'I have heard of your King Conrad's excesses, his need of jewelled clothing and cushioned beds.' His lip curled in disdain.

Dragonetz couldn't help himself, despite the shocked gasp of disapproval from Bar Philipos beside him at anyone contradicting Nur ad-Din. 'I owe allegiance to King Louis of France, not King Conrad,' he pointed out politely.

Apparently as unmoved by such presumption as by the very existence of Louis, Nur ad-Din swept the Frankish King into a tent-corner with one gesture of his arm and another sardonic curl of the lip. 'Louis, Guy, I don't remember all these Frankish names. Conrad brought an army to take our lands and then he took the army away again. Enough! We have no need to talk of the distant past but rather to celebrate a man's courage today and break bread together. Sit.'

A little disconcerted at this dismissal of events which seemed all too recent to Dragonetz, he nevertheless curbed his response and sat. Nur ad-Din's entourage was introduced to him as each sat down on the coarse weave blankets.

'My uncle, Chirkouh,' announced Nur ad-Din. *Who killed the Prince of Antioch in full combat, and presented the body to his nephew,* Dragonetz mentally added while his mouth spoke the words of greeting.

When the full complement of Dragonetz' enemies had joined him for dinner, he took a moment to look into the shadows, at the invisible ones, the guards and servants. Eyes cast down, the shadow people formed three times the number of men eating. Those waiting to serve food were all young boys, as in Christian halls, where it was a stage in their progression to manhood.

Pre-pubescent, the boys were pretty as girls, long-lashed and dark eyed, smooth and gold-skinned, dark curls covered only by woven caps, slim arms shooting out from their robes like frightened rabbits and then hiding again in the folds. Even a man such as Dragonetz could appreciate such innocent beauty aesthetically but he could sense the less objective response in Bar Philipos, who was also appraising the boys. All so beautiful, all but one.

He was bigger than the other boys but a second look showed that he was merely older than they were, well into puberty to judge by his ravaged skin. Dragonetz instinctively stroked his own jawline, which still showed the pits of adolescence. This particular ugly duckling did not hold promise for the future however. Dumpy and flat-faced, his looks promised a short, fat man as outcome. And yet there was something about him, about the way he carried himself. Around him was just enough space to show that the other boys kept their distance – or he kept them at a distance.

Curious as to why such a boy would be among these ornaments of the true faith, Dragonetz studied him longer, realising that not only was the boy completely at ease in his own body – unusual enough in a youth – but he was looking steadily back at Dragonetz himself. It was a shock to meet those eyes, measuring him from the safety of the shadows, and to know for sure that this was not an invisible one, whoever he might be.

Bar Philipos clapped his hands and the pack-horses' burdens were unrolled before the Muslim leader, carpets and silks, a velvet pouch of jewels 'for your wives, may they be fruitful.'

The finest produce from Damascus' markets lay at Nur ad-Din's feet. All had been unrolled for his inspection, except two box-shaped packages, wrapped in brocade, which Bar Philipos signalled his servants to leave for the Muslim leader's personal attention.

Saying, 'I thank you for these riches on behalf of my people, for whom I am but their treasurer,' Nur ad-Din kept the basket of ripe fruit and the two unopened packages beside him. Dragonetz could guess what was in one of them but not the other. His curiosity was not to be satisfied until after their 'feast'.

Nur ad-Din signed to one of his men, who promptly stood and declaimed some verses of poetry. 'Sanai,' Dragonetz thought aloud, identifying the Persian author of the poetry, and earning a nod of approval from Nur ad-Din.

'Belief and doubt spring from the same source,
Your double-thinking heart.
Of course the way is long when
You hesitate over the first step.
Just one single step towards Him
Who offers you a kingdom
When you bow the knee.'

This edification continued at intervals throughout the meal, which was surprisingly frugal. Breaking bread meant just that, a wholesome meal of unleavened rounds and a meat stew, lamb or goat most probably, tasty but simple. The wineskin was not only a surprise but a disappointment. Dragonetz hid his reaction to the plain taste of water on his tongue. A glance at Bar Philipos showed that he'd expected no more, despite his own penchant for fruity, red, Syrian wines.

Dragonetz felt a strange longing. Even the black honeyed drink would have been more enjoyable than this nothingness swirling round his mouth. He was a blade that needed blunting this night, and a little alcohol or Bar Philipos' herbs would have relaxed him. As it was, he was endlessly holding on to Sadeek, rearing before a black bull, twisting away from death, his heart pounded to dust.

'… I was born here you know,' he heard Nur ad-Din saying.

Dragonetz forced himself to concentrate. 'Damascus,' he stated.

'It is my birthplace and –'Nur ad-Din's shrug expressed whatever an informed man might want to read into it. Affection, desire, responsibility, understanding. A shrug could be rendered even more eloquent by the words that followed. 'I have never camped outside the city walls to threaten my people. I came because I heard the cries of fellow Muslims when their homes and livelihoods were taken by the Franks. I will always come when they have no-one to defend them.'

Although Nur ad-Din was looking at Dragonetz when he spoke,

the words were clearly meant to touch Bar Philipos, who had made it clear often enough to his Christian prisoner that the Damascan ruler was no Unur. When Unur was alive, Damascus had not needed, nor wanted Nur ad-Din. But now they had no-one to defend them? Mixing the past with the present was clever because things had changed and reading the past through the present justified all Nur ad-Din's past actions. Wasn't that exactly what Dragonetz himself had been doing?

'Allah has given me the power to protect all my people and when the citizens of Damascus beg me to make their walls strong again, I will hear their prayers. I am no Infidel to force my own people.'

Dragonetz could sense only approval from Bar Philipos beside him. Was he confident that Nur ad-Din would respect the Christians of Damascus if he became overlord? Despite his declaration of Jihad? Or was the Syrian trying to curry enough favour to protect himself from any persecution in the future. Probably both, Dragonetz suspected as he mopped gravy with a hunk of sour, brown bread.

It was hard not to compare this frugal meal with the banquets of Louis and Aliénor, even on campaign. Not only did they insist on silverware, platters and knives, their courses were as complicated as if they were still in Paris and their cooks were more essential in their eyes than their commanders. After their stay in Byzantium, they'd added forks to their sophistication, and if their coffers had allowed, they'd have swopped silverware for gold plate, notwithstanding the weight and toll on the horses.

Nur ad-Din was right. Wagonloads of bric-a-brac had weighed down the Crusaders. But that's what made a king different. He had to look like a king and be treated like a king, to be a king. If he dressed as an ordinary man, would anyone respect him? Would their armies have fought as well for a mere man? The Lord's anointed must surely be treated as such?

At Louis' banquets there would have been a real feast, even in a tent. He would have sat in a wooden chair, a makeshift throne but a throne nevertheless. And there would have been singing. Dragonetz heard the songs in his head, the lyrics he'd have chosen to hearten the weary, fire the cowardly, inspire the plodders. Whether he'd sung himself, or another of Aliénor's troubadours had offered entertainment, there had been no shortage of music. And if he should sing for Nur ad-Din? What would he choose? Marcabru's call to arms in the Holy Land? A crude ditty? A love song? There was no sign of woman or girl in the tent, any more than there had been during the show.

'I've heard that your court includes many poets,' Dragonetz opened cautiously. 'Do they set their words to music.'

That curl of the lips again. 'I know of your reputation with the oud, my Lord Dragonetz, but you waste your talents on such trivia. I need no string-plucking from my poets, to distract them from the words they interpret from Allah's truth, which is beyond words.'

The silence also spoke beyond words and it was Nur ad-Din who broke it. 'You can't be expected to understand,' he declared graciously. 'But it seems to me you know something of horses. Why do you ride a stallion? And what is his lineage.'

The mood lightened all round and the talk turned to horse breeding and training, and the techniques by which Dragonetz had carried out the manoeuvres in the day's show. Nur ad-Din spoke of his plans to build a hippodrome in Aleppo to rival that in Byzantium, which supposedly held thirty-five thousand spectators and a four-chariot track. Dragonetz confirmed this and responded politely to an invitation to display his own skills in the new hippodrome when it opened. At every opportunity he praised Shunnar and Aakif but somehow their names went unheard, conversation flowing round them as if they were turds in a river, known to be there but politely ignored. For Dragonetz' own skills and exploits, no praise was too high.

The boys came and went, offering more stew, more flatbreads, each server to his designated place. The one serving Bar Philipos suffered the man's breath too near his face as the lad bent over, a hairy hand steadying the smooth arm as the boy served, chunky fingers testing the unblemished skin like a roll of brocade in the market. The boy's minute, instinctive jerk away was punished with those fingers clamping in a pinch. The boy froze and the fingers released him but the fine skin showed the pressure-marks. No-one noticed. Conversation flowed as before. One of Nur ad-Din's men had progressed further with his waiter. If anything, the other boy accentuated his availability in response, flirting his lithe body as he bent more than was necessary. Was this expected behaviour? At one gesture more explicit than another, Dragonetz caught the same sardonic curl of Nur ad-Din's mouth as he'd shown when speaking of the Franks, or of music. Disapproval then. But tolerance of other men's base needs. His stomach churning, Dragonetz looked anywhere he could bear to, at Nur ad-Din, who was ordering the fruit to be served, calm and distant. At the stocky, older youth who served the Muslim leader.

Nur ad-Din caught the youth's arm to stop him. For a terrible moment Dragonetz thought he would be privy to some act of perversion, even from the light of the true faith, but though there was affection in the gesture and the voice, Nur ad-Din's words rescued Dragonetz from his worst imaginings. 'You may speak to Lord Dragonetz, my boy. Yesterday he was my enemy, today we break bread in his honour, tomorrow only Allah knows. Maybe you will face him across a table one day – or across a battlefield. Lord Dragonetz, I present my nephew, Salah ad-Din.'

'May our paths cross in honour.' The youth's voice had broken and its gravelly timbre already held an authority greater than his years. Suddenly his face seemed the least of him and Dragonetz suspected that no-one would be talking of his lack of beauty in the future. Salah ad-Din bowed in courtesy to Dragonetz, finely judged to show respect but not humility and Dragonetz returned the compliment, exactly.

'My brother's son is newly with me, to learn all I can teach. And first, he must learn that we all serve one greater than us.'

Salah ad-Din bowed, deeply this time, with every sign of genuine respect, and he returned to his duties, smooth but never invisible.

The formalities of the meal were completed, the debris cleared and the servants returned to their shadows, responding instantly to a finger-snap if need be. Nur ad-Din showed no sign of postprandial sleepiness and Dragonetz' experience with royal banquets had left him immune to the after-effects of a full stomach.

He was keeping an eye on the two unopened gifts, hatching futile plans to snatch them, un-noticed by the grim, unblinking guards, run for the door-flap, steal a ready-saddled horse, duck the volley of bolts and arrows to gallop through the darkness towards – towards what? – breaking both the horse's neck and his own in the first cursed irrigation channel they hit. Luckily he didn't have to tax his brain with devising a slightly more practical plan as it was too late. The packages were now on the blanket, between him and Nur ad-Din. The Muslim looked at Bar Philipos, received some kind of confirmation, and dismissed the Syrian and his own men to take their ease in the recesses of the tent. From the corner of his eye, Dragonetz was aware of Bar Philipos finger-clicking a boy towards him as he lounged on a blanket.

Nur ad-Din unwrapped the first package. As soon as Dragonetz saw the board divided into eight squares by eight, he knew what would be in the wooden box, but he could not have imagined the craftsmanship of the shatranj pieces that emerged. Nur ad-Din held each one for a moment's appreciation before placing it on the appropriate square. Abstract forms and size distinguished between rukh and baidak, faras and shah, but the artist had worked his heart into the exquisite, carved, ivory balls on which each character was balanced. As if the ivory had been spun sugar, fine strands linked repeated patterns of leaf, star and shell in an infinite honeycomb. Nur ad-Din held the shah a long time, just looking at it, and his eyes glistened as he offered the piece to Dragonetz so he could have a closer view.

The size of the shah allowed the artist room for not only stylised motifs but also a quotation, the curves of the Arabic as beautiful as the interlaced leaves. Dragonetz turned the piece to follow the miniature script. He read aloud,

'Who hath created seven heavens, one above the other;
Thou wilt find no flaw in the creation of the Merciful One;

Look again; seest thou a single flaw?'

The Koran, surely, but what splendid, justified arrogance, for the artist to liken his own creation to God's.

Once again, Nur ad-Din read his mind. 'No, not arrogance. A man's talents come from Allah and to marvel at them is to worship the great creator. Look deeper.'

From the impatient gesture, Dragonetz realised that the order was literal, and he looked again at the ivory ball. Impossibly, another carved ball was inside that, and another, and another, 'unto the seventh heaven,' Dragonetz said softly. Ivory carved into seven balls, each one turning inside the other. He had seen enough in Damascus' markets to know this must be Chinese craft, to Muslim commission and design, travelling the silk road to reach this man who declared himself both mere vassal and ruler of the eastern world. He gently set the shah down, the last piece on the board. The game was about to begin.

Nur ad-Din unwrapped the second package. Within the brocade was oiled sailcloth, which revealed a book that Dragonetz could describe with his eyes shut. As Nur ad-Din reverentially turned the pages, of which Dragonetz knew there were four hundred and ninety-one, the three columns of script, the aged colour of the parchment, all was visible in the torchlight. 'The Keter Aram Sola,' breathed Nur ad-Din.'

'But surely it is a Torah, of special value to those of Jewish faith?' Dragonetz queried.

'It is a rare and precious form of the word, a priceless book. Did you, a mere Infidel, not gasp at the beauty of the shah and the perfection of the words from the Koran? How could I not see the perfection of this book?' He picked up the shah with his right hand, the book open in front of him. 'Bar Philipos tells me that the book is not within his gift but that it is within yours. I will treasure it as it should be treasured. Your mission is to deliver this book safely and there is no safer keeping than mine. You have found me, the one the book is seeking through you.' His eyes and tone mesmerised Dragonetz, speaking only truth. But not the only truth. Candle-light flickered over the open pages and picked out the annotations in the margins, the work of Aaron Ben Ascher to enable the music of the Torah to be heard, to turn words into heavenly harmonies for the faithful.

Reluctantly, Dragonetz shook his head, accepting his burden. 'Just as you are treasurer for your people's riches, so the book is in my charge but not mine to dispose of, except to the chosen one of Jewish faith. To the Jews it is not just priceless, it is sacred.'

Nur ad-Din's face darkened. He held the shah towards Dragonetz, the light playing on the carving, worth ten-fold ransom for a knight in the one piece. 'Then let there be an exchange of equal value, this unique and sacred shatranj set for the book.'

'I have given my answer.'

There was a dangerous silence. 'It is your way when there is a dispute to use trial by combat? To let God decide?'

'It is,' assented Dragonetz cautiously, wondering whether he would get his foolish wish to measure up to Nur ad-Din in only oil and loincloths, and hoping that God would feel in the mood for miracles. His experience suggested that solid muscle and years of training helped enormously in God's decisions.

'Then we will play shatranj for the book, and let God decide. If you win, the book is yours and you will travel to Jerusalem unhindered. If I win, you give the book to me, freely.' Nur ad-Din's tone brooked no disagreement and Dragonetz was already desperately studying the pieces, to make their forms so familiar to him that he would waste no time mistaking the stylised elephant for the horseman. The odds would probably have been better in a wrestling match! Coldly, he weighed up his own strengths and weaknesses, placed all known strategies in mental formations, to be called on as needed, like his detachments in a land battle. At least the pieces were as unfamiliar to Nur ad-Din as they were to him. A deliberate ploy on the part of Bar Philipos, to even the odds? How much of this had been planned from the start? Was Bar Philipos expecting Dragonetz to win or to lose? There was no time to consider the subtleties of the Syrian's mind.

'We will play the ten-move start,' Nur ad-Din told him, moving a baidak. Dragonetz would have preferred a slow start and time to judge his opponent's style but he accepted the rule and swiftly made his ten moves, none over the half-way line, so that both sides had formed their battle lines. Then the match began. The two men knelt over the gameboard, neither succumbing to the other's rhythm, but each taking whatever time he chose to respond.

Ten moves into the mid-game Dragonetz knew his advantage and had already lost it. Whereas he had assumed Nur ad-Din to be outstanding, and had played no risky moves, his opponent had underestimated him and wasted moves to test him. This had gained Dragonetz the tiniest edge in control of the board but the tightening of Nur ad-Din's lips told him there would be no more leeway. The time for sacrifices was coming and Dragonetz knew his choices off by heart; horsemen more valuable in opening and mid-game, governor-fers more valuable in the endgame but one of each more desirable than losing two of either.

It looked as if Nur ad-Din was willing to sacrifice a horseman. He looked thoughtfully at the piece he'd made vulnerable. 'Unur was also your opponent once.' They both knew that Unur could only be considered the winner of that particular battle. 'They tell a funny story of Unur. Perhaps you've heard it? For his entertainment, his guests loosed a lion and a lamb into the courtyard for him to watch their antics. Contrary to all expectation, the lamb ran bleating at the lion, who was terrified at the bold creature making strange sounds, and who fled. The lamb chased the lion round the courtyard and Unur ordered that the lamb's courage be celebrated and the lamb itself kept alive.'

'And the lion?' asked Dragonetz, guessing the answer.

'Cowardice is punished by death, always. You showed great courage today, my Lord Dragonetz, as well as unexpected skill.'

So he was the lamb. Once more, Dragonetz tried to give credit where it was due. 'The guards, Aakif and Shunnur, showed no less, and my honour is their honour,' he started, only to be cut off.

'They disappointed me.' Dragonetz was learning to read that

mouth. 'Had they been braver, they would have – and should have – outridden you. Cowardice is punished by death, always.'

Dragonetz was a soldier and this time Nur ad-Din would not read his eyes or his mind. He bent over the board and took his opponent's horseman, placing him beyond the chequered squares, out of the game forever. 'Your move,' he said, while his heart told him, *'A friend cannot be considered a friend until he is tested on three occasions; in time of need, behind your back, and after your death.'* and the words of another dead friend accused him *'Why do you always have to win?!'* He knew the answer now, leadership and guilt, intertwined like leaves and stars in ivory. *It's who I am.* He postponed the grieving until he'd won this game and focused once more on five moves ahead, when he would know for sure the outcome. Nur ad-Din took his Governor. 'Check,' he said. They were into the endgame.

Fewer options, more deadly choices, and Nur ad-Din was taking his time over every move now. Dragonetz was sure he had every option covered and allowed his focus to drift around the tent, the sounds of chit-chat and laughter crossing the barriers of his earlier intensity. A couple of men were analysing the chess game in whispers, close enough to see the board but far enough away to avoid distracting the players. Judging by their faces, the outcome was still uncertain and their bets likewise. Dragonetz' gaze scanned the small groups, not needing to hear the words to see their moods highlighted in warm light and only half-hid in the shadows.

He shut his eyes and heard the music of the tent, the pool of silence enclosing him and his opponent, the amicable drone of male talk, bees on flowers, gathering news. His ears told him there was another note, soprano and anguished, suppressed tears, not a man. Eyes open, Dragonetz couldn't hear it, but the plea for help vibrated in him, demanded his attention. The boy who'd served Bar Philipos was standing in front of the Syrian, no longer looking down but fixing Dragonetz with a wide, black stare, empty as the pits of hell, silent as endurance. Half-hidden behind him, Bar Philipos' hands pursued God knew what exploration, unchecked.

'Check,' drew Dragonetz' attention back to the board but not before his sharp-eyed opponent had noticed the direction of his gaze and drawn his own conclusions.

'Do you want him?' Nur ad-Din asked casually.

'I lack a page boy,' Dragonetz shrugged, lightly. 'But no doubt he has a better future as a man in your service.'

'They tell me he sings like a canary.' A curl of the lip. 'I have no interest in him or his singing so they'll sell him on when they've cut his manhood to keep his voice sweet. It's probably easier than rendering him mute.' He gestured impatiently. 'I'll get another serving-boy, one who keeps his mouth closed.'

'A fine future.' Dragonetz' voice was colourless. 'But not as a man.'

A thought struck Nur ad-Din. 'Shall I give him the choice? He may keep his tongue or his manhood and choose where the cut falls.' Before Dragonetz could reply he added, 'Or shall we change the bet, my Lord Dragonetz. Would you like this boy, in exchange for the Keter Aram Sola? Whoever wins our game? Come here, boy.' The boy came. 'Sing for the Infidel.' His eyes never leaving Dragonetz' face, the boy took a ragged breath and sang a couple of cracked notes, wincing at his own output. Nur ad-Din frowned and the boy shut his eyes, drawing the music from inside himself, singing a practice scale in all boyish sweetness, before starting a love song.

'Enough!' interrupted Nur ad-Din, slamming his hand on the blanket and the note, cut off in full soar, hung in the air. 'Well?' he challenged Dragonetz, who looked at the shatranj board and tried to shut all music out of his head.

'Nur ad-Din's reputation for justice has travelled oceans,' he began slowly, as if a life hung on each word, 'and we agreed that God would decide the fate of the book, through our combat. Such an agreement cannot be broken.' Dragonetz felt, rather than saw, a trembling in the frail limbs of the child beside him. He continued in the same measured tone. 'Should my munificent host decide to honour his unworthy guest with a gift, to complete the most memorable day of this Infidel's life, I would be happy to relieve you of your inadequate servant, with his irritating voice. Nur ad-Din's reputation for generosity equals that for justice.'

The frown lines cleared in the Muslim's forehead. 'I have men paid to flatter me,' he observed, and Dragonetz knew he'd failed. 'Nevertheless it pleases me to give you this nothing of a gift, this boy.' Dragonetz felt the melody play in his own heartbeat. 'If, by the grace of Allah, you win, you shall have book and boy. Your move.'

To the onlooker, Dragonetz had lost control. Each quick move was forced by a check to his shah. Yet Bar Philipos was black with anger at his protégé's moves, and there was no smile on Nur ad-Din's face as he made slow choices. Both had seen further ahead and no way out but to follow the path of Dragonetz' making and hope for a mistake. There was no mistake. In the one move that Dragonetz was under respite from check, he retaliated. Now it was Nur ad-Din's turn to seek shelter but each option was worse than another until Dragonetz moved his horseman, uncovering the concealed check and blocking the shah's only potential escape.

Nur ad-Din toppled his shah onto its side and laughed aloud. 'The knight has me!' he declared. 'May I learn from this lesson and may Allah's will be done!'

Inshallah,' Dragonetz agreed, sensing no change in the trembling boy beside him. If anything, he was hiding even greater fear, as he reached out and tried to stroke his new master's arm suggestively, letting slip his robe to show a shoulder. Hiding his revulsion at this coquettish behaviour in a child, Dragonetz suddenly realised what the boy had been trained to do, why he might be afraid and yet behave in such a way. Of course! Dragonetz cursed himself for a fool and turned to the boy, speaking coldly. 'You, wrap up this book. You have new duties to learn before you sing for others and you must give up this catamite behaviour. It is not my habit and it spoils your voice.' He managed a lip-curl worthy of Nur ad-Din himself and was rewarded by the alacrity with which the boy jumped to work.

Another boy was eyeing Dragonetz, still measuring him, while men stood to organize leaving and farewells, following Nur ad-Din's clear signal that the evening was over. Bar Philipos made curt farewells, told Dragonetz to find his way back with the two guards waiting for him 'and the new page boy', and left, his irritation trailing sour behind him. Dragonetz was about to follow but the boy Salah ad-Din gestured to him to wait. After brief words with his uncle, the youth told Dragonetz he'd escort him, and his precious book, safely from the camp.

Nur ad-Din was already elsewhere in his thoughts, and his final words to Dragonetz were the prayer for close of day. 'We have reached the evening and at this very time unto Allah belongs all sovereignty and all praise is for Allah. My Lord, I ask for the good of this night and the good of what follows it and I take refuge in You from the evil of this night and the evil of what follows it.'

'Amen,' said Dragonetz, and left the light of the true faith, taking with him two guards whose names he didn't know, one unladen pack-horse, a precious book and a small human being with a tendency to skip every few steps. The youth Salah ad-Din spoke to the boy and the guards, told the knight, 'They will wait for you at the edge of the camp. There is someone who wishes to meet you.' Dragonetz no longer cared whether there was a trap or another feast awaiting him, but accepted what came. 'Inshallah,' he said.

'What would you have done?' Salah ad-Din asked him. 'If my uncle had refused you the boy?'

Dragonetz didn't have to think. The moves had been in his head. 'Set fire to the tent,' he said. 'Grabbed the boy and the book and run.'

Salah ad-Din nodded. 'And if you'd had to choose? Between the boy and the book?'

'I don't choose between,' said Dragonetz. 'Life without honour is no life.'

The youth led him around the perimeter of the camp, expertly skirting guards and campfires, until they reached bushes behind a large tent, where Dragonetz was told to wait. Salah ad-Din melted into darkness and Dragonetz was left alone to consider whether he would prefer knife or garrotte as an ending. He had time to conclude once more that he didn't want to choose between, when the tent flap beside him was lifted and Salah ad-Din's voice told him to crawl underneath.

The opulence and femininity came as a shock after Nur ad-Din's spartan surroundings. As his eyes adjusted to the light, Dragonetz took in cushions and brocades, sweetmeats and fruit, and books left open where their readers had abandoned them. One such reader was inspecting him, veiled from head to toe, with only her dancing eyes to suggest what she might look like. Another veiled woman was keeping watch between her mistress and the closed flap of the tent's opening, where the shadows of two guards and their scimitars loomed twice life-size.

'My aunt, Ismat ad-Din Khatun; my Lord Dragonetz,' Salah ad-Din introduced them.

Ismat ad-Din Khatun, daughter of Unur and Damascus, married to Nur ad-Din as part of their alliance and balancing act. Payment to Nur ad-Din for leaving Damascus independent, promise to Nur ad-Din of his claim for the future. A woman revered in Damascus for her learning, for the university she had founded, for spreading the Sunni faith. Childless, as were all Nur ad-Din's wives, which made Salah ad-Din his heir. And yet, Dragonetz could sense only friendship between childless wife and her nephew the heir, closer to her in age than her husband. So young, so important.

'I don't usually start off on my knees when I meet beautiful women,' Dragonetz gave her his lop-sided smile, gesturing at his clumsy entry under the tent flap.

Her eyes sparkled. 'It is not permitted that men visit me and my women but I wanted to see you because of what Salah ad-Din has told me about you. He knows what the other boys suffer. He told me what you did for the little one who is unsuited to this life of brutes. My nephew is my eyes and ears in the world of men.'

'For now,' her nephew told her gently. 'Until my servant days are over. I am a man now.'

Her eyes clouded briefly, then snapped again. 'All the better for our plans. And for Damascus.' A pause. 'I have eyes and ears in the world of women too. Is there a woman has cause to hate you, Dragonetz?'

Love, passion, hatred – so close together, like sisters. 'At least one, Khatun.'

She nodded. 'Word has reached me that it was a woman's orders, if not her hand, that loosed a bull on you this day.'

'Then she brought me glory and the greater pleasure of meeting you.'

'I don't think that was her intention,' was the dry reply. 'Be careful, my Lord.'

'My thanks for the warning.' As if on cue, Salah ad-Din passed a box to Dragonetz, one of those brought by Bar Philipos as gifts for Nur ad-Din. The knight took the hint gratefully, having already realised what the occasion demanded and what he lacked, hoping that the box didn't contain an abacus or other masculine object. 'Khatun, I have brought a small present for you.' Her childish delight on finding the squares of sugared jelly so popular in Damascus confirmed Salah ad-Din's good judgement.

The expressive eyes narrowed. Why would a woman ever need to show more of herself to enchant a man? 'Salah ad-Din told me all about you. Will you make me a promise?'

'Only if it has honour, and I can keep it, Khatun.'

'Then stay away from Damascus. You failed to take it but you have grown since then. You know how to win. If you are asked to take it now, refuse. You know it is not yours! You know Damascus! I do not ask you to fight with us, only to not fight against us!'

'I cannot promise that, Khatun. I owe fealty to my own lord, as you do to yours.' Her eyes dropped. 'But I will keep your words in my heart, as I keep this city that I have come to know and love.'

'Then I will settle for that,' she told him, 'and should you want to get word to me, speak to Salah ad-Din. His thoughts are my thoughts. Take this and go now, before my other women return from the pointless errands I sent them on.' She pressed something into his hand and he caught her small fingers in his, bent his lips in homage, concealed the token in the folds of his robe. He crawled back out under the tent, waited for Salah ad-Din, walked thoughtfully back round the edge of the encampment. At one point he noticed crates upon crates, apparently filled with small livestock. 'Provisions?' he asked.

'No. Pigeons,' replied Salah ad-Din, and then they reached Bar Philipos' guards, and a boy whose face gleamed like the moon. 'Should we meet again...' Salah ad-Din hesitated.

Dragonetz smiled at him, and repeated the youth's words when they'd been presented. 'May our paths meet in honour.'

Salah ad-Din bowed. Dragonetz offered his right hand and it was shyly taken, in the handshake fashionable among knights, then the heir to the Muslim world vanished in the night. Dragonetz shivered. In the past, the divisions between Moorish tribes had enabled Christian victories, especially during the crusade that had won Jerusalem sixty years ago. What if someone strong could unify them? First Nur ad-Din, then Salah ad-Din. Would the victories stop at Damascus? *Night thoughts,* Dragonetz told himself, *born of a tiring day.*

'Walk like a man, not a rabbit,' he rebuked his new page boy, smiling to himself.

'Yes, my Lord,' came the reply, spoken like the words, 'my wife' by a man newly wed.

'My lord Dragonetz says he needs help to sleep after such a full day and has requested some honey drink with herbs,' the servant reported to his master as instructed, with regard to all of my Lord Dragonetz' activities.

'Give it to him,' replied Bar Philipos between gritted teeth. 'And if the bastard never wakes up, so be it.' But of course, he would wake up, and they would travel together to Jerusalem, the next marketplace for a knight and a precious book.

This evening, Dragonetz had bested Nur ad-Din, the man who'd paid Bar Philipos to kill him, and the light of the true faith had not been pleased. If Nur ad-Din hadn't been assured beforehand that the poppy would remove this troublesome piece from the board, the

Syrian would have suffered more than the humiliation of seeing his boy given to Dragonetz. If the bet over the book hadn't been so public, it was unlikely that either the knight or the Torah would have left the tent. But Nur ad-Din had a reputation to maintain and Dragonetz was too public a figure to dispatch like a pair of cowardly guards. It had, however, been made very clear to Bar Philipos that the poppy had better do its work or Damascus would lose a merchant.

Although he was sweating from the knowledge of Nur ad-Din's displeasure, Bar Philipos was not resigning from the game. Another buyer remained in the market and might well prove equal to Nur ad-Din. De Rançon's mistress in Jerusalem had paid well to keep Dragonetz out of play. Now she wanted the knight in Jerusalem, with the book of course. She'd made it clear that the time to choose sides had now come and if Dragonetz chose wrongly, she no longer wanted him kept out of the game. She wanted him dead. If she couldn't have him, no-one else would.

If the knight was in such a hurry to reach Jerusalem, on his own head be it. The shoots of liking for his remarkable prisoner had withered under Nur ad-Din's petty revenge and Bar Philipos would always hold the winning piece; honeyed black tea. The servant bowed smoothly and left to fulfil his orders. His master looked at the willing boy on his cushions and some of his tension eased in anticipation. But he'd wanted the other one! To hell with Dragonetz and Nur ad-Din with him!

Through bush and briar, over hill and dale, the black knight had ridden with his Moorish companion for days without end, till their minds were twinned as their mounts. Twice they'd found a wayfarer in the wilderness; twice they'd been told the Lady's castle lay ahead, further, always further. Ahead, always ahead. Perhaps there had been a time Dragonetz longed for the end of the journey but now he let the road lead him. He had food, water, a friend by his side and a quest. Each day he woke knowing his purpose in life. He loved Estela so he would find her. And then? He would rescue her of course. And then? Stupid questions! He needed to find her. And hold her in his arms. It couldn't be more straightforward.

'Dragonetz.' Malik interrupted his thoughts, drawing his attention to a figure moving towards them on foot, accompanied by the sound of a handbell, hooded and robed, like a monk, but this was no brother. Dragonetz instinctively drew back but his soldier's discipline controlled the urge for flight. The figure grew closer, ringing the warning bell, giving them the chance to get out of the way. Malik and Dragonetz waited, like statues, their very stillness betraying tension.

The hand shaking the bell was invisible in the long, drooping brown sleeves, the face hidden deep in the hood's shadows. Not one ounce of flesh showed, thank God, but the nose was never the fool of the other senses. Nothing could hide the smell. Worsened by an overlay of sweet herbs, was the rancid odour of stale meat, rotting flesh, a fly-feast. And a voice from the tomb, crying 'Unclean.'

They did not move. Dragging its feet, impossible to identify as man or woman, well beyond the distinction mattering, the figure was beside them on the path. A leper. Not just a memento mori but a death-bringer, a death-ringer. The warning bell tolled uselessly and that voice of dust and ashes spoke to them. 'Your chivalry does you honour, Sirs, but many would call it foolish.'

'I am a knight of the Grail, good sir,' Dragonetz replied, 'and if you cross our path in this wilderness, there is a purpose to it. We seek the dwelling of a Lady, known in these parts as the Lady of the Waterfall, although to us she has other names.'

'A little water, my Lords, please, in charity.'

Both men moved at the same time, each trying to prevent the other from contact with the leper and his contagious death, but Dragonetz was faster. He passed his waterskin to the folded sleeve, carefully doubled over who-knew-what remained of a hand. The leather bottle vanished inside the hood. Glugs and slurps from who-knew-what kind of broken mouth stained the silence. The bottle reappeared, was offered back to Dragonetz.

'Keep it,' he said, seeming courteous, but not being so. There were limits. 'My brother and I can share.' Strange brothers, he and this turbaned Muslim, yet so it was. Dragonetz breathed again as the bottle disappeared back into brown serge folds of clothing.

'You are nigh on the place and person you seek,' sighed the leper, like the creak of willow roots shifting in a storm. 'And yet she is not the person you seek. You must win her. And yet you will not want to. The lady will greet you at the castle, as dazzling as you remember her, love laughing at you in her eyes, promising you a night to remember.

You will want nothing more than one night with your lady and she will come to you. And you will have a night to remember, a night such as many have not survived. There is a curse upon this lady, so that in your arms she will change into all manner of monster.

Be you steadfast and hold her, no matter what you perceive in your arms, cock-crow shall find you lying with your own true lady. Should you flinch and let go, it is you who will be lost forever.'

Dragonetz felt the knot of fear in his belly loosen. Was that all?! He laughed. 'Shape shifting and fantasies! You have repaid me full, good Sir, and tomorrow morning, my Lady will be in my arms.'

'God be with you, my Lord.' The leper held out his long brown sleeve and shook the bell. 'Unclean,' he called as he lurched onwards. Malik said nothing but kept pace with Dragonetz, who was spurred on by his hopes and the sight of two ethereal turrets suddenly visible above silver birch and ash trees.

As if in a dream, Dragonetz rode through the open portcullis, up to the castle entrance. He walked between two rows of livery-clad servants, lined up as if they were expecting him, and at the top of the steps he threw himself to his knees, unable to meet the eyes of the most beautiful woman he'd ever seen.

She would always be the most beautiful woman he'd ever seen. Her hair, more black and silken than Sadeek's coat, was plaited and coiled in loops that invited him to remove the pins, shake out the tresses. Her slippers peeped out from scalloped hems, all rose-pink, with variegated silk favours. He kissed the hand offered, he raised his eyes to hers. Great golden rings in smooth, honeyed skin, laughter greeting him in her eyes, in the upturned bloom of her mouth and in the voice he remembered. 'You've kept me waiting, Dragonetz,' she teased him. 'I've been waiting a long time.'

And then there were sweetmeats and banqueting, music and singing, the two of them playing games of reminiscence and anticipation, all the duets imagined and unimaginable, leading to the one his body was starved for. As he lay in bed waiting for her, he thought he would die if she didn't come to him, so intense was his need. When she was finally there, in only the black of her hair and the gold of her skin, he worshipped her, pulled her close, ripened to bursting as he found the place he belonged, as he whispered her name, kissed the angled bone of her shoulder and found...

... brown serge cloth in his mouth and the foetid smell of rotting flesh in his nostrils, where a second earlier there had been young skin and rose-water. His body convulsed but his mental discipline held. His arms stayed round the creature, who croaked 'Do you love me, Dragonetz? Really love me?' He shut his eyes, conjured up Estela in all her beauty and sweetness, told himself all else was illusion and held on. 'Yes,' he said.

Even with his eyes squeezed shut, he could feel the changes in the form in his arms. It was dry, scaly, slithery, running many forked tongues along his skin. 'Do you love me, Dragonetz?' the creature hissed. All desire turned to disgust, his ripeness withered, but he held his arms steady round his bedfellow. 'Yes,' he said. He felt the flicker of tongue inside his head, stirring his memories, gathering ammunition for further assault and he repeated the leper's words to himself, over and over, reminding himself that all was illusion.

Illusion, he protected his mind from his senses, while his arms held his mother, a fire-ball, a horned goat, an icy river that stopped his breath, took him to the brink of drowning, only to change once more into human flesh. Sheer exuberance in his triumph flicked his eyes open and his laughter died in his throat. 'I'm going to hurt you a little bit,' said Bar Philipos, spittle lodging in his beard, 'but you enjoy that, don't you, my pretty boy,' and he rubbed his naked, unmistakeably eager male body against Dragonetz. 'You do love me, don't you?' he asked, with the same mocking irony he'd used in their games of chess.

'No!' Dragonetz screamed, fending the man off with his hands, leaping out of bed, retching, looking with horror at the man in the bed, who was still laughing as he shifted shape. Then the smile turned to white-faced horror and a woman's tears. His own Estela stared at him, doomed, betrayed, and the cock crowed dawn. Even as he rushed back to her, his Lady shimmered, as did the bed and the chamber, crumbling around him with no noise, no dust and not a vestige remaining. He was in a clearing, holding Sadeek's reins, Malik at his side, looking at him with infinite pity, waiting for him to speak.

'She changed too much for me.' The confession was a thousand swordblades through Dragonetz' heart. He couldn't look at the other man.

The judgement wasn't one. 'We must pray you have a second chance. Allah is merciful.'

Dragonetz would rather not depend on Allah. He remembered the leper's words. 'I am lost,' he said but he mounted anyway and rode onwards, no longer knowing what he sought.

CHAPTER TWELVE

As it happened, Estela barely had time to find out that the newcomers were from Oltra mar before one of them sought her out. She was just concluding a music lesson with Bèatriz in an alcove of the Hall when a page brought his message that a lord sought permission to wait on Estela.

Eyes sparkling at the prospect of distraction, Bèatriz told the page to bid the man enter.

'We have finished for this morning anyway,' she told Estela. 'I need to work on that second strophe myself before I try it again with the melody.'

'My lady, you are moving beyond my capacity to teach you,' Estela replied gravely, standing up to make sure that the visitor would give respect as due, to the seated Comtessa-to-be.

'But I have much yet to learn –' Bèatriz broke off from the mutual compliments to observe the young man entering the room. His garb immediately marked him as recently returned from abroad, partly from the extravagant fabrics used, partly from the fact that their cut was outmoded. His bliaut, the outer tunic, was shorter than was now fashionable and bloused over a simple belt instead of being cut tight to the body with the belt wrapped at the waist and knotted. However, the quaint cut of his clothes did nothing to detract from the strong, pleasing form of the body underneath them.

When he threw himself to one knee in a fluid, extravagant gesture, in front of the two young women, the movement was elegant and controlled. His courtier's pose, one knee on the ground, one bent at the perfect angle to his upright torso, showed off the calf muscle strongly delineated in his perfect silk hose. When he took the hand Bèatriz daintily offered him and pressed his lips to it, the sleeve of his bliaut fell back to reveal contrasting silk and the striped inner tunic, the chainse, underneath.

'My Lady Bèatriz,' he smiled up at her and gave Estela the chance to admire an open face, weathered browner than its natural colour, curly brown hair like a bird's nest framing a teasing mouth and the most remarkable eyes she'd ever seen. Some trick of the light played their hue from grey to green to blue to brown, dancing the colours into a medley.

'My Lord de Rançon,' Bèatriz rebuked him playfully, 'this is not the court of Jerusalem and we do not ask that our courtiers prostrate themselves on a morning visit.'

'You should.' The mouth twitched. 'For the view from here is decidedly worth the suffering of my kneecap.' There was no ambiguity about the way he looked at the stone flag and ran his gaze slowly from the tip of Estela's slipper peeping out her gown, slowly slowly curving his way up her invisible ankle, her knee, her thigh, her cinched hips, her swelling breasts, her throat and then she took the full brunt of those remarkable eyes.

Estela flushed crimson, wondering whether such a look could really strip her, see the very dagger sewn into her underskirt, but she held his gaze steadily. She would not give this man, impudent as he was, the satisfaction of outstaring her. She concentrated, unblinking, on those eyes, in each of which she saw not one, not two but three reflections of herself. Reflections of reflections of reflections, as in a sorcerer's crystal ball. A young woman curving thin and wispy, losing form and substance, vanishing into blue, brown, green, grey. Was this all she was? De Rançon smiled, blinked and looked away. She almost sat down, as if her legs had given way when the contact was broken.

'He told me you were beautiful,' de Rançon murmured, his Poitiers accent overlain with sun-tones from elsewhere, 'but how could I have imagined...'

Estela waited. She was familiar with such play-acting in the troubadour world and, now that he was no longer looking into her eyes, she had regained her poise. It was, after all, not unpleasant to watch an attractive man pretend to be smitten with instant love, teasing her with what he was not saying.

'Of course he is in love with you,' de Rançon continued. 'Who would not be? Such beauty, such grace, and such talent, I am told. It all makes sense now.'

It was Bèatriz' patience which cracked first, no doubt weakened by the fact that the extravagant compliments were not aimed in her direction. 'I'm glad it all makes sense to you, Sir, but it makes none whatsoever to me! God's body, get off your knees and speak like a man, not like a puzzle! I have no wish to solve you and neither does my Lady Estela!'

Rather than objecting to Bèatriz speaking for her, Estela queried softly, 'He?'

Those eyes fixed her again. 'My friend, Lord Dragonetz. He has sent me to you with urgent messages.' This time she did sit down, on the stool against which her lute was propped.

Bèatriz was clearly disappointed. Dragonetz was old news and of little interest compared with guest lists and dowry coffers. Her pout suggested that the prospect of romance and intrigue had removed itself Oltra mar and so she had better things to do. 'Then I must leave you to discuss your business. Make sure you also prepare the duets we discussed,' Bèatriz ordered grandly and she fitted action to words, leaving Estela alone with Geoffroi de Rançon, while castle life fussed around them, through chambers and passages, past the open doors that led to them and from them.

With the same muscled grace, Geoffroi de Rançon pulled a stool up beside Estela, close enough to be unsettling without being so close as to be impolite. The angle between them meant that she could comfortably look at the doorway, only sneaking glances at his face from time to time. She suddenly found the doorway extremely interesting.

'I'm sorry,' he said disarmingly. 'I feel that I know you from the way Dragonetz has described you to me, the black silk of your hair, the gold of your eyes, every ... feature of your body. I forgot that I am a stranger to you while I know you as well as if you were the love of my life, not of my friend's.'

Estela was uncomfortable at the idea of being discussed in such a manner, and she could not prevent the colour in her cheeks but she was used enough to courtly compliments to control her voice, with a hint of rebuke. 'As my Lord Dragonetz' friend, you are welcome, my Lord de Rançon, and I am impatient to hear your news. But duty comes first. The Comtesssa spoke of duets?'

'She wishes us to sing together. I am no Dragonetz but in his absence I am thought adequate. Would you sing with me?'

Sing. With someone else. Estela felt sick at the thought, her ribs squeezing away her breath in refusal. 'Of course I shall perform as the Comtessa wishes,' she replied tonelessly.

If de Rançon was disappointed at the manner of her response, he was too smooth to show it. 'The honour is mine. But of course you want to know about Dragonetz.'

Estela waited, her hands clasped lightly in her lap, betraying nothing.

'He is well,' smiled de Rançon. 'He has spent some time in Damascus.' Estela knew nothing of Oltra mar geography but she assumed this was on Dragonetz' route from St Jean d'Acre, where he would land – that much she knew – to mission's end in Jerusalem. 'I met him there, being on business from my Queen, and we passed the time together sportingly, as you can imagine.' He laughed, a young man's laughter, suggesting late nights, wine and poetry, gambling and girls.

Estela could indeed imagine. Dragonetz had never promised faithfulness with his body, but she'd been worrying, wondering if his enemies had caught up with him, killed him even. She'd been carrying Musca, growing ever lumpier, then facing the threat from Miquel, protecting his family, while he'd been, while he'd been ... 'Go on,' she said.

Apparently oblivious to his effect, de Rançon continued gaily. 'You know Dragonetz! He was poking into everything, wanting to know how steel and silk were made, how roses grew, what the difference was between the Syriac language and Arabic, so he could speak both better.'

Estela smiled, despite herself. 'Yes, that sounds like Dragonetz.'

'He even got into a horseback contest with two guardsmen, had all the locals betting on the outcome. I heard the whole city turned out to watch.'

'And he won.' Estela stated the obvious. What had Arnaut asked him that time on the river bank, when they'd competed to retrieve her token? *Why do you always have to win?*

'Not just the contest,' confirmed de Rançon, 'but hearts too, men and ... everyone.' He changed his intended sentence after only the slightest hesitation but Estela missed nothing. 'I was gone ahead of him to Jerusalem but word reached me even there of the show he put on, some story of risking death against a raging bull.'

'Yes, that sounds like Dragonetz,' repeated Estela, like a mechanical figurine, one of the wire characters on the water-clock he had sent her as a present, striking a tinny brrring each time she was made to surface.

'I'll get the full story out of him when he gets to Jerusalem.'

'He's on his way there? Or was when you left him?' Jerusalem was the end of Dragonetz' road Oltra mar, the end of his road away from her. He was safe, he could return. Then they would be together again and everything would be the way it had been before.

'Yes, all was well and he was on his way to Jerusalem, where we shall meet up.'

'You're going back?' Estela looked at him, wondering. The way he spoke of such vast distances as if they were a trip to market.

'Better than that, my Lady.' Eye contact was still a shock. Green today, reflecting her own pale, bemused expression. Perhaps it was his diamond buttons that made strange mirrors of those irises. 'Much better than that!' he teased her. 'All goes so well that Dragonetz wants you to join him in Jerusalem, to sing with him for Queen Mélisende, to be at his side. You are to return with me, after we perform for the Comtessa and as soon as you have prepared your baggage. We need to embark before the autumn weather disturbs the seaways.'

'It is not possible,' Estela murmured. Then the doubts hit her. What did she know of this de Rançon. It was all too easy. Dragonetz well, successful, wanting her beside him. A dream come true, even if it did mean travelling to the ends of the earth to be with him. Dreams didn't come true.

As if he'd read her mind, de Rançon added. 'I forgot! Dragonetz told me that you were wise and would be cautious of any supposed messenger from him. He has so many enemies! So I was to give you guarantee that these are his wishes by naming his old friends al-Hisba and Arnaut and to ask you to come in the name of Boethius. Does that make sense to you?'

Estela looked into the clear, honest eyes – blue now. Only Dragonetz could have mentioned Boethius, a reminder of a very private moment. She need have no doubts. She smiled. 'Yes, it makes perfect sense. I will make ready to leave.' Saying the words made them real and she felt the weight dropping from her shoulders.

She would leave the threat of Miquel, she would leave the tedium of wedding preparations – after soothing Bèatriz' ruffled pride – she would take her lute and her voice, and adventure after Dragonetz. She could tell him about Musca and they'd return together, triumphant, a family. She must send word to Raoulf. She must find the chest, the medium size one, and pack whatever was suitable for the climate Oltra mar. What was the climate Oltra mar? Warmer than snowy Dia in winter, for sure, or there would not be peaches.

'And you, my Lady?' de Rançon asked. 'You look well but a little tired. Is there some worry I could take from you? Wolf or usurer, tell me and I will dispatch him from your life in a second! What of your news, since Dragonetz last saw you? Tell me all. He sent me to you only because he can't come himself. Pretend I am indeed Dragonetz until such time as I can re-unite the two of you.'

Silence filled with childbirth and attempted murder, a baby in safekeeping. Estela opened her mouth to share all this with Dragonetz' friend, as she would have done with Arnaut, or even al-Hisba. But it was so complicated she didn't know where to start. And shouldn't Dragonetz hear of his son from her first? Maybe later, she would start to tell her story. Maybe on a long sea voyage. 'Nothing of moment,' Estela told him and they spent some time discussing songs before parting for the day, each with a lighter step than before their meeting.

As it turned out, explaining her plans to Bèatriz was easier than convincing Gilles that a trip Oltra mar was necessary. He did not accept the response she gave to his every objection, 'Dragonetz requires it.' Instead, he dwelled on the time passed since Dragonetz had sent the message; on all that could have gone wrong in between, all that could go wrong still, both for Dragonetz himself and for Estela on the journey; on the circular logic that Dragonetz wouldn't put her at such risk if he loved her; and so on.

Until Estela lost her temper, blazed indignant over the danger she was in already from a murderous brother, so that she would in fact be safer in Jerusalem with the protection of Occitania's finest swordsman. And as for Gilles' mistrust of de Rançon, what could a wrinkled peasant know of courtly behaviour! Extravagant compliments were the norm, a mere politeness! As if she, Estela couldn't look after herself, as she had done before Gilles turned up in Narbonne!

To which Gilles retorted that she didn't need to go to Dragonetz for protection if she could look after herself. As they both knew it would, the argument finished with Estela's bald statement that she was going anyway, and Gilles' equally defiant riposte that he was going with her. And on that 'Well then!' note, they refused to speak to each other for at least a day, and then pretended there was no disagreement, Gilles continuing in his usual obedience to his Liege, albeit a Liege he had looked after since she was a baby.

Bèatriz was disappointed to lose her troubadour before the wedding but when the advantages of this were hinted to her, notably her own capacity to shine without other women songbirds sharing the limelight, it was possible for her to be pleased at Estela's good fortune in being summoned by Queen Mélisende. For so de Rançon had presented matters to Bèatriz, and he assured Estela that it was no more than truth.

Although he'd presented Estela with the private message from Dragonetz, it was Queen Mélisende's wish that the two of them join her court as troubadours, which had led Dragonetz to send such a message. Estela struggled to take in all that she was being told. She knew nothing of politics Oltra mar – another matter to put right on the long sea voyage, she told herself.

However, it seemed only natural that the Queen would want Dragonetz at her court, as had Aliénor, as had Ermengarda. At the thought of the golden lady of Narbonne, who had drawn Dragonetz very close to her, Estela hoped that Queen Mélisende was as wrinkled as she ought to be at the age of forty-six. It was also natural that the Queen would be happy with the partnership that Estela and Dragonetz made as troubadours but to be worthy of the court in Jerusalem, Estela needed some practice. Luck had given her someone to practice with. Ignoring every reflex that said, 'This is no Dragonetz', Estela threw herself into working with de Rançon.

There was so little time to prepare that it made sense to choose from the traditional lays that they both knew well, rather than adventure into Estela's work, which of course was new to de Rançon. Although no troubadour, happily admitting that he composed nothing himself, de Rançon was no mean musician and his singing voice was an agile tenor, capable of runs and trills that would have defeated Dragonetz' rich baritone.

Humming as she stitched another infernal piece of linen for Bèatriz' trousseau, Estela smiled to herself, remembering some twist of the lyric they had contrived to amuse the audience, or an unexpected split of strophes between the two of them, which changed the meaning along with the voice. She knew the alchemy of music would work between them and Bèatriz would have a farewell performance from her troubadour to prepare the way for all the celebrations planned for the coming months.

There had been only one sour note in their rehearsals. Estela had lost herself in Rudel's beautiful song, eyes tight shut, thinking how soon she would be in Dragonetz' arms. As the last notes died, Estela still dreaming of her 'amor de lonh', de Rançon laughed and said conversationally, 'As Dragonetz tells the story, Rudel died in the arms of a whore, paid to play the lady of Tripoli so the poor fool could die happy. The illusions of love!'

'But everyone knows the story, how he loved the Comtesse de Tripoli just from hearing about her, how he fell ill on his way Oltra mar but reached the shore, only to die in his lover's arms.'

'My sweet, romantic Estela, I am sure you must be right,' de Rançon had teased. 'It would certainly spoil the story if the man had died of the dysentery in a whore's arms. No, the more I think on it, the more I am sure you must be right and Dragonetz wrong. You know what Dragonetz is like!'

The ground on which she walked seemed suddenly shaky to Estela, as if the small cracks in the paving were growing large. Did she know what Dragonetz was like? Sometimes, listening to de Rançon, she felt she was hearing about a stranger. Was this what men were like when alone together? Cynicism and crude jokes? What had Dragonetz really said about her, Estela? That she was a whore playing the lady? She flushed. Suddenly anything seemed possible.

'I've changed my mind. We'll leave 'amor de lonh' out of the programme. Everyone sings it,' she told de Rançon, who looked sharply at her but said nothing. She liked his sensitivity. She was growing used to his manner, the way he adapted his company to her mood, the luminous gaze. When she was with him, she felt like she was the centre of his universe, beautiful, talented. Of course, he was merely representing his friend, but it was only human to enjoy such attentions. He had even won over Gilles, by sheer practicality.

'You can't take coffers. Not even one coffer,' Gilles told her bluntly. 'De Rançon has told me what's involved in this journey and if you take half of what you want, you won't see Dragonetz for another two years. We want you to ride light, a real horse not a palfrey, and just saddle-bags on pack-horses, no wagons. If we camp overnight that will save time too. I told him you were game for it. Are you, Roxie?'

'Of course!' she told him, silently dismissing gowns and jewels, presents to smooth her way Oltra mar. She would not leave her healing box, nor the pathfinder runic brooch, but she could not take her water-clock, the only memento of Dragonetz remaining to her. She would take the little paper book, a present from Malik in which her songs were written, and a quill. She could use the charcoal from their campfires for ink. She had so few personal possessions for one of her age and status.

'De Rançon says you can buy clothes in Acre, or in Jerusalem, and the climate will be mild so there is no need of your Dia wools, just some light gowns, underthings, a few toiletries and your cloak.' It made Estela feel strange to think of the two men discussing her so intimately.

'Riding,' she said. Obviously, with a 'real' horse she would be riding astride, her usual custom, although she had ridden side-saddle in the company of a baggage-train, and on a suitably docile palfrey. Riding astride required full, circular skirts, and they dirtied so from horse sweat. A long journey would rub her legs raw too. She made her mind up. 'I want a thick pair of men's hose,' she told Gilles. In response to his air of startled query, she explained, 'To wear underneath a riding gown. It's not just horses who get saddle-sore.' He nodded.

She considered the journey. Aboard ship, there would be no problem. Ordinary day clothes would suffice and she saw no need to pack anything for performance or show. She would indeed need coin to purchase court clothes once she was Oltra mar. She mentally put the jewels back in her saddle-bags – she would need the wherewithal to barter.

'How will we travel from Acre to Jerusalem?' she asked Gilles, feeling more comfortable at showing her ignorance to her man than to her new friend. 'Camel train' was the short reply. Estela concluded that there was only so much planning that a woman could do in advance and she concentrated instead on something she did know about. Her voice had fully recovered from emotional strain and lack of use, her eyes were no longer melancholy pits above purple shadows. She was ready to sing for the Lords of Dia one last time.

CHAPTER THIRTEEN

E stela curtseyed yet again, while the applause continued unabated round the Great Hall of Dia. Her right hand was lightly imprisoned in her partner's and de Rançon raised it high, acknowledging her and their audience. Her oud clutched firmly under her left arm, Estela steeled her thoughts away from another hall, another man at her side. There was always closeness from singing a duet, matching rhythms and playing with harmonies, and Estela was not immune to de Rançon's glittering energy, the heat of his hand enclosing her own. However, she had enough experience of performance to distinguish the fever-rush that came after she'd lost herself in song and listeners' spellbound faces, from the feelings that could outface the morning sun. There was only one man she wanted to wake with of a morning, every morning.

De Rançon raised their hands one last time for the audience to yell appreciation and the volume diminished enough to let the duo know it was time to cede the floor.

'Thank you,' de Rançon told her, kissing the captive hand before he released it, bowing to her in personal homage before clearing a way for her back to their prestigious seats, at one end of the high table. Still hot from the touch of his lips, Estela's adventurous hand brushed against the hard gold buckle fastening a sash swathed round her hips and the burning sensation made her jump. Her pathfinder brooch was a prize gifted to her in a tournay of song at Narbonne, by a Viking Prince, and its runes supposedly held powers. When a fortune-teller had tried to read Estela's future, the pathfinder had blocked her visions. Not that Estela believed such rubbish and the prophecy given when the pathfinder had been removed merely played on Estela's guilt and fears. Mere generalities that would be true for everyone.

Her hand still stung a little from the contact, a warning, if she were feeling fanciful. The pathfinder showed roads, crossroads and choices. She hadn't looked at it or thought about it for months, her decisions all driven from the head, all inevitable. If there were no choices, there was no benefit to holding the great brooch, tracing each possibility along the path runes, wondering which way she should go. Was there a choice now, she wondered? Something she was missing?

She eased herself behind the trestle table, accepted the compliments passed on to her via the courtiers sitting between her and the rulers of Dia, central at table. One space showed the absence of Bèatriz, who was to conclude the entertainment and who was already tuning her mandora. She was no longer the shy youngster whom Estela had taken under her wing at the court of Narbonne over a year ago. The heiress of Dia showed all the assurance of her birth and education as she waited for hush and then filled the farthest corners of the hall with the opening lines of one of her own compositions.

A love song, noted Estela without surprise. Equally predictable was the way the singer's eyes were drawn to the high table as she sang, not to her parents but to a young man paying tribute to Dia from his own realm further south. Raimbaut d'Aurenja, who had squired Bèatriz at the extravagant Court of Love staged in Narbonne, a year ago. Much of an age with Bèatriz, the heir to Aurenja had filled out, losing – or hiding – the air of being poised for flight which had struck Estela when she had first seen him. An honoured guest in Dia, he nodded his dark head to the melody, smiling at the singer. Some things had not changed in a year and expedient marriages were unlikely to alter the alchemy between these two. Already a troubadour of note, Raimbaut was certainly capable of appreciating Bèatriz' talents. And there was no doubt that she was talented. *Time for me to leave the floor to Bèatriz permanently*, Estela told the pathfinder.

'A sweet voice, but lacks maturity,' whispered de Rançon in her ear and Estela's stomach lurched. That was exactly what Dragonetz had said about her own singing when they'd first met.

'Her lyrics are beautiful,' Estela responded, truthfully.

'Granted. And she has good technique. How could she not, with you as a teacher? But you have a woman's voice. You sing with a woman's feelings. She's still a girl.'

Estela bit her lip and said nothing. The pages refilled the jugs with celebration wine, the specialty of this cold province, and Estela took a sweet draught of the sparkling white liquid. She shivered.

Eyes fixed on the flames dancing in the braziers, her companion murmured, as if to himself. 'They tell me this wine has been made here for hundreds and hundreds of years, that Pliny the Elder wrote of how the Voconce tribes placed jugs of white wine in the rivers in autumn and lifted them in spring to find them alchemised and effervescent.

My Lady,' he turned his gaze on her but she refused to meet his eyes, 'I think you have alchemised in Dia. You are, and are not, as Dragonetz described you. You have been alone in deep currents in the chill of Dia winter and something has changed.'

'I can hide nothing from you,' Estela laughed, though one corner of her mouth disobeyed her attempt at levity. 'I am all froth and fizz like the Clairette.'

His voice urgent, his eyes still fixed on her, de Rançon said, 'I have heard tales of a cave in the Vercors mountains, an hour's climb from here on horse, where the ice never melts but forms strange sculptures, unicorns and maidens, narwhals and lovers.

Should a man take his lady there, lay her on ice and warm her with his own body, so she feels chill and heat, ice and passion, the tingle of cold... it is said that they may reach out at such a moment and a jug of Clairette will appear.

One sip each from this jug will fill them with the ice of its making and the fire of its opening so that they are fused inseparably, forever.'

Estela gasped as chill exploded against her arm, tingling every small hair, rushing confusion through her senses until she realised it was merely the jug of Clairette held wickedly against her bare flesh.

'Of course, it's just a local story,' smiled de Rançon. 'Would you like some more wine?' Wordless, Estela held out her goblet and met his eyes. *Diamonds*, she thought, *prisms, straight lines and wrong-coloured rainbows, misdirections, reflecting what's not there... ice, being stroked with ice, open to ice...* She shivered again.

'Are you all right?' de Rançon asked her, all concern.

'I'll be glad to head south for warmer weather and not face another winter here! No more talk of ice, please. Tell me about Oltra mar and the peoples there, and about Dragonetz.' Estela stroked pathfinder absent-mindedly but found nor ice nor fire in the touch. If the great brooch had been a cat it would have been purring in her lap, self-absorbed. Not like a white dog, who would have raised one eye, watching, always watching, to see what worried his mistress and where the threat might be.

Estela's last performance at the court of Dia was followed by packing and leave-taking. The former was supervised by Gilles, impervious to Estela's tears over what must be left; the latter was organised by Estela, impervious to the people who must be left. Comte Isoard, grizzled and expressionless, accepted her explanation that she was invited to sing at the court of Jerusalem and could not turn down such an honour, Lady Bèatriz having graciously given consent.

Estela fended off a polite enquiry about her son's wellbeing in Paris and her answer seemed enough to satisfy the Comtessa's curiosity. Isoard's wife, Bèatriz' mother, was a woman who disappeared into the background, whether from experience or nature Estela didn't know, but there was an absence of personality that made connection difficult. Not so with Bèatriz, who flung herself tearfully into Estela's arms, recalling their meeting in Narbonne, their music lessons.

Estela disentangled herself from the young woman's embrace and laughed at her fears. 'It has been a long time since you needed either a teacher or another trobairitz at this court!' She shook her head. 'Your melodies lilt through my head and stay there, every note just. And your way with rhyme is unmatched! The coblas in that last song you performed – wonderful! Estela threw back her head and sang from memory,

> 'Ab joi et ab joven m'apais
> E jois et joven m'apaia
> Car mos amics es lo plus gais
> Per qu'ieu sui coindet'e gaia.'

> 'On youth and joy I thrive
> Aye more joyful, youthful
> Because my friend's alive
> With mischief, never rueful.'

The coblas doblas are so clever, so much work, but the result appears so effortless! The words make me want to dance, make me feel like a girl again.' She whirled Bèatriz into some dance steps, singing the next lines badly, out of breath from twirling. 'You have a great talent, Bèatriz.'

The young heiress flushed with pleasure. 'Do you really think so? You sing so much better than I do.'

'Your voice is improving all the time. And your songs are as good as anyone's!' Estela told her firmly.

'I wrote that song for Raimbaut,' Bèatriz confessed shyly.

Estela tried to look surprised. 'And I'm sure he appreciates it.'

'He does.' The oval face was serious. 'He suggested I try a flute accompaniment.'

Troubadours! thought Estela, remembering with a pang her own mix of music and love talk with Dragonetz. Actually, the flute would work well with Bèatriz' voice. 'I think he might be right. Just for some phrases though.' She hummed a trill. 'There.'

'I thank you.' Bèatriz' eyes glowed. 'I will always remember what you've given me.' Once more the future Comtessa of Dia, she held out an imperious hand to be kissed in leave-taking. Estela hid a smile as she made obeisance. Bèatriz clearly couldn't wait for Estela to leave, so she could score some phrases for the flute. Troubadours! It was time to go, leaving Bèatriz to her marriage and her estate, her lover and her songs, whatever the future might hold for her.

De Rançon's party assembled at dawn, ready to depart as soon as the gates were opened and to make the most of a day's travel. Without a backward glance, Estela dug her heels into the temperamental roan charger she'd been given as a mount, more suited to her size than those the men rode but clearly still a war horse, no palfrey. She thanked God and Gilles for woollen hose and for her training with her father's fast hunters, and let the horse follow his instincts, matching his running walk to that of his fellows as the road opened up.

From Dia the band followed the river Droma west on the trade route towards Lion, the very road that Raoulf had pretended to take. Was it really such a short time ago? How much had changed! De Rançon had briefed Estela and Gilles as to the planned route and received curt nods from both in agreement to the punishing ride. A hard first day would take them to the fortified town of Crest, but there was no intention of seeking shelter behind those walls with the lord of Crest.

Time spent in chateaux or abbeys would add wasted days, exchanging news, explanations and courtesies. No, the plan was that the party, comprising a dozen armed men, plus de Rançon, Estela and Gilles, would camp off the road each night, soldier fashion. Estela saw no need to point out that this would not be her first such night, nor that a saddle-bag for a pillow and a thick woollen cloak for blanket were an improvement on her past experience. She merely gave her assent. Gilles hesitated, concerned for Estela's safety without a city wall, but a withering response from de Rançon regarding the training – and discipline – of his men, silenced him. This was no longer the de Rançon of sparkling eyes and words but a seasoned Crusader, who gave clear, practical orders to his men and got instant obedience.

Two hours' riding, then a break, water and onwards. Another two hours, break and bread, water and onwards. At this stage in early autumn the river had recovered from summer drought but was still gentle enough to access from the stony shoals lining its banks. Another month and full spate would make travellers' lives more difficult. Two hours' ride, water and onwards, the rhythm of heart and hooves pounding. So the day cantered its long stride to dusk and the looming square keep of Crest, dominating the valley from a distance.

De Rançon led the band off the road to a clearing and signaled the men to halt. They dismounted; tied horses to trees, removed bridles and saddles, then started the business of setting up camp, with practised ease. Three men took the horses loosely by the reins, to take them down to water. Estela knew enough about horses to know they'd need grooming and night blankets to prevent any harm from chilling sweat. Lucky horses. The woollen hose had protected her legs, the circular skirt had sat comfortably around her as she rode, but her garments had absorbed a day's worth of sweat – horse and human combined. By the end of a week's travel in this manner, she'd have sweat-striped skirts and it was better not to think about her hose. She'd just have to slip out of them each evening and let them dry before starting another day's lather. All that was unimportant compared with her means of travel, the horse.

Gilles had already dismounted, was using his stump of an arm to hold his own horse and was reaching out to help Estela down, clearly intending to take her horse too and tend to both. She flushed with both shame and pride, because he was worth ten two-handed men, and because he thought that she would let him do her work in looking after her own horse.

'No indeed!' she told him. 'I shall do the work needed.'

Gilles regarded her steadily, holding her as she slipped off the high saddle, holding her as she carried on slipping, her legs giving way completely and dropping her in a confused pile on the ground.

'Bound to happen, when you're out of practice,' he told her brutally, removing saddle-bags and combining the two sets of horse reins. He clicked encouraging noises to the horses as he led them delicately round the crumpled girl. 'Get up slowly,' he instructed over his shoulder. 'Your legs will shake for a bit, your thighs and calves will feel mangle-wrung but you'll live to ride again tomorrow.' Estela groaned at the thought, more than at her aching legs. Arnica and lavender oil, she thought. What she needed was a clump of trees and half an hour's privacy to rub an embrocation into her legs. Then she needed to be carried around on a litter by six strong men.

As if summoned, de Rançon was beside her, holding out a hand to help her stand. He refrained from asking how she was, for which kindness she would be eternally grateful. Standing, but wobbly, she told him succinctly what she needed from her saddle-bags and watched while he found her healing box. She hobbled on his arm to a carefully chosen thicket and, with de Rançon keeping watch, his back firmly turned, Estela first relieved herself – no mean task with her leg muscles screaming – then peeled off the hose and rubbed life back into her legs, along with her precious ointment. She should be careful not to use too much on the first day, she thought, as she rubbed in some more. On the other hand, if she didn't save her legs today, there wouldn't be a second day. She rubbed one more fingertip's worth of lavender and arnica into her thighs then dropped the long skirts over her naked legs and put the boots on her bare feet.

De Rançon was still as a statue waiting for her to emerge, jumping when she tapped his shoulder. She gave him her best smile and she meant it. Sometimes, practicality was worth more than a fine singing voice and a handsome face, and de Rançon had been perfect. He bowed apologies at leaving her and went to arrange fire, food and night watch, while Estela allowed herself to merely sit against a tree-trunk, her legs stretched full out, convinced that she would never move again.

Travel has its own natural laws, breaking taboos and habits, making friends of strangers. Chaperoned only by a one-handed man, in the company of unknown soldiers, Estela felt safer than she had since the moment her brother appeared in her doorway. The pain in her legs, which she'd been sure was life-threatening, had dulled to an ache, and the smell of meat turning on a campfire suddenly made her stomach declare itself void and desperate for exactly the food available. Gnawing on a bone in the light of the fire (near which her hose were discreetly drying on an impromptu rack of sticks), a cup of wine warming her insides, Estela could suddenly understand what Dragonetz had meant when he said he felt 'unknotted' from camping with his men.

Everything was simple. Horses tended, basic human needs satisfied, nothing else had to be done. There were no politics, no palace intrigues, no delicate conversations required. Travelling changed time. The future was the next day's ride and beyond that was irrelevant. The past was a story for telling round a campfire. Men were munching and slurping, flames crackling and the stars above offered all the entertainment required. Was Dragonetz looking at the same stars? Wondering about his place in the universe?

Estela lay back and watched as the sky blackened and increasing numbers of diamonds pierced the velvet. She didn't know the names of the constellations so she made them up, drawing imaginary lines to make pictures of a sword, a horse, her mother. She could read her own story in the stars if she kept looking. Pleasantly weary from the exercise and the wine, her hunger fully satisfied, Estela lost count of the stars and the men's voices became a brook babbling in the distance. She fell asleep where she lay, with her head pillowed on a saddle-bag.

'Estela,' a voice prompted her, followed by a gentle nudge. The horizon was already pinking up and as Estela stirred for the new day, she realised she'd been covered with a blanket and the campfire had died down long since. She shivered a little in the autumn chill of the Diois region, a breath of mountain always in the night air. That would change as the party crossed the invisible line south of Lion, near Valença, where the evening breeze would ruffle her hair with a lover's warmth, even in October.

Gilles stood guard over her privacy as she slipped down to the river for a quick sluice and donned her woollen hose once more. The roan was already saddled by the time she returned to camp and there would be two hours' riding before they broke fast with a hunk of bread, somewhere near, or even on, the great Roman road south. Four days travel on the Via Agrippa should get them to Arle, if all went to plan, and then another two days to the port of Marselha in the Golf dau Leon, where a boat awaited them. Estela's heart sank at the thought of another six days' hard riding but already she was finding the rhythm of her great horse and sparing them both the awkward jolting of the previous day.

The weather was kind to them so it was only sweat that drenched Estela's skirt and hose, not the rains that could easily have slowed their journey. The last time Estela had taken these roads, it had been in the sedate company of Bèatriz' entourage, returning to Dia from Narbonne, where Bèatriz had been under Ermengarda's guardianship. They had taken a month then to do much the same journey that Estela was now expected to do in a week. And she would, too, she told herself as she eked out lavender and arnica embrocation onto her aching legs each evening.

The road south followed another river, the Ròse much larger and more difficult of access than the Droma, so the men filled their waterskins whenever they could, to provide for the stretches where the banks were too steep. On the third evening they camped near the town of Monteleimar and Estela had enough energy left to chat to de Rançon. He had been attentive but formal on the journey so far, alert for any possibility of danger in the strangers they passed or overtook, in the choice of campsite. One eye was always on his men and on the condition of their horses, and he gave the impression that if he thought of Estela at all it was as a kind of saddle-bag, a little cumbersome and to be got from Dia to Marselha without damage. He seemed open enough to Estela's questions though, when she plucked up courage to pose them.

'Are there wolves?' she asked him, watching the fire die into embers now it had fulfilled its cooking function. The southern nights needed no more than a blanket to keep them warm at night.

De Rançon chewed absently on a twig, lying relaxed. Estela thought that chainmail and leather jerkin suited him better than the flamboyant outfits in which he'd graced Bèatriz' court. He looked leaner, more masculine, his unruly brown curls loosed from the coif he wore while riding. Although he continued looking into the fire, the corners of his mouth twitched in amusement.

'You're afraid we'll get torn to pieces when the fire goes out? No, the wolves are in the mountains either side of the valley but they have full bellies at this time of year and won't come so close to men's gatherings until the famines of deep winter force them. Men are more dangerous to other men than are wolves, my Lady.' His eyes caught a red flicker as the fire crackled into last life, painting shadows along his fine-boned face. A man-wolf. Estela had heard of such things but didn't believe in them. Night in a forest was not the best time to discuss such matters however and she changed the subject.

'You and Dragonetz must have grown up near each other. Were you friends then? And you were on crusade together. What was it like? How did you end up at the Court of Jerusalem serving Mélisende? What is she like?' Once the questions started, they poured out from her unstoppered mouth.

'Halt!' protested de Rançon. 'Yes, Lord Dragon – the father of your Dragonetz – has an estate neighbouring ours at Rançon so our paths naturally crossed at tournays. We were both squires, learning our duties, but Dragonetz is two years older than I, and you know what boys are like at that age.' His voice was dry, uncritical. 'Older boys pick on younger boys. No, we weren't friends.'

'But you're friends now,' Estela hurried him on to a more enjoyable part of the story. 'So was it during the crusade that you grew to know each other?'

De Rançon was slow to respond, choosing words carefully, as if each one had to be weighed for truth, giving her no more and no less than she asked. 'Being two years younger still mattered, even during the crusade, and I was the Commander's son, an unpleasant combination for an ambitious young knight to stomach, in so far as he was aware of me at all. I think his attention was all for his liege, Aliénor.'

There was a careful lack of inflexion in his voice, a lack of innuendo, but Estela needed none to guess at the past relationship between the young knight and the beautiful queen. She knew every one of Dragonetz' songs, had known them long before she met him, and she knew perfectly well he'd written many of them for Aliénor. She also knew that any passion between them had long ago changed into something else, loyalty and memories, nothing of which she need be jealous. She was more troubled by the implication that Dragonetz had been a bully, spiteful and petty. It didn't fit the man she knew. Or thought she knew.

'My father was an exceptional leader.' Estela noted the past tense. 'He trained Dragonetz, led him and all of us young knights in sorties in Aquitaine, on Aliénor's business with would-be rebels. While she was in court at Paris, there were always those in Aquitaine who thought themselves strong enough to take her duchy. My father proved them wrong, again and again. When the call came to take the cross, my father was at Aliénor's side, willing to lead for her, and to die for her, willing for his son – me – to do likewise.'

'Men do feel like that about the Queen,' murmured Estela.

'Then you understand how it was for Dragonetz,' said de Rançon, as if apologising for what might be unwelcome revelations. 'He was moonstruck and wanted more than just being her troubadour. And as well as his personal hopes, he wanted to be her Commander.' He hesitated a long moment, again weighing his words, and in that same flat tone, he said, 'His scouts reported to him that there were Seljuq warriors in wait near Mount Cadmus and he saw his opportunity. He said nothing of these troops to his Commander, my father, but let him fall into the trap of obedience to the Queen, who wanted to continue marching and make camp further on. A good decision – if you didn't know of the Seljuq troops! Dragonetz used all his skills in acting to plead with the Queen not to march on, defying her and his Commander – a noble gesture of self-sacrifice if he hadn't been sure of profiting later. Of course, my father chastised him for disobedience, thereby sealing his own fate.

Dragonetz galloped back in secret to the pass, timing it late enough to act the hero with King Louis in full battle, rather than early enough to save the lives that were lost that day. And my father was dismissed in shame for his 'error', replaced by Dragonetz. I was dismissed with him and we rode back together to Rançon, leaving the Crusaders to do their miserable best.' He shrugged. Estela was shocked into silence, part of her wanting to say it couldn't be true, part of her recognising that it could be. Dragonetz was indeed ambitious, and he had become Aliénor's Commander, very young, by what means she knew not, but she knew him capable of clever politics. Her stomach lurched. This was not the Dragonetz she knew!

'I don't know why I'm telling you this,' the voice continued, lighter. 'Campfire talk! As you say, Dragonetz and I are friends now and the past matters not one jot. He has changed. He did a fine job as Commander and I respect him for that.'

Estela couldn't help asking, 'Don't you resent him, for what happened to your father?' *And for boyhood slights,* she thought, remembering her brother's grievances, carried for years like treasures and rotting his mind with slow-drip poison.

The reply was immediate. 'I am bigger than that,' he said simply. 'A man cannot let every act of politics and intrigue eat away at him or he ends up with less honour than the target of his vengeance.'

'That is the truth!' declared Estela, full of admiration, as her inmost thoughts were spoken by the man beside her. 'Dragonetz is lucky to have you!'

For the first time there was a trace of bitterness in de Rançon's tone. 'I wish he thought so,' he said, then lightened again. 'But perhaps I'm the lucky one.' He turned his full smile on her but she couldn't read his eyes in the shadows. 'I am the one travelling with you.'

Smoothly, expecting no response and keeping the tone light, he continued, 'As for my service to the Queen of Jerusalem, now here is a story you'll enjoy.' Skating lightly over the fact that, thanks to Dragonetz, his family name was out of favour in his native country, he explained how he'd been drawn to return to the Holy Land and welcomed at court. He then indulged Estela with some gossip about Mélisende that left her round-eyed and laughing with disbelief, until the natural moment came to bid goodnight and seek what privacy for sleep was afforded in a camp. Estela lay awake long into the night and she wasn't thinking of the alleged peccadillos of the Queen of Jerusalem.

As for de Rançon, an onlooker would have guessed by the angelic smile on his sleeping lips that he was every bit the perfect knight Estela thought him to be.

Getting up in the morning was already an established routine and the party was soon on the road again, aiming for somewhere near Avinhon. The day after that should take them to the end of the Via Agrippa at Arle, where it was crossed by the east-west Via Domitia. Westwards, the road would take them to Narbonne. The backroads from Narbonne went to the estate of Johans de Villeneuve, where Txamusca was tugging thoughtfully on the ear of a large white dog, but Estela would be going east, not west.

'Roxie, Estela,' Gilles interrupted her wayward thoughts. He often used both names, having never got used to her troubadour name but trying his best to show respect. He reined in, matching her horse's pace so he could ride beside her. As usual, respect didn't exclude giving his opinions bluntly. 'How well do you know Lord Dragonetz? I don't like what we heard of him last night!'

Nor I thought Estela, instinctively seeking the comfort of the ring he had left her but it was no longer round her neck. Of course, it was with Musca. Without showing a trace of her own doubts, she answered staunchly, 'I've known him through more trials than some couples meet in a lifetime and his honour is without question!'

Gilles picked up on 'is'. 'Maybe. But it seems to me like it was under question, perhaps long before you knew him, but I don't like what that says about him. I don't think de Rançon's a liar.'

'And I don't think it's your place to speak ill of the father of my child, when he's too far away to speak for himself!'

Gilles had braved her temper often enough to ignore the threatened storm. 'All I'm saying, Roxie, is what I always say. A sword can be pretty enough and break. Test the weapon well before you rely on it. I don't want us riding to Jerusalem for some bootlicker who sings well. You can do better than that.'

'Go back to Dia then! I'm not nine years old!' Estela dug her boots viciously into her mount's side to put distance between herself and her irritating man. She was careful to keep near enough to the soldiers for the rest of the day's journey but Gilles caught her alone once they'd set up camp and the stubborn set of her face didn't stop him speaking.

'I'm sorry,' he said. 'They were harsh words. And I came late to Narbonne so all I saw of Lord Dragonetz was his heels disappearing abroad after his mill burnt to ashes and his friend was killed. That, and leaving you carrying a child, don't notch points in his favour with me.'

He held up a hand to stop her angry response. 'I know, I know. He didn't know you were carrying and he couldn't help the other business. I know you have feelings for him. It's only natural. But things change, and de Rançon is a good sort. He tries to hide them but he has feelings for you, deeper than the silly compliments you all play as games.

Maybe this journey will give you thinking time. I mean no more than that you'll use your head when you see Lord Dragonetz again, before rushing into something just because there used to be something there to rush into. I'm only thinking about what's best for you.'

'Well, don't,' she told him, still cold. 'The subject is closed. And if you can't behave appropriately then I shall turn you off!' They both knew she wouldn't dismiss to impoverished death a man who'd given one hand to protect her and would give the other if need be, but it was a measure of her anger that she said it all and Gilles merely bowed his head in acceptance.

Chat around the campfire made no mention of Dragonetz, nor disgraced lords, nor queens, but that didn't mean they were absent from people's thoughts. *And no,* Estela agreed silently with Gilles, *I don't think de Rançon is a liar. I wish he were.*

CHAPTER FOURTEEN

The end of the Via Agrippa caught them by surprise, so accustomed had they become to that inexorable trek south. The suddenness of it, seeing the road stretching in two opposite directions, threw Estela off-balance. She realised that she had a choice and, unconsciously stroking the pathfinder clipped to her riding gown, she ignored the rest of the party turning left and kicked her horse into turning right instead. Musca was so close.

All she had to do was ride for a day and she could watch his milky smile, smell his yeasty baby skin, hold him in her arms, where he should be. He would gurgle while she dug her fingers into handfuls of warm white fur and sat her baby on Nici's back, playing ponies. If she could have just one day with her son and her dog, free from doubts and decisions. It would be easy enough to go to Marselha two days later. All she had to do was ride.

' Roxie!' called Gilles, spotting her break away, and looping a cumbersome turn to chase after her. She rode faster. De Rançon was faster still, wheeling expertly and galloping westwards after the fugitive. He wasted no time calling after her, but spurred his great destrier alongside her, dust clouds enveloping both riders as he reached for her reins and gently slowed both horses.

'Easy, there, easy.' Estela didn't know whether he was

speaking to the horse or to her and she didn't care. She felt the salt of tears running into her mouth and she didn't care. The choice was gone. She couldn't tell de Rançon where she wanted to go and why. She couldn't give up on Dragonetz, who was waiting for her.

'Something spooked him?' de Rançon asked gently, still holding her reins as he walked the horses round, to take a gentle pace eastwards again.

White, tear-streaked, defeated, Estela merely nodded and swallowed the insult to her horsemanship, reclaiming the reins, concentrating on the big roan and his anxiety. They caught up with the rest of the party, returned to the rhythm of the road, heading away, always away.

'Think instead about what you're going to,' Gilles' quiet words cut into the miserable pounding of hooves in Estela's head.

'Only a day away!' The words bled from her.

'More like four days, assuming you survived the road on your own. If we'd taken the detour as a party, that would be the best part of a fortnight late at Marselha and we're already into the chance of autumn storms and poor sailing. And for what? To rip open wounds that haven't healed? Seeing him for a day would only make it worse to leave again.'

'I know. It was just too strong for me.'

'I've told you before how much like your mother you are. Just keep steady. She'd be very proud of you. Two days and you'll be on that ship, heading towards Dragonetz and then there will be nothing to fight any more.'

'To be so close!' In saying the words, Estela was letting go, knowing the moment had gone, knowing her son might as well be an ocean away already. As long as he was safe, what did it matter?

'Are you all right now?' De Rançon's voice made Estela jump. She'd not been aware of him riding alongside, so deft was his manoeuvring of the destrier. She wondered how much he'd heard but he gave no sign of finding her words strange so she answered on the level of the question asked.

'I don't know what came over him,' she replied, 'but I should have handled him better. I'm fine now, just a bit shaken.'

'The smallest thing'll spook a horse. Could've been a snake underfoot, wind waving a rag in a bush, who knows. If you need a break to recover, just say the word.'

'No!' Estela spoke more sharply than she'd intended. 'I'm fine. I just want to get to Marselha and get on that ship.' De Rançon gave a brief nod and galloped off to exchange words with his men at the front. The pace picked up again and the world was once more two hours' riding, pause, water, two hours' riding, pause, water, food.

The long downhill ride into Marselha at sunset, giving a panoramic view of blue sea, olive trees and twisted pines, gave Estela time to recover her sense of adventure. Nothing could have prepared her for the crowds and bustle of the busy port. After nights camping in woods, and days on horseback, so many people walking purposefully through so many steep streets made Estela think of an anthill, strange creatures rushing on pre-ordained paths, criss-crossing without contact. If someone had blocked a street with an upturned cart, would the flow of creatures have continued unabated, creating an alternative route by sheer weight of numbers?

Muscles hardened by days in the saddle, Estela no longer felt as if she'd survived a penance when the sun dipped for night, but she did suddenly feel unbelievably filthy. She balked at the idea of going on board ship for weeks of further makeshift toilet when all around her was evidence of civilisation.

A quick word with de Rançon and Gilles gave her the go-ahead and within an hour of settling matters, Estela was testing the heat of her bathwater in a clean, comfortable inn, her sweat-stained riding-gown and woollen hose abandoned in a heap. Appalled at the risk to health of bathing so late in the day, a servant nevertheless scurried to fetch yet one more bucket of steaming water, to top up my lady's bath.

Never had Estela so much appreciated southern sophistication, the drops of rose-water and the soft olive oil soap, produced in Marselha itself, with which she scrubbed and scrubbed her skin pink. Should she die the next day, at least she would have known this bath! Towelled dry, glowing with the scented oil she'd rubbed on after the bath, she fell asleep in a bed of roses, too exhausted to worry about past or future choices.

Waking at dawn was habitual for Estela and she was in her travelling gown and ready before Gilles knocked at her door. If she needed something suitable for a long ride again, she would buy clothes in Acre, as no form of torture could force her back into the blackened dress and hose which she'd peeled off the night before. Definitely for burning! She left them for the servants to dispose of and followed Gilles, her saddle bag over his shoulder giving him a strange double-headed silhouette as they walked down to the docks. The salt-sea-smell of fresh fish hung on the air and already the fishermen were setting out what they'd netted the previous night, for the early market. Not even in Narbonne had Estela seen such variety, and those fish already dead were still bright-eyed and silvery-scaled, glittering in the first rays of sunshine.

The sunshine also caught the ships on the far side of the harbour, glinting on the masts, pennants and crow's nests of the merchant roundships, which formed the majority of the large ships docked. Estela was expecting one of these to be their destination but Gilles stopped at a galley, the banks of resting oars bobbing on the tide like idling feet. They both knew that the lighter galley, the most usual warship, was more vulnerable itself to attack but faster and easier to manoeuvre, without the dependence on wind and tide that limited the roundships, those bulky floating fortresses. A galley was also far more expensive than a merchantman. The flotilla of small boats around the galley, unloading supplies, looked like courtiers buzzing round their queen.

'Venetian.' Gilles was like a small boy sailing his first wooden stick down the river, glowing with excitement. In that one word was implied 'the king of ships crafted by master shipmakers'. Estela had lived in Narbonne long enough to absorb some knowledge about ships, on which all trade depended, but she hoped she wouldn't have to suffer too much detail of undecked hulls, freeboard height or keel lengths. Gilles' awed repetition of 'Venetian, made in the Arsenale itself,' suggested her hope was doomed. She stopped to take a look around the docks, a last look at her homeland before stepping onto the ship that would carry her away from everything she'd ever known.

The harbour was so full, it was a miracle that each ship held its mooring and that each zig-zagging small boat, whether incoming fishing vessel or outgoing pilot boat, avoided capsize. The city curved around the hillside, above the rocky shore of its ancient harbour. To the east was the oldest part, the white of Roman columns standing out on the hillside, but the ancient gods had ceded to Saint Vincenç of Marselha, whose abbey seemed to have borrowed its stark lines from its classical ancestors. Further round to the west were the new merchants' houses, a hotch-potch of structures and streets, with the largest and most fashionable highest up the hillside. Estela imagined herself living in a grand villa at the top of the hill, with a view across the bay. On a clear day she could probably see Antioch! Resolutely, she turned and stepped onto the boards, ignoring the dip and sway as she marched aboard the galley, crossing the gap at the board's end without mishap, reassured by a judicious helping hand from de Rançon.

As it turned out, neither Gilles nor anyone else bored Estela with facts about shipbuilding because from the moment the ship left the harbour, 'dip and sway' became 'heave'. As the ship heaved, so did Estela. Allocated a cabin somewhere in the bowels of the ship, she stayed in hiding there and refused to come out. She became unpleasantly intimate with the bucket provided for her. She left her bed only to totter between bunk and bucket, pleading with the lord of the universe to end her life, now, quickly. No answer came from the wainscot round the cabin walls, nor from the crew members who rushed in and out to change buckets. The silent deckhands also left food and water, which only evoked more groans from the miserable depths of the bunk.

Gilles ventured into Estela's hell-hole to tell her it was just like riding a horse; once she was into the rhythm of the long ship, she'd ride with it, instead of against it, like she was doing. Groans were the only reponse. After what could have been years of this mole-like existence, a knock on Estela's door was followed by de Rançon's entrance.

'Just want to be alone,' Estela moaned weakly, looking at him through half-closed eyes.

'I'm sure you do,' he told her, with a marked lack of sympathy that snapped her eyes open in an angry glare. De Rançon ignored buckets and stench, showing a complete insensitivity to her condition. That in itself should have warned her. 'It's time to get up now, Estela.'

'Noooooooo,' she groaned, shutting her eyes again, only to find her arm gripped firmly and raised so that she had no option but to rise into sitting, then standing position. A vague instinct to reach for the knife always in her undershift barely broke through the waves of nausea from changing position. She vomited over de Rançon's boots but he didn't even look down, never mind release the vice-like grip.

'I can't go out like this,' she protested, indicating her crumpled clothing.

'You can.' De Rançon pulled a light mantle from its hook and swept it round Estela's shoulders, covering all underneath. She registered the fact that someone had ranged her belongings while she lay at death's door, and there seemed to be new items there too. A green gown and matching ribbons drew her attention. If she survived, maybe she could try them on... The grip marched her out of the cabin door, supporting her but with no tenderness.

She'd given up on groans and merely concentrated on getting up the wooden steps and onto the deck, where she would at least be able to vomit into the sea rather than disgrace herself again. The salt breeze smacked into her face as she surfaced from below decks, making her gasp. And then she gasped again, this time at the sight of the open sea ahead.

This was her first sea voyage, her first sight of the wide blue 'mar' in so many songs. She was on her way Oltra mar on a Venetian ship. The ship's pennant streamed in the breeze, depicting the lion of St Mark. It lifted one proud paw in gold on a red background, announcing the boat's provenance to other seafarers. Estela could just make out the intricate carving of the prow and recalled Gilles' excitement at being on a Venetian ship. For the first time since stepping onto the boat, a feeling other than bile rose inside her. 'What's it called?'

'The Santo Spirito.' De Rançon let go of her, casting her adrift. She felt the swell of the sea, was aware of the furrow breaking against the keel, as she looked always towards the horizon, the edge of the world. The wind must be with them as the broad bottom of the great triangular sail swelled and filled, adding to the rowers' momentum.

'What will happen when we reach it?' she asked. 'Will we fall off?'

'We won't reach it. The horizon is further away than you think and our charts show us where the land is that we need for our stops.'

Now that Estela looked more carefully, there were blobs in the misty distance. 'Land?' she asked.

De Rançon laughed. 'I think you were too occupied to notice but we stopped at Messina to restock and now we should have enough to reach Antioch, if the weather is with us. If not, Sicily and Cyprus are options. We have a good pilot and he has good charts – the rest is down to wind and weather.'

Estela gulped in the freshness, her face stinging pleasantly, as if gently scrubbed clean. She felt the rise and fall of the ship and realised, astonished, that Gilles was right. 'It is like riding a horse!'

'Then you'll forgive my rude method for bringing you up here, my Lady?'

She looked steadily into his eyes. Never would she be prepared for their strangeness, shimmering now with sea and waves, reflected clouds, an ocean demanding her attention. She could never be prepared but she could at least hide her reaction. 'Forgiveness must be earned, Monseigneur de Rançon,' she told him in her haughtiest tone.

'Then perhaps you would join me with the Captain at table this evening and I will set to work.'

Table. Food. Estela was suddenly ravenous, her empty stomach gurgling a protest.' I think that will be possible,' she said graciously. She would wear the green gown and ribbons. And she would eat a lot. And she didn't want to die any more.

Having found her sea-legs, Estela also found enjoyment in being the only woman aboard ship. The discipline established by De Rançon, and by the Captain, ensured that she was shown nothing but respect by the busy, silent crew, and Gilles was never far from her side. Nevertheless, she was aware of flattering glances and the quality of silence lightened where she walked. She remembered a story in which an enchanted princess left trails of rose petals in her wake wherever she walked. It felt like that, as if Estela were surrounded by invisible petals, a feminine aura that sweetened the atmosphere.

She was well aware that her reputation would not be the more respectable for this journey but as a troubadour she cared little for conventional reputation, and as a wife she was protected from all but her husband's disapproval. Estela's patrons had chosen her husband carefully, and made the conditions clear. She knew that Johans de Villeneuve was content with the privileges heaped on him by his liege Ermengarda and would never seek to claim a husband's rights or show a husband's anger at the actions of a wife who was known only by her professional name of Estela de Matin. No, there would be no recriminations from her husband, however she behaved, so Estela's only constraints were self-imposed, however much Gilles might offer his views.

Dining with the Captain was a daily pleasure, offering seafaring stories with varying degrees of credibility, full of ice-rocks and meta-morphosed fish-women. De Rançon contributed racy anecdotes of life

Oltra mar but also showed an unexpected interest in seamanship, raising debates about the link between tides and the moon or the possibility that different stars could be seen from different seas. In hesitant Latin, Estela scrambled to contribute, from what she could recall of her own classical education and her conversations with Dragonetz and al-Hisba.

Sometimes her comments were well-received; sometimes not. She offended the Captain deeply with her casual implication that the oarsmen were slaves and criminals. On the contrary, he told her, such practice was illegal in the Serenissima and Venetian families vied to contribute rowers to man their famous ships. The fame of the ships depended not just on the building skills of the Arsenale but also on the strength of Venetian rowing, which was developed through contests in the laguna that all Venice would gather to watch. Slaves indeed!

Estela also offended the pilot, with her eager request to look at his charts. Every male eye round the table fixed her in horror, as if she'd asked him to drop his hose, rather than let her see a map. The pilot was too overcome to speak, and it was de Rançon who explained that a pilot's charts were his most precious and personal possession, his trade secrets. Which is why their pilot was so valued, because he knew of currents and rocks, streams and doldrums, charted only by him. Such knowledge was not to be shared with anyone but the Captain of any particular voyage, and only such knowledge as was relevant. The Captain looked uncomfortable at the idea of what he didn't know, and Estela hid her disappointment with an attempt to regain the approval she'd lost.

This time, she fared better, amazing not only the Venetians with her praise for their trades other than ships, their alum industry and bookbinding in particular. It soon became obvious that Estela's technical knowledge on these subjects outstripped the men's, although she carefully held back when she realised this and emphasised her admiration for the Serenissima. The Venetians were almost purring as she ladled on the cream and another glass or two – or three – of wine, restored good humour to the table. *They'd have all known a lot more about alum and book-binding if they'd spent as much time as she had at Dragonetz' paper mill,* thought Estela. She determined to use this voyage to learn just as much about ships, charts and stars, and to turn her Latin into Italian as fluent as de Rançon's.

Warm from wine and surprisingly good food, Estela sought the deck when she left table, not ready to go to her cabin yet. She waved imperiously to Gilles, who dogged her as always, to leave her alone. When he saw de Rançon join her at the railing, Gilles nodded and slipped away. It was a relief to relax into Occitan, not to worry about saying the wrong thing.

'You can see more and more stars the longer you look,' she said, wondering at the deep black of the night sky.

'Behind the stars you can see are the ones you can't, the fixed stars. And among them the primum mobile.' De Rançon was so close she could feel the heat of his arm against her side and he sounded serious, no trace of his usual laughter, no compliments. Just a man standing beside her, looking at the stars, wondering.

'What's the primum mobile?'

'The one that makes everything happen. The one that makes the celestial spheres move, take their places, perform a dance across our heavens. The prime mover.'

'But if we can't see it, how do we know it's there?' objected Estela. She shivered and he placed an arm round her shoulders, covering her with his cloak, enclosing their two bodies together under its warmth. She shivered again, breathing in the scent of the Marselha soap he had used to shave with. As he spoke, his lips close to her ear, she could smell the trace of wine on his breath, sweet with herbs – rosemary she thought.

'We can see its effect,' he murmured. 'We know where it is from what the others do.'

Estela turned abruptly, needing to check his expression. Closer to his face even than she'd thought, her mouth found his and tasted it. Rosemary, confirmed, as he hesitated then responded, his arms holding her hard and close, harder and closer. Estela's whole body remembered what should happen next and begged for more. It had been a long long time and she was at sea, ready to drown.

She stumbled as the kiss broke and de Rançon stepped back, putting night air between them. 'I'm sorry, my Lady. Too much wine was responsible. Forgive me. I'll escort you to your cabin.'

His formality and distance made it impossible for Estela to say anything, do anything other than take the arm that was politely offered. In silence they walked along the deck to the ladder below but de Rançon stopped short, apparently needing to say something difficult before they parted.

'My Lady. Estela.' She waited, still as a ship's figurehead. For once he looked away from her, ducking his head with the effort of finding the words. Then he seemed to take courage, with his usual steady gaze, a crescent moon floating in each eye. 'I might regret telling you this but as we are both dedicated to reuniting you and Dragonetz...'

His eyes told her this was the truth and she felt the first flush of shame dowsing her lust. She had encouraged him to dishonour them both! 'When I said that all was well, I didn't want to trouble you with my worries, and I thought it best you see Dragonetz for yourself... but now, I think it better that you know... Dragonetz,' he hesitated again, 'is not the man he was. I fear some illness of the mind. It is even possible that he will deny sending for you.'

He gave a sad smile. 'It is even possible that he will say I am no friend of his.' He flung out both hands in a gesture showing his own impotence. 'But maybe I'm being pessimistic. Maybe whatever curse was hanging over him has lifted.' He smiled resolutely. 'One thing is certain. That he loves you. That you mean everything to him. He needs you. And we will get you to him safely.' He bowed. 'Good night, my Lady. Sleep well.'

Too shamed to speak, Estela dropped a curtsey and rushed down to her cabin, latching the door. As if that would protect her when the evil was inside the cabin. Inside her. She did not sleep well.

De Rançon hung over the rail, gripping it with hands that shook slightly, letting the spray sober him. He was irritated by his own lack of self-control but he needed a few minutes before going to his bunk in the cabin he shared with the Captain. It was not surprising that he should have reacted to the passion of a beautiful woman throwing herself into his arms but he had not expected so much desire, such personalised desire to flood him in response. Maybe he had let his guard slip during his delicate courtship of Estela. Maybe she had found some chink in his armour, with her engaging curiosity, her brave spirit, her angel's voice. A pretty face and woman's curves meant nothing to him but something, something had touched him more deeply. And it would not do.

He'd had to picture his father's face to escape from that dangerous kiss. His father's face on Mount Cadmus, chiseled, proud; his father's face as he'd last seen it, sunken in firelight, etched with bitter lines, a portrait of failure and disgrace.

However long he spent at the court of Mélisende, however fêted he was as her courtier, his father's face haunted de Rançon, along with the parting words from elder to younger. 'Go as far as you like, leave me, but you carry our cursed name with you. Should a man whisper behind your back, you'll know he speaks of de Rançon, a name without honour. Should a woman turn you down, you'll know she fears contagion.'

That's how it's been for me since Dragonetz los Pros' – he spat out the nickname like poison – turned the Duchesse against me with his plots and pretty face. Place no trust in queens!' Again he spat. 'Better dead than a de Rançon.'

Two years alone with his father, his father's demons, his father's cold servants and absence of all friends, had taught de Rançon self-control. And much more. His mother had left the family home soon after her husband's return from Oltra mar but whether it was fear of contagion from disgrace that drove her, or whether it was the ugly tempers that stormed through the chateau, who could say. Only de Rançon, the son, was left to suffer.

The day came when he decided his father would be no worse off without him and he went to Jerusalem, to continue in the family tradition and serve a queen. This one however was no mere wife of a king, but queen in her own right, and widowed, making her doubly powerful. De Rançon thrived on the court politics, realised that the disaster at Mount Cadmus was just one event in a series of bad decisions, in a catastrophic campaign. No-one wants to remember failure and no-one at the court of Jerusalem considered any aspect of the second crusade as successful, except perhaps the Queen staying out of it. De Rançon was able to live as if the crusade had never happened, which suited him fine.

And then came word from his Damascus contact, Bar Philipos. De Rançon was wooing the citizens of Damascus through this man, with promises from Mélisende, of armies and treasure-coffers, should Damascus accept the rule of Jerusalem. It was clear that Damascus could not remain independent, not with Nur ad-Din's sorties from Aleppo growing ever stronger, not with the Franks equally avaricious from the south.

De Rançon had won enough respect from Bar Philipos to be informed that the balance would be tipped sooner than they had thought, unless they could contain one irritating knight, the Commander currently imprisoned in Bar Philipos' own house in Damascus. The man they called Dragonetz los Pros. And he had a book with him, worth a kingdom, sacred to the Jews, and valuable to anyone who collected art, perhaps to a queen, who already possessed a priceless psalter and would surely appreciate another art treasure.

That's when de Rançon knew his duty to his ruined father, knew the purpose of his own existence, and he swore an oath against his own life. After a long, private audience with the Queen, in which he revealed none of his interest in Dragonetz but understood all of the Queen's, de Rançon joined Bar Philipos in Damascus.

Mélisende had made her instructions clear; get the book and keep the knight out of play, while she considered her next move. No-one else was to have either. Not Nur ad-Din, but especially not her rebellious son Baudouin. Bar Philipos was obviously in touch with Nur ad-Din, playing the delicate game of preserving Damascus, and between them he and de Rançon had neutered Dragonetz, keeping two clients happy. One who'd paid to have Dragonetz killed; one who'd paid to keep him safe but out of the way.

They were into the mid-game now. Nur ad-Din would expect the death sentence he'd paid for to be carried out, discreetly of course, via the opium that poisoned Dragonetz more every day. Mélisende no longer wanted Dragonetz kept safe and out of play but wanted him in Jerusalem and hers. Or of course, dead. So Dragonetz and the book were on their way to Jerusalem. Should he say no to Mélisende, he would write his own death sentence. Bar Philipos could report to Nur ad-Din that his task was fulfilled and de Rançon could report likewise to Mélisende, who would by then have the book. Nur ad-Din had missed his chance with the book, which was all as it should be.

There was only one little matter for de Rançon to consider, as primum mobile in this exquisite movement. How could he cause Dragonetz the most pain before ensuring his death? This needed his full attention during the weeks before his party reached Jerusalem. How was Estela best used? Should he fuck her? His body gave an involuntary response at the thought. Or should he continue to play perfect?

Would misplaced accusation on Dragonetz' part cause deeper damage, widen the crack between him and Estela that de Rançon was so carefully creating? Make Dragonetz himself drive Estela ever closer to his enemy while he could only watch helplessly? Or would it hurt him more to watch the physical evidence of his slut betraying him? For of course she was a slut. All women were. His mother had abandoned his father, taken the world's side against him. De Rançon should beware the spell Estela had almost cast. He was not a man for the cosy hearth. Not since Dragonetz had wrecked what was once his home.

Pondering his revenge would pass the time nicely between here and Jerusalem. Then the endgame would begin.

CHAPTER FIFTEEN

Dragonetz was unhappy about leaving Sadeek in the Damascus stable but the hands had confirmed Bar Philipos' curt information. From Damascus to Jerusalem, six days by camel across desert and rock, with water in short supply. Not a journey on which to risk a glossy-coated high-bred destrier. Sadeek bridled flirtatiously under the brown hand smoothing his nose but clearly accepted his carer, so Dragonetz left him with a murmured adieu and a promise to return.

The Bar Philipos household was in a frenzy of preparation, clerks preparing inventories, shouting instructions to the porters who piled goods in courtyards and entrances, then made them disappear. Dragonetz glimpsed fleeces and silverware, brocades and knives, in the ever-changing landscape of his living-quarters. No longer his prison, the house revealed its architectural secrets to the curious knight. Although the orthodox cross of Christianity featured on some chamber walls, the arches and tile patterns proclaimed the more mathematical symbolism of the east. The sound of water, bubbling in private courtyards, was never far away and favoured contemplation more than the icon-cluttered chapel that served for family prayer.

Wearing the comfortable robes and leather sandals he'd adopted for anonymity in the city, Dragonetz took refuge in one such corner, on a stone bench amid blind vines. The pebbles had been colour-matched for exact hues to create grey-brown arabesques around the roots of an old wisteria, seemingly grown from pebbles, not earth. Everywhere, the eye was drawn to patterns and symmetry, purpose and mathematical beauty, while the ever-present water tinkled its message of eternal life, an absence of self.

Dragonetz resisted the urge to kneel, to formulate a convention of prayer, and instead let his mind open to God's will all around him, as he had in the vigil before his knighthood, and in the times since, when he had felt the need of guidance. He reached out for the pattern and for his purpose in it, hearing pebbles and arabesques as melodies, phrases repeating. Whatever happened, the songs of his life could not be unsung; whatever happened, as long as he lived, there would be more songs.

He had no idea how much time passed but Dragonetz was suddenly aware of people shouting, outside his garden. 'Take that load to the camel-herders and tell them get the palanquins strapped up.' 'Keep those separate – they're provisions for the journey.' 'Have you tallied the wine-skins?' The practical details focused Dragonetz' thoughts on his own plans for the journey and although he still felt that inner peace he'd been part of, briefly, his mind returned to this world and its demands. He too needed porters. He needed some special crates, a present from the Khatun, taken to the camel train and he needed some different, equally special goods, placed in safety for his return.

Now was the time to harvest the goodwill he'd sown amongst the craftsmen of Damascus, when he'd spent hours questioning them about their skills, showing his own willingness to get his hands dirty. He'd made them laugh with his attempts at pot-throwing, his clay bowls collapsing into mis-shapes. He'd surprised them with his delicacy in peeling a sliver from two plant stems and tying the open wounds together, in the miraculous marriage of plants that the rose-grower called 'grafting'. He'd earned respect both for his muscular body and his use of a forge when he stripped off and sweated over the filigree on a sword-blade. He'd achieved one curving initial, the letter D with as much pride as if he'd traced a tattoo over the whole blade, as the master swordsmith then demonstrated in front of him. Now was the time to remind that master-swordsmith of their agreement.

Dragonetz was leaving Damascus, forever if his plans worked out, and he wanted to be sure his work here had not been wasted. When he'd won their trust, he had shown the rose-grower and the sword-smith his token from the Khatun, that daughter of the city. Such a token guaranteed that Dragonetz' offers would be taken seriously, and he'd given them time to contact the Khatun and confirm his credibility. Now he needed to make the future arrangements clear. There would be plenty of time on a six-day camel journey to consider what he would do afterwards, in Jerusalem.

'Find Muganni and send him to me,' Dragonetz told one of the house servants. The boy-singer had asked for a new name from his master to fit with his new life and now responded only to the Arabic word for singer, Muganni. Dragonetz had no idea what he was going to do with the boy long term but for now he had no choice but to make the most of the slavish adulation, until he could fashion more independence.

As a messenger, Muganni was the perfect combination of loyalty, intelligence and anonymity. He would flicker through the streets unseen, let the swordsmith and the rose-grower know what Drag-onetz expected, and how he would contact them from Jerusalem. He would ensure that the precious boxes, with their live cargo cooing in alarm, were delivered from the Khatun's store to the camel train, as Dragonetz' private property.

The boy approached his master in a loping run, throwing himself at Dragonetz' feet in a semi-audible apology for his tardiness. 'I have work for you, Muganni,' Dragonetz told him. The boy looked up with a sunbeam smile. Dragonetz sighed. 'And stand up, for God's sake. I'm not an Emperor.'

With no change in the smile, Muganni jumped to his feet. 'Yes Effendi, no Effendi,' he assured Dragonetz. And then, hesitantly, 'What's an Emperor?' Dragonetz sighed again.

Outside the city walls, a sea of camels shimmered in tasselled saddles and packloads, the morning sun glinting on embroidery and scimitars, as a hundred anonymous men wrapped their scarves tighter against the wind, ready for departure. The camels spat their annoyance, frothing through their bridles, while harnesses were double-checked and the doors opened to each palanquin, which swayed like an eagle's nest on a rose-bush, impossibly perched on camel-back. Merchants' wives or daughters, noblewomen travelling to Jerusalem, would have the extra comfort of their padded box during the journey, protecting them from the damage caused by the extremes of weather and men's glances.

Watching the equally anonymous figures, presumed female from the way they slipped through the small openings of their cushioned cages, Dragonetz shuddered. There was something claustrophobic about such a mode of transport. He copied his fellows, tightened the swathes of fabric round his nose and mouth, only his eyes unprotected, and he mounted the kneeling camel to which he was shown with a grunt and the wave of a goad. The angle was impossible. He had the feeling he would fall forward over the beast's nose at any moment and then, with a whack of the goad, the camel lurched to its feet and Dragonetz clutched the saddle as well as the reins, convinced he was heading over its back-end into a humiliating heap. Once the camel was upright, he felt unnaturally high, accustomed as he was to horses, but at least the horizon was level again.

All round him, camels were whacked into standing up, and Dragonetz could see everyone else thrown forward and back as the beasts heaved to their feet. Some were attached to each other with ropes, others free, and, with surprising speed, the amorphous mass became a procession, picking a route through the orchards, heading into the wilderness.

Twisting his head for a last look back at the city, Dragonetz took stock of how much he'd changed since his first view of Damascus, with the crusading army. How ignorant of the city he'd been, of its mix of peoples, of its sophistication, of its independence. To think he'd fought to 'liberate' this city! He'd believed the priests who promised him redemption in exchange for death in the holy cause. He hadn't died; instead he'd returned home, weighted with new sins. No wonder Bar Philipos treated him with contempt.

As he settled into the long stride of the camel, less demanding than that of a horse, Dragonetz had plenty of time to think. Holding the reins was a mere sinecure as the camel followed its fellows in a rhythm meant for long distance, no hint of distraction for tasty low leaves or a bird flashing skywards. Onward past the irrigation channels to dry earth and rock, then sand and rock, then sand and sand. The road from Damascus, the very journey that St Paul had taken, in reverse. Was this to be an epiphany for Dragonetz too? He felt light-headed with the prospect of adventure, his time in the garden still shaping an inner peace. The very names of places they would pass on the journey held childhood magic from the bible stories; the River Jordan, the Sea of Galilee and finally Jerusalem itself. He would see the Holy City again and, despite his responsibility for a mission and a book, despite oaths sworn, his spirits rose boyishly at the prospect.

Meeting Jerusalem's Queen played no small part in Dragonetz' excitement, however dangerous for him such a meeting was likely to be. What had Bar Philipos said? That if Dragonetz accepted one of the offers that would be made to him, he would tip the balance. He'd already turned down Nur ad-Din. What offers would come to him in Jerusalem, where a royal mother and son were at odds? And what price would he pay for a refusal? Somehow, he had to keep his head and find the Jew who would take the book and free him from his oath and his poverty.

Dragonetz was certain that the Syrian would try to make him offer the book to the Queen, whose appreciation of fine art was every bit as developed as Nur ad-Din's. The question for Bar Philipos would be what Damascus could gain from Mélisende, or her son, if forced to choose between Nur ad-Din and Jerusalem as ruler. Dragonetz knew enough of Bar Philipos' game to know his own place in it, an item for sale in the market-place, to protect Damascus.

And what did he want for himself? Did he want to be the 'world-changer' Bar Philipos had named him? Did he want to have a thousand trained men under his command? His pulse quickened at the thought. He had been cooped up in Damascus for too long and he needed action. So Dragonetz' mind turned as the camels paced ever onwards until the sun marked day's end, sinking lower on the right. Ahead of him, the tight caravan was already dispersing into clusters of kneeling camels and the first tents were being erected in the shelter of rocks that loomed black in the lengthening shadows.

Once he'd eased his muscles back into walking without the feeling that a drawbridge was wedged between his legs, Dragonetz stood outside the tent he'd been allocated and kept out of the way, observing. The invisible occupants of palanquins were shielded as they emerged from their cocoons, flashing an ankle or a bracelet in the awkwardness of getting out of the tiny doorways.

Hatred flashed towards Dragonetz from one such occupant, and he didn't need to recognise her brown eyes, all that was visible in the travelling robes, to know Yalda was among their company. No doubt she would be an asset to her father's trading. A great asset, he thought with momentary regret for their trysts, quickly replaced with the memory of the Khatun's warning that a woman was responsible for the release of the bull intended to kill him. He'd not doubted who that woman was. He could even understand her motives, having grown close enough to her, even if only through skin-heat, to feel the recoil when he sent her away. What he couldn't understand, or forgive, was the consequence to the two guards. Aakif and Shunaar had died because of her petty revenge, men whose families she claimed she knew. Feeling once more the hatred in her glance, Dragonetz suddenly realised she might feel the same way; blame him for the men's death.

As she waited, unsure which was the women's tent, Yalda was joined by a flurry of servants, ushering another slight figure from palanquin to female company. A vicious gust of wind whipped her face free of its hood and scarves and as she flailed at the recalcitrant material, streaming in pennants, Dragonetz saw that she was light-skinned, blue-eyed and ill. Even from a distance, he could see that her skin bagged and sagged, undernourished; her grizzled hair was knotted in tangles older than today's wind; the skin around one eye still bore the unmistakeable yellowing of deep bruising, caused by a fist if Dragonetz were any judge; and as her eyes met his, as if drawn to the quiet watcher, he flinched from their emptiness, soul-less beyond the worst despair. Then her servants were around her, covering her in seemly fashion, guiding her with the other women to the tent where they would spend the night. Dragonetz shivered. If that were a merchant's wife, the knight hoped his only dealings with the merchant would be at the end of a lance.

'An experience, isn't it.' Bar Philipos dropped to the ground beside Dragonetz and assumed the cross-legged position in which so many of his countrymen seemed most comfortable. Out of politeness, Dragonetz sat beside him, preferring to stretch out his long legs. Camel-riding had cramped him quite enough for one day. Other men joined them, in easy silence or spoken half-thoughts, as is the way of travellers breaking bread at the end of a hard day's ride. 'You will never see the stars brighter. In the desert, you can see your way more clearly in the skies than on the ground.'

Dragonetz searched the stars for answers but their alien brilliance told him only that he was nothing, a grain of sand, a breath of wind, here for a day only. Was Estela looking at the same stars? Did she think of him or had life brought her some distraction with desire in his eyes? The spheres would sing their song, regardless.

'Muganni,' he summoned and his shadow was instantly beside him, bowing and smiling. 'Fetch my oud.'

Dragonetz stroked the familiar curves, tuned the strings and strummed a few chords, before launching into the first song that came to mind, of love far away.

'Lanqand il jorn son lon en may
M'es bels douz chans d'aulhelz de lonh,
E qand me sui partitz de lay
Remembra.m d'un amor de lonh,'

'When days are long in May
I hear
the sweet-tongued birds so far away
And near
Things leave me dreaming
Only of my love so far away'

The plaintive Occitan echoed against the rocks. More and more travellers joined the group around the singer, hunkering down to listen. Even the women's tent opened to let shadowy figures hover nearer the song. The most spell-bound was Muganni, his eyes full of desert stars as he edged closer to his master, forgetful of his proper place, mouthing the foreign words as if his life depended on them. A song is never merely the words and music created by the composer. It comes from the soul of the singer, through the place and time of the singing, to reach the soul of the listener.

'Mas so q'ieu vuoill m'es tant ahis
Toz sia mauditz lo pairis
Qe.m fadet q'ieu non fos amatz!'

'But my desires can never be,
The Father wills that my love
Loves not me.'

The final words faded into the desert night, their sweet melancholy so powerful that at first the noise seemed but a continuation of the song. Then the woman's sobbing jarred, desperately real. As if flood-gates had opened, the wailing from the women's tent surged in uncontrolled waves, diminishing as soothing chatter from many voices drowned the sound of misery. No-one commented. No-one so much as caught anyone else's eye, looking a question.

'Muganni,' Dragonetz ordered, passing his precious oud to the bright-eyed lad.

There was no false modesty as the boy re-tuned the instrument for

Arab minor keys, tested it and lost himself in the old songs that had the camel-drivers and merchants alike nodding their heads, dreamy-eyed. Dragonetz closed his eyes and heard, underneath the Arab training, a soprano as angelic as he'd ever come across. Estela's soprano was richer, womanly. Dragonetz imagined them singing together. His voice would blend with either of them but he could imagine nothing but clashes from the two sopranos together. Suddenly, inexplicably, he felt depressed. He didn't want to listen to music any more. He reached for the feeling he'd had in the garden and found only worries churning endlessly in the pit of his stomach. As soon as he could politely do so, he retired to his bedroll, but the black humour followed him into his dreams.

'Why do you no longer seek the Grail?' al-Hisba demanded.

'You presume on an old friendship,' Dragonetz told him, controlling the urge to hit the man. He was seated on a golden throne, in a pavilion of multi-coloured silks, his dragon devices flying at the entrance and embroidered on the brocade cushions scattered on the carpets underfoot. 'I am the King. I don't need to seek the Grail because others do it for me. And don't purse your lips like that, man. You go too far!' Five of his guards had swords drawn the instant Dragonetz shouted and he allowed them that moment, weapons pointed at al-Hisba, to make their relative status clear.

Al-Hisba didn't flinch or speak. He bowed and left. For good, Dragonetz hoped. He didn't need sour-faced morality in his new life. He clicked his fingers and gold platters appeared, heaped with his favourite sweetmeats and spiced pies. Another click of his fingers and girls wearing transparent scarves wove bright movements across the room. Music of any kind was of course banned; it weakened a man. And there was no room in his court for weakness.

A pretty youth in dragon livery approached him with a message. 'Your Highness, the Queen says...' The message was so private that the youth whispered the words in Dragonetz' ear and his body responded instantly to the teasing double meanings. He clicked his fingers and his courtiers vanished, leaving him alone with the Queen on the piled cushions. Her silks conveniently unwrapped at his touch and her body opened easily to his, blue eyes encouraging him to further exploration, her hands following their own adventures. Everything a man could want, everything, he told an imaginary al-Hisba as he let go of all he was, lost himself in skin and need, climax on climax until his body was air. Until his body was gossamer. Until his body was wrapped tightly in gossamer, spider threads.

The Queen was shaking her head, sadly, her blue eyes bulging, her face becoming hairier, darker. 'You are the white knight,' she told him gently, as if teaching a particularly stupid child something even he should have known. 'And I am the black Queen, the black widow.'

He still didn't understand, even as her limbs multiplied, eight legs deftly tying the ends of the threads which bound him. Infinitely patient, she told him, 'I'm going to eat you alive…' and her face expanded into a mouth, sucking him into sticky blackness, dripping with saliva.

He was sweating and feverish when Muganni woke him, and grew worse during the day, struggling to merely stay awake as the camel carried his dead weight. The tremor in his hands worsened, and his left leg seemed possessed, suddenly kicking out, beyond his control. His head was hot and full of spiders. At the noonday break, he ordered Muganni to lash him to the saddle, ensuring that if he did lose consciousness, he would still be carried along. He had no idea whether he was asleep or awake during a journey that could have been twenty years or one day before he was helped to a bedroll at the night's camp.

'Drink this,' the boy told him, with no trace of the usual grin. He drank, he slept and in the morning he was completely fine – better than that; he brimmed with health and the urge to carry out all his plans. He'd never felt as physically fit or as mentally sharp.

He smiled at Muganni. 'Those were good herbs'.

There was no answering smile. Grim-faced, the boy told him, 'Those were not good herbs.'

'What do you mean?'

Muganni glanced around him, at the other men stirring in the tent, preparing for departure. 'We need to talk, Effendi,' he murmured, 'in private.'

At first, Dragonetz called the boy a liar. Anything rather than believe he spoke the truth and that Dragonetz was consumed by a poison that would kill him if he stopped taking it, and kill him if he carried on. Fear in his eyes, whether for himself or his master, or both, Muganni explained that the poppy was used to help boys through the pain of castration. He would have taken it himself if Dragonetz had not bought him a different life. But some of the boys he'd known had carried on taking the poppy after the cutting was over. They'd wanted relief, from pain, from despair, from the memory of old men's bodies forcing their own. But the poppy was dangerous, created illness and need, and this was how it was for his master now. Muganni knew the signs that the poppy was taking a man and he had seen them in Dragonetz.

'What signs?' Every question was torture that must be faced.

'Your eyes go wrong. They have the away-stare. You are falling asleep sometimes, in the day. At night you shout in wild dreams. What you suffered yesterday was from going without longer than your body can manage. I made a mistake.' The liquid brown eyes regarded Dragonetz steadily, despite the fear.

'You're dosing me with this poison?!' The anger rush was easier than the other feelings Dragonetz did not want to deal with.

'It was in the honey tea you were given. I knew the smell. I thought you ordered it, not knowing it was bad for you, so I stopped it reaching you. I've been giving you a little poppy only, to cut it down, to clean you, but yesterday your body said I had not given you enough. I thought you had chosen to take the poppy.' The boy looked at him and Dragonetz could only imagine how much of the horror he felt, showed in his face. 'You didn't know.' Muganni's face reflected the horror. 'Tell me who I should kill, Effendi. Who has done this thing?'

Yes, killing would feel good, thought Dragonetz, looking at the innocent young face offering to murder for him. Unfortunately, killing would do nothing to help Dragonetz or his plans. 'No. They don't know I'm aware of…' he gestured, still finding it difficult to say the word, '… this. That gives me an advantage.' Again he asked the question Muganni had already answered. 'What if I just stop taking it?'

'Like yesterday but worse.'

'But I could get past that after a time? Be free?'

'Maybe. If you are locked up, with people around who can help you, and yet ignore your screams for help, with no-one who will listen to you promising anything – anything! – to get the poppy. Sometimes a man dies anyway.' There was only pity and honesty in those brown eyes but the sentence they delivered could not have been more cruel.

With one of those disconcerting returns to the behaviour he'd been taught in Nur ad-Din's camp, the boy laid his head against Dragonetz' chest, throwing his thin arms around him, expressing his feelings in the only ways he knew. Gently, Dragonetz gave the boy a fatherly hug and disengaged. It was a long, slow process, teaching Muganni how a boy and a man should behave together. Dragonetz didn't want to destroy the boy's capacity to express any emotion physically and yet it was hard not to react against the imitation of a woman's touch, with its wrongness.

'How are you getting the poppy?' Dragonetz suddenly realised how costly it must be and that Muganni had no means.

'When you sent me to the Khatun, I told Salah ad-Din. He will not speak of it,' he hastened to reassure Dragonetz, not realising the humiliation caused. 'He took enough from the store, told me to say to you that it is a gift not a purchase, that he knows you cannot promise more than you did to the Khatun, that he hopes you live but only you can outwit your death.'

'You have kept all this from me.' Dragonetz was more amazed than angry.

'Salah ad-Din said I would know the time to talk to you. And I thought the poppy was your choice not a doom upon you.'

Clear-headed, no doubt because of his recent dose! Dragonetz weighed his options and found them wanting. 'Can you keep me functioning for two months?'

'I think so.' Muganni frowned. 'But every week the poison gains hold, takes more of your essence, makes it harder for you to escape. You will need stronger doses. And in two months it will be even more dangerous to cleanse you than now.'

'It is worth the risk.'

Muganni hesitated, looking away, then made some decision. 'There is something else. I have hash, from the Man of the Mountain.' Dragonetz' ignorance must have shown in his face and the boy explained, 'Hash is also a drug, a kind one, which can take pain and lighten the spirits, make a man feel strong before battle, enough to take on a hundred men. I think we might be able to slow the increase in poppy by using hash, if you know the signs and can dose yourself at the right times.'

'A kind drug?' Dragonetz' every instinct revolted against adding yet another poison to his system. 'The Man of the Mountain?'

'I am Hashashin. I was taken from my people and now I belong to you but I know how to find them, where they hide in the mountains and where they hide in plain view, amongst their enemies in the cities. The Man of the Mountain is our Leader and he taught us how to use hash, for special occasions and battles. It fires men up, then it leaves them clean. That's what I mean by a good drug.'

'Your enemies?' asked Dragonetz, wondering what weird tribe his young servant came from.

'Those with different beliefs, who will not allow ours to exist. And those whose names we are given, to deliver their fate. We are Isma'ili.'

Dragonetz had not heard of the Hashashin but he was aware of the Isma'ili, hated by other Muslim sects, living in cast-out communities, fighting according to their own interests, even, so it was rumoured, in alliance with the Crusaders. But their usual ways of fighting were through targeting individuals, through stealth and even at night, so alien to army tactics that Dragonetz had dismissed the people as outlaws. Muganni leaned close to Dragonetz, whispered a name and a password in his ear.

'If the time comes that you would like the man killed, who did this to you, write down these two words, with the man's name, and give your wish to any beggar on the street. All know that such messages are for the Hashashin, that the bearer will be rewarded. Your words say that the Hashashin owe you this favour and there will be no payment asked.'

Studying the serious face, Dragonetz realised that the offer to kill for him had been no idle threat. Muganni was Hashashin. 'You do not belong to me,' he told the boy. 'You are free to go to your people.'

'And leave you to your death? Say these words to me again, in two months' time, and I will consider what is owed.'

'Thank you,' Dragonetz said and then laughed sourly.

'Effendi?'

'St Paul,' Dragonetz told him, knowing he wouldn't understand. 'It seems the two of us had our moment of revelation in exactly the same place on this road.'

'Effendi.' Muganni's face closed up into that of the perfect serving-boy, humouring his lord, and he went about his business. Dragonetz was left with the verbal equivalent of a signed contract for a man's murder, to be used when and on whom he chose; and with a body that was destroying itself, minute by minute. The only thing to do, as he'd already decided, was to mount his camel and ride for Jerusalem and its widow-queen, following where the train led.

CHAPTER SIXTEEN

L ast time he'd seen Jerusalem he'd been too bitter to notice. How could you enter Jerusalem without a thousand stories for company? All those bible stories and crusading veterans' tales. For a minute, Dragonetz imagined how the first Crusaders must have felt when they claimed the Holy City for Christian rule. Their pride and awe at fulfilling their sacred mission, the miracle of their success. Then he remembered the pride of those same veterans in 'dispatching' the thousands of Jewish and Muslim families who lived in Jerusalem.

He was no longer the young Crusader who'd come to fight the Infidel and he would never again be able to go to war without counting the cost in human lives. Human, not just Christian. He shook his head, like a dog shakes off a shower, willing away the unwanted images, knowing he made his life complicated by such heretical thoughts. Instead, he let his soldier's experience automatically signal the city's defensive strengths and weaknesses to him, as he rode towards it with the vantage point of an attacking army.

Everything about Jerusalem was square, from the four-walled shape of the city to the battlements and towers. Squarest of all was the Tower of David, a keep dominating the skyline, apparently impregnable. It would be to the Tower of David that the important residents would retreat if the outer walls gave way to mangonets, trebuchels, or force of numbers scaling the walls. He appraised the city again and corrected his first impression. Not all buildings were square. He recognised the Dome du Rocher. Not as high as the tower, the huge gold roof, curved like a Saracen helmet even to the decorative peak, proclaimed the city's Arab history. Its neighbour, in duller grey, also built as a mosque. No doubt their names had been different in the past, to suit their previous use.

Then the great walls loomed close and Dragonetz lost sight of the city interior. The train stopped outside the city walls, breaking formation and performing the usual undulation of camels kneeling and men dismounting. Although no longer afraid he'd topple off, Dragonetz couldn't say he was used to the extreme motion as his beast dropped to its knees.

Horses and wagons came out to meet them, to carry high-born riders and goods into the city. Servants were accompanying their masters on foot, filing past the guards at the Damascus gate and through the city walls, out of sight. Dragonetz mounted, feeling a little strange at first on the Frankish saddle after days on a camel, preceded by horse-riding for months with Moorish tack. Bar Philipos and Yalda rode beside him, while Muganni loped easily in the rear, alongside the other servants and the laden pack-horses. No doubt there was more than one wagon with Bar Philipos' goods, following them into the city.

The Damascus Gate opened into the quarter dominated by the ex-mosques and Arab-style housing but they quickly moved past these and headed to the right, amongst many churches and few houses. Clean, paved streets stretched out in every direction but the impression of well-organised design was disrupted by equal numbers of relic-sellers, food vendors, their customers and the numerous beggars who littered the streets. Dragonetz had never seen so many people.

'Thank the Lord we're here out of the season for pilgrims,' murmured Bar Philipos, kicking away a man whose cupped hands and whining plea for a coin had intruded on the Syrian's physical space.

'The thigh-bone of Saint John,' offered a peddler dressed in monkish garb. 'Guaranteed to cure all ills.'

'And the third such thigh-bone in this street alone,' muttered Dragonetz, any remaining illusions about the holiness of the city taking a severe beating. 'Could there really be more people in this city in the summer?'

'From April to October, the pilgrims come in their thousands. Every pilgrim lodging is full, at triple the usual price, and any accommodation in the city is hard to find. I've heard that Rome is no longer as efficacious, and Santiago de Compostela was always a poor-man's choice, so, now the Church of the Holy Sepulchre can be visited, what Christian would not choose Jerusalem?'

It was so easy to fall into easy habits of conversation with Bar Philipos, learning from his extensive knowledge of these lands and their peoples. Since he'd been a captive, because he'd been a captive, Dragonetz had put unsavoury facts about the Syrian to one side of his mind and had profited from their contact. Anyone watching them would have thought them friends. That habitual relationship had become second-nature to Dragonetz, even though he now felt dirty at the contact.

How was it possible for him to chat in this way, knowing the Syrian's abuse of boys just like the one who gambolled along, protected by, and protecting, his new master? Knowing that he had dosed his captive with slow death, smiling throughout? Dragonetz felt sick at his own capacity for mummery. *This,* he told himself, *is about survival and alliances, when deep in enemy territory. I could whisper this man's name, with the password, into the right ears, and his life would be over. This is not me, who makes polite conversation with such a man. And yet.*

And yet, that is exactly what disturbed Dragonetz most. There was a part of him that respected Bar Philipos' passionate commitment to Damascus, a city that – thanks to the Syrian – Dragonetz had grown to love. That same part of him could appreciate Bar Philipos as a politician, while despising him as a human being. How was it possible to distinguish between the two? How could you hate a man, for what he'd done to others and for what he'd done to you, and also admire him as a strategist?

'Our roads must part here.' Bar Philipos broke into his thoughts as if reading them. 'See.' He nodded towards the grand walls and entrance to their right. 'The Church of the Holy Sepulchre.' Confused, wondering whether he was supposed to perform a pilgrim's thanks for safe journey, Dragonetz waited. That such a suggestion should come from Bar Philipos! 'And opposite,' the Syrian continued, looking left, 'the hospital, where the knights of Saint John are expecting you. They have lodgings for pilgrims, some empty in October, and you are expected. I go to stay with family.'

The Hospital could easily be recognised as such by the crowds of people, some being carried, many with makeshift bandages and in varying stages of sickness and bodily weakness, all gathering round the entrances to a long building, almost as grand as the holy monument opposite. Dragonetz saw flashes of the characteristic, monkish tabards worn by the knights Hospitaler, black with white, eight-point crosses. The Hospitalers were organising their would-be patients, sending urgent cases one way, holding others in waiting. The original structure of the building was that of a monastery but there were additions, including a small but beautiful church, dedicated to John the Baptist. Just past the complex of Hospital buildings was a private entrance and it was here that Bar Philipos stopped.

Dragonetz could not move a limb, lost, uncertain. The Syrian told him, 'I gathered that the Templers have been over-zealous in trying to recruit you, and that the Hospitalers would offer a more restful place to stay.' Adolescent resentment filled Dragonetz. What else did the man know about him?! From Yalda, no doubt! Or from the poppy dreams, over which he had no control. Still, he sat there. 'You are a free man,' said Bar Philipos and it was only then, with those five words, that Dragonetz felt his imprisonment, the weight of it shackling his mind as much as his movements, the daily constraints. He felt the tremors starting in his hands and caught Muganni's eye. The boy nodded imperceptibly.

Bar Philipos gave a curt order to one of his servants, who brought a pack-horse towards them, laden with what Dragonetz instantly recognised as his own saddle-bags, with extra goods stacked above them. 'You will find *everything* is there, *all* your possessions,' the Syrian told him, 'and we will have audience together with Queen Mélisende, two days from now, to discuss the matter of Damascus. You have been my guest for several months and we have much information to share with the Queen. And of course I have told her of the special gift you bring for her.'

'You don't fear for what I might say?' Dragonetz ventured.

'I trust your judgement, my Lord,' was the smooth reply, and if Dragonetz hadn't known of the contingency plan to dispose of him, he would have admired the other's confidence more – or perhaps less. Bar Philipos kicked his horse on, and the last Dragonetz saw of the party was one sullen glance from the swathes of black fabric hiding all but Yalda's eyes.

'My Lord Dragonetz.' A young Hospitaler smiled his greeting, then ordered black-clad servants to take the horses and show Muganni to the prepared lodging. 'It is such an honour to have you here. We have all heard of your crusade, how you became Commander on Mount Cadmus and so young!' Wearily, Dragonetz suffered the starry-eyed young man to lead him to a clean, sparse chamber where Muganni had already aired the bed and placed a night chemise on it.

'What am I thinking?!' The Hospitaler, who'd introduced himself as Francis de Blaincourt, stopped mid-flow. 'You must be so tired after the journey.'

'I am,' Dragonetz responded shortly. 'Please excuse me but I think I must sleep as long as I can this night.'

'I see your boy has prepared a posset for you already,' smiled de Blaincourt. 'Then I wish you good night and will see you at matins.' Before he had pulled the heavy oak door to, Dragonetz had already lost control of his hands. Muganni held the 'posset' to his master's lips and helped him drink, ignoring the tears forcing their way out of closed eyelids, then he supported Dragonetz to the bed. 'You will be yourself in the morning,' Muganni promised in soft Arabic, but no-one heard him. Dragonetz was already deeply elsewhere.

Not at matins, nor prime, but closer to terce and lunch-time, Dragonetz emerged from his stupor. After sluicing himself awake at the wash-basin, with the pitcher provided, he unpacked the saddle-bags and parcels. He watched Muganni fold unwanted clothes into the chest.

'The crates!' he exclaimed.

The boy's teeth gleamed as he reassured his master, 'The pigeons are in the care of the knights' falconer. I went back to the camel-herders last night to have them brought here.' Dragonetz breathed again, glad he'd paid handsomely for his cargo to be kept safe. The Khatun's gift – for she would never have insulted him with the word 'bribe', whatever she hoped – was only partly in the pigeons them-selves and was irreplaceable.

Inspecting his armour for rust or damage, Dragonetz was pleased to find it had been oiled and had no stiffness in the joints. Unlike himself. He donned his mail hauberk over his long-sleeved linen under-tunic and britches, then paused, looking at the tabards and chemises, belts and stockings. They looked so foreign to him.

Instead he reached for one of the loose, striped robes that had been his daywear for months, slipped it over the hauberk and tied a cord round his waist. Another day wearing the comfortable garb of Damascus would harm no-one, he thought as his feet made their habitual way into leather sandals. He probably looked much like a Hospitaler, or a pilgrim. His Damascene sword belted round his hips, he was ready for Jerusalem. He let Muganni find young Francis de Blaincourt, who was only too happy to escort Dragonetz to the refec-tory, where unleavened bread and sheep cheese tasted as good as any banquet, especially washed down with good red wine from the hill-vineyards of Homs.

Silence did not appear to be one of the vows taken by the Hospitalers but, with a full stomach, Dragonetz found de Blaincourt's chatter entertaining rather than irritating, and he was able to turn it to his advantage. By the end of the meal, he knew that Queen Mélisende's good-looking Constable was rumoured to be more than her right-hand man. Dragonetz was also fully informed as to the Hospitalers' organisation into knights, men-at-arms and chaplains, and the strength of the newly formed militia, an army to rival the Templars – so de Blaincourt informed him with pride. The rivalry between Hospitalers and their red-cross brethren, the Templars, was not news to Dragonetz and he was not sure whether lodging with the Hospitalers would weigh in his favour or against him.

The Templar Grand Master would be none too pleased when he heard but Bar Philipos was quite right. Because of their work in the Hospital, the Knights of St John still preserved a reputation for adherence to their vows, and for neutrality. Whether this would change as their militia grew stronger, was a good question. What was certain was that the Templars' power had already grown well beyond neutrality; their ingenious banking system, from which Dragonetz had profited in the past, made their vow of poverty a joke. They were an easy target for tavern jokes regarding their other vows too, but such jests were rarely made in front of the Templars themselves. Their skill at arms was not a joke.

Dragonetz had been approached several times by Templar Commanders, including the Grand Master himself, Everard des Barres, when they were Crusaders together, but the offers had never convinced him. Not that the offers hadn't been tempting! But he could never shake the feeling that he would be signing away his soul, even with de Barres, a man after his own heart, in a way beyond anything he had known with Aliénor as his liege.

De Barres had rescued King Louis from his own folly more than once in the first year of the crusade and then, like Dragonetz, returned home with the defeated army, disillusioned. Whereas Dragonetz had invested his energy in a paper mill, De Barres' reaction to the humiliating campaign had been to retire from the world and join the monastery at Clairvaux. Dragonetz didn't know his successor,

Bernard de Tremelay, but he did know that the new Grand Master had been leader in all but name since de Barres left the Holy Land, and the title had been ratified by vote four months ago.

Given the fragile relationships between the two orders of knights, and his own reputation (of which he was informed hourly by de Blaincourt) it was no surprise to Dragonetz that the Hospitalers' Grand Master, Raymond de Puy, requested his presence.

When he entered the austere chamber to which de Blaincourt escorted him, Dragonetz found himself alone with one of the most powerful men in Jerusalem. A man in his sixties, with a bald head and a curly grey beard, the Dauphinois Raymond de Puy addressed Dragonetz in their native Occitan, which instantly created a feeling of intimacy. This was reinforced by de Puy's Hospitaler garb, the same as all the knights wore, and his unassuming manner.

Inviting Dragonetz to draw up a stool and sit with him, de Puy spoke with a twinkle in his eye. 'De Blaincourt tells me we have a legend among us, a cross between the Lancelot of the new Frankish ballads, and a Perseus, who dispatched the Damascene minotaur while hanging upside down from a stirrup.'

Dragonetz smiled. 'I fear he exaggerates, most worshipful master. The stirrup acrobatics were separate from the killing of the minotaur.'

'Nevertheless,' de Puy returned the smile but showed the steel within, 'this makes your choice of allegiance interesting to my order.'

Dragonetz let the silence speak.

'I will speak frankly. I am concerned, as are many others, at the way the Templars' power grows, beyond any checks. They serve the throne because they choose to do so but they make it clear that they are above the law and own no authority but the Pope's. The Pope is a long, long way from here and his authority weighs lightly. Until recently, the Templar army went unchallenged, which works well when we are united against the infidel; not so well in truce-times where power seeks more power, more land and more wealth.

There must be a balance to such power and we can provide it. I am at fault for letting our order concentrate on our hospices and development of skills in care of the sick, leaving the military duties to

the Templars unless war called us to arms. No more! We are
expanding our militia, and training them to be unbeatable, to offer the
counter-balance. We need the best training, and you can give us that.
Will you join us?

I can't offer you wealth. Nor prestige or power such as you would
gain with the Templars themselves. There is little earthly reward in
doing God's work but the knowledge that you fight for what is right.
You would have a thousand young men like de Blaincourt, to shape
for the good, with a knight's skills, used for a knight's purpose, not
for greed. What do you say? Will you join us?'

Dragonetz bit his lips to prevent the 'Oc' of assent escaping. To say
yes and give up the responsibilities he carried, to obey orders, doing
what he did best, working for someone he respected... No wonder de
Puy had reached the position he had, when he inspired such an urge
in a stranger. However, the instinct to accept de Puy's offer did not
further his plan.

'I take the question as a great compliment,' he replied slowly, 'and
I will think seriously about it.'

Disappointment flashed across de Puy's face. They both knew the
answer was 'non' but the older man was wise enough not to press.
Instead, he clasped both Dragonetz' hands in his own, then blessed
him, leaving a stronger feeling of guilt and debt than any recrimina-
tion could have done.

Dragonetz needed to dress for court. Several times he picked up the
clothes he had worn in the past, then put them back down, while
Muganni waited passively. Then he gave them to the boy, to fold and
put back in the chest, and instead selected a clean robe, with long,
loose sleeves and embroidered trim. It was so much more comfortable, left him so much more freedom of movement than his Occitan
garb. He told himself that his attire was not so different from the
Hospitalers and he knew that the court of Jerusalem had a far greater
range of nationalities among its courtiers than that of Paris, where

even a southern flourish in dress would attract disapproval. So Aliénor had found, to her cost.

Musing on the two courts, Dragonetz imagined the scene when Aliénor had been presented to Mélisende, three years earlier. That must have been some competition in jewels and entourage. How Aliénor must have envied the woman who was queen in her own right, not through some weak husband. Indeed, as a widow, whose king-son had barely reached majority, Mélisende held absolute power. This might not be what her father had envisaged when he left his throne jointly to his daughter and her carefully chosen Frankish husband, Foulques. No doubt the father had imagined his daughter supporting her husband, securing the throne until it could be passed on to her son Baudouin, on Foulques' death. If so, Mélisende's father had known little of his daughter, who fought inch by inch, surviving scandal and war, to rule as Foulques' equal – more than equal, many said, as blood heir to the old king.

A hunting accident had ended Foulques' reign two years before the Crusaders came Oltra mar but Mélisende was in no hurry to proclaim her son king in anything but name. His coming of age at fifteen came and went with no change to the balance of power. King Baudouin did his mother's bidding, although he had more than proved his manhood, leading his army alongside Dragonetz in the crusade. Maybe Aliénor had taken another lesson from Mélisende's example; a queen's power could be extended and strengthened through a son and heir. Aliénor's frustration at birthing only daughters was boundless, while Mélisende rejoiced in two sons, Baudouin and his younger brother Amaury. However, at twenty-one, King Baudouin was surely chafing at the bit.

When discussing politics with Bar Philipos, Dragonetz had asked the Syrian's judgement on the King and Queen, if friction grew to a matter of choosing between the two. His reply had been that Mélisende was proven, an ally of Damascus, and Baudouin untried. For that, his mother must be blamed – she could not keep her son like a hunting cat on a leash. That he rebelled against this spoke for his manhood and his honour. Sooner or later Baudouin would come to power and, if he were to keep it, he would need to learn from Mélisende how to make an ally of Damascus while there was still time. If Mélisende would not resolve the growing conflict between her and her son, then her subjects must, and the sooner the better for all Christian Franks.

Having been Bar Philipos' 'guest' for some months, Dragonetz would be expected to know and share the latest news from Damascus. As a Christian knight, he owed fealty to the court of Jerusalem, to both Queen Mélisende and King Baudouin. He had already heard and rejected de Puy's invitation; whether the Templar Grand Master would also make his bid for Dragonetz, remained to be seen. Maybe all Dragonetz' previous rejections of the Templar offers had left a clear message and he would not be asked again. That would be one less buyer in the marketplace to which Bar Philipos had brought him. Brought him and the book. Except that the book was not for sale. Whether he was, remained to be seen.

A full gathering of the court faced Dragonetz, when he was summoned to audience with the Queen. He had not been invited to court on his previous visit to the city and he noted the eastern décor of the palace, carpets and gilt statues, servants in livery, and all manner of people. He'd been right about the variety of dress, from baggy-trousered Arabs to sober clerics, from fully covering veils to flirtatiously slashed kirtles. This was indeed very different from Louis' court in Paris.

The throne room itself was lined with people Dragonetz assumed to be the great and the fashionable of the city, who barely glanced at him as they competed with each other for attention. Regally tall – in that, she and Aliénor were well-matched – Mélisende was dressed richly but simply in a red robe, ruched all down the front. She wore the golden coronet of Jerusalem encircling a white wimple. Her olive face spoke of her Syrian mother but the blue Frankish eyes made a striking contrast. Her hair swung in a long reddish-brown rope below the wimple and hinted that widowhood weighed lightly on this woman, now in her forties, but still showing the beauty for which she was famed. She watched Dragonetz approach, then accepted his obeisance with easy grace and started the presentations with an introduction to the woman who stood beside her, equally tall but painfully thin.

'My Lord Dragonetz; the Comtesse de Tripoli. My sister tells me your voice would make pets of the desert snakes, enslaving anyone who hears you sing. She regrets that she was indisposed and unable to thank you as you deserved for your exquisite performance on the journey from Damascus.'

Startled, Dragonetz recognised the mysterious woman from the camel train, the woman who had sobbed in the night as his song ended. The 'far love', the peerless woman for whom the song had been written, and who was standing here before him, bruises not yet faded on her face, eyes still fixed on some abyss.

Hodierne, Comtesse de Tripoli, would have looked very like her sister if her existence were happier but her hair had been allowed to grey and knot, her face was sallow with starvation and misery, and her drab robe hung loose on the thin frame. What had turned the beauty of the ballad to this shadow? He bowed deeply to Hodierne, choosing his words with care. 'To inspire such a song is more notable than merely to sing it. Wherever there is song, the Comtesse de Tripoli is a byword for all that is fair in a woman.'

Then she did focus on him, tears in her eyes. Her voice barely reached him, as if she was afraid even to speak. 'I think the Comtesse de Tripoli has indeed become a byword.'

Squeezing Hodierne's arm, both in support and in signal that she need not exert herself, Mélisende spoke for her. 'My sister has not been well and is come to court for a cure of some months' duration.'

'Some months!' exclaimed Hodierne. Then her voice dropped back to its whisper. 'No, no, I daren't stay so long. My Lord of Tripoli would not approve. I must do as he wishes or …'

Mélisende flashed fire and spoke to her sister in quick Armenian, presumably the language of their childhood. 'My lord of Tripoli will accept whatever his queen orders! You will return to your … lord… when you are well enough and not before!' She spat Tripoli's title as if it poisoned her tongue to pronounce it and suddenly Dragonetz understood the bruises, the fear, the anxiety to please. The Queen put a hand on the arm of the black-haired courtier beside her, as easy with him as she had been in touching her sister. 'Manassés,' she said, her tone once more husky and honeyed, 'please see the Comtesse de Tripoli accompanied to her chamber.' Mélisende smiled warmly at Hodierne, then apologetically at Dragonetz. 'She wanted so much to meet you after hearing you sing but it is too soon after illness and journey for her to be abroad.'

Meekly, Hodierne followed her sister's wishes, and her sister's Constable, gathering enough force to breathe, 'I hope you will sing for me again,' as she passed Dragonetz.

'It will be my pleasure,' he responded, bowing. Then he was distracted from the mystery of Hodierne by a bear-hug that lacked all courtly procedure. 'Dragonetz!'

'Baudouin,' replied Dragonetz, extricating himself from the enthusiastic greeting and studying a man who'd filled out from the young comrade-in-arms of three years ago. At eighteen, King Baudouin had led the army of Jerusalem in support of King Louis and the Emperor Conrad. He had proved himself in battle, a popular leader and comrade. The way he greeted Dragonetz now was a reminder of the time they were brothers-in-arms.

Did he imagine a frown darkening Mélisende's expression at Baudouin's exuberance? If so, there was no trace of it as she spoke. 'I see you and my son, Baudouin, already know each other. I am sure you have much to discuss. Let me just present my son Amaury, before I leave you to talk of men's matters.'

No-one was fooled by the implication that Mélisende had no interest in 'men's matters' but the withdrawal was graceful. Dragonetz bowed to Amaury before the young man followed his mother. He was a reserved youth, quietly observing others and staying in the background. Probably the background was a safe place to stay, for a younger son. Mélisende gave her parting orders. 'We have a private audience this afternoon, my Lord Dragonetz. Yohana Bar Philipos will join us. I will send for you.'

'Your Grace.' Dragonetz bowed and was dragged off by Baudouin, past the throngs, along the corridors and into a pleasant ante-chamber where they could sit undisturbed. Although he had the energy of youth, Baudouin was as politically astute as he was physically hardened, and he cut to the quick of all the news Dragonetz brought from Damascus.

'She won, over Damascus. We should never have laid siege.' Dragonetz had no need to ask who 'she' was. Although she had allowed Baudouin and his troops to join the siege of Damascus, Mélisende had refused to join the Crusaders, keeping her truce with the city. Dragonetz now strongly suspected that many of Baudouin's troops had worked against the siege, but there was no point accusing Baudouin of double-dealing. It was evident that he had lost popularity from leading his section of militia against the city. Any double-dealing had been either his mother's doing, or individuals backing their own interests against the land-grabbing newcomers. Either way, Mélisende had profited.

'So Nur ad-Din sits waiting for Damascus to fall into his hand, like one of the city's juicy plums. But you don't think he will use force.' Dragonetz confirmed his view. 'We can't afford to lose access to Damascus. Its trade is too precious and its position too central,' Baudouin mused aloud, 'but we can't take it by force.'

'Definitely not. Even the attempt would be all the excuse Nur ad-Din would need to 'protect' the city and if Jerusalem pushed the citizens of Damascus to choose between armies, they would jump into the Muslim's arms. The siege made no friends in the city and Jerusalem is dipped in the same crusading dye, even if Queen Mélisende has kept her personal reputation separate.'

'So our best hope is to support the city's independence?'

'I think so but the attempt is doomed with Unur gone. The current Atabeg is too weak to hold the city together. Bar Philipos and his fellow-merchants are wielding the real power. While you have time, you need to make your trading links so intertwined that Damascus cannot do without Jerusalem.'

Baudouin's frown deepened. 'Not so easy as the other way round.'

'You must find ways.' There was no point putting honey on the pill.

'I need to think, talk to some of our key merchants. This is a new way of thinking to me. The Grand Masters of both orders speak to me of armies, training, strongholds and castles. Their answer is always more knights and new fortifications.' Dragonetz said nothing, reading the other man's attraction to military solutions. He would have been the same at that age.

'There is a need for training and armies,' Baudouin continued. He hesitated, then the words came out in a rush. 'By the rood, Dragonetz, I need to be honest with you or I can't say this at all! If you carry tales then so be it. I cannot live like this any more.' He got up and paced the room in his agitation.

'There is no reasoning with her! She has me running errands wherever she wants to send soldiers, she lets me listen to 'men's matters' but she holds the real power in a grip of iron. I've been pushing for six years now just to have my rights. She has stopped saying, 'when you're of age', now I'm of age!

Instead, she asks what fault I find with the job she does as queen, says that she values any insight I care to give her. And that's not it at all! I am just tangled even more in her threads. The worst of it is that she even uses my respect for her to keep me from what should be mine. I love her – damn her! – but she has gone too far for too long.

Then there is Manassés.' The name hissed from Baudouin's lips and Dragonetz had no need to ask how the man felt about his mother's… Constable. 'She will not listen to anything I say about the man, or about what people think. She assumes I'm jealous! But he has tipped the balance and I am approached daily by one lord after another, begging me to put a stop to the situation, to take up the throne, my birthright. Dragonetz, I cannot continue like this and the day is coming when I must act, with force if need be. Sometimes I think that's what she's after, that she's testing me, that she actually wants me to show force.'

Dragonetz' unspoken fear must have shown in his eyes for Baudouin hastened to add, 'Not violence against my mother's person, but force against her men, starting with Manassés. I have armies at my disposal, I have the whole city of Antioch under my control, and more than half of Jerusalem would rise on behalf of my just claim. When I make my move, there can be no doubt of the outcome.

Dragonetz, will you join me? There is no-one I would rather have as my Commander. I know you have freed yourself from Aliénor's service and I know your worth. The armies of Jerusalem and Antioch would be yours to train and command. I am Regent for Antioch since the Prince was killed and as yet the widow is free. When she marries again, I will have to hand over Antioch to her husband, as it should be. Marry Antioch and you will rule a state as powerful as my own. I can't think of any man I would rather have as Prince of Antioch than you and I can make this happen!'

Dragonetz imagined himself at the head of King Baudouin's armies, Prince of Antioch, successor to the golden giant, both in the kingdom and in the widow's bed. Raymond of Antioch might have been older than his wife Constance, but there had been no doubting her passion for him. Dragonetz had seen the young wife, trying to hide her outrage at her husband's behaviour with his niece, Aliénor. She had behaved with more dignity than Aliénor's husband Louis, but who knew what had been said behind closed doors. After all, it was through marrying Constance, when she was still a child, that Raymond de Poitiers had become Prince of Antioch.

Constance was Mélisende's niece and if she had a tenth of her aunt's spirit, she would make a fiery wife, fit partner to rule a principality. Dragonetz racked his memory for more detail of his bride-to-be. A pretty thing, his own age. Four children, so she had proved herself. But that meant complications for any children they might have together. Still, a grand marriage that would bring a smile to his father's face. His parents had been nagging him for years to choose a bride and an Oltra mar princess, with Antioch in her dowry, was a choice to take your breath away.

As to leading the Christian armies; Dragonetz had nothing but respect and liking for Baudouin. He would happily offer his sword to such a leader. Training soldiers, planning campaigns, weighing politics against battle, was what Dragonetz did best. With a pang he remembered his paper mill, his attempt to find something else he did best, something that would make the world a more civilised place. And where had that got him?! Maybe he should accept what his fate was telling him; he was a fighter. His only choice in life was who to fight for. Surely there could be no-one worthier than Baudouin; nor more on offer to him and his line, in reputation and wealth?

'I will think seriously on it,' he told Baudouin, and, this time, he meant it.

'He's not there, Effendi,' Muganni said.

'Hell and damnation! What do you mean 'not there'?!' Dragonetz had hoped for peaceful thinking time before he faced his private audience with the Queen but, instead, he was presented with another complication. He'd never expected the endgame to be easy. He'd been prepared for Bar Philipos to have him followed and to try to prevent him passing on the book but he'd not considered the possibility that his Jewish contact would not be there.

'I followed all your orders, Effendi. I went to the dyeworks.'

'Was it the right dyeworks?' Dragonetz interrupted.

'There is only one dyeworks in Jerusalem. The Jews pay the Queen to have the only dyeworks. So I went to the Jewish quarter, to the dyeworks and yes, your Abdon Yerushalmi works there. But he's been in Egypt since January on family matters.' Parrot-fashion, the boy recited what he had been told. 'He's supposed to be back for Chanukkah, their festival, which starts three days after the Ides of December.' Muganni resumed in a natural voice. 'He's needed at the dyeworks because he's overseer, and he promised he would be back for the festival, so, Allah willing, he will be back.'

Dragonetz started to laugh, a shrill cackling sound that escaped his control and spiralled higher, ugly. Muganni winced. 'It's the hash,' he told Dragonetz. 'Sometimes the hash laughs when there is nothing humorous.'

'Oh but there is,' wheezed Dragonetz. 'Being kidnapped has made no difference to me at all. If I'd come straight to Jerusalem I'd still be waiting for Yerushalmi's return, exactly as I'm doing now.' He rasped to a calmer note, breathing heavily. 'But I wouldn't be living with this poison in me.'

'Who can say, my Lord.' Muganni shrugged. 'The paths not written can never be taken. There is no virtue in thinking of them.'

'I need to be here until Yerushalmi is back. You must check daily, to see whether he has returned. We might be lucky and he'll be here tomorrow. We might be unlucky and he won't be back till mid-December. Do you have enough poppy? Enough hash?'

'It will not be cheap but I know where to get it.' The boy hesitated. 'That is not the problem…'

'I know. You told me.' Dragonetz was curt. 'There is no choice. And the wherewithal is no problem, however much it costs. I have very rich friends.' And then he began laughing again. Muganni hid his thoughts under long lashes, bowed and left his master giggling on the bed, taking what rest he could before facing Mélisende.

Robes had many advantages, Dragonetz thought, as he hid a parcel in a pouch, underneath the loose folds. Bar Philipos had made it clear that Mélisende was expecting to see the Keter Aram Sola, so he would not disappoint either of them. It was well known that the Queen was a connoisseur and patron of the arts, owning one of the finest psalters ever created, a present from her husband. There was no doubt that she would be willing to pay a high price for the Torah, both in commitments to Damascus (Bar Philipos' aim) and in tangible personal benefits to Dragonetz.

He sighed. In theory, he had not one solidus to his name, indeed was deep in debt until he delivered the Torah to Yerushalmi and earned the reward promised by the Jewish money-lender, Raavad. When he handed over the book, all debts due from his sabotaged paper mill would be cancelled, and a fat sum would acknowledge the success of a dangerous mission. He would be a free man, his oath fulfilled and honour restored, free to accept the amazing future offered him by King Baudouin. If he could get the poppy out of his system, and without losing his reputation in the process.

In the mean-time, he actually had rather more than one solidus to his name. The 'very rich friends' were no idle boast. Dragonetz was starting to lose track of the gifts reaching him, not 'bribes' of course. Perish the thought. In all courtesy, he could not refuse the gifts of his superiors, and still they arrived.

Bar Philipos had played the generous host throughout Dragonetz' captivity and he knew that if he tried to tell Mélisende that he'd been kidnapped and held against his will, it would be difficult to explain the freedom or the largesse that had provided the Damascene sword at his hip. Another sticky thread in which he'd been tangled, Dragonetz realised bitterly. There was no accusation he could make against the Syrian that would not make him seem foolish or worse. So he accepted the coffers, full of jewels, brocades and best Damascene daggers, which arrived in his Hospital lodging, 'to remind him of the good people of Damascus.' So went the bid from Bar Philipos and the other merchants of that city.

Then there was the casket from de Puy, full of coins, 'for your daily needs while you are our guest', balanced by the case from the Templar Grand Master, containing the jawbone of St Roch, and accompanied by a promissary note to be drawn on the Templar bank, and naming a sum that made Dragonetz blench, so large was it. St Roch was no accidental choice and Dragonetz smiled, remembering that the Occitan-born saint had been born with a miraculous red cross birthmarked on his chest.

Latest offerings were more coffers, two from Baudouin and – again a pleasing symmetry – two from Baudouin's mother. 'To make your stay in our kingdom more agreeable,' was the first message; 'May you take Jerusalem to your heart as we do' was the second. Never had Dragonetz been so cherished a guest to so many hosts, at the same time. Never had he felt the distinction between 'guest' and 'prisoner' so fine, not even when he was in Bar Philipos' house.

Sticky threads indeed and he must test his footing every step of the way if he were to stay alive. Let one rich, powerful friend believe he had chosen one of the others, and he would suddenly find himself unpopular to all but the chosen one. Unpopular could well mean his name whispered with a password to a beggar on a street corner, a stranger with a cord or a knife on a dark night.

Bar Philipos, of course, knew he only had to wait. He would be wanting his money's worth, short term; Dragonetz arguing for Damascan independence, and the book buying it. Bar Philipos was too afraid of the curse to take the book himself but if he ever realised he couldn't manipulate Dragonetz, who knew what he would risk, for Damascus. The irony was that Dragonetz did support Damascan independence, did love that city and its people. If Bar Philipos had left him free, never bound him with the poppy, Dragonetz would have been an even stronger ally for the city.

A thought struck him. 'When did you last intercept a poppy drink?'

'In the house, before we left for the camels, Effendi.'

'And how often were they being given?'

'Every week, Effendi, but I can't tell what the dose was. I only know what I give you and I try to keep it low.'

'You do well, Muganni. I couldn't manage without you.' The boy beamed. 'Bar Philipos thinks I've had no poppy for over a week. He won't know for sure how soon I will react to lack of the poison. So in a week, maybe two, he will expect to see me ill, or he will know I have found the poppy elsewhere. Maybe we can pretend an illness, keep him guessing.'

'Maybe, Effendi.' Muganni looked doubtful but said nothing, his eyes large with pity.

'Speak,' Dragonetz ordered.

'Feigning illness is easy. But if you recover, he will know you have found the poppy.'

'If I stay out of view for a few days?'

'No, Effendi. A man does not recover in a few days. Nor does he look well when he recovers.'

Dragonetz was on the verge of asking how long. Of asking how 'not well' But however horrifying the answer, he must go through the experience in the future, after the endgame. He could not afford the time, nor the illness, before he had delivered the book.

'The Queen of Jerusalem expects me,' he said shortly, and the subject was closed.

CHAPTER SEVENTEEN

The private chamber in which Mélisende received Dragonetz and Bar Philipos had thick walls, one solid door and no windows. Muganni earned a scowl from the Syrian as he took up his place outside the door, beside the other servants, shut firmly out. Manassés was at the Queen's side and drew up stools upholstered in tapestry for them to sit on. Dragonetz had to force himself to treat someone's art in such a crude manner.

He was acutely aware of the hawks and horses, deer and knights, peeking out from the others' rear ends. The desire to giggle welled up and he reminded himself of the effects of hash and the need for self-control. He sobered up listening to Bar Philipos give the same analysis of Damascus, almost word for word, as he had given to Baudouin that morning. In a word, trade not war, while there was still time. Obviously, the Syrian didn't mention his close ties with Nur ad-Din, nor that he was keeping his options open with both the potential future overlords of Damascus.

'Dragonetz?' The Queen turned her sharp blue gaze on him.

He could only reinforce what Bar Philipos had said, adding the detail of what he'd observed in the city; its defensive strength was unchanged – and he should know! – but Mujir ad-Din was too weak to hold the city together and was likely to fall from power sooner rather than later, to his own military commander, or to Nur ad-Din. To Jerusalem? Dragonetz explained once more why the people of Damascus would rather have Nur ad-Din if that was the choice they were given, and Bar Philipos nodded his satisfaction, like a tutor at his star pupil's first performance in public.

'The book, Lord Dragonetz,' he urged, explaining to the Queen, 'I have told you of the book that has come into Lord Dragonetz' possession. The Keter Aram Sola, an ancient Torah, a priceless treasure. A connoisseur such as yourself cannot look on it without awe. I have told my Lord that the proper place for such an art treasure is in your Grace's collection, and that you could not but appreciate the role of Damascus in bringing you this, and other such treasures in the future.'

Inwardly, Dragonetz cringed, but this was the game. He had to play along, as far as he could, for the time he needed. Reaching into his robe, he pulled out the pouch, extricated the oilskin parcel and unwrapped the book. He placed the Torah carefully on another tapestry stool, open, facing the Queen, and this time he felt no compunction at hiding the cross-stitched huntsmen. He could not help remembering Nur ad-Din's reverence on seeing the book. Mélisende's expression was more like a child with a platter of sweetmeats, wanting it, and definitely not wanting to share. She ran a long, tapered finger delicately over the annotations in the margin. 'By Aaron Ben Asher, you say, some great Jewish religious?'

'So I was told, your Grace,' Dragonetz said. 'And the book is a holy object to the Jewish community. It is their bible and the notes are unique. They tell them the music of how the Torah should be read.'

'As does my psalter, Lord Dragonetz. I understand.' He could see she didn't understand at all and the frustration welled up. This was more than a pretty, valuable book! 'Your Grace,' he attempted, 'this bible belongs to the Jewish community. It must be returned to them.' He was making no mention of missions and dyeworks, neither in front of Bar Philipos, nor if he saw the Queen alone. Cupidity and power were a dangerous combination.

She gave him one of her disarming smiles. Or at least a smile that was intended to be disarming and might have worked on a younger Dragonetz. 'You can trust me to look to the interest of my Jewish citizens. Thanks to me, the Jews have the monopoly on dyeworks in Jerusalem, and for a piffling annual rent.

They have their living quarters and the right to follow their own misguided faith. In offering the book to me, Lord Dragonetz, you ensure that all the Jews who visit my city, not just those who live here, will see this treasure – for, you may trust me; I shall make it available to public view.

I want all my citizens to see this book and what better place than the Cathedral.' Her eyes gleamed with excitement. 'The renovations should be finished this year and what better way to draw people into God's house, people of all faiths, than to show the Torah beside the Psalter, and our holy relics. This book is too precious for private ownership. It should be a state possession.' Her voice dripped honey, her face was open and guileless.

Dragonetz let his expression show how deeply he was struck by these new ideas. Never trust someone who tells you she can be trusted, and tells you twice. Sticky sticky threads. In his imagination, Dragonetz cut through them. State possessions belonged to the Queen. So much for 'no private ownership'. Ping! A thread cut.

Public view could be once in twenty years. Ping! Another thread cut. Piffling annual rent did not describe the sum Muganni had quoted to his master as what the Jews paid for their monopoly. Ping! A third thread.

And Jewish rights were far outnumbered by constraints on Jews. There were reasons why Jewish families were moving to Egypt. Ping! Dragonetz was free.

His smile was every bit as disingenuous as the Queen's. 'This indeed gives me much to think about and I'm sure will be welcome news to the Jewish community, as it will save them a large sum of money.' That shook Bar Philipos and made Dragonetz' smile genuine. 'And it will gain them the Torah, to all intents and purposes. What is Jerusalem's is theirs.'

'Quite so,' smiled Mélisende, 'so, not to be too indelicate, shall we discuss what I can offer you in return for what is, of course, priceless.'

'Not yet,' smiled back Dragonetz, 'for I need a little time first to share with the Jewish community this wonderful news, so that they fully appreciate all your Grace is giving them.'

The Queen's smile faltered. Perhaps Dragonetz should have avoided the word 'share'. 'Is that necessary?'

'Oh yes,' replied Dragonetz. 'Trust me.'

'Of course,' said the Queen. 'We will discuss this again, then, soon.'

'Of course,' said Dragonetz, carefully removing the book from under Mélisende's last caress, and returning it to the safety of his pouch, beneath his robe and out of sight.

Mélisende sighed. Then she said briskly. 'I have other matters to discuss with Dragonetz, privately.' Bar Philipos immediately stood to leave and bowed farewell. Manassés looked a question at his queen. 'Yes, yes, you too,' she told him impatiently. 'This is private, family business.' If she'd slapped him in the face, the expression would have been the same and Manassés quit the room in an evident temper, half-shouldering Bar Philipos out the way.

'Young men,' Mélisende apologised with a shrug as the door slammed. Then she smiled. Dragonetz hid a sigh. Just when he'd thought the battle of the smiles was over… 'It is about a young man that I wish to talk to you. I have to be frank with you or I can't ask you what I need to. I love my son very much but he's overstepping the mark, becoming a threat to the throne instead of biding his time till he can sit on it.'

'Your Grace,' Dragonetz ventured cautiously, 'he is one and twenty. It is the custom for a man to take on a man's role before such an age.'

'He can be a man,' flashed Mélisende, 'but he is not ready to be king! And I have no intention of giving up my kingdom into the hands of a callow youth. Do you really believe him more capable of ruling than I am? Because he is male?!'

Dragonetz decided it was safest to take the question as rhetorical.

'Your Grace, at what age do you think he will be ready to rule?'

'When he can best me in strategy. When he can defeat me in battle. When he can force me to give up the kingdom to him. Until then, he is too weak to rule! My father, Baudouin's grandfather, was willing to let his five-year-old daughter, my youngest sister, be raped by her Infidel guards rather than give his cities over to crazed ransom demands. That is the kind of decision a ruler has to make. Baudouin hasn't made one difficult choice in his whole life.'

'What is it you want of me?' Dragonetz asked quietly, thinking that Baudouin was currently choosing between his mother and his kingdom.

'The pace is stepping up between my son and me. I want you on my side, Dragonetz. Jerusalem's army is mine, not Baudouin's. I want you to lead it, not my son. He can look after his regency in Antioch and play soldiers there if he wants. You will lead my army and the militia of the two orders will defer to you, riding to arms where you say they must, training as you say they must.'

'Your Grace, neither the Hospitalers nor the Templars will defer to any other than the Grand Master.'

'But the Grand Master will defer to coffers and castles.' She smiled triumphantly. 'You know what I say is true, Dragonetz. The purse-strings will hold the Masters close to me, as will their own best inter-ests. Our armies must unite. Nur ad-Din gets ever stronger and we mustn't forget those cursed Seljuqs. The two orders will fight along-side us, without question, and if you are my chosen leader, they will accept that, and you.'

'The Constable?' he queried.

'Manassés won't like it,' she assented. 'He leads my private armies and I will have to limit his military role. But he is not the commander that you are, and the people are turning against him.' Dragonetz had a shrewd idea as to why the people were turning against him.

She clasped his hands and gazed earnestly into his eyes, beseech-ing. 'Please, Dragonetz. I offer you a proper place in this kingdom, worthy of you. I offer you a title, lands.' She hesitated, then, still clasping his hands, she continued, 'The Kingdom of Tripoli.'

Truly shocked, Dragonetz said, 'As far as I know, Raymond Toulouse of Tripoli is in good health.'

'That need not continue. There are many diseases in this land, many ailments of the stomach that sadly cause death. Raymond of Tripoli deserves a dog's death for what he has done to my sister. Should such a death happen, no-one would mourn him. And I understand you have no love for the Toulouse family, to which he belongs.'

'That is past history, your Grace, in another country.'

'But still.'

'It would be a strange coincidence if a Toulouse of Tripoli died in the same manner as his relative, Alphonse Jourdain?' Dragonetz remembered only too well the rumours when Jourdain had died, poisoned, a Toulouse with a better claim to Tripoli than the illegitimate Raymond. The fifteen-year-old Comte de Toulouse had believed it to be Aliénor and Dragonetz who'd killed his father.

Dragonetz had even wondered himself whether it was Aliénor's doing, in her hatred of Toulouse. Others claimed that Raymond of Tripoli had protected his claim to the state by murdering his relative. Yet others claimed that Mélisende had ordered the murder. Dragonetz chose his words very carefully, wondering exactly what he was being told. 'People might talk about such a coincidence.'

The Queen released Dragonetz' hands, dismissing people's talk with an airy wave. She'd certainly been subject to enough of it during her reign and survived. 'Let them talk. If Raymond were to die of some stomach malady, then people would say someone took revenge for his murder of Jourdain. Or that he had fallen out with his ex-ally Nur ad-Din, and everyone knows heathen methods of resolving dispute. Nur ad-Din's father died the same way. All would be neat and easily understood.

Yes,' she mused, 'I like the idea that Nur ad-Din would be blamed. Should Raymond die, his widow would need a man I trusted as husband, someone who could hold Tripoli, but who could also restore her spirits. You are such a man. Do we understand each other?'

'We do.'

'And your answer is?'

'I will give it serious thought,' said Dragonetz automatically.

Mélisende nodded. 'We will discuss the matter again. And make it your business to attend to the Comtesse de Tripoli. She likes your singing.'

'The Comtesse is gracious,' murmured Dragonetz, bowing his leave.

In bed that night, unable to sleep for his galloping thoughts, Dragonetz tried to order what he'd learned of the two major players in this game. Baudouin was preparing to do battle with his mother, whose idea of love was to hang onto power till he could wrest it from her. Dragonetz was the current rope in this tug-of-war, required to take a side and lead its armies against the other.

If he chose Baudouin, who had youth on his side and must win in the end, Dragonetz would have armies to lead, and Antioch for a kingdom, with pretty young Constance to wife.

If he chose Mélisende, the wilier of the two, she would murder Raymond of Tripoli and Dragonetz would have armies to lead, the state of Tripoli and the tragic, faded beauty of a widow to be his wife. Mélisende could protect him against Baudouin; could Baudouin protect him against poison? Of a certainty it had been Mélisende who'd had Jourdain murdered; she'd all but admitted it. The consequences of going against Mélisende's interests couldn't have been presented to him more clearly. However, it was a relief to Dragonetz that, after all, it had not been Aliénor who stooped to such a method.

The next few weeks were going to be interesting. He felt like a wealthy demoiselle, paying equal attention to all her suitors until she'd made up her mind which of them to accept – if any. He finally fell asleep trying to decide if he'd rather be a Prince on the coast or a mere Comte, inland, ruler of the most secure of the three Crusader states.

So began a feverish dance round court politics, conversations with everyone and intimacy with no-one. What Dragonetz had not expected was to find genuine pleasure in the company of the Comtesse de Tripoli. The changes in her were marked, after only a few days in Jerusalem. Her hair was now glossy in its demure plait, with the same reddish sheen as her sister's; her skin was scrubbed to a smooth glow; and although her eyes still held a sadness, they observed the world shrewdly. Like the powdered bruises, the void was covered over for the moment. It would take time before her figure filled out but already she had a healthier colour from eating well.

When Hodierne first spoke with Dragonetz, she avoided his eyes, glancing round the hall like a mouse seeking the cat. He treated her just like such a timid animal, avoiding the flirtations that any court lady would have expected, gently offering thoughts on music and city life, to draw her out. Little by little, she responded and Dragonetz glimpsed the girl Hodierne had been before her marriage, intelligent and light-hearted, taking for granted that she was a princess and would be treated as such. What had happened?

Bar Philipos remained a useful source of information. According to him, Hodierne had been as much the whore as her two sisters. However, even he exempted the youngest from the epithet, the sister who'd been sacrificed by her father and was now an Abbess. From her many lovers, Hodierne had chosen to marry Raymond of Tripoli. Or been told by the Queen her sister that it suited Jerusalem for Hodierne to marry Raymond of Tripoli. It amounted to the same thing.

Unfortunately for Hodierne, the couple's first child had been born eight months after the wedding, and Raymond had very naturally repudiated the baby. Hodierne had of course claimed the baby was her husband's and she'd named the ill-fated baby Mélisende, in desperate hope that the Queen's name would protect the little girl from her father's righteous hatred.

Vain hope. Not only did Raymond repudiate the child but he quite rightly realised he could not trust the mother, and he constrained and chastised her as any husband would such a wife. Raymond could at least guarantee the parentage of his son and by such surveillance he made sure that no-one would make the sign of horns or laugh at him behind his back.

Dragonetz listened to Bar Philipos in horror and could only pity the girl who'd been doomed to such a marriage. He was even gentler in his attempts to make her smile and when he succeeded, he felt a greater sense of achievement than in all the conversations over trade and soldiery with Jerusalem's leaders. What hurt him was the way in which Hodierne cut short a smile or her rare laughter, hiding her mouth and her pleasure with her hand, like a cur awaiting the whip.

Unlike her sister, she never indulged in double-meanings, or lingering glances. She never said a critical word about her husband, however much fear was in her eyes when she mentioned him. Instead, as she grew more at ease with Dragonetz, and discussion of song lyrics led to more personal comments, Hodierne spoke of her love for Raymond, and her shame at not being able to please him, to be a better wife. Dragonetz was sick to the stomach, listening. Such a relationship was beyond his understanding and sometimes he felt that the best thing possible for Hodierne would be Mélisende's solution for Tripoli.

It was while Dragonetz was in such a conversation with Hodierne, that there was the sort of stir in the hall indicating newcomers. Anyone used to court could identify the moving ripple of hush and gossip that accompanied an arrival. Dragonetz had heard the same mass response when he had walked the length of the hall to meet the Queen and he recognised it straight away.

Turning to view the source of the disturbance, and already preparing some witty remarks for Hodierne's entertainment, he had a back view of a lady on the arm of a gallant, being presented to the Queen. The woman was tall, waist-length dark hair plaited neatly and falling below a rich head-dress. Her robe was midnight blue velveteen with cream lace trimmings, and her deep, graceful curtsey proclaimed her confidence in court manners. The gallant was equally fashionable, his tabard in the same velveteen, with hose of the same blue, and he was even more at ease in his surroundings, talking to Mélisende in an animated manner that made the Queen laugh. Their co-ordinated clothes, youth and energy made them a pretty couple.

Then Mélisende and her entourage looked towards Dragonetz himself, and with more nodding and smiles, the newcomers were heading towards him. 'She is very beautiful,' murmured Hodierne. Dragonetz couldn't speak. He wondered whether he were dropping into some daytime poppy-dream but the woman walking towards him showed no tendency to turn into mist. Her steps were dainty and very real. Her face could be placed exactly onto his memory of another face, although he had forgotten the mole on her left chin and her mouth was fuller, redder than he remembered, her eyes more hypnotic. It was her eyes that had first captured him, topaz and swirling. Then he had heard her sing. The couple reached his side.

'I rode a camel,' the woman told him, beaming with pride. 'Their knees get callused from all that getting up and down so people can mount them.'

'Estela.' His voice broke with emotion. He was horrified. How could he protect her when he could barely keep his own footing in this crazy dance? 'What in heaven's name are you doing here?!'

Her smile faltered and she looked for reassurance to the man beside her, on whose arm she was still hanging. He nodded to her. Encouragement? Perhaps. But there was something else there, a hint of a reminder, something the man had told Estela previously.

'We couldn't get here any more quickly,' she told him, a mix of apology and resentment that he didn't appreciate the journey she'd had. Oh but he did. He could imagine the journey she'd had! And there was no way he'd have wanted her to make such a journey! Why wasn't she safe in Dia? 'I came as soon as I knew you wanted me to,' she continued, 'And your friend has been everything you could have wanted him to be.' She bestowed a smile on her companion that turned Dragonetz' guts to the purest of poison. In that instant, he could understand every action that Raymond of Tripoli had taken.

'I don't know –' he burst out but some instinct caught the smug expression of victory on the man's face and he changed *'who this grin-*

ning idiot is' to 'what I'm thinking of! What a wonderful surprise to see you both. I really can't believe you're here.' He clapped a hand on the bastard's back, hard, smiling through gritted teeth, enjoying the flicker of disappointment. *You don't get me that easily, he admonished silently. Not after weeks in the spider's web.*

'Would you introduce your friends to me?' the gentle voice of Hodierne interrupted, no longer a mouse-breath, but still low and self-conscious.

'Estela de Matin, renowned trobairitz and a dear dear friend of mine, whom I had thought to be at the court of Dia; meet the Comtesse de Tripoli.'

'Rudel's Comtesse de Tripoli?!' asked Estela, her eyes round.

'The very same,' replied Hodierne, sadness vying with amusement.

Then everyone waited for Dragonetz to introduce Estela's companion. The pause lengthened, while Dragonetz wondered who the hell the man was and whether he'd have to get Estela to make the presentation, arousing everyone's suspicions and no doubt pleasing the stranger.

'De Rançon!' interrupted a youth in silk stripes, ignoring the frowns of the man he greeted with great enthusiasm. 'I didn't know you were back! You promised me we'd fly the new goshawk together and she's been blooded six months and more! Where did you get to?' It dawned on him that he was interrupting and he flushed. 'Excuse me. I'm just so glad he's back and we can have some sport again.'

'We will indeed have some sport, Barday,' de Rançon said drily, 'but it seems it will not be today.'

Undeterred, Barday said, 'I'll be at the Pilgrims' Haven this evening. I shall see you there, I hope.' Without waiting for an answer he left them.

'My Lady Hodierne,' Dragonetz started smoothly, as if the interruption had not taken place, 'may I present another dear friend, Geoffroi de Rançon, a comrade-in-arms from the crusades, who served with both me and Jaufre Rudel, and who can add to our evening's entertainment with his singing.'

'Then we shall have fine entertainment after tomorrow night's banquet. I shall ask my sister to announce your performance. You will sing for us, won't you?' Her voice tailed off. Always the hesitation, the fear that she was over-stepping the mark.

'Of course, my Lady,' Dragonetz reassured her and caught Estela's eye but she was already accepting the invitation, for both herself and de Rançon. Another injection of poison in the guts. What in the name of the father and all the saints was going on?!

'We must take our leave,' de Rançon told them, with an exquisite bow.

'I must hear more about the camels.' Dragonetz gazed intently at Estela, willing her to see below the surface, to understand that he loved her, that he was afraid for her, that he couldn't have her in his rooms because she'd see his times of sickness. 'I cannot offer you accommodation, because I have simple lodgings in the knights' hospital,' was what he actually said.

'Estela has no need of accommodation,' de Rançon informed him. *Did that man really have to speak for her?!*

'I am the Queen's guest,' Estela smiled at him. 'I find there are certain advantages in being a troubadour, including a chamber to myself.' Her eyes said 'Come to me there' and Dragonetz felt all his careful plans collapsing. Someone had bound Estela in the stickiest of threads and wanted him to watch as his every movement jiggled her closer to the predator. 'Someone' had a name; Geoffroi de Rançon. Dragonetz bowed his goodbyes to the couple, lingering over Estela's hand in a kiss, breaking into a million impotent fragments, his brain chanting *'Geoffroi de Rançon, my 'friend', Estela here, why, why, why?!'*

Throughout the afternoon's polite conversations, Dragonetz put the pieces together. There were still holes but what he'd worked out made a kind of horrible sense. He remembered de Rançon vaguely, a youth always in his commander-father's shadow, not allowed to blow his nose without permission and usually criticised for the manner in which he did so. De Rançon senior had been as rough on his son as he'd been on the rest of his troops.

On Mount Cadmus, Commander de Rançon had made the biggest

mistake of his career and paid a big price, losing his post and his honour along with the thousands of men who'd died, needlessly. Dragonetz didn't see himself as a hero but he knew other people did, and he also knew that more people would have died, possibly Louis himself, if Dragonetz hadn't disobeyed orders. For which his reward was to take over the post of Aliénor's Commander. How was he seen by Commander de Rançon's son, who accompanied his father home, disgraced? It didn't take a genius to work out that de Rançon was unlikely to love the man who'd replaced his father. No 'friend' then!

Starting from the premise that de Rançon was his smiling enemy, and had tricked his way into Estela's confidence, Dragonetz puzzled his way further into the labyrinth of possibilities. De Rançon had gone to a lot of trouble to bring Estela to Jerusalem. They seemed close. Dragonetz stilled the surge of venom at the thought and concentrated on logic. He could not afford the luxury of emotions, yet.

Maybe de Rançon wanted Estela; her feelings for Dragonetz were an obstacle so the trip to Jerusalem was to oust the ex-lover and leave room for the new one? Maybe. If that were so, de Rançon was passionately in love – and unscrupulous in his methods of getting the object of his desire. Estela obviously trusted de Rançon, so Dragonetz must tread very carefully if he were not to accidentally play into the bastard's hands! If only he knew what lies Estela had been told.

Then there was the possibility that Estela was unwittingly a hostage, a means to control Dragonetz. His enquiries during polite conversations had ascertained that de Rançon was Mélisende's man. Could the Queen be looking for a hold on Dragonetz, in case he chose Baudouin? Mélisende was capable of anything! But how would she have known about Estela? Had gossip about the two of them reached the court of Jerusalem? Unlikely.

Or it was possible that de Rançon's enmity against Dragonetz was personal, and Estela was merely a pawn. Why so complicated? If de Rançon held a grudge because of some perceived injury to his father, wasn't he man enough to hold Dragonetz to account personally, swords drawn? And what injury? That Dragonetz had judged a military situation better than his Commander? That he'd taken Commander de Rançon's place? If a son took revenge every time his father made a mistake or was replaced by a younger man, the world would be littered with dead bodies. Was that what de Rançon's plan was? Dragonetz dead? Or disgraced, like de Rançon's father had been? It didn't quite add up. Something was missing

Which sent him back to the idea that de Rançon wanted Estela. That it was all about passion. In which case, everything turned on Estela and her feelings. Dragonetz faced the hardest thoughts. Did she still love him? Would she still love him if she knew the poison in him and what it was capable of?

Muganni had told him that if, when, the poppy supply was stopped, Dragonetz would do anything to get some. *Anything,* the boy had said. *You will beg, steal, cheat. Friendship will mean nothing to you and you would kill your lover to get poppy. You will be so far from yourself that no-one can afford to care about you, for their own sake, until you come through the other side of the cravings. If you come through the other side.*

'He's worse than I feared.' De Rançon shook his head sadly. He and Estela had found a secluded alcove in the palace to discuss the practical matters relating to her baggage, which had weighed down two camels with absolute necessities, including ten new dresses for court, purchased in Acre.

They also discussed the detail of her first performance for the Queen. Estela wanted to get everything right and de Rançon was the ideal advisor, both knowledgeable and entertaining on the subject of the court of Jerusalem. It was so easy to talk to him, a continuation of their shipboard friendship, their Arabic lessons, their endless camel ride. De Rançon had been the perfect knight, never referring to Estela's moment of weakness, nor seeking to make it happen again. His eyes burned with feelings that he never allowed to taint his duty to Dragonetz and Estela admired him for that, and was not completely immune to the attentions of such an attractive man. Sometimes, she almost wished him less perfect, and then she would remind herself of her whole reason for being in Jerusalem.

Dragonetz. She'd hidden her shock on seeing him but she still could not believe her lover had become this bearded stranger in eastern robes, his eyes touched with wildness as if he were using belladonna. Once he'd recognised her, his expression had been odd, not the welcome she had expected. As if it was painful for him to see her.

He'd been odd with his friend too. Although de Rançon's warning that Dragonetz might not recognize him had proved wrong, there had been no warmth, no appreciation. When she thought of the hardships of the journey, the way de Rançon had protected her for thousands of miles, controlling his own feelings and thinking only of his friend's needs, she felt quite angry with Dragonetz. No appreciation at all!

And yet, he was the father of her child, the man she loved, and in loyalty she would not say all she felt, even to this true friend. 'He didn't seem quite well,' she conceded. 'You are right about him needing us.'

De Rançon looked grave, turning away from her as if mulling over what he might or might not say. 'Speak freely, dear friend,' Estela said. 'There is something you are still keeping from me and it is easier for me to help my love if I know everything.'

'This is very painful for me to talk about … Here in the east there are heathen ways of living that can seem attractive to a man. Every pleasure of the flesh and senses can be bought, and a man has to be strong to resist all that is on offer, when the example of so many at court makes the depraved seem ordinary. The longer people are here, the more they accept the unacceptable. Christian values are forgotten in the temptations. I've seen it so often now. A man will taste something new, for the adventure, and then he gets drawn further and further from the true path. Sometimes it's the smoke that starts them off.'

'Smoke?' Estela queried.

'It's an Arab habit. Men use a pipe to take in substances that make them feel lighter, happier.' *The wildness in his eyes?* wondered Estela. *Has Dragonetz indeed been smoking some substance?*

'And that leads to worse… a man's instincts can get the better of him…'

'Women. I know there are slaves, dancers, all kinds of women here,' said Estela firmly. 'Dragonetz is no monk.' Then she coloured, afraid she might have offended her companion, given that he had been womanless in all the time she'd been with him, despite her provocation.

De Rançon seemed not to react, too lost in the difficulty of what he was trying to say. 'Not women,' he said quietly. 'Have you seen the little boy who accompanies Dragonetz everywhere, the way they look at each other, the way they touch…'

'I don't understand. This is some Arab servant boy, I think? Many men have servant boys. I don't know what you mean.'

'No, of course you don't. You could not know of the reasons some men have boy servants, very pretty boy servants, nor the ways in which such boys are brought up, to know how to give every pleasure to a man, in the ways a woman should, and more …'

'No!' Estela cried out, horrified as de Rançon's meaning dawned on her.

'I'm sorry, my Lady.' He turned to her, holding her hands, looking deep into her eyes, his own full of pain at causing so much hurt. 'You wanted to know what we are dealing with and what we must rescue Dragonetz from. He is in deep.' De Rançon shook his head, grieving. 'But together we can rescue him. Let's say no more about it. Let's speak of your songs for tomorrow.'

Her head reeling, Estela suggested her programme, accepted some changes that would please the Queen better, in de Rançon's view. All the time, she was asking herself, did she want to 'rescue' this stranger? Drugs?

Small boys? Her skin crawled with revulsion.

CHAPTER EIGHTEEN

'Of course you should be there, as my attendant.' Dragonetz ruffled the boy's hair with affection and Muganni's smile lit up the chamber. The boy automatically responded to the touch by stroking his master's arm and Dragonetz gently caught the wandering hand, shaking his head.

There had been progress but the ways that Muganni had been taught to behave with older men were deeply ingrained. Dragonetz always tried to hide his instinctive recoil, patiently letting the boy know what was normal between boy and man, and what was not.

'You need to hear others sing, to analyse their breathing, their phrasing and the way they hold back or unleash the notes to convey emotion.' His training of the boy had been erratic, because of time constraints and his own mood swings, which he controlled less well in private than in public. Despite that, Muganni's control over his voice was growing and he was so eager to learn that he seemed to absorb knowledge from the very air. He had picked up enough Occitan to copy and understand the songs his master played to himself and his Frankish was broken but could communicate well enough.

When Dragonetz felt tired, but not able to sleep, it soothed his spirit to have the boy sing for him, but he preferred the liquid sound of Arabic to the oddity of Muganni's Occitan. There was no question about leaving Muganni behind when an evening of song was planned at court. A voice like his should be treasured and, as his tutor, Dragonetz was responsible for how the boy developed, and for how the world saw him.

'Finest robes and trousers,' he instructed Muganni, who always wore the loose pants and over-robe typical of his people. Dragonetz himself decided it was time to say goodbye to his own robes, and to his beard. The boy had fetched warm water in the ewer and there was soap on the basin. How many months had it been since he'd performed what used to be an automatic daily routine? He couldn't even remember when he'd stopped shaving. Was it when the guards stopped doing it for him and he'd had the freedom to do it himself? His hair grew quickly and stubble had always formed on his swarthy skin by the end of the day.

Now his beard was thick and pointed, eastern-fashion. He smiled to himself. At least he had not followed the eastern philosopher's fashion and left his beard untrimmed, to grow as it willed, with enough tangles to home mice without anyone noticing. As his dagger blade cut through lather and hair, exposing the pale skin, Dragonetz stripped off the layers of his Damascan self.

He no longer knew what lay underneath but he had to try every method he could think of to change the expression of doubt he'd caught on Estela's face, and to wipe the smugness off de Rançon's. If a shave and a tabard could make a difference, then so be it. His fingers traced their accustomed route round his jaw and rinsed off the last of the lather. Not one drop of blood, he noted with satisfaction, choosing not to imagine what his chin would be like if he'd not been at the peak of his poppy dose.

Dragonetz laced his undershirt and donned a crimson tabard with gold embroidery and black fur trim, black hose and soft, calfskin boots, also black. He felt a fraud. Shutting his eyes, he conjured up a garden, water ever-trickling whether he was in the garden or not, and, drawing deep from the memory, he found the fatalism to meet whatever an evening's entertainment at the court of Queen Mélisende might bring.

Whereas the French court impressed, the court of Jerusalem dazzled, and its queen was always the brilliant at the centre. She was sparkling this evening, both in her dress, and in her conversation, to judge by the reactions of the circle closest to her. Closest of all was, of course, Manassés, his jewelled doublet rivalling the queen's necklace, and in matching diamonds. Discretion played little part in their relationship.

An oriental luxury distinguished the furnishings of the banquet hall from any in France or the Occitan lands. Sconces were ornate metal rather than plain iron; the rich wall-hangings had Arabic quotations amid the stylised, interwoven patterns; the silverware boasted equally intricate designs and the knives were best Damascene steel, filigree gleaming in the candle-light; even the tables denied their relationship to foreign cousins by the impossible slimness of legs that tapered to claw feet, instead of the sturdy trunks that usually supported trestle tables in Frankish halls. And the inevitable cushions, to allow those who wished to lounge or sit cross-legged, relaxing after their meal. If any one habit marked the difference between east and west, it was that of sitting on the floor, or rather on priceless cushions and carpets, an extravagance to Occitan eyes.

Amongst the pale-skinned Frankish courtiers in their flamboyant colours, were darker races in more sober robes and turbans, a cultural mix that could only be found Oltra mar. Dragonetz now knew some of the Franks by name and affiliation and he identified them as his gaze swept the hall; Guy de Beyrouth, Philippe de Naplouse, Balian d'Ibelin, Hélinand de Tiberiade... all of them united in wanting rid of the Constable, powerful allies if Dragonetz were to accept Baudouin's offer, and powerful enemies were he to accept Mélisende's. His imagination still played with the futures that might have been his but Estela had brought the cold mistral of reality with her. His fear that she should see him with the sickness upon him brought home to him how deeply he was in the poppy's power.

Muganni had tried to tell him, when he had lain sweating and desperate for the potion, that he was taking stronger, more frequent doses but it was easy to brush off the words of a small boy. It was easy during the days following a dose, after the initial stupor, to pretend he was as much in control of himself as he'd always been. Seeing Estela had told him otherwise. Never had he wanted so much to be at her side, to be everything a man could be to a woman. Never had he felt so inadequate. He had to finish this mission, hand over the book, and retreat fast somewhere he could clean his system of the drugs and become himself again. Maybe the mountain stronghold of the Hashashins would take him, where Muganni's people lived. They had knowledge of such things and Muganni could take him there. He smiled at the boy, who took his hand and smiled back, glowing with anticipation at the prospect of a festival of song. Dragonetz gave an inward sigh, shook his head slightly and disengaged his hand from the boy's, patting him on the head to soften the rejection.

At that moment, Dragonetz caught sight of Estela. He recognised her one-handed man, Gilles, before it dawned on him that the black-haired beauty, gorgeous in crimson finery that matched his own, was his very own lover. Did he still have the right to call her that, he wondered, observing her arm resting lightly on that of the gallant beside her. De Rançon. Apparently as much in Gilles' good grace as in Estela's. They formed part of the circle around Mélisende, as was natural, given that de Rançon was her man and Estela was to star in the performance after dinner.

'Deep in thought, my Lord?' The low, grave tones of Hodierne called for Dragonetz' attention.

As gentle with Hodierne as he was with Muganni, he answered, 'I was remembering another hall, another entertainment.'

'Will you, too, sing for us tonight?'

'I think not,' was all he said, but he yearned for the music he and Estela had made together.

'If her voice is as beautiful as she is, I think this evening will be memorable.' Hodierne's eyes followed his, watching the graceful way in which Estela accepted courtesies from the court nobility. 'She has the bearing of a princess.' Dragonetz imagined Hodierne at Estela's age in this very hall, vivacious as her elder sister, teasing her many suitors and thinking life would always treat her as a princess.

'It is easier for a girl to play the princess, than for a woman.' He gave Hodierne the compliment of his full attention. 'If my memory serves me well, Estela's voice will indeed please you.'

'The bitter-sweetness of memories,' Hodierne sighed. 'What we were, what we could have been, what cannot be...'

'Stay here in Jerusalem,' Dragonetz urged her impulsively, emboldened by the risks he took daily. What was one more? 'Each day you are here, you regain your health. You become once more the woman so loved that your song will never die.'

Hodierne flushed. Retreating to her mouse's voice, she whispered, 'If only my husband loved me... but he has told me, so often, for so many years, why I must be punished. It must be true. I must deserve it. And I must go home, soon, whatever my sister says.'

All the bile Dragonetz had swallowed, flooded him: the months imprisoned; the casual murder of Aakif and Shunnar; Yalda and her sister's honeyed lies; de Rançon laughing and gazing into Estela's eyes; Muganni's corrupt childhood; and the poppy killing him, Bar Philipos' slow murder working through Dragonetz' own body, poisoning his every thought, probably responsible for the very rush of emotion he was feeling now.

What had Muganni said to him? What he should do if he decided to have his murderer killed? He held the power of life or death over his worst enemy. Bar Philipos? Or this man, de Rançon, always hanging around Estela? Another rush of hatred filled him. Which should it be? With the bizarre logic of the poppy, one of his knight's vows jumped into his mind; to protect the weak and defenceless.

He spoke to Hodierne so quietly that no-one else could hear him. 'Forgive me for speaking honestly, my Lady, but my honour demands it. You don't deserve such treatment! You must believe Mélisende, if not me. No man has the right to do such things to any woman. You were near death with such abuse. If you go home, if he lays hand to you again, your life is at risk. If you must go home, if your duty to your family is so strong, then you must take this weapon with you, to use in self-defence.' Then Dragonetz whispered a name in her ear, a name to be passed on via the city beggars, in Jerusalem or Tripoli, with a password and a second name, the target. Two names to seal a man's fate. 'Send these two names to the Hashashin,' he whispered, 'if need be.'

Hodierne flinched and went white but she showed no anger at his criminal suggestion. 'I might get a little dog,' she said conversationally. 'When my little sister was released from the men who... the men who held her hostage – did you know she was only five?' Dragonetz nodded. 'She was still hostage, in her mind, until a Muslim doctor gave her a little brown dog. She called him 'l'Architecte'. Strange fancy for a little girl but she left childhood behind her in Aleppo.

I think she told that little dog everything she couldn't tell us and then the healing started, in so far as she could be healed. Now,' Hodierne shrugged, 'now she is Mother Abbess in the fine convent Mélisende endows with every artefact she is allowed to. Ivette tries to stop her but Mélisende is an unstoppable force.' She smiled weakly. 'And Ivette's faith in God is her strength. Perhaps I will get a little brown dog. And I will talk to my sisters. Before I go home to my son, and to my daughter.'

Dragonetz felt a weight lifting. He would no longer be tempted to a dishonourable measure himself and it eased his conscience to give the Comtesse de Tripoli an option that might save her life. Especially as he knew he would close the door the queen had opened, the door to a future in which Dragonetz himself took Hodierne to wife, and in which no harm came to her ever again. He remembered the void in her eyes, the bruised face and skeletal body he'd glimpsed on the caravan train. At least he had given her an option that would save her life, should she be brave enough.

'We should go to the high table now,' she said mildly, leading the way.

High table was more of an ordeal for Dragonetz than usual. In addition to balancing the various factions, convincing each one that it was the most attractive to him, he also had to deal with de Rançon and Estela sending knowing looks at him and each other. He might as well have been eating straw for all the pleasure he took in the rice dishes, yellow with saffron and golden raisins, and piled high with spiced lamb; the exotic fruits that were unknown to him before travelling Oltra mar, sugared pineapple, lotus fruit and coconut; sweet and savoury appetisers of liquorice, candied jellies, pistachios, olives and m'tabbal, an aubergine mousse. He dutifully washed it all down with a goblet of the fruity red wine from the Judean hills, while his mind turned over the puzzle of de Rançon and his mouth made polite, even witty, conversation. Then a court poet opened the entertainment, declaiming the wonders of Jerusalem throughout the dessert courses. At least the poetry spared Dragonetz from chatter.

He didn't have to look at Estela to be aware of every move she made, every smile, every glance in his direction – and there were many such. When he did risk looking at her, the connection between them melted his resolve to keep his distance, to keep her safe from the web in which he was caught, to keep her far from the poison's effect on him, and from whatever might happen when he stopped taking it.

He responded to the questions in her eyes with what he hoped was reassurance. *I love you* his unruly thoughts told her. *You'll be wonderful. You always are.* So many ghosts kept him company; another hall, another queen, Estela and he singing together, Estela and he doing everything together – lovers, friends, partners. They'd thought it was forever. And here she was, so close, so sophisticated and yet still his Estela, the little beauty spot beside her mouth, the animation as she spoke to those around her, the scar on her left shoulder, hidden underneath her clothes; he knew her better than he knew himself.

Standing to attention behind Dragonetz' chair, Muganni sensed his master's tension and instinctively reached forward, to knead and relax the tight neck muscles. Just as naturally, Dragonetz half-turned, stopped the boy's hands with his own and motioned 'no' with the tiniest of gestures.

The whole movement had taken only seconds but that was long

enough to spark significant looks between de Rançon and Estela, who flushed and looked away from Dragonetz. *By the rood!* he thought, exasperated at the undercurrents he didn't understand. *All I need is some crazy rumour that I'm going to adopt Muganni as heir and all the marriage plans being made for me will take a battering.* He felt the familiar bubble of drug-fuelled laughter but controlled himself. *Damn de Rançon to hell!*

Eventually, it was Estela's turn to perform, last, as became the star of the evening's entertainment. From the moment she rose from table, picked up her oud and took the floor, Estela's quality as a performer was unmistakeable. Poised, seeming taller as she drew all eyes towards her, she tuned her oud and let the whispers of 'hush', 'she's going to start', create silence that rippled out from her to the furthest corners of the hall, to the servants who paused with their trays at the back, wanting to hear this famous troubadour.

If Dragonetz had not fully realised how much Estela had matured and how much her reputation had grown, it was brought home to him now. The girl he'd tutored was now the guest of the Queen of Jerusalem, the star of the court's entertainment. A lesser man might have felt envy, or at least concern at being eclipsed, but Dragonetz knew his own talents and felt nothing but joy at the reception given Estela.

Then the voice that haunted his dreams breathed sweetness into the Great Hall, a voice by turns poignant with love and loss, flirtatious with springtime and nostalgic with winter, satirical over hypocrisy and celebratory over courage. Estela sang her listeners through a range of emotions that stripped them all to their common humanity, taking them far away from the court of Jerusalem and daily trivia to a world that was on a grander scale. If Dragonetz had tears in his eyes, he was not alone. He glanced behind him and saw Muganni oblivious to everything other than the singer and the song, the boy's lips shaping the words of songs he knew, his eyes large and glistening.

As the audience breathed and sighed in collective response, Dragonetz regained enough detachment to assess his ex-student's performance. With a professional appreciation of the singer's need to draw breath and change register, he approved the selection of songs and the transitions, but Estela surprised even him when she sang her own work, the song of Arnaut and al-Hisba.

The tears overflowed as he relived the story of his friends' courageous fight, and Arnaut's murder. Even as Estela's voice pierced his heart, he was aware of the technical skill in a narrative lyric that mastered new forms and he knew she had truly become what she set out to be; no mere jongleur, singing other people's songs, but a troubadour, whose work would be memorised and passed on to others for years to come.

Throughout her performance, Estela had looked towards de Rançon as much as towards Dragonetz but for the song of Arnaut and al-Hisba, her eyes sought only him.

This was a song they had lived together and she sang it for him, however many others were in the hall. It was a bold choice, to sing in the court of Jerusalem about a Muslim defending a Christian against a band of murderers.

'*Esquena amb esquena, els companys van lluitar,*
Fraires en les armes diferents.
Dividit per la seva forma de pensar
Units contra un dany comu.

Un dels homes va aixecar la mitja lluna
Un dels homes va aixecar la creu
I va obrir les dues fulles de la justicia
En el camp de batalla de la pèrdua.'

'Back to back, the comrades fought,
Brothers in different arms,
Divided by the way they thought,
United 'gainst a common harm.

One man raised the crescent,
One man raised the cross,
But both blades swung for justice
On the battlefield of loss.'

The silence stretched after the last notes took Arnaut's life, until Dragonetz feared that Estela had misjudged her audience and touched on matters too sensitive for the mix of races and religions in the hall. He needn't have worried. As Estela curtsied, signifying the performance was over, the audience erupted in applause, in a swell of approving comments, in the reaction of people waking from the extremes of emotion.

She acknowledged the response, calm and still, at the centre, but as she raised her head again, she sought one person only. Unable to speak, had he tried, Dragonetz held his hands over his head, exaggerated a slow clap, held his arms out to her in praise, mouthed 'Bravo,' and blew her a kiss.

Then, finally, she smiled and turned her gaze to the Queen, to the courtiers, to everyone, as she picked up her oud, ready to go back to her place at high table, beside de Rançon. Her attention was already on her dinner partner, who was standing and gesturing. His meaning became clearer as he walked round the table towards her, suggesting that she perform one more song. With him. A duet. Dragonetz' insides churned black murder.

As Estela hesitated, before de Rançon reached her, a small figure tugged on her arm, demanding her attention, and the hall hushed again, anticipating more entertainment. With sick recognition, confirmed by looking behind him to find only an absence, Dragonetz wondered how on God's earth he was going to rescue Muganni from whatever folly had got into his head this time.

Dragonetz rose to intervene and was close enough to hear Estela's halting Arabic in response to the boy's question, but not close enough to prevent Estela announcing to the hallfull, in her clear voice, 'You have been so kind, such a good audience, that I request your patience for one more song.' She bent and checked something with the boy, then nodded. 'Muganni and I will perform an old favourite for you but with a difference. As this is a land of many languages, I will sing in my mother tongue and Muganni will sing in his.' The Queen nodded her approval.

It will never work, thought Dragonetz, forcing room for himself to sit on a bench between two aggrieved courtiers, who nevertheless made the best of it and in their turn pressured those further along. De Rançon, who had been so close to his own duet with Estela, also pushed his way to a seat, his usual amiable expression replaced by murderous rage. Dragonetz' own such feelings eased considerably. *Good,* he thought, turning his full attention to the duo. His spirits dipped again. *Two sopranos. Their voices will clash horribly.*

Then the magic started again, the hush and Estela's opening notes, singing their song.

> *'Us cavaliers si jazia*
> *Ab la res que plus volia'*

> 'A-bed beside his lady-love,
> Her own true knight stopped kissing.
> 'My sweet, my own, what shall we do?
> Day is nigh and night is over
> We must be parted, my self missing
> All the day away from you.'

How could he not remember the first time Estela had sung his aubade, standing beside the ditch she'd slept in, singing for her very life? And then they'd sung together the words he'd written, partners in public and lovers in private, until the last night together when he'd left at dawn and the words of the song had come true.

Lost in memories, Dragonetz nevertheless heard what these two matchless singers were doing to his composition. Estela left time between each line for Muganni's melancholy Arabic to thread its way into a round, shaping an Oltra mar echo, like the Muezzin at dawn. The two voices, the woman's rich with experience, the boy's of angelic purity, followed each other and shared the song. Not only did it work, it made Dragonetz' hair stand on end with its sheer brilliance. And the boy must have translated the song himself, working from his slow Occitan to find the lyric in his native Arabic.

'My sweet, my own, what shall we do?
Day is nigh and night is over
We must be parted, my self missing
All the day away from you.'

The last words of the song flowed over him, in Occitan and then in Arabic, as the lovers parted. Muganni brought the song to a close, his eyes shut, lost in the world of his music. Estela whispered something in his ear, he nodded, his face aglow, and she held up her hand to stop the applause that was breaking out.

'The troubadour who wrote this beautiful song is right here with us,' she announced. 'My Lord Dragonetz, will you sing the last verse with us?' Encouraged by the audience, and by a small boy's face, Dragonetz stood by the table, reading Estela's face, following her intake of breath to start on cue, and this time the harmonies of male baritone and female soprano formed the Occitan duet, with the boy's Arabic echo like a commentary by the gods. This time it was Dragonetz who shut his eyes, knowing where Estela's every breath would fall, feeling her with him as no-one else had ever been or ever could be.

Muganni rushed the last notes in his excitement but Dragonetz doubted whether anyone would criticise him, as the audience erupted once more. Estela took the boy's hand and held it high to present him to the audience for their acknowledgement. She bowed her head to him in her own homage to his talent and he dipped awkwardly to her, to the Queen, in all directions, then he made his escape. He bounded towards Dragonetz, who still stood where he had sung, beside the table, and he charged into his arms, expecting a hug. For once, he was not disappointed. Dragonetz wrapped his arms around the boy. 'You did well,' he told him. 'You did very well.'

'This is the best, the most important day of my life,' Muganni told him. 'I must go back to being your servant now.' He imitated the expressionless face of the other servants in the hall and he took up the standard pose, but his downward-cast eyes still danced and his body fizzed with energy.

Dragonetz couldn't look away from Estela. The music still flowed between them, bursting the dams to a thousand memories. The way she looked at him, the way she smiled as the boy hugged him, suggested that shadows had cleared from her mind too. 'Come to me tonight,' she mouthed, across all the people between them, and he just nodded, helpless in the flood. Then she was claimed by the Queen and her entourage. Dragonetz had his own admiring following to fend off, and Muganni to explain, hampered by Muganni's tendency to explain himself. Tonight, his master felt indulgent and, with anyone who would listen, the boy discussed his choice of one Arabic phrase over another for his translation.

Sweeping the room to find de Rançon, Dragonetz placed him at last, in conversation with Bar Philipos. Queen's business no doubt. As the Syrian was accompanied by his daughter, Dragonetz felt no urge to approach them and find out more. The next time he looked, de Rançon was nowhere to be seen, and Dragonetz had more important matters to think about.

They made love with words and with their finger-tips, with kisses and laughter, with shared memories and new discoveries, with the hunger of abstinence and then taking their time, with imagination and experience. Touch erased the awkwardness of a year apart, at least for this first night back together. Questions were asked but answers evaded. Some things were too important to announce with, 'I should say, in passing, that since we last saw each other...'

In a satiated pause, stroking the long curve of smooth olive skin, from shoulder to thigh, Dragonetz noticed Estela's pathfinder clasp, discarded on the pile of their clothes that tumbled together on the floor, as their owners had done in the course of play.

'The pathfinder clasp,' he observed idly. 'You still wear it. Do you remember the fortune-teller in Narbonne, who said it blocked her visions?'

'Mmm,' responded a sleepy voice. 'Too many paths, my choice...'

Then Dragonetz realised there was something that Estela wasn't wearing, that hadn't come off with the froth of lace, silk and linen. His hand stopped its circling caress, lying lightly on her haunch. 'My ring,' he said. 'You're not wearing my ring. Where is it?'

Her body tensed under his hand. 'I didn't want to risk it getting lost on the journey,' she said. 'I left it with Raoulf.'

'The ring was meant to protect you on any such journey! As was Raoulf. It makes no sense to leave either of them behind.'

'Ow,' she reproved him mildly, shifting her position and making him aware how much pressure he'd been exerting. 'Raoulf had other duties and de Rançon was my escort. And Gilles was with me. You know what he's like – if he had no arms at all, he'd bite anyone who tried to hurt me.'

'Like that big dog of yours... what was his name?'

'Nici. I left him with Raoulf.'

'You left a lot with Raoulf.' He tried to keep the sarcasm out of his tone and softened the comment with, 'I'm surprised Nici went with Raoulf. He seemed to be very clear as to who his master was – or mistress, in this case.'

Estela massaged her lover's neck and back, and lower, turning him to allow more intimate contact. 'There has been no-one else,' she murmured. 'There is no-one but you.' He believed her, his faith encouraged but not determined by his physical reactions. His spurt of anger vanished as suddenly as it had come, just another drug-induced mood swing. He sensed some mystery around the signet ring but he had forgotten how to trust someone, forgotten that explanations could be innocent.

'I can't believe that there's been no-one else for you,' she teased him, not waiting for an answer (thank the Lord) but continuing, 'Do you find me... changed, physically?'

'More beautiful,' he responded, automatically, wondering where the insecurity had come from. He was unable to tell her how reassuring it was for him to touch her very human body, to feel a patch of rough skin, to see a crooked tooth, instead of the crazed perfection of his poppy-dreams.

She didn't press further, accepting his physical reassurance that he wanted her as much as he ever had. After playing together again, she rolled away from him. 'You must be taking some potent herbs to keep your desire so strong. I give in – I need to rest a while!'

He could have told her then, that at this stage of his weekly cycle, it was highly probable the 'potent herbs' he took did indeed delay his jouissance. However, when he had just taken the poppy, in ever stronger dose, not even Estela herself would be able to raise his interest. Shame flooded him. No, he could not tell her. He would rather the poison kill him. He buried his face in the scent of her neck, breathing in eastern spices, sandalwood and jasmine he thought, blended with sweat.

'New perfume,' he murmured.

'From St Jean d'Acre, when we'd disembarked and were waiting for the camel train to be organised. De Rançon took me to the best merchants.'

Dragonetz ignored the automatic kick in his guts at the name. He stroked her long, black hair. 'Tell me about the camel ride... while we recover...'

She was sleeping when he left. Afraid to fall asleep himself, in case his dreams betrayed him, he slipped out the chamber, through deserted corridors and empty streets, back to his lonely bed. He was tormented by thoughts of her waking alone and wondering whether he really cared. A present on her pillow would have added insult, as would a casual meeting later in the day, as if what was between them was mere sneak-in-the-night. Unable to come up with a better solution, Dragonetz sent the only other person he trusted, to keep guard outside the lady's chamber and then give her his apology, and his invitation. Muganni left the warm bedroll by his master's door, and headed off at a dogtrot, with his usual youthful enthusiasm. What he made of a message that mixed camels and the music of the spheres, Dragonetz cared not, as long as Estela got the message and kept the private rendez-vous, later that same day. He shut his eyes and took what sleep he could.

CHAPTER NINETEEN

W hat to tell and what not, after so long apart? Dragonetz gave the bald facts of his imprisonment and listened to the detail of Bèatriz' wedding plans. He briefly outlined Muganni's history and listened to the various ways in which de Rançon had behaved heroically. Perhaps it was just as well that Muganni interrupted the tête-à-tête at the exact moment when Estela was describing how de Rançon had taught her Arabic or the sound of gritted teeth might have become obvious.

Bowing to Estela, Muganni launched into speech. 'You wanted me to let you know straight away, Effendi.' He had to pause to catch his breath and Dragonetz motioned him to speak freely. 'The Jew is back from Egypt. I don't like him. He told me to stop singing, that music is a childish distraction from what is important.'

Endgame. Soon, it would all be over. 'Then I don't like him either. But this is business. Go back to the dyeworks and speak with him in private. Tell him that the Christian knight brings him a gift from Raavad of Narbonne, as promised. Tell him to be at the dyeworks tomorrow at vespers and I will come to him there.'

'Effendi.' Muganni bowed and was gone.

'The book,' stated Estela. When Dragonetz had left her in Narbonne, he had told her everything about his mission. 'You give this man the book and your debts are cancelled. You'll have kept your oath and you'll be free again.' She reached across to take his hands in her own, her happiness at his restored fortunes shining in her face. 'And we can go home.'

'Free,' agreed Dragonetz, hiding his unease. After all, he'd never expected the endgame to be simple. Bar Philipos would of course be tracking him. In fact, Dragonetz was relying on the fact that the Syrian would also be at the dyeworks when vespers was rung. All that was needed was a good excuse to kill the man. In Dragonetz' opinion, an attempt to steal the book might very well lead to a fight, and self-defence would count as a very good reason indeed. Of course, he didn't mention any of this to Estela, but kissed her hand lightly as they parted. She told him she understood he'd need to rest during the night, that they had all the time in the world to be together, and he'd pretended she was right, even while he sensed the poison clogging his blood and his thoughts. Tomorrow it would all be over, one way or the other.

As he rolled up his pack and stashed it on the bed he'd claimed in the servants' quarters, Gilles cursed Dragonetz for existing. Estela's relationship with de Rançon had been developing nicely into more than friendship and every step of their long journey together had increased Gilles' respect for Mélisende's knight.

He was the sort of leader who drove his men hard and himself harder; who could handle his own weapons well and also take a strategic view; and who treated Estela like a queen. The perfect match for the woman who, in Gilles' eyes, was more than a queen. She was the motherless little girl he'd been a father to, when her own proved wanting, and she was the spirited woman who'd travelled across seas and desert without complaining. And all to meet up with this Dragonetz!

Gilles had known little of Dragonetz before the knight had to leave Narbonne, penniless and on some secret, heathen mission.

Estela's love was evident but she wouldn't be the first girl to fall for a sweet-talking – or even sweet-singing – rogue. Gilles had taught her how to judge the quality of a weapon, and not to judge by appearances, but he still preferred to double-check her judgement, and he didn't like what he had found out about the man she had chosen.

De Rançon had tried loyally to hide his friend's shortcomings but Gilles had understood much from what was left unsaid. Whatever Dragonetz had been before coming Oltra mar, he was now a dissolute womaniser – perhaps worse, judging by the way he and that boy behaved! One look at him in those robes, and with that beard, and anyone could see he was no Christian knight any more. Changing his dress back and shaving wouldn't change what was underneath and it wouldn't fool Gilles. It was all very well Estela making songs about it but friendship between a Christian and a Moor was just plain wrong, and likely to turn a man, and no doubt that had been the start of it with Dragonetz. Then, coming here had made things worse.

Servants always knew what was going on. They were invisible to their masters but that didn't stop them hearing very interesting conversations. The trick was to get them to tell you what you wanted to know. And Gilles knew lots of ways to make other servants talk. He could be so harmless, so hail-fellow-well-met, and so generous with a jug of wine. Along with some crude detail on the Queen's use of a good-looking young man (the second time, mind you! At least this time she wasn't a married woman, but still!) Gilles found out that Dragonetz was a big man at court, with talk of some high-up marriage for him, and land here, Oltra mar. Gilles doubted that Dragonetz had mentioned any of this to Estela.

Other whispers in the servants' quarters were about the oddness of the boy. Some said he was a djinn, who cast spells that kept his master strong. Everyone agreed that Dragonetz would hide away in his room for a day or two, with only Muganni tending him, and then the knight would emerge, full of energy, and after that the cycle would repeat. There were men who changed into beasts and had potions to keep them man-like; maybe Dragonetz was one of those. Maybe his name came with a family curse... Gilles was sceptical about Dragonetz turning into a scaled beast but then, you never knew, and hiding away was very odd behaviour.

Then there was the question of how Dragonetz had behaved with Estela. The word 'love' had often served a man whose only interest was between a woman's legs. There could be no doubt that Dragonetz had found his way to that sweet place and then left Estela with child while he traipsed round the Holy Land, having God-knew-what adventures. And how was he treating her after she'd shown courage beyond her sex, facing all the dangers of their journey for his sake? He'd tumbled her, that was how, and not even stayed the night.

Poor de Rançon. No wonder he was keeping away, knowing how unworthy Dragonetz was of Estela but too loyal to take his place. Too loyal, even though, if Dragonetz deigned to notice his friend at all, it was with that sardonic sneer of his. Well, Gilles was not going to keep out of things. He didn't trust Dragonetz and when he'd followed the boy the day before, his suspicions were confirmed. There was no good reason for a Christian knight to be meeting a Jew at sundown in a dyeworks and Gilles was going to make sure he was there, to find out exactly what was going on. When he had all the information he needed, he'd cut this bond between Dragonetz and Estela, and help de Rançon take his rightful place. Then she'd have someone who treated her right, not someone who – this was the final torch to his bonfire of outrage – not someone who didn't even think Estela worth a second night! After over a year apart!

Wearing an anonymous brown cloak, Gilles stomped an angry path to the dyeworks in the Jewish quarter, as the sun grew low. The vats in the courtyard had been covered and the workers had already downed tools for the day when he got there, but the gates were still open. It was easy to find a suitable dark doorway, outside the empty clerk's room, where he could stand in the shadows. Then all he had to do was wait and watch.

First to appear was a man wearing robes and a turban, with a companion fully covered, in the manner of some heathen women. The man seemed to know his way round the dyeworks and checked the covers on the vats before standing openly in the courtyard, waiting.

The woman kept to the side, by the buildings, her black robe blending into the shadows.

Then Dragonetz arrived on foot, his hauberk flashing silver under his cloak and his head covered in the mail hood. No courtesy visit then. He was accompanied by the Arab imp, who was sent out of the way, to hop impatiently on one leg, so close to Gilles that he could almost have reached out and touched the boy.

'Yerushalmi?' queried Dragonetz, his voice deep and echoing slightly.

'I am Yerushalmi,' the turbaned man confirmed. 'Lord Dragonetz?'

'I have something for you from Raavad.' From under his cloak, Dragonetz extracted a parcel. 'A wise man asked me to give this book into your keeping. *Blessed be he who preserves it and cursed be he who steals it, and cursed be he who sells it, and cursed be he who pawns it. It may not be sold and it may not be defiled.*'

'May the blessing be upon you,' Yerushalmi replied. He unfastened a strap from round his neck and took a leather bag from underneath his cloak. 'This was given to me for you in exchange for all you have done for us.' He handed the leather bag to Dragonetz and the knight accepted it, as Yerushalmi had accepted the parcel, without showing the ill-manners of looking within.

Gilles missed the next exchange because he noticed another man arrive on the scene, moving stealthily, as if he'd been following Dragonetz. The newcomer was robed and wore a swathe of fabric round his head but it was not a turban like the Jew's. Whether he and the Jew were in league, Gilles had no idea, but he recognised the meaning of an outstretched dagger in a man's hand, and whatever he thought of Dragonetz, he would not see him taken down from behind.

He hissed at the boy, who looked at him, startled. 'Your master needs help,' he told the boy urgently, 'Get de Rançon, tell him to come quickly.'

With one glance at the man approaching the courtyard, dagger out, the boy nodded and ran.

'Dragonetz!' yelled Gilles, coming out of the shadows, drawing his own dagger. With his one hand, he could only manage one weapon, but he could still throw a dagger straight and true, even in this waning light.

Dragonetz turned first to the robed man who'd followed him. 'So glad you could join us, Bar Philipos.' Then he sighed. 'Gilles. This is an unexpected pleasure. I would be very grateful if you would return to guard your mistress. In fact, I'm relying on it.'

Gilles didn't bother responding as Dragonetz' attention switched to Yerushalmi's companion, who'd moved out of the shadows and rolled down the hood to reveal a young woman's face, black hair and flashing brown eyes.

'Yalda!' exclaimed Bar Philipos.

Dragonetz drawled, 'One surprise after another. I assume you're here to finish off what the little black bull didn't?'

'You flatter yourself.' Yalda stood beside the Jew, who was holding tightly to the parcel Dragonetz had given him. 'I'm here because of him.' She jerked her head at Bar Philipos, who seemed unable to move. 'You can't believe it, can you?' she jeered at him. 'Well it's true. Another daughter goes to the Jews. Only you won't beat this one till you kill her.'

She looked at Dragonetz then. 'I told you she died because of love. She was going to run away with Yerushalmi and marry him until *he* found out. Then he did what he always did with us, if we weren't 'good daughters'. Only you got carried away, didn't you, *father*.

But it all turned out for the best because you covered it up so well, and you could use the death against this stupid knight.' She laughed, raw and bitter. 'What does it feel like to have been played, Dragonetz?! Don't you want to kill him yet? Don't you understand why I do?!'

Yerushalmi put his arm round her, shushing her, speaking in his measured way. 'These matters are behind us now. We will take the Keter Aram Sola to Maimonides and I will study it with him in Egypt, somewhere Jews don't have to beg permission to scratch a living, somewhere 'vespers' will be but a memory,' he gave an ironic glance towards Dragonetz, 'and we will live in our words and observe our religion.'

It was the Jew's words, or unruffled tone, that sparked Bar Philipos out of his shock. 'I should have killed you too! You can take my second harlot daughter and damn her to hell with all Jewry, but you're not having the book!'

He attempted to rush Yerushalmi but Dragonetz was too quick and a sword blocked the way, swinging dangerously. Bar Philipos seemed to regain control. 'I can wait,' he said. 'De Rançon will be here any minute with your whore and you'll have the choice, my Lord.' He gave a sarcastic bow. 'Give us the book or your Estela will die, efficiently I suspect, knowing de Rançon.' He must have seen murder in Dragonetz' eyes because he threw his dagger away. 'Would you kill an unarmed man?' he mocked.

'Go,' Dragonetz told the Jew and the girl. 'Go quickly.'

Then Gilles realised what he'd done and swore aloud as he saw Estela walking towards the dyeworks, with de Rançon. No doubt Muganni had found them en route. He was skipping alongside de Rançon and Estela's hand rested lightly on her companion's mailed arm, her face anxious – for Dragonetz, no doubt. De Rançon moved with graceful assurance, despite the weight in armour he carried. Sword out, murmuring words of reassurance to Estela, he reached the scene, just as Yalda picked up the dagger Bar Philipos had discarded and stuck it between her father's shoulder-blades.

Staggering towards de Rançon, the Syrian held out his arms and tried to speak. If, like Estela, he hadn't known better, Gilles would have been impressed at the speed with which de Rançon assessed where the danger to his friend was coming from.

The Syrian only got as far as 'De Rançon...' in talking to his partner, before he was run through by an efficient sword-stroke, which turned his words into the bloody gurgle of a dying man. De Rançon had finished what Yalda began.

'He wasn't armed,' Dragonetz said drily, his body tensed pre-fight, waiting de Rançon's next move. Estela was behind de Rançon, who only had to move back a few steps to reach her and run her through, with nothing Dragonetz could do to stop him. She stood there, trusting, happy that de Rançon had saved his friend's life.

Swopping dagger for sword, Gilles edged backwards, one tiny movement at a time, slowly trying to move out of de Rançon's peripheral view, while the man's attention was focused on Dragonetz. He was sure Dragonetz could see what he was trying to do but the knight didn't betray him by so much as a flicker of his eyes. Instead, he turned his attention to Yalda, who was staring at her father's dead body, impassive.

'You have what you came for,' Dragonetz told her, 'but what I don't understand...' Anyone who knew him would have been put on guard by the casual, insulting drawl.

He opened his cloak, giving her a clear view of the gap between hauberk and hood, the bare target of his insolent face. 'What I really don't understand, is why you have to fuck every man your sister has.'

Yalda screamed, pulled the dagger from her father's back and would have thrown it at Dragonetz had not Muganni hung onto her arm, preventing her and shouting. 'He's trying to kill himself. He's using you to kill himself. It's the drugs. He can't help what he says.' Yerushalmi moved to hold the girl, taking the dagger, calming her in soft, foreign words.

Gilles used the distraction to reach Estela and drag her backwards till he could put himself and his sword between her and de Rançon. The latter acknowledged the move with a twisted smile. Gilles knew he was no match for de Rançon but Dragonetz was at least an equal, and de Rançon was caught between them. Estela was no longer the easy hostage she had been.

'I don't understand,' Estela kept saying. 'Get off my foot!' but Gilles had no intention of letting her free to go to de Rançon and it was too complicated to explain to her now. Unable to hold her and the sword, he'd settled for standing on the fashionable long pointed end of her boot, pinning her down neatly.

'You *must* stay here,' he told her, urgently.

'My dear Estela,' de Rançon told her, putting down his bloody sword, 'it will be all right. I'm here.' So it was to be play-acting, thought Gilles grimly, with Estela as the audience and everyone else watching, to see what trick the bastard would pull next.

Dragonetz nodded to Gilles, and that little gesture of gratitude and reassurance was enough from such a man. They would get out of this! 'Go, Yerushalmi,' Dragonetz told him again.

The Jew looked towards Bar Philipos' crumpled body. 'The curse has delivered justice. Maimonides teaches that we should eschew vengeance, but even so, Yalda and I will know greater peace in our new life for having truly finished with this one. Come, Yalda,' he said and the couple retreated into the dyeworks building, locking a door behind them. De Rançon followed them with his eyes.

'Effendi,' yelled Muganni. Dragonetz had crumpled to a heap on cobbles, apparently asleep. 'It is the drug,' the boy told them, placing the leather bag under his master's head. 'It takes him against his will to the poppy-world for a short time and then he wakes, groggy as if from too much wine. He needs a litter to take him back to his lodging.'

De Rançon and Gilles weighed each other up, coldly. With Dragonetz unconscious, de Rançon could kill them all. 'Dragonetz!' cried Estela and rushed, one-shoed, to her lover's side, too fast for de Rançon to catch her, if he'd tried. Gilles moved to block de Rançon's access to the couple but at most he could only buy time against such a swordsman.

Oblivious to all danger, Estela ordered, 'De Rançon, go to the hospital. Get a litter out here, as soon as you can!'

Gilles readied himself to give his life for his mistress, praying that the city guard would turn up, drunk Templars, thieves, anybody! But instead, inexplicably, de Rançon put his sword up and left. Gilles had no idea where de Rançon would go or what he would do, so he sent Muganni 'to get Dragonetz' chamber ready' and (sotto voce in the boy's ear) to get the Hospitalers to send a litter.

If the boy was confused by the duplication of litters, he gave no sign, merely his customary 'Yes, Effendi' and he was off, leaving Estela cradling Dragonetz' head in her lap, and Gilles clutching a leather bag, his heart full of silent apologies and prayers.

Like the stone walls and closed door of Dragonetz' chamber, Estela and Gilles heard all that was said but stayed silent. A little weak still and lying on the bed, Dragonetz was nevertheless lucid as he outlined the way he had been drugged, the effect in hallucinations and sleep, the sickness when he had no poppy or reduced the dose. Muganni showed Estela and Gilles the poppy pods and the ground hash that he was using. He told them the quantities that Dragonetz needed to avoid being sick.

'But poppy is dangerous,' he warned. 'Sometimes it is stronger than others, even with the same proportions of pods to water. You will see by the colour of the infusion and you must be careful – an overdose will kill. I use the hash to make a little happiness.'

Never had someone spoken of happiness with as serious an expression. 'At some stages of the cycle the poppy makes depression and anxiety, and because we are trying to keep the dose low, there are sometimes pains too. The hash gives a little relief.'

Muganni made Estela recite the method and proportions of preparing the concoction until he was satisfied that she had them memorised and Dragonetz smiled weakly at the boy. 'You have done well, my boy.'

Then Estela realised why she had to learn the preparation of the drugs. 'You are leaving,' she said to Muganni.

'I have some jobs to do for the master and then he bids me go to my people in the mountains. I am Hashashin and I will be free.' There was pride and excitement in his voice but something else too.

'You were always free with me,' Dragonetz told him, opening his arms. The boy went to the bed and hugged his master, the way Dragonetz had taught him, as men hug, as father and son hug. Estela thought it a pity that de Rançon couldn't see them now or he would realise how mistaken he had been about the relationship between Dragonetz and Muganni.

They released each other, patted each other heartily on the back, and Dragonetz smiled his approval. If his eyes were a little moist, then no doubt, like their redness, it was an effect of the drugs.

'You are leaving too,' Muganni told Gilles and Estela.

'For the mountains?'

Muganni looked at his master with regret. 'It is not possible. The Hashashin face many threats and my Lord would draw down on us a force that would finish us. We can only survive by hiding and there is nowhere Oltra mar that a man like my Lord can hide. Everyone will seek him. He must go home, somewhere he can be isolated for the time it takes.' And then Muganni told them what had to be done to purge Dragonetz of the drugs and what the risks were.

White-faced, Estela asked, 'How will we get him home?'

'I am still here, you know,' Dragonetz complained. Everyone ignored him.

'My Lord planned all this. In the event that he survived the meeting at the dyeworks, there is a camel train, leaving tomorrow at dawn, with two litters, one for my Lord and one for my Lady.'

'I'd rather ride a camel than be in one of those coffins!' interrupted Estela.

'As my Lady wishes,' bowed Muganni. At St Jean d'Acre there will be a ship waiting for you.'

Estela's eyes were round. 'The cost!' she said 'How could you have paid so many men to travel in the stormy season. Camel trains! A ship!'

'Didn't I tell you?' Laughter struggled to emerge in the tired eyes. 'I'm unbelievably rich. Look.' He passed her the leather bag, which had been beside him on the bed. 'Go, Muganni.'

'No, wait!' a thought struck Estela. 'Muganni could tell de Rançon that we're leaving, so he can come with us. We could do with the extra protection.' She dropped her eyes, hiding the suggestion that Dragonetz' weakness left them vulnerable.

Gilles and Dragonetz exchanged looks. 'No,' said Dragonetz. 'De Rançon is the Queen's man and it would put him in an impossible position. Mélisende will be livid when she knows I've gone. She had plans for me. De Rançon will be able to say, honestly, that he knew nothing and he'll keep his place at court. Go, Muganni.' The boy left. Gilles was gazing fixedly at Dragonetz, with respect.

Estela still felt unsure about leaving de Rançon out of their plans. She started to open the bag. 'The Jew's teacher is right, you know, about eschewing revenge. De Rançon said something similar when we were travelling. So difficult to surmount those feelings and so admirable, don't you think? Oh. My!' She'd opened the velvet pouch inside the bag and spilled a dozen or more fine-cut jewels over the bed. 'I hope you counted them!' she said, gathering them up again, admiring the glitter as different facets caught the light, and putting them back safely in the bag. 'Twenty?' she queried, drawing the string tight. 'They must be worth a fortune!'

Dragonetz nodded. 'Read the parchments.'

Estela pulled two rolled parchments out of the bag. The first was as expected, signed by Raavad and writing off all debts against his loan to buy the land and material for his paper mill. 'You're free!' Estela beamed at her lover.

'Read on.'

The second parchment took longer to read and was signed Malik-al-Judhami of the Banu Hud. *Al-Hisba!* thought Estela as she read his message.

Dearest friend of my mind,

Forgive my deceit but if I had not got you out of Narbonne, you would not be alive, and I could not let the world lose a mind such as yours.

If you read this, then you have completed your task for Raavad and enough time has passed for you to come home without fear of the assassin. When you do come back, you have wealth beyond your dreams. Before the paper mill burned, I shipped all the paper to Venice. We were right about the potential of paper and the payments are waiting for you with Raavad, who has full accounts. The summer's work bore the harvest you deserve and you can now reap the rewards.

The Christian Church will never allow you to make paper again but what

we learned together will find a use, in some other form. You will find another
project and you have the money to invest in it.

I am sometimes in Narbonne on business so perhaps our paths will cross
once more. I hope so.

Inshallah

Malik-al-Judhami of the Banu Hud

'You're rich.'

'That's what I said.' Dragonetz gave her a boyish grin. 'So now you
really love me, don't you.' She moved close to him, put her arms
round him in a very unmanly way, laid her head on his chest and
sobbed.

At dawn, the guards on the Damascus gate let a party of three adults
leave the city. Robed, in travel headgear, and carrying only three bags,
the small group walked to the camp outside the walls, where the camel
drivers were already fastening saddles to camel backs. Two litters were
also buckled tight but they remained empty, at least for the first day.
Both Dragonetz and Estela preferred to ride in the open, although each
nagged the other at regular intervals, to take the enclosed option.

'I'll buy you more dresses,' Dragonetz promised as Estela
mourned all the new finery, abandoned in the palace of Jerusalem.
She had been banned from returning there, both by Dragonetz and by
Gilles, and she had accepted that their flight had to be secret, but she
kept remembering one item after another.

'My tortoise-shell comb,' she said glumly. 'After all those weeks in
the same sweaty dress, with nothing, I could finally look like a girl
again. And here I am stuck on a damned camel once more.'

'Ladies don't swear,' Dragonetz told her.

Estela proved volubly that she was no lady and they continued to
distract each other from what lay unsaid between them, but which
weighed heavily on both.

At one point, Estela asked, 'Sisters?' and Dragonetz told her simply of the drug illusions, of bedding Yalda, of his discoveries about the girl he'd thought had died for him.

As if aligning two portraits of the same man, Estela matched what she learned against her memories of the man she'd fallen in love with in Narbonne. She remembered how hard he'd tried not to love her, fearing she'd get hurt, and she understood this better. She also matched what she was told against a third picture, the one de Rançon had painted as they travelled together. Some things fitted; some things didn't. She shrugged off the discrepancies. De Rançon had misinterpreted what he saw, not knowing Muganni's background and not knowing that Dragonetz had been drugged against his will.

How Dragonetz had treated de Rançon in the past and indeed how he was treating him now, remained a puzzle to Estela so she didn't dwell on what she couldn't interpret. There was enough to worry about. She had to maintain the correct dose of the drugs to get this man home, across weeks over desert and sea, and then she had to wean him off the poppy. None of the herbal lore she'd gleaned from her mother had prepared her for such a task.

When they set up camp at the end of the first day's travel, the travellers could see the darkness swirling behind them and the sky above, starless black. 'Sandstorm,' confirmed the camel drivers. 'I think we will outrun it but the way behind is closed for days.'

When Gilles caught a private moment with Dragonetz, he started with his apologies. 'So you were played too,' Dragonetz drawled. 'De Rançon impressed you, didn't he. So much more the right man for Estela than I am, don't you think? Such a pity it turned out he was a treacherous bastard, working with that… pig.'

'When are you going to tell her? About de Rançon? Or do you want me to?' Gilles owed Dragonetz the choice, given his misjudgement of the man.

'I can't. Neither of us can. De Rançon barbed his hooks and if either of us tries to draw them out the poison will remain. If we speak against him, Estela will take his part all the more and any doubts he set in her mind about me will become certainties. She has seen him do nothing but behave in a courageous, loyal, chivalrous way.'

Grim-faced, Gilles acknowledged the truth of this.

'With any luck, we've left him behind. And not just for a few days. If not, at least you can tell me the worst. What has been said about me?'

Hesitant at first, Gilles began the catalogue of petty spite, arrogance and dissolution which described Dragonetz, as seen through de Rançon's clever inferences. Neither man took pleasure in the tale.

De Rançon directed soldiers into one house after another, enjoying the screams of the occupants at the invasion into their homes. The sound of smashing crockery and furniture was music to de Rançon's ears. Someone would pay for this evening's comedy of errors, he promised himself.

From the moment Yalda stuck a knife in her father, rendering him useless, all that careful work, months of planning, had been for nothing. It should have been so simple. He would have had Estela, to threaten and swop for the book. Dragonetz would have capitulated straight away and given the Torah to Bar Philipos, who could have dealt with the Jew and the book. The Syrian would have enjoyed dealing with the Jew, his hatred of the entire race being evident to anyone who knew him. In his imagination, de Rançon played the game as it should have been.

Instead, first the Syrian's daughter, then that clod of a manservant had intervened – pieces which should never have been on the board – and the game-plan was wrecked. The book was vanishing out of his reach with the mealy-mouthed Jew while Dragonetz lay unconscious from drugs, protected by a woman, a small boy and a one-handed man. De Rançon was renowned – renowned, he reminded his imaginary listeners – for his skills as a knight and now the revenge he'd dreamed of was reduced to skewering an unconscious man, already dying of drugs. This wasn't how it was supposed to be. Dragonetz would live long enough for de Rançon to make him suffer before he died. Instead, de Rançon chose to chase the book, while the trail was still hot.

One of Mélisende's Guards rushed out a house to report, breathlessly, 'My Lord, they're hiding in the synagogue.'

'Then get all your men and capture them!' roared de Rançon.

The soldier hesitated, then, 'Yes, my Lord.'

De Rançon had been right. Turning over the Jewish Quarter, men who knew their work had found Yerushalmi quickly enough. Within the hour, the Jew and Yalda were intimate with the instruments of torture maintained by Queen Mélisende for special guests at the palace. Men, who also knew their work, applied carefully judged degrees of pain and pressure, while de Rançon paced the passageways. The book had not been on the Jew when he was found with the woman, hiding by the altar – where no woman was allowed, de Rançon had pointed out to them. Yerushalmi said he'd passed on the book, that it was safer for someone else to take it to Egypt. Yalda said she didn't know who he'd given it to. Lies, de Rançon had thought. All lies.

But morning had come and the Queen's torturer reported to de Rançon, with his apologies, that the woman had not known who the book had gone to, or had died without saying. The good news was that the Jew had given up a name before they put him out of his misery. De Rançon barely waited for the last syllable before he was off hunting in the Jewish Quarter once more, with the same result; a successful capture, but no book, and more work in the Queen's torture-chamber, more pacing the passageways. Red-eyed and fuzzy-headed from lack of sleep, de Rançon walked another restless night before, finally, the report came to him.

When it did, he smacked his gauntlet across the man's face in frustration but someone in his line of work would hardly flinch at a blow to the face and the Queen's torturer merely repeated, 'He gave it to someone else. That's all he would say. We used everything.'

'You should have kept him alive and started again!'

'You wanted the information in a hurry.' The man shrugged,

explaining the obvious to a debutante. 'Can't do both. You should've said if you were willing to wait.'

Dropping with fatigue, de Rançon returned to his lodgings to sleep. He could order random raids on the Jewish quarter, and he could give instructions to search every Jew leaving the city for a book stolen from Queen Mélisende, but he knew the odds were against finding it. The Jews would wait till things had quietened down then the Torah would head for Egypt. As for his business with Dragonetz, that could surely wait, the state Dragonetz had been in when last seen.

By the time de Rançon knew he should have checked earlier, it was too late. He'd had no inkling that there was an escape plan, and Dragonetz had seemed too ill for any sudden action. De Rançon admitted it; he'd missed the move. When he realised Estela and Gilles were missing, he checked on Dragonetz and followed the trail to the Damascus Gate and a camel train en route for the coast. He'd almost laughed at the crazy daring of the plan. It was so much like something he would have done. He would have followed them on racing camel, or even horseback, had the sandstorm not made the final judgement on his chances of catching them. It was not to be.

All de Rançon could do now, was to consider the position in which he was left. He still had all his credibility with Estela and he would find a way to use that in the future. Bar Philipos had become a liability, and the timing of his death had raised de Rançon's credit with Estela, at the same time as solving a problem. It wouldn't do to have Queen Mélisende know how closely her loyal knight had worked with Nur ad-Din in Damascus.

On the other hand, the Queen was going to be very disappointed. She'd wanted the book, she'd wanted Dragonetz and she'd relied on de Rançon to deliver both. However, if word went out on the streets that thanks to their gracious ruler, a priceless Torah had been delivered to the Jewish citizens of Jerusalem and was on its way to Egypt for study, that would be received very favourably by the Jewish community, and might even be seen as a positive outcome by the Queen. De Rançon wrote the scenario in his head. Bar Philipos was the thief, intercepted and executed by the Queen's man – de Rançon himself – who also trapped his partner, the daughter, and obtained her confessions to this crime. Then, at the Queen's command, de Rançon had delivered the priceless book to its rightful owners.

The big problem was that large numbers of Jewish families had been raided by the Queen's Guard. Then they must revisit the Jewish Quarter, with largesse and apologies, explaining that Bar Philipos and his daughter had been in league to steal the Queen's book. De Rançon had tried nobly to prevent them, and had returned the book to the Jew who would carry it safely for study in Egypt.

Of course, this Jew's name must remain secret to protect him, when he carried such a precious object, but he travelled with the blessing of Queen Mélisende. There were a few more details to be tidied up, monies and threats, in the required proportions, to the families of Yerushalmi and the other Jew who'd died under torture, but the story had enough of a ring to it to be spread as truth by those whose palms were greased well enough. Yes, he rather thought he could sell that version to the Queen and to the city. He sounded rather fine in it, there was no-one to contradict him, and it wasn't so far from the truth.

As to the Queen wanting Dragonetz; she had made it clear when she sent de Rançon to Damascus that she wanted Dragonetz leading her armies or dead. Dragonetz would not be leading her armies but neither would he be leading anyone else's, thanks to the good work of Bar Philipos. The poppy would most likely finish Dragonetz, but on the slim chance that it didn't, de Rançon would be only too happy to take on the Queen's alternative wish. In fact, if he'd killed Dragonetz in the dyeworks, the match would be over, without him having seen the man suffer. De Rançon had enjoyed the admiration he saw in Estela's eyes. She still believed in him, and therefore believed in all he'd said about Dragonetz. She was hooked and all he had to do was reel her in, while Dragonetz watched, helpless. If he survived the poppy, of course. De Rançon was starting to hope that Dragonetz *would* survive.

So much potential in Estela. It would be a waste not to combine business with pleasure and he had unfinished business with the slut. Bar Philipos was right about women – sometimes useful and always disposable. De Rançon didn't like unfinished business, or unsolved mysteries, and there had been something on the journey, something he'd meant to revisit... what was it again?

He retraced their ride in his imagination, till he came to the turn for Marselha. That was it! The chit had wanted to go right, towards Narbonne, and Gilles had known why. She was very emotional about it too. So there was something Narbonne-way that Estela was very attached to. He smiled. Attachments were useful. They could be used to hurt people.

Which reminded him. Another piece of unfinished business. And this time there would be no mistakes.

Muganni was singing as he skipped along the cobble-stones, the sort of song a boy sings to himself when all is right with his world. He'd finished his errands for Dragonetz the day before, luckily, as the pigeons would never have been able to take off in today's sandstorm. He had followed instructions carefully, putting a duplicate of the same message in each of fifteen tiny leather pouches, buckled in turn to all fifteen pigeons 'to make sure that at least one gets to the Khatun'.

He had held each one high above his head, cupped in both hands, feeling the plump breast and fragile heartbeat under the feathers and he had loosed them, to beat their noisy wingstroke away from the city and back to Damascus, where their keeper would feed them, care for them and take the messages to the Khatun. Whatever the Khatun knew, so would Salah ad-Din, and Muganni imagined them reading the message. He knew what the words said but they made no sense to him at all.

'All as planned. My sword sleeps. Damascus chooses without me. Swordsmith, rose-grower and horse, please. Acre. Inshallah' and there was a tiny dragon's head as signature. There was no need for Dragonetz

to worry if the message fell into the wrong hands, thought Muganni; the worry was whether it would be understood at all, even in the right hands. When they left Damascus they'd had twenty-four pigeons so Dragonetz must have sent some earlier. No doubt the combination of messages would make sense to someone. And the pigeons would be home.

As he'd set each one free, Muganni's own heart had lightened, as if he were flying a little way with each one. Home. Free. His steps echoed on the cobbles as he skipped and sang. He'd been wrong in the Great Hall. This was the happiest day of his life. If the sandstorm hadn't stopped him, he would have gone to the mountains today, but tomorrow would do. Tomorrow he would be back with his people. One day made no difference.

He didn't see the man lurking in the shadows, nor have any forewarning of the knife that slit his throat from behind. As in the alleyways of most cities, people could turn blind and deaf, melt away into air, at a hint of trouble, and whoever might have been heading that way, found other streets to turn into when they saw the unmistakeable shape of one man holding another, followed by one figure collapsing to the ground.

Had there been a watcher, the witness would have heard the murderer say, 'Sing now,' as he kicked the corpse into the gutter and then bent to pick up something glittering that rolled out of the boy's clothes. The city saw nothing and heard nothing; merely absorbed one more bloodstain into its stone streets.

CHAPTER TWENTY

There was no doubt that money opened doors, or more importantly hired a camel train and then a ship. Estela had already seen the impact of Queen Mélisende's wealth, when she was travelling with de Rançon, but it made her quite giddy to think that Dragonetz could pay for all this and not even count the cost. She had kept to the same dose of drug that Muganni had been giving, until they left Jerusalem, and Dragonetz was on an up moment when they reached Acre, organising vast quantities of goods to go aboard the ship. Not just goods, either. Robed men also waited Dragonetz at the port.

'Estela.' Dragonetz called her over, his face alight with enthusiasm. 'Before you go shopping, I want you to meet two of the finest craftsmen in Damascus, or rather in Occitania, for they are travelling with us.' And then he introduced her to a swordsmith and a grower of roses 'big as platters, frothy with petals and scented like the harems of Solomon.' Estela learned that she would have gardens full of Damask roses, the envy of every court in Christendom and that she would have a new dagger to replace the one in her undershift.

'Dragonetz!' she rebuked him, flushing, but there was no stopping him in this mood. The swordsmith made no reference to where the dagger was to reside but told her it would be his pleasure to pattern such a weapon in the Damascene manner, and that my Lady could choose the designs she wanted. That definitely caught Estela's attention and she was deep in questions about swirls and initials when Dragonetz darted off again, murmuring, 'Sadeek,' as he left. As if that explained everything. Which of course it did, to Estela.

'His horse,' she explained to the bemused craftsmen. 'I sometimes think he loves that horse more than –' she blushed – 'more than anything,' she finished lamely, wondering if intoxication was contagious.

And then Dragonetz was back with them. 'My horse,' he said, and Estela smiled to herself.

The rose-grower fished in his robes and brought out a small square of parchment, like those put into the capsules of carrier pigeons. 'Salah ad-Din gave me this message for you,' he said in his deep, serious voice. The craftsmen bowed and left to organise crates of metal and rose bushes, and their families. The two wives and a bevy of children hovered anxiously by the huge crates, waiting for embarkation.

Dragonetz didn't stop Estela reading over his shoulder, her own Arabic now capable of translating such a short, incomprehensible message. It looked like a couplet from a poem.

'Leave as my honoured friend.
Return as my honoured foe.
Salah ad-Din'

'What does it mean?'

'It means I've survived the Holy Land twice and am not welcome here a third time. Thank the Lord there is little sign of another crusade. This man Salah ad-Din has something about him ... and he will be leader after Nur ad-Din. I don't envy the commander who meets Salah ad-Din on the field in the future.' Estela's face must have shown how lost she was, for Dragonetz finished, 'I'll explain it all later,' and then he rushed off to supervise more loading and unloading.

All this frenetic energy did Dragonetz no harm and Estela knew what must follow, so she made no attempt to calm him down. In addition to the usual drop from his current state into depression, if she followed Muganni's advice, he would be unwell, if not worse. Once they were aboard ship, Muganni had advised that she cut down the quantity of drugs, little by little, to try to make it easier when he stopped completely. The hash would help to combat depression and pains, but not enough to make complete withdrawal possible.

That had to wait until Dragonetz could be placed in a secure room, and tended by friends who would also be his guards and physicians. Estela dreaded the scenes for which Muganni had prepared her, but as yet they seemed impossible. How could her Dragonetz ever be so crazed by drug-want that he could turn against her? She put the possibility aside in her mind and concentrated on the present; boarding ship, getting over the vomit-inducing swell of the sea, and maintaining Dragonetz in some kind of stable condition until they got him back.

As it turned out, Estela found her sea-legs quickly, thanks to her previous voyage and de Rançon's tough kindness. Dragonetz seemed unimpressed by her account of how de Rançon had rescued her from near-death below decks but then he seemed to ride the waves as he rode Sadeek, a natural. That did not spare him a different sort of sickness.

As Estela experimented with the dose of poppy, Dragonetz was sometimes nauseous, other times garrulous and confused. Estela would lie beside him on the narrow ship's bunk, holding him. Not only had he lost any desire for her, he seemed unaware that desire existed or that he'd ever felt any. He liked her holding him though, and murmured about her warmth. He sometimes felt very cold, shivering, however many blankets she used. At other times he threw off all coverings. Estela increased the poppy dose when she felt he was not coping – or that she wasn't.

Conversations were random, usually an outpouring by Dragonetz on something that interested him, particularly roses, steel and pigeons, with Estela encouraging him and asking questions.

'The pattern welding is expert but not new to me,' he informed her. 'What makes Damascene steel unique is some secret ingredient. The swordsmiths wouldn't tell me what it is – my own won't even tell me! – but I think it comes from India. There is as much aboard ship as was in stock but when we run out, we'll have to organise a trade route ourselves.'

'You have contacts Oltra mar. Maybe the swordsmith himself can organise something via Damascus. Or maybe de Rançon can. Queen Mélisende must have trade with the east.' Estela encouraged all his projects and engaged his lively mind in planning the future and in finding solutions for all the problems that didn't matter, as far as she was concerned. Running out of the secret ingredient for Damascene steel was as irrelevant as the possibility that all the rose-bushes would die on the journey, or that Occitan pigeons would have no homing instinct.

'You mustn't over-water,' he told her. 'It kills as many plants as under-watering. And salt water kills them straight away. You should see the joining of plants, the way Khalid cuts the root and joins them, to get the best of both types. It is the closest thing to magic I have ever seen.'

'Let's go and see Khalid. He can tell us how the roses are doing.' She would go with him to talk to the rose-grower and the sword-smith, to take a turn round the deck, where Dragonetz could learn about the tack the captain planned to take in a forthcoming storm, or the origins of the crew-members. As long as he was learning, planning or in hot debate, Dragonetz was almost himself. It was the other times, when he lay wooden or shaking in her arms, that Estela was frightened for him, though not yet frightened for herself. He would recite obscure Persian poems to her, Khayyam and Sanai.

'You blazed through my heart and opened
Me like a rose in full bloom
And I lay at your feet, dead,
Until permitted to live once more.
Freedom meant nothing until

I offered you everything.
Now I am truly free.'

Despite the time of year, the storms treated them lightly and, probably because it was winter, they crossed no pirates. They reached Marselha on a cold, winter day with the Mistral to welcome them home, chopping the waves into a nightmare for the pilot boats unloading their ship. Estela breathed a sigh of relief on reaching dry land and had to remind herself that her work was yet to come. Once again, money made all things possible, but even so it took several days before Gilles could find a property to lease, which met Dragonetz' requirements: 'large, as befits the rank of a nobleman; secluded so that screaming will go un-noticed; with at least one room that can be locked and keep a prisoner secure; and with a walled garden.' Gilles saw fit to keep some of these details to himself when enquiring locally for empty properties.

While Gilles sought somewhere for them to live, Dragonetz ensured that his craftsmen, and their families, were established in suitable premises, in a quarter where Arabic was common. This was not nearly as difficult in Marselha as Gilles' task. On his first day asking around about lodging, he had let it be known that they would need servants for their time 'near Marselha' and the result was a steady stream of potential candidates for Estela to interview. She chose those who struck her as discreet as well as experienced and once the household was established in the villa Gilles had found for them, she sent two of her new men on urgent messages.

One went to Johans de Villeneuve, with a message for Raoulf, letting him know that Dragonetz and she were safe, at the address given, and that they were all to stay where they were until further word from Estela. The other message went to Raavad, to let him know Dragonetz had returned and would indeed require the monies due to him. Inside this missive was another, for Malik, but this one was different from the others. *'Come quickly,'* it said. *'Dragonetz needs you. I need you. Estela'* She had no real hope that he would be able to reach them soon enough but if anyone could reach Malik, it would be

Raavad. And Malik's skills could make all the difference. Now that the time had come, Estela was scared.

'To our new home and to the future!' Dragonetz raised his goblet, his eyes bloodshot and wild, unbalancing a little as he stood to make the toast on their last evening at the inn.

'To the future,' echoed Gilles and Estela, standing, raising their glasses with his.

'What the hell is up with that damned dog now?!' No-one was stupid enough to answer Raoulf's rhetorical outburst, except perhaps the dog, who increased the volume of his barking. It was as if the dog knew his mistress was home, close enough to reach in a day's travel.

Raoulf could understand all the barking earlier in the day when the messenger showed up. Nici was the sort of dog who would protect his family from a passing fly, his deep bark warning off any miscreant within the entire valley. Usually the dog would do his duty and then, satisfied he'd frightened the living daylights out of any threat in hearing, he'd drop to a satisfied sleeping-hearthrug position by the babies' crib. Today, however, there had been the excitement over the messenger's arrival, with the news that Estela and Dragonetz were both safe and near Marselha. 'Thank God!' Prima said when Raoulf told her the news, and she hugged both babies so tightly she made them cry. Nici had faced the approach to the house, barking at the stranger riding up long before Raoulf could see what all the noise was about, and then he'd quietened when Raoulf greeted the messenger. All as it should be.

But then, this afternoon, Nici had started again, his hackles up and barking incessantly, which set the babies off screaming and drove Raoulf outside to chop wood. He could still hear Nici from the yard but at least he could vent his annoyance with the axe on the chopping-block. Although they were getting too heavy for her to carry both for long, Prima had hoisted the babies up, one on each hip, and come out to join him. She sat on a low stone wall, making the most of the burst of winter sunshine, the babies well wrapped and sheltered from the chill wind. Of course, Nici came out with them, circling anxiously, nipping the air behind Prima's ankles then barking into the wind, until she gave up and went inside again.

Raoulf could hear the barking and crying until he thought he'd explode. He gave up on the chopping, grabbed a rope and went into the room where all the noise was. Nici didn't fight when the rope was placed round his neck and he allowed himself to be dragged outside and tied to a tree but his ears were back. He was not happy. As soon as Raoulf stomped indoors, the dog started off again, his great bark echoing for miles.

'He's never been like this before,' Prima said, mildly, as she shooshed the babies and gave them turns at the breast to calm them before sleep.

'Bloody dog,' muttered Raoulf between gritted teeth, his head still pounding with regular woofbeats.

'How long do you think before we take Musca to his mother?'

'No idea.' Raoulf was irritated with both Estela and Dragonetz. He'd been left as nursemaid while they adventured round the Holy Land and now he was to wait in the middle of nowhere until their highnesses decided he could be sent for. Left with a stupid beast that barked its head off, a couple of wailing babies and a woman who thought the world centred on their feeding habits! No, that was unfair, he chided himself, having taken full advantage of Prima's generous body in a more adult fashion. She was a kind girl, and discreet.

Raoulf had wondered what reception they would get from Johans de Villeneuve, when they arrived with a message from his wife Estela asking him to shelter them and 'his' baby Txamusca. However, everything had been extremely civilised. De Villeneuve had amazed them with his practical generosity and with his absence.

Raoulf, Prima, the babies and, by default, Nici, were given a wing of the bastide which formed de Villeneuve's home. Servants were sent to them to ascertain their needs and provide for them, food being sent to them in one of their chambers. The de Villeneuve estate made room for the little family and went on with its own, very separate life as if Raoulf, Prima and the babies didn't exist. In fact, Nici was better integrated with the de Villeneuves than Raoulf or Prima as the huge dog went on occasional scrounging and play expeditions with the bastide curs and hunting dogs.

If Prima had not already had her suspicions, de Villeneuve's behaviour would have made her wonder if he were indeed Txamusca's father, and when Raoulf told her the truth, she accepted it without question, for which Raoulf was very grateful. He found it tricky enough negotiating the wolf-trap of secrets placed in his care by that precious duo. Dragonetz and Estela suffered some more choice epithets. He'd rather be fighting a host of Saracens than 'protecting' Dragonetz' son against non-existent enemies in a chilly castle in December! He envied the soldiers who'd accompanied him from Dia, and who were now back home in Aquitaine, behaving as men. Recognising that Prima was going to take the brunt of his mood if he didn't go out, Gilles told her he needed to exercise his horse and he headed for the stables, with their calming smell of straw and wax, horse dung and sweat.

Raoulf was already galloping across the garrigue in his imagination and he didn't notice that the barking had stopped. He was adjusting the girth on his saddle when he heard Prima scream. 'Take the horse!' he told a stable boy, then grabbed his sword from where he'd dumped it against the wall, and ran back across the courtyard.

Sword drawn, he entered the room where he expected to find Prima and the babies. He could make no sense of what was going on. In a growling whirlwind of white fur and snapping teeth, the chewed rope swinging around him, Nici had gone crazy and was on his back legs, attacking Prima, whose scream was choking and who kept trying to hit at an arm locked round her throat.

'Nici!' screamed Raoulf, within an inch of running the mad dog through with his sword, and then his battle instinct told him what he was really seeing, showed him the man hidden behind Prima and Nici. The man's other hand held a knife and he was stabbing at Nici but the dog would not let go of whatever human part he had his teeth locked into, growling and shaking his prey.

Raoulf watched the writhing mass, waiting in despair for a clear sight of his target, then in a last burst of energy Prima flung her head backwards against her assailant and Nici pushed with all his force, never letting go with his teeth.

The threesome toppled onto the edge of the hearth, where the logs Raoulf had cut earlier kept a merry dance against the winter's cold. This time it wasn't Prima who screamed, but a man, his voice unnaturally high with pain. Nici let go, Prima rolled away from the heat and Raoulf hauled the unconscious body away from the fire, beating down the attempt of a near flame to follow the flesh it had already singed.

'My brave girl.' Raoulf put his arms round Prima. 'Are you all right?'

'Good enough,' she croaked, slowly getting to her feet, ashes and bits of torn gown scattered over face and body. 'It wasn't me he wanted.' Safe in the crib, the babies wailed their complaint against a world that had woken them up yet again, and the sound was music to his ears.

Then Raoulf went to the great dog, who'd heaved himself over so he could lie beside the crib. He was licking himself, so he was alive, thought Raoulf stupidly. 'My good, brave dog,' he murmured and Nici thumped his tail once. Then Raoulf saw the slashes where the knife had caught the dog and his stomach lurched. He had seen such wounds in battle. Most were cuts that might heal if they didn't get infected but one was very deep.

'Strip that gown off,' Raoulf ordered Prima and never had she taken off her clothes for him with such alacrity. The gown was already in strips and Raoulf tied it round the dog's middle, tight enough to slow the blood and close the worst wound a bit. It would stop him from dying today. Nici let Raoulf tend to him, looking at him with trusting brown eyes, then went back to cleaning his paws and licking his lips. Raoulf hoped it was Miquel's blood in the dog's mouth.

The identity of the assailant was confirmed when Raoulf finally turned his attention to the man laid out on the floor, unconscious still but not dead. He smelled of burnt flesh and there were trickles of blood on his head, where he'd hit the hearth, and on his neck, from bite-marks. Raoulf would not kill an unarmed man, especially when that man was Estela's brother, but neither would he spend time on the care of a child-murderer. Let the fates decide what would happen to Miquel.

'Get fresh clothes on,' he ordered Prima. 'Throw everything you need for yourself and the babies into a box. We're going to join Estela and Dragonetz whether they like it or not.'

'What about Nici?' she asked. 'He saved our lives.'

'He's going with us. I'll get a wagon and he can travel in that with you and the babies. With any luck he'll last till he sees his mistress again one last time. I owe him that.'

Estela still couldn't believe that her message had borne such fruit. Was al-Hisba – Malik – really sitting there, cross-legged on the carpets in an ante-chamber of their new home? Dragonetz had insisted on carpets and cushions, opening crates himself until he found what he wanted amongst the various goods he'd bought in Acre. He was sitting in the same fashion as Malik, apparently comfortable like that, and the scowl on his face had nothing to do with lack of a stool.

Estela sighed and shifted position again, trying to work out what a lady was to do with her skirts when sitting on the floor. She really must get furniture that suited her sense of propriety, into all the rooms, not just items that met the needs of Dragonetz' odd, new habits. He really was angry with her for sending to Malik, angry with her for telling Malik about the poppy, angry with her for existing, it seemed.

For days now they had been arguing. Now that the time had come to clear the poppy from his system, Dragonetz had changed his mind. He didn't see the need, he said, telling her that as long as she kept to the correct dose, he felt fine. It was only when she got the dose wrong that he felt unwell. And if she couldn't get the dose right, he was perfectly capable of dosing himself. 'When you're unconscious?' she blazed at him. 'You'll look after yourself then too?'

'That's only happened twice!' he fired back.

'And will happen more and more. You know what Muganni told us.'

'He is only a little boy.'

'A little boy with the head of an old man. He has more knowledge of such things than any Christian doctor. And he kept you alive.'

'And I'm grateful. I'm alive. I'm fine, so don't worry and don't fuss over me!'

Never had Estela been so glad to see Malik. 'Tell me again,' she said, holding on to the little miracle, like a child to a favourite story. 'You were with Raavad...'

'I was with Raavad,' he indulged her, in his slow accented Occitan.

'No,' she told him, 'speak Arabic. I can understand you and speak it myself. Not well, but I can speak it.'

He began again and she realised how different a man is when he speaks his mother-tongue. Now, she was able to hear his authority, his confidence in his own skills, as he told her about the medical care Raavad had needed for his family and so he had stayed longer in Narbonne than planned, passing on his knowledge to the Jewish doctor who'd observed him. And then he'd had Estela's message, so he'd brought the deeds from Raavad for Dragonetz...' The knight gave a curt nod to acknowledge the service. 'And here we are.'

'I'm sure you're keen to rejoin your family,' Dragonetz told him, 'and however much a pleasure to see you again, we won't hold you here. As you've seen, Estela has been worrying over nothing.' She gasped at the rudeness of sending Malik away and at the presumption of the word 'we' but most of all she was afraid. She didn't know how to get this stranger to do what he must do. She was cutting down on the poppy dose and Dragonetz grew daily more aggressive and unpredictable. Her eyes pleaded with Malik but she dared not speak.

'I will not trouble you for long, my Lord,' Malik said smoothly.

'Perhaps my Lady would like to show me to my chamber?' My lady certainly would, thought Estela, seeing the last chance for a very private conversation, and Dragonetz had one of his fits of indifference, showing no further interest in either of them. At that moment a servant burst in, announcing a wagonful of people and one of them wounded. Estela and Malik were needed urgently.

When Malik realised that the dagger-victim was a dog, he point-blank refused to treat the animal, nearly coming to blows with Raoulf.

'Dogs are unclean,' repeated Malik, not even looking at the creature in the wagon. Estela had hugged Prima and the babies, dripped tears of relief all over Musca and kissed him till she made him squirm, then sent them off to be fed and found a comfortable room, with drawers for makeshift cribs. She was now in the wagon with Nici, unwrapping the bloody rags, assessing the damage. A white feathered tail wearily banged the wooden floor of the wagon, in an attempt at greeting, as his mistress checked him over. Estela emerged from the open wagon-back, blood-flecked and grim.

'Milos, get hot water and clean rags.' The servant rushed off and Estela sent her maid to get her healing box from her coffer of clothes but she knew without looking how depleted and faded her herbs were. It had been a very long time since she had helped the midwife in Dia and although she had stocked up on oils and dried medicaments in the east, the fresh herbs had withered.

'What happened?' she asked and Raoulf told her, in spare, self-incriminating words. He had grown complacent, Miquel had attacked, and Nici had saved all their lives. Malik listened, impassive. 'And now this 'friend' of ours won't help him because he's a dog! Nici didn't stop and say 'I won't help them because they're only men'!'

'Malik?' she turned to him, unwilling to plead, knowing him to be the sort of man who'd take badly to an attempt to play on his emotions. She spoke to him in his own language, choosing each word with care. 'I can wash the blood off the surface of the wounds but one of them is deep and will not heal over of its own accord before Nici, my dog, has bled to death. I cannot seal this wound but I know you can, if you choose.' She took a deep breath, sensing no change in her friend's response. He would help her with Dragonetz, his attitude said, but a dog was untouchable.

Where was Dragonetz? she wondered. *Why wasn't he checking on what all the fuss was about? Please, Malik,* she thought but didn't say. 'I know this is wrong by your religion. I know that we have different beliefs underneath all that we share. I know that you have already given us more than anyone could expect of a friend and that I can never repay the debt I already owe you. But I ask you to consider two questions. If this were your horse, would you let him die when you could save him? As you feel about your horse, so do I feel about this brave, loving dog of mine.'

'A dog is not a horse. Nor is *your* dog *my* horse,' replied the Arab, his eyes gleaming with the pleasure of a logical contest, or with something else, as he listened to the stilted Arabic. 'What is the second question?'

Estela shut her eyes and prayed for inspiration. There was no second question. What stupid notion had made her say such a thing? She racked her brains. Malik's objection was based on his religious beliefs... She remembered her mother tending to women who refused treatment because it went against God's will. What had her mother told her? *'If they quote scripture at you, quote it back at them until you win.'* Then she knew what to say, and surely she'd listened to enough Persian poetry on a long ship voyage to make this convincing. Estela looked Malik straight in the eyes as she began, 'I might have some of the words wrong but did not the poet say,

> *'All gifts are from Allah*
> *Be not proud of what was never yours*
> *But give when Allah calls to you.*
> *What seems to you a wounded dog*
> *Is the way to the walled garden*
> *If Allah wills.'*

Malik regarded her in grave silence, then nodded and said, 'Inshallah. So be it. I will try to heal this infidel dog.'

Estela flung her arms round him, her thanks choking in her throat. Then they set to work. The wagon was as good a place to operate as any and Malik had his surgeon's kit but he shook his head at Estela's impatience.

'Something to dull pain,' he told her. 'Even if we tie his muzzle closed so he can't bite, we can't hold a beast this size still and what I do will hurt him. Also, we need to clean the inside of the wound properly or it will putrefy from within, however pretty it looks on the outside.'

'Why?' asked Estela. 'Why does it matter if it's clean? Surely the blood will carry the impurities away and if we balance the humours, his body will heal.'

Malik looked at her as if she were a child trying to mend a broken doll with mud. 'Infection comes from dirt,' he told her. 'We must have clean hands, clean rags and we must put an antiseptic into the wound. Lavender oil would do.'

'Diluted?' queried Estela, aware of the horrific extravagance of using lavender oil. Her mind was in turmoil, mortified and confused at the notion of cleanliness mattering. How many times had she tended to women with no thought of washing her hands, or using 'antiseptic'? There was so much to learn from Arab medical knowledge.

'Neat,' said Malik shortly.

'I know what we can use to dull the pain!' Estela rushed off to retrieve a little of the store of poppy given to her by Muganni. She mixed it with chicken broth and brought the bowl back to the wagon, where she found Malik laying out his instruments. Estela had never seen surgery before and she thought Malik's equipment looked like a sewing kit, with metal hooks and needles, even thread.

'Poppy tea,' she told him, 'or rather poppy soup. Nici must weigh about the same as Dragonetz so I think I know the right dose. And I can get Nici to drink this. I know I can.' The big tail thumped at the sound of his name and Estela disappeared into the wagon, helping the dog into a position where he could sup from the bowl, which he did, with great enthusiasm.

'Poppy tea? Dragonetz?' asked Raoulf.

'I'll explain afterwards,' Estela told him. 'Just let us attend to Nici first.'

When the dog's eyes closed and he didn't respond to touch, Estela bound his muzzle, just to be on the safe side, and Malik set to work. Estela passed him swabs and tools, held the wounds open for cleaning, instructed servants to bring a change of water, with soap. She watched closely, while he cleansed the wound as deeply as he could, using enough lavender oil to pay a year's rent on a cottage. Then, with impossible dexterity, Malik sewed up the gash with needle and thread, just like mending a rip in a blanket.

'The stitches will need to be cut out,' he said, 'in two weeks, when the tear has closed over. Meanwhile he needs to be watched, not to rip it open because it itches. Some oozing between the stitches is normal, and good, and a little lavender oil each day will keep infection at bay.' He checked the more superficial wounds on the dog's torso and neck. 'There are some burns.'

'He fell against the fireplace,' Raoulf confirmed.

'The lavender oil will help the burns heal too, but spread honey on them, also. Its properties are soothing and healing for burns. If he doesn't lick it off. And be careful that he eats and drinks, light things at first. With people, broth is good, eggs and chicken. I don't know anything about dogs.' He had finished. He clambered out of the wagon and stretched.

Estela suddenly realised how stiff her back was from nursing in a cramped space and she imagined how Malik must feel. 'You need a drink yourself,' she told him. 'And thank you.'

'I think he'll be all right.'

'Poppy tea? Dragonetz?' persisted Raoulf and suddenly Estela had a sick presentiment, a guess as to why Dragonetz had not made an appearance. If she was right, she'd need help.

'Gilles, Raoulf, Malik, come with me. I need to find Dragonetz.'

They found him sitting on the floor in a corner of the room where

Estela had left her stock of poppy open on the bag in which it was usually hidden. She'd not believed Muganni when he'd warned her that a man's addiction would lead him to search for the drug but she'd taken precautions, just in case. And now, the poppy was spilled over the floor and there was an empty cup beside Dragonetz, who was laughing, his eyes drooping, red and wild.

'I told you I can dose myself,' he mocked her. 'Raoulf, good of you to come and see us.'

'What in God's name?' Raoulf's face showed his horror but Dragonetz just laughed at him.

'He's possessed,' explained Gilles, crossing himself.

'No, he's not,' snapped Estela. The last thing she needed was Raoulf charging off to the city and finding some priest to carry out an exorcism. 'He was given the drug in Damascus, when he was prisoner, and didn't know, and we're here to cure him.'

The laughter evaporated as quickly as it had come. Grey-faced, Dragonetz spoke like a voice from the tomb. 'Help me. It is time to lock me in a room. Estela, do what Muganni said. Don't do anything I say. Don't believe anything I say. Only what Estela says. She knows…' Then his head slumped and he left them.

Estela rushed to him and checked his pulse. 'Alive,' she told them. 'The room has been prepared these three days and we have no choice now. If we love him, this is what we must do…' In cold, hard words she told them all that Muganni had said must be done. It would be harder for Dragonetz because he had increased the amount of poison in his system, undoing all their careful work in gradual reduction.

The three men carried Dragonetz to a room bare of anything that he might use to hurt himself and they locked him in. This would take at least a week to work or it would kill him. Estela and Malik sat down to work out what herbs might ease the terrible symptoms of withdrawal, physical and mental. Gilles and Raoulf worked out a timetable of food and surveillance that would leave not a mouse-hole of opportunity for escape.

And in the small hours of the night, when she couldn't sleep, when she didn't dare risk Prima's wrath by disturbing Musca for yet one more cuddle, one more milky scent of his skin, Estela sat beside a large white dog, on a blanket in a recess. Malik had told her she would be better leaving Dragonetz' nursing to him, letting him clear up the shit and vomit that were part of the withdrawal sickness, whatever herbs he used to alleviate the symptoms. He told her that love did not always survive the messy business of being ill, that physical disgust could replace desire. Estela hadn't needed to think twice. 'That's not love, that's sugar on cakes,' she told him. 'Mine is real.'

She stroked the dog's head, from the short hairs of his muzzle to the lion's ruff around his neck. She buried her head in the white fur, murmuring, 'Get better, please get better.'

CHAPTER TWENTY-ONE

Dragonetz gave Sadeek his head, galloping alone across the open moorland, chased by a storm that was already rolling black clouds over his head and dense fog over the terrain. Galloping was dangerous but his heart was black as the storm. As far as he knew, his friends were all dead, either from chasing the Grail or from the enemies they met during the pursuit. Why should he continue? Because of an oath to a king? What would be left of the kingdom when all the knights were dead, chasing dreams?

He was weary, his legs ached and he had no wish to be caught in the storm. Ahead, he could see a domed shelter, a stone shepherd's bourrie appearing and disappearing amidst the thick swirls of fog. That would have to do, as he had no idea where there was anything other than Godforsaken wasteland. Just as he had no need to spur Sadeek, so the destrier knew to slow down as they approached the place Dragonetz thought the bourrie must be.

He was not wrong but as the bourrie appeared once more, so did something else. A wild-eyed giant in body armour stood between Dragonetz and the bourrie, swirling a mace in one hand and an axe in the other. Battle-trained as he was, Sadeek reared in fright, as a flash of lightning silhouetted the nightmare being in front of them. Then the horse steadied, brave enough even for this last fight. For Dragonetz had no doubts that this would be the last.

The heavens opened in a cacophony of thunder and a light-show that turned the torrential downpour into pink spears, churning the grass to mud. Dragonetz charged at the giant, lance in hand, hoping to find a weak spot in the armour, between neck and helm. There was no chance of felling this monster by force; he must have been twenty feet tall and seemed to grow as Dragonetz neared. It was not his imagination. Not only did the giant grow as Dragonetz approached, so did the reach of his mace, which swiped both Dragonetz' legs. The ache turned into stabbing pain, so intense Dragonetz screamed.

Voices in the fog spoke like the thunder itself, rolling sounds into his head where they resonated before finally turning into words.

'His legs hurt.'

'Try the hash.'

'He's already had as much as I dare give.'

'It's not strong enough.'

'Nothing's strong enough'

The voices flickered through his head and flashed across the sky. They were right about one thing. Nothing and no-one was strong enough but he would die fighting. He asked the impossible of Sadeek once more and charged against the giant but this time he kept riding, till he was inside the reach of the lethal chain and using his sword to find just one chink in the mail, stabbing and stabbing, his legs giving way underneath him. It was almost a relief when arms like tree trunks wrapped around him so he was crushed against metal, smelling the blood-scent of iron, rubbed raw even through his own armour, unable to breathe. Then the arms released him. A giant hand picked him up and hurled him screaming into the eye of the storm.

'He's worse,' the thunder said

'It must run its course,' said the lightning and he was not dead yet, but carried through the skies on the storm, riding the black cloud. 'Sadeek,' he murmured to the cloud, which whinnied and descended to a landing giddy as a camel kneeling. He dismounted, his legs still hurting.

He was standing in the family graveyard at Ruffec, one cypress planted inside it, dark green in mourning. The iron gate was shut behind him, and he couldn't see over the high wall enclosing twelve graves, eleven with headstones, and one open, ready for a burial.

There should be nine graves, not eleven. He knew the names and inscriptions off by heart, of his father's parents, and his grandfather's siblings, just as he knew the coppice beyond the wall, where he'd hidden to avoid church-going when he was a naughty seven-year-old.

He peered at the inscriptions on the two new graves; his father and his mother. He didn't remember them dying. The pains in his legs intensified and his head throbbed again.

'You are not alone.' It wasn't the thunder but a woman he thought he knew, gliding towards him. She looked like a rose, all beautiful layers in full bloom. Her name popped into his head and he rolled it on his tongue. It wasn't a bit like thunder. Estela.

'We're here, with you.' Al-Hisba was with Estela, his dark face and robes a contrast to the rose pink. Dragonetz wondered why they looked so worried.

'It is time,' he said and let himself fall backwards into the open grave. He felt a momentary pang of guilt that his would be the last grave in the family. No-one would tend his grave and the cemetery would become overgrown with ivy, the stones cracked and blackened. He had not done his duty, not married, not sired an heir – though God knew his parents had nagged him often enough. He let such thoughts slip away, with all other pains. It was too late. 'Stay with us.' Estela's voice. He shut his eyes and let go of the real world, floating away.

Floating far from his body in the grave, Dragonetz drifted over the fields to a river so broad he could not see the other side. The water flowed dark and slow, each drop irrelevant in the illusion called river. He dipped his hand into river and it came out covered in drops of water. He was just a drop of water and the river would carry on flowing.

Across the river towards him, gliding over the surface, came the barque he was expecting. Three fées in black veils and gowns stood tall and slim in the prow, whispering his name in a summons that would have found him wherever he was. Behind them, in the stern, glowed the Grail light and Dragonetz knew that he had only to touch each fée and name her, and he could leave the river bank behind, embark for the land of the Grail.

As the barque neared, Dragonetz heard once more the Grail music, its multiple harmonies and vast scope dampened by the river mist but unforgettable. All Dragonetz' bitterness evaporated at the *rightness* of the sound. One of the figures on the barque stretched out towards him as the barque touched the bank. Dragonetz leaned out himself and touched the cold, white hand, saying 'Morgan.' She inhaled deeply as if breathing him in and she moved aside to let her sisters come in front of her.

Then Dragonetz was pulled rudely back from the barque, the moment spoilt, his way blocked so that he could not reach the fées who awaited him. Nor could they step out of the barque and come to him. The music and the fées called him but he would have to get past a black knight and a small boy. This knight, however, was no giant but a slighter man than Dragonetz when he took his armour off, as he did, piling it into a heap on the grass.

'Will you fight me again, my friend?' asked Arnaut, the other-worldly blueness crackling around his eyes. 'It is not your time. Go back. You don't have the right to let go. You owe me a life – your life. You must live it.'

Unable to move, caught up in the spell of the music but unsettled by Arnaut's words and presence, Dragonetz waited for the other person to speak.

Muganni hopped on one foot, his eyes as changed as Arnaut's. 'It is not your time,' he said, changing foot. 'Go back. You don't have the right to let go. You owe me a life – your life. You must live it.'

Still Dragonetz did not move. As the music grew quieter, he realised that it was the barque that had moved, floating ever further away from him, as the mists covered them all up. Then he wept for all he had lost and closed his eyes to find sleep.

'Can you find me something to write with?' Dragonetz asked.

Estela looked at Malik, afraid to hope, but he nodded. The crisis had passed.

'What for?' she asked, curious.

A shadow of irritation passed across his face as if it should have been obvious to her. 'To write the music down,' he said. 'I think seven voices would make something like, don't you? You were both there. You heard it.' He was obviously frustrated at how slow they were.

'We were both there,' confirmed Estela slowly.

'We heard the music,' agreed Malik, 'If you write it down, we might be able to help shape it.'

'That's what I thought,' sighed Dragonetz with relief, while Estela went to fetch her pen and her precious paper book, leaving the door unlocked, announcing to everyone she passed that the master would be joining them for evening meal.

It was one of those crazy winter afternoons when the sunshine was almost too warm for sitting outside. The stone walls glowed golden and Dragonetz imagined his roses growing there, or in some other walled garden, wherever it should be. He must get down to the city and see his rose-grower, and his swordsmith. There were business matters to clarify. But for now, it was enough just to be here, to be himself.

The dreams still lingered in his waking mind. He hummed phrases and changed the composition every day but his score was taking shape. He'd never written anything spiritual before but he thought he knew the very person to turn the work into performance. He remembered a monk at the Templar stronghold at Douzens, someone al-Hisba had worked with before joining Dragonetz. The monk was a man who would understand, who would find the singers and the setting for the chorale. But it all could wait.

What could not wait was what he must say to Estela. He had turned his dreams over and over, seeking meaning, denying meaning, until he thought his head would explode. He had dark moods, moments when he felt that part of himself had left this world when he'd touched Morgan le Fay, and then he would shake off such superstitious thoughts, knowing that it was the poppy that had touched him, and left its traces. But the dreams lingered in his imagination and it troubled him that Muganni had appeared in such a guise, with Arnaut. In the same way he felt the rightness of the Grail music, he couldn't shake the feeling of wrongness about the dream-Muganni. He needed to know that Muganni was fine, that he'd reached the mountains safely. If only a pigeon could wing its way between them!

His throat tightened as he remembered their meeting in Nur ad-Din's tent, the boy's vulnerability underneath the veneer of training, his inability to hide his feelings. Dragonetz had seen every emotion pass through those luminous round eyes, from loathing and fear to joyous fulfilment. Recalling Muganni's beautiful voice in the Arabic dawn song, accompanying Estela, still brought shivers of appreciation. No-one who'd been in court that evening would forget the boy, or his talent. And yet he'd thanked Dragonetz daily, when thanks were due the other way round. A slip of a boy, who'd saved his master's life with his knowledge and nursing. Who'd saved it yet again in the dream-world that led out of this one. Wherever Muganni was now, the child would be singing like an angel.

Foreboding chilled Dragonetz once more, but there was nothing he could do about that feeling at present so he shook it off again. There was something he could do about the other realisation that had come to him. Seeing the family graveyard, seeing his own grave, he had believed for the first time in his own mortality. He was no longer a young man, as his parents had told him often enough. His parents who, thank God! were still alive as far as he knew.

'Dragonetz, there's something important I must tell you. I've left it too long and it's not getting any easier.' Estela was watching the babies as they rolled on the grass, pulled an occasional handful, which their nursemaid patiently retrieved from their mouths. Bemused at having such a household at all, Dragonetz had not asked for an explanation of the children who'd suddenly appeared. Some by-blows of Raoulf, he assumed, observing the way his man treated Prima. They wouldn't be the first, although usually Raoulf moved on to the next pretty serving-girl, leaving what he saw as ample compensation for a broken heart and a baby. Dragonetz wondered idly how many little Raoulfs were scattered around the Holy Land. Some soldiers were like that. Which reminded him of what he must say to Estela.

He interrupted her. 'There's something I have to say something to you first.' The babies chuckled and babbled as they explored a world where every clod of earth and each leaf was a novelty. 'I owe you my life. No amount of thanks could suffice.' The words sounded cold and formal to his ears after all they had been through together.

She shook her head. 'No, it was Muganni who saved your life. If he had not prepared me for what it would be like, what we must do, Malik and I would never have managed.'

Maybe that was what lay beneath his dream, Dragonetz wondered. He did owe his life to Muganni. There was no reason to worry about the boy, who would be among the Hashashin at this very minute. He tried again to tell Estela what he must. 'You are my life. I can't imagine a life without you in it. But…' Her face was as stone. 'But I also have a duty to Ruffec. I must take a wife and get heirs. I will not live forever, Estela,' he didn't dare touch her, 'do you understand? It needn't spoil what we have now.' He cursed the plea in his voice.

'I understand,' she said, looking straight ahead, a statue.

'What was it you wanted to say?' he asked.

'Nothing,' she replied. A robin hopped near one of the babies, sending the infant into an ecstasy of gurgling as he crawled surprisingly quickly across the grass after the bobbing bird, towards the stone steps. He stretched out his hand to make the grab, the robin took flight and Dragonetz saw the danger just as Prima yelled 'Txam-usca!' as if calling a baby's name would prevent an accident.

In a few, quick strides, Dragonetz had scooped up the little man just before he started the inevitable head-over-heels tumble. A signet ring on a chain swung free of the baby's clothing as he was righted. Dragonetz kept the child in his arms, not needing a closer look at the ring. A baby called Txamusca, fire born of the dragon.

'It's all right, Prima,' Estela soothed the distressed nurse, who offered to take Musca from Dragonetz. He shook his head and turned to Estela, clutching his precious burden.

'My love,' he said, 'why didn't you tell me?'

'How could I?' she said, turning those expressive eyes full on him. 'How could I add to your troubles before you were safe? How can I now complicate your plans for Ruffec? I will not hold you hostage. I want you to be free.' Then he understood everything. And he knew why she had worried about her body disappointing him. Some questions had easy answers. Tucking Musca under one arm, he leaned over and kissed Estela on the mouth, not a polite kiss but a lingering promise of more, answered in kind.

'Later,' he murmured, breaking off with reluctance. 'This thing wriggles.' He sat down on the stone bench beside her, dandling his son on his lap, at peace in the walled garden.

'A walled garden is the Muslim symbol for paradise,' she informed him.

'I believe so,' he replied gravely, 'but the poet did not say anything whatsoever about a wounded dog.'

'Oh!' she blushed. 'Did you overhear? No... you couldn't have.' There was no need to say where Dragonetz had been at the time.

'Malik told me,' he grinned at her.

'You mean he didn't believe me?!' She was indignant. 'I thought I was very convincing!'

'You were very convincing,' Dragonetz assured her. 'Malik has warned me that a nest of scorpions is less dangerous than you when you have your mind set on something.'

'Presumably that's a compliment?'

'I believe so,' he said, evoking a radiant beam from Musca by tickling the palm of his tiny hand. The robin landed again, gave its one-eyed check for danger before engaging in a tug-of-war with a doomed worm. The cobbled paths round the garden drew the eye in soothing patterns, loops and diamonds, interweaving to return always as a circle. A walled garden could be a symbol of paradise.

EPILOGUE

APRIL 1152

Queen Mélisende of Jerusalem was leaving Tripoli, knowing that her sister's temporary respite would be over once she left. Even Baudouin agreed that nothing would change Raymond of Tripoli. So Mélisende took measures to ensure that the respite would be permanent. On her sister's behalf, she spoke the name and a password that Hodierne had whispered to her in Jerusalem. Mélisende made sure the words reached the right people, and she was a day's ride out of Tripoli when its Comte was murdered by the Hashashin.

The Queen of Jerusalem then made extremely generous donations to her other sister's abbey, and was promised that the prayers for her soul would be made daily, by those whose virtue must surely count with the Lord. Having sought absolution for what she had done, and for what she was about to do, Mélisende penned a missive to Raymond of Toulouse, announcing the unfortunate death of his relative, and the happy reign of the new Comte de Tripoli, Hodierne's son, under the governance of his mother. She also mentioned that the murder of Toulouse's father could now be traced to the hand of the dead man, Raymond of Tripoli, so all might rest assured that justice had been done.

Having neatly blamed the murder of one of her victims, on another of them, Mélisende prepared for a night with Manassés and for war with her son.

HISTORICAL NOTE

Dragonetz and Estela are fictional characters living in real 12th century events. Whenever actual historical figures appear in the story (see list at the back of the book), I have kept within historical evidence and only imagined events and details that could indeed have happened. If I've made mistakes in the research, then I plead 'novelist'.

Within the story, I have used my research and answered some of the questions posed by historians. Everyone agrees that the Second Crusade was a failure from the Crusaders' viewpoint but what caused the military disasters at Mount Cadmus and in the siege of Damascus? Who had Alphonse Jourdain murdered and why? Dragonetz' adventures include my answers to these questions.

The real historical characters include an amazing woman; Mélisende, the Queen of Jerusalem, queen in her own right and ruler of all the Crusader States. Geoffroi de Rançon really was the Commander of Aliénor's Guard at Mount Cadmus and he was indeed dismissed in disgrace afterwards. He did have a son, although dates are a little contradictory so I have suited my story with regard to Geoffroi Junior.

The rare Torah of the story is the book known today as the Aleppo Codex, and it is perfectly possible that an adventurous spirit took it from the Jewish community in Provence to Maimonides in Egypt.

Much debate has taken place about the Hashashins, who gave rise to the term 'assassins'. Some say their alleged use of hash arises from a linguistic misunderstanding; others cite oral tradition as suggesting otherwise. This is a romantic novel so you can guess which version suited me best.

Working in four languages is confusing enough, let alone adding the random choices of medieval spellings. I've tried to give the flavour of the different languages by my choices so, for instance, I've used the Occitan spellings of French place-names such as Lyon (Lion) and Marseille (Marselha). The name Txamusca should be pronounced 'Sh-a-moose-ka' but you can say it how you like! Welcome to my version of the 12th century…

HISTORICAL CHARACTERS APPEARING
IN THE SERIES SO FAR:

- *Aaron ben Asher* – Jewish sage, who annotated the sacred Torah known as the Keter Aram Sola / the Aleppo Codex
- *Aliénor of Aquitaine/ Eleanor of Aquitaine*, Duchess of Aquitaine and Queen of France
- *Abraham ben Isaac/ Raavad II* – Jewish leader in Narbonne
- *Alphonse*, nicknamed 'Jourdain' / 'Jordan', Comte de Toulouse, father of Raymond, killed by poison in Caesarea in 1148
- *Alphonso,* King of Castile, Emperor of Spain – died in 1144 leaving his estate to the Templars
- *Amaury* – younger son of Mélisende
- *Archbishop of Narbonne*, Pierre d'Anduze – brother of Ermengarda's husband
- *Archbishop Suger* – royal prelate in Paris, adviser to King Louis
- *Baudouin*, King of Jerusalem – Mélisende's son
- *Bèatriz* the future Comtesssa de Dia / Comtesse de Die and famous troubairitz
- *Bernard de Clairvaux* – advisor to Louis, abbot leading and reforming the Cistercian order
- *Bernard d'Anduze* – Ermengarda's titular husband, brother of the Archbishop of Narbonne
- *Bernard de Tremelay,* Templar Grand Master 1151
- *Chirkhouh* – Nur ad-Din's general, killed Prince Raymond of Antioch
- *Constance* – widow of the Prince of Antioch, Mélisende's niece
- *Conrad* – Holy Roman Emperor, ruler of the Germanic peoples
- *Ermengarde/Ermengarda* – Viscomtesse of Narbonne

- *Everard des Barres*, Grand Master of the Templars during the Second Crusade
- *Foulques*, King of Jerusalem by marriage to Mélisende – died 1146
- *Geoffroi de Rançon (the father)*, Commander of Aliénor's Guard 1148
- *Geoffroi de Rançon (the son)*
- *Guilhelm de Poitiers* – married Bèatriz
- *Hodierne*, Comtesse de Tripoli – sister of Mélisende, Queen of Jerusalem,
- *Isoard*, Comte de Die/Dia – Bèatriz' father (very little known about Bèatriz)
- *Ismat ad-Dhin* – Nur ad-Din's wife, Unur's daughter
- *Joscelyn*, Comte d'Edessa – deserted and lost the city to Muslim forces, starting the Second Crusade
- *Jarl Rognvaldr Kali Kolsson* – Prince of Orkney
- *Louis VII* – King of France, married to Aliénor
- *de Maurienne*, Comte – uncle and adviser to Louis VII
- *Maimonides* – Jewish philosopher
- *Manuel Komnenos/Comnenus* – Emperor of Byzantium
- *Manassés* – Constable of Jerusalem
- *Mélisende* – Queen of Jerusalem
- *Mujir ad-Din* – ruler of Damascus, 1151
- *Nur ad-Din* – Muslim Atabeg (ruler and general), uncle of Saladin
- *Pope Eugene III*
- *Raimon Trencavel*, brother to Roger and Comte de Carcassonne on his brother's death in 1150
- *Ramon Berenguer*, Comte de Barcelona, Prince of Aragan and Overlord of Provence
- *Raymond V*, Comte de Toulouse
- *Raymond Comte de Tripoli*, Hodierne's husband and relation of Toulouse, killed by Assassins in 1152
- *Raymon/Raimon/Raymond, Prince of Antioch* – Aliénor's uncle and rumoured lover, killed by Saracen troops in 1148

- *Raymond and Stephania of les Baux* – rulers in Provence
- *Raymond de Puy* – Hospitalers' Grand Master 1151
- *Roger Trencavel*, Comte de Carcassonne – died in 1150
- *Saint Paul/ Saul of Tarsus* – famously converted on the road to Damascus
- *Salah ad-Din/Saladin* – Muslim leader during the Third Crusade
- *Sicard de Llautrec* – ally of Toulouse
- *Unur* – Muslim general, defended Damascus in the Second Crusade
- *Zengi/Imad ad-Din Zengi* – father of Nur ad-Din, murdered in 1146
- *The Hashashins/Assassins* – the Isma'ili Muslim sect
- *the troubadours* – Jaufre Rudel, Marcabru, Cercamon, Peire Rogier from the Auvergne, Raimbaut d'Aurenja/Raymon of Orange, Guiraut de Bornelh
- *Persian poets* – Omar Khayyam, Sanai
- In charge of the Templar Commandery at Douzens – Peter Radels, Master; Isarn of Molaria and Bernard of Roquefort, joint commanders

THE CRUSADER LANDS

AFTER THE SECOND CRUSADE

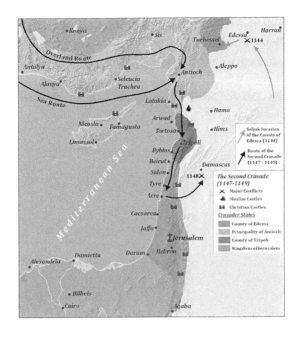

ACKNOWLEDGMENTS

Many thanks to:

my editor, Lesley Geekie Dawe;
my critical friends, Babs, Fan, Jane, Karen C, Karen M, Kris, Moon,
Steve, and the Impeccable Editor, for your invaluable input and
support;
and to everyone in the Dieulefit Writers' Group for the fun we've had
with our writing.

Historical sources that were particularly useful were:

The second crusade 1148 – David Nicolle
Ermengard of Narbonne, the World of the Troubadours – Frederic L
Cheyette
Eleanor of Aquitaine – Alison Weir
Blondel's Song – David Boyle
Holy Warriors – Jonathan Phillips
The Crusades – Thomas Asbridge
Mélisende de Jérusalem – Elyane Gorsira
Les Croisades vues par des arabes – Amin Maalouf
L'Orient des Croisades – Georges Tate
Troubadours et cours d'amour – J Lafitte-Houssat
Ecrivains anticonformistes du moyen-âge occitan – René Nelli
La Fleur Inverse – Jacques Roubaud
Voix de femmes au Moyen Age – Danielle Régnier-Bohler
Les Troubadours – Henri Davenson

ABOUT THE AUTHOR

I'm a Welsh writer and photographer living in the south of France with two scruffy dogs, a beehive named 'Endeavour', a Nikon D750 and a man. I taught English in Wales for many years and my claim to fame is that I was the first woman to be a secondary headteacher in Carmarthenshire. I'm mother or stepmother to five children so life has been pretty hectic.

I've published all kinds of books, both with traditional publishers and self-published. You'll find everything under my name from prize-winning poetry and novels, military history, translated books on dog training, to a cookery book on goat cheese. My work with top dog-trainer Michel Hasbrouck has taken me deep into the world of dogs with problems, and inspired one of my novels. With Scottish parents, an English birthplace and French residence, I can usually support the winning team on most sporting occasions.

www.jeangill.com

facebook.com/writerjeangill
twitter.com/writerjeangill
instagram.com/writerjeangill
goodreads.com/JeanGill

The follow-up to her memoir *How Blue is My Valley* about moving to France from rainy Wales, tells the true story of how Jean

- nearly became a certified dog trainer.
- should have been certified and became a beekeeper.
- developed from keen photographer to hold her first exhibition.
- held 12th century Damascene steel.
- looks for adventure in whatever comes her way.

PLAINT FOR PROVENCE

1152: LES-BAUX-DE-PROVENCE

If you enjoyed *Bladesong*, don't miss the further adventures of Dragonetz and Estela in *Plaint for Provence: Book 3 of The Troubadours Quartet.*

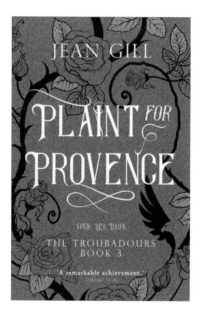

Shortlisted for the Chaucer Awards,
FINALIST in The Wishing Shelf Awards,
Historical Novel Society Editor's Choice

'By far the best historical novel I've read this year' – **Rabia Tanveer, Readers Favorite, Dec 2015**

If peace fails inProvence, Dragonetz' sword must decide the winner and friends will die.

CHAPTER 1 SAMPLE

PLAINT FOR PROVENCE

If someone drinks a great quantity of wine in order to quench his thirst, he induces senseless behavior (as happened with Lot). Thus it is more healthful and sane for a thirsty person to drink water, rather than wine, to quench his thirst.

Physica, Plants

'Him.' The boy's head swivelled towards the drinkers at the far table.

'Dolt!' Geral hissed. 'What have I told you? God's body! Don't look at him. Make it natural. Just follow me – and follow my lead. Best you say as little as possible.' He sighed again, stuck with the youngster as his partner, all limbs and credulity but tall enough to breathe down the back of Geral's neck as they threaded a route across the crowded inn to squeeze a place beside their target on his bench.

Their task was made easier by the fact that the man in the corner was not only alone; he reeked of misery and isolation so that all those nearest had instinctively turned their backs on him and shifted to make space. The man also stood out because he was in uniform, a red tabard, grubby from travel but nevertheless a slap in the face for the ordinary working men around him. If he'd had the presence to carry the rank his tabard declared, or bought a flagon for the table, he might have found himself singing 'Marie's a-courting' in good company. Instead, he was nursing a mug, a pitcher and a black look.

'Dolt,' muttered Geral, not about the boy this time. Briefly, he wondered if the man was indeed some Lord's Fool, indulging in some off-duty misery, but if so, he would have either been out of livery or wearing the other signs of his trade. No, this was a messenger, like himself, but naïve or vain enough to adopt the new trend of wearing uniform, advertising his provenance and mission to anyone who cared to look. And it was Geral's job to look, to ensure his own message reached the right ears, unhampered by others. He knew that livery from somewhere, somewhen, and his little finger told him it meant trouble. The little finger he'd broken, when he was six and fell from the apple tree, was never wrong.

'Greetings, master,' he interrupted misery incarnate. 'Bertran here,' he waved his tankard vaguely towards the boy looming awkwardly beside him, 'was much taken with your costume and wondered how a man of your standing came to be in our drinking haunt. It being my task to educate the boy, and to take every chance of letting him hear from his betters, why, I thought we could benefit from an exchange of news while you are here and, it seems, lacking company.' Geral gave his most winning smile, a little dented by the lack of teeth on one side but usually a successful accompaniment to flattery and the messenger's magic word, 'news'.

The man straightened a little and contemplated his fellow-drinkers with bleary eyes. As he sat up, the silk of his tabard rippled a golden lion into view, its tongue and claws tipped blue against the red background.

'Aquitaine!' exclaimed Geral. 'God's bones but you're a long way from home, man. On the Queen's business, I should think, and a weary one to judge from your face.'

The other man's face set into even deeper lines, grime etching the hollows of his cheeks. 'Sit,' he gestured.

Geral introduced himself as he obeyed and clambered opposite the other man onto the bench, spreading enough to make another place. 'And the boy's Bertran. We're in the same business, you and me.'

'You wear no colours.'

'My Liege is local, not worthy of your attention.' Geral shrugged, grateful that his minor Liege wasn't there to hear him and consign him to the highest dungeon in Provence, where men learned quickly that 'deepest' wasn't always the most terrifying where dungeons were concerned. 'But I know Marselha and can perhaps save you time and trouble in your errand. All in good time, all in good time. I've a thirst on me would drain the harbour. You!' He grabbed a server, commandeered a pitcher of wine and two goblets, pouring a small amount for Bertran, and a generous amount for himself and the man from Aquitaine.

'Simon.' The man offered his name like a miser giving alms but it was a start.

'I've seen a few tough assignments in my time,' Geral confided, 'and here I am to tell the tale.' He checked that Bertran was giving proper attention and was reassured by the round-eyed curiosity. 'If this lad pins his ears back and learns what I teach him, he can take my place and welcome, when it's my turn to sit by the fire.' He spoke to Bertran with a glance now and then at Simon, to include him as a fellow-expert.

'You start by carrying the women's messages; fetch the midwife, fetch the priest, tell a man there's a boy born…'

'Aye,' nodded Bertran, interrupting enthusiastically. 'One time I took a hunting dog as a present from our Lady, a long way down the coast. Rex his name was, black tip to his tail.' He finally noticed Geral's glare and blushed his way into silence. Thank God the boy was more interested in giving the dog's name than his Lady's. Giving that information away was not part of Geral's plan, not until he knew whether it would be to his advantage or not. He suspected not.

He continued, warming to his theme, and having kicked Bertran hard under the table. 'Bad news is what gets you killed. If you're not crafty. Suppose you bring message of a death?' He watched Simon out of the corner of his eye but there was no reaction. So it wasn't a death that was worrying the messenger from Aquitaine. 'How do you break the news without a bit of your body being broken in return?' he paused, a good teacher.

Bertran's face screwed up in thought. 'I'd stand a good way back when I said the news and I'd say it fast-like, then maybe run?'

A flicker of amusement shimmered across Simon's face and he sat straighter, apparently distracted from the weight he carried. Geral sighed and shook his head. 'Think, man, what impression that would leave on some poor, bereaved human. No, no, no, you must carry the death in your person as if it's your own dog that died, like this.' And he schooled his features into his special face for 'I am the bearer of sad, sad news.'

Bertran clapped his hands with admiration. 'I must do this. Is it so?' and his own baby-faced smoothness contorted into a gargoyle around his twinkling blue eyes.

'Almost,' lied Geral. ''Tis practice you need.' He felt another lift of spirits in the man opposite him, a barely concealed twitch of the mouth, and he emptied the pitcher of wine, calling for another. Tickling a fish was ever slow business to start with and a quick catch at the right time. Timing was everything.

'And when you tell of a death, then judge the telling of it to suit the hearer. If the dead one was loved, then the death was heroic and painless – make it so. If the dead one was hated, the last moments were all cowardice and pain. And if the death was not personal but a public change...' No, there was definitely no reaction from Simon. So, the red queen was not dead. What mission was the man on that brought him so far south? 'Then you must tell it for the advantage of the hearer. Find the good in it for his status. Find a future invitation to greatness from the man who has replaced the dead one.'

'But that would mean telling a lie.' The boy's eyes were saucers.

'No indeed.' *A lie is the least of what you will do as messenger*, Geral thought, *if you want to stay among the living*. 'No indeed, for the future is unknown and it might well be that the new power will bring good to your hearer. You must just imagine it to be so, when you give the message, whatever that message may be. And remember that when one flower fades, another takes its place.' Aha! That found an echo in Simon's thoughts. The fish shimmered silver below Geral's hand and he grabbed it.

'I hear there has been such a replacement in Aquitaine,' he hazarded aloud.

'You know then.' Simon's face and tone were exactly right for proclaiming a loved one's death.

'Not the detail.' Geral reeled him in smoothly and kicked Bertran once more under the table, just to make sure.

'It all happened so quickly.' Once he'd opened up, Simon spouted like a gutter in a storm.

Printed in Great Britain
by Amazon

49821382R10182